I0550556

A Chance of Clouds

© 2013 Lianna Shen, 1st Edition

Table of Contents

- 1 - Taipei, 1978

What a woman chooses to wear on the night her life begins is an important decision. For twenty-five-year-old Polly, that night is tonight, and she has chosen to wear her most respectable dress: A taupe wool shift with a high collar, that hits just below the knee. It is not the most comfortable dress she owns, nor is it the most fashionable. But she has chosen it nonetheless.

She's clutching a black leather satchel under her arm, and has wrapped a soft golden scarf around her neck – a final parting gift from her Godmother, and last minute addition to her ensemble. It's her first time riding an airplane, and she drums one fingernail on the armrest of her seat as she waits, seated beside her new husband at the Taipei Airport's international terminal.

Oh, how she longs to kick off her shoes, roll down her scratchy stockings, and itch herself with her manicured fingernails, but looking around at the fancy travellers, she doubts that would be proper. Feeling overheated, she cools her face down with a bamboo fan, inhaling the subtle fragrance of the wood, mixing with the smoke from her husband's cigarette.

Only hours ago, she had married him on the terrace of his parents' modest home, dressed in crimson and gold silk. She was the perfect Taiwanese bride, beaming under a brilliant red canopy. The groom - the dashing and auspicious Peter Young, wore a bespoke charcoal tuxedo, with his black frame glasses tucked into the breast pocket.

Later, there had been a succulent feast of rare abalone, shark fin soup, and other expensive delicacies at one of the swankier restaurants in Taipei. The Young Family invited almost everyone they knew in the city. Polly's parents have been dead for years, so the King Family's guest list defaulted to Polly's

Godparents, and their friends. And with her sisters living in America, Polly's personal guests consisted only of a few former schoolmates, a favorite cousin, and a sprinkling of distant relatives.

Instead of taking a honeymoon, Polly and Peter have decided to start their new life immediately – which means leaving Taipei, and taking an airplane to their new home in Canada. Peter has already secured a little house with his savings - a combination of money from his generous father, and the small salaries he has managed to bank so far in life.

With the *hongbao* money they've received as gifts from the wedding guests, they have a decent nest egg to start this new life. Peter has started a promising new job with a small oil and gas company in Calgary, Alberta, and Polly is excited to go snowshoeing. She can't imagine it to be very difficult.

While she is pleased to be moving to Canada, it is not what she expected. When Peter proposed, he had told her that they would be building a new life together in America. She can't say she knows the difference, and perhaps it is very much the same thing, but she is anxious. She has never seen snow, doesn't speak English, and her closest relatives will be her sisters in New York, which is a whole country away.

She looks over at her new husband, searching for some reassurance, gazing at his intense profile. A thick vein in his forehead throbs in concentration as he reads the *New York Times* – an American newspaper that the stewardesses had been handing out. Several other foreign men, dressed in suits, are reading the same newspaper. A rush of pride hits her and she straightens her spine with a smile. Her new husband is very capable.

Fears and doubts now pushed into the back of her head, Polly rises confidently from her seat when their plane is called. With Peter leading, she takes his hand and walks four inches behind him to the heavy glass doors, and together they push through to the tarmac outside. A giant airplane – a 747, Peter tells her – sits majestically on the runway, shining like a giant bullet. The airline's emblem gleams vibrantly on the tail; a giant red plum blossom painted in what looks to be watercolors. Staring up at the giant vessel, she takes a deep breath and imagines herself as the Oriental Grace Kelly, walking up the steps of the airplane with her princely husband, leaving the only country she has ever known, to live in a distant land.

After a fourteen-hour flight, they arrive in San Francisco for a short layover. She is excited to deplane and witness the city where Tony Bennett left his heart. She is disappointed when she cannot see the famous Golden Gate Bridge from the airport windows, or anything else, for that matter. Gazing out at the foggy sky, she turns away with a heavy sigh and decides to people watch instead. To her surprise and comfort, she sees many Orientals around. One man, who looks to be Japanese, is sweeping the floors in the terminal waiting area. An older Chinese lady is working the cash register at the magazine stand, where she stops to buy a fashion magazine. Though she can read very little English, Polly plans on being fully versed in the latest North American fashions. Perhaps Peter can read it to her on the next flight, which promises to be less than four hours.

They arrive in Calgary late at night. It is September, and the air is already cooling with the first signs of a very long winter. Peter had already settled in several months earlier, readying their new home with enough furniture and amenities to be move-in ready. After collecting their luggage, they take a blacktop taxi from the airport straight to their new home. It takes less than fifteen minutes, and there are almost no other cars on the single lane road.

The little house Peter has bought is in a lower middle-class neighborhood – he paid only twenty thousand Canadian dollars for it, in cash. It is a *bung-a-low*, says Peter, which means there is only one level. Polly dislikes the ridiculous word immediately, ducking her head through the door, looking up at the low ceilings with a frown. The ceilings at her Godparents' apartment in Taipei were at least nine feet high.

Her Godparents had been very encouraging about Polly and Peter moving to Canada. *It's very beautiful there*, they had assured her, and they showed her pictures of moose, bears, and evergreen trees in an encyclopedia they had pulled from the shelf. They told her that Canadians drank a delicious, sweet sap from giant maple trees, and that *Calgary*, her new destined home, was wedged between the Rocky Mountains and endless kilometers of prairie land.

When they drive around the city the next day in the white Ford Capri that Peter had bought months earlier, all Polly can see are bare little sapling trees, dry, yellow hills, and farms dotted with grazing cows with white and brown coats.

"I thought cows were brown," Polly says, slightly bewildered. "These cows look strange."

Peter laughs. "They have brown cows here too. But the spotted ones taste better."

Polly raises an eyebrow, not sure whether or not to believe him. But they've been married for less than a week so she decides not to argue.

The city's only saving grace, in Polly's eyes, is its cloudless, azure blue sky, which ironically makes everything else dull in comparison. To make matters worse, within a couple weeks, the chilly fall weather turns downright cold, and Polly finds herself knitting heavy wool sweaters, sitting by the rickety heater, shivering.

Peter begins his new job straight away, leaving Polly plenty of time to unpack and turn their home into the cozy dwelling she had envisioned. She hasn't learned to drive yet, so her only form of transportation during the day is the city bus, which runs only a few routes around the their area of the city. She makes do, boarding the bus with one paper bag of groceries at a time, clutching the bottom in case the contents decide to burst through and splatter across the sidewalk – a lesson learned after the fact.

On Halloween, this strange holiday where children dress up as ghosts in white sheets and ring their neighbors' doors for candy, the neighborhood teenagers decide to toss raw eggs at the Youngs' new house and drape the crabapple tree in the front yard with toilet paper. Overnight, the eggs freeze to the glass windows, and Polly spends the next day scraping off the mess with a metal spatula, leaving scratches on the windows and turning her fingers numb with cold. What a terrible, terrible holiday.

To Polly's surprise, Peter is very much a chain smoker and the house reeks of cigarettes in the evenings. During the day Polly opens all the windows and cranks the heater up full blast, causing their power bill to go through the roof. When Peter confronts her about the bill, she shrugs despondently and tells him to stop smoking.

Peter is ever the ambitious businessman, and now wears his glasses on a full-time basis, urging his colleagues to take him seriously. He's so focused on his career that he can hardly remember which day he is supposed to leave the trash out, and doesn't have the capacity to memorize their postal code, which he thinks, is an unnecessarily complex jumble of numbers and letters. On occasions when their full address is requested over the telephone by family and friends wanting to send them a package, he hands the telephone to Polly, who has phonetically perfected the pronunciation of their new address, spelling, postal code and all.

As spring comes, melting away the snow, and bright yellow dandelions begin popping up at the edge of their lawn, Polly seems to come alive as well. She makes a small group of friends - a mix of Oriental immigrant wives from other countries – most prominently, Hong Kong. She ends up learning English by watching soap operas – *General Hospital* is her favorite - and becomes fluent in Cantonese as well, thanks to her weekly mahjong games with her new friends.

They are married for four years before Polly becomes pregnant and subsequently gives birth to their first child. They name him Peter Junior. By then, Peter Senior has advanced in his company to become a partner - the youngest, and only Oriental of the group. He moves his growing family to a quiet neighborhood in an up-and-coming suburb. Polly insists that their new house have at least two levels, and they settle on a three story, white stucco house, complete with a basement.

Peter Junior enjoys two years of his mother's undivided doting attention before his younger sister Claudia is born. As Peter Jr. and Claudia grow, Polly becomes a most devoted mother. Her children come before everything, and she is obsessed with giving them the best – from music and speech lessons, to toys, to schools. She insists that the family be baptized in order for the children to attend the top-tier school in their district, which happens to be a Catholic school.

Life is simply perfect for Polly, who is no longer just an orphan maiden from a faraway country. Her husband is successful, her children well mannered, sharp and studious. As a young man, Peter Jr. becomes the spitting image of his father, and little Claudia is a graceful combination of her both parents. She is blessed with her father's perpetually sun-kissed skin, paired with the delicate features of her mother.

While the children are at school, Polly spends her days obsessively cleaning the house, cooking elaborate meals, and once a day, she watches *General Hospital* on the large television in the living room, continuing her language education. It is on one of these days, when she is standing at the mailbox during a commercial break and shuffling through the mail, that she sees a familiar scrawl. It's on a letter addressed to her husband: *Mr. Peter Young.* Her stomach turns violently, as she knows that the elegant handwriting belongs to only one person, and she has not seen that person in over fifteen years.

Hands shaking, she carries the letter along with the rest of the mail inside and proceeds to the kitchen. They had just remodeled it the year before, and the marble countertops are always gleaming, thanks to Polly's incessant wiping.

She fills the kettle and heats it on the stove. When it starts to steam, she carefully holds the letter over the spout, as she's seen done countless times in the movies. Once the flap puffs up, she peels the rest of the envelope open to extract its contents.

The letter, written on thin loose-leaf, is crisply folded twice. She opens it warily, not in the least bit knowing what to expect. Reading slowly, she absorbs and translates every English word in her head to her native tongue.

When she finishes, she brings a hand to her chest, feeling her heart beat rapidly. She gingerly grasps the side of the counter, smudging the marble as a result. Steadying herself, she drums her fingernails a few times, takes a deep breath. She folds the letter back up and returns it into the envelope. She is about to look for some glue, when she has a better idea.

She strolls down the hallway to her husband's office. The door opens with a creak to reveal floor-to-ceiling mahogany bookshelves and a large, grandiose desk in the middle of the floor. It is an organized mess, with piles of paper everywhere, and a mountain of unopened mail on his desk. She sees what she's looking for in the corner of the room, next to a trash bin.

Walking over to the waist-high contraption, she pauses, looking for the on-switch. She finds it on the side of the machine and flicks it on. It roars to life with a single green light.

Like she's watched Peter do after he's paid their bills, she holds the envelope to the machine, until it catches. She jumps up in surprise as the machine eats it up, shredding the envelope and its contents into a thousand tiny, inconceivable pieces.

With a pang of guilt, she switches the shredder to the off position and turns to leave the office. On her way out she catches sight of a picture on Peter's desk.

It's a picture of the two of them, before they were married, on the night they were engaged. She is wearing a faded mauve dress, her hair is curled Farrah Fawcett-style away from her face, and she is holding the crook of Peter's elbow, smiling charmingly at the camera. He is standing quite straight, though his stance is relaxed. One would never know that he were mere minutes away from proposing to his future wife.

The person taking the picture had apparently said something funny. Peter's expression is of pure amusement, his mouth in an open smile with his top teeth visible. His eyes are squinting and full of mirth. You can almost hear the laughter in his face.

Polly tries to remember what was said that had received such a reaction. But for the life of her, she remembers nothing, except that when the picture was taken, all she was thinking about was how she so desperately wished the photographer would go away, so that she and Peter could have the rest of the night to themselves.

- 2 - January 2004, Calgary

It's the middle of Claudia's senior year, and is she about to be expelled from her high school. Her mother and father are sitting on either side of her in the principal's office, with their hands clutched together.

Claudia looks up at the plaster ceiling that is probably rampant with asbestos, holding in her tears. Damn this place. All her life she has worked so hard, trying to be the best at everything – especially academics – and now, six months away from graduation, she is being told to leave.

A straight-A student with perfect attendance, Claudia has been involved in an unfortunate event on school grounds. It has been labeled as "unnecessary, voluntary violence" on the memo she is holding, written in the secretary's flowery handwriting. She has only been out of the hospital for a day, eager to return to her studies; she missed a couple of important tests. The secretary had called the Young residence early in the morning to request Mr. and Mrs. Young's presence at nine a.m. sharp, to meet with the school principal, Mr. Percy.

And here they are, in Mr. Percy's office, and he is telling them that Claudia is no longer welcome at St. Agnes, and that she will have to find another school to attend for the remainder of the school year.

"This is ridiculous," Claudia's father sputters. "My daughter has one of the top averages in her entire class. She is enrolled in all AP classes and plays in the school orchestra. Those girls are the ones who should be punished, not Claudia." He ruthlessly bangs his fist on the large oak desk, unable to contain his anger. "I can not accept this."

Mr. Percy holds up his hands in a signal of defeat. "I am deeply sorry, Mr. Young. I completely understand where you are coming from. But the fact of the matter is, *those girls* do not attend my school – in fact they don't attend any school – so we have to rely on the legal system to punish them, which I'm aware is happening, as it should. But in Claudia's case..."

Mrs. Young interjects with a loud, long sigh. She shoots Mr. Percy a dirty, painful stare, and uncrosses and re-crosses her legs leisurely, squeaking the chair. She is not happy with this man and she wants him to know it. Claudia stifles a smile and looks down, after catching a look at her mom's eyes, filled with fierce love, like a mother bear.

Mr. Percy clears his throat. "If I may continue...in Claudia's case, her involvement, regardless of her innocence, puts our school in a precarious position. We have a zero tolerance rule for violence, and as it stands, we have witnesses that say she did strike a hand..."

"Of course she did! You expect her to stand and cower while she gets beat up, under your watch?" Mr. Young shakes his head, incredulous. "This is a mistake. But perhaps you're right. She can't remain at this school...a school where she is not protected, and menacing criminals can enter school grounds at will and inflict harm." He sets his mouth in a firm line.

"Let's go, Claudia. Polly." He stands, buttoning up his overcoat. "This school is not worthy of you."

He turns to walk out the door, while Mr. Percy pretends to busy himself with organizing papers on his desk. Mrs. Young follows. At the door, Claudia turns to Mr. Percy.

"Mr. Percy," Claudia says. It comes out in a warble, so she clears her throat and repeats herself. "Mr. Percy. I just want to make sure that this does not blemish my high school record, and that my academic standing will not be impacted. I'm expecting a scholarship for University."

Mr. Percy nods. "Academically, everything is as it was, Claudia," he says. "You will simply continue your studies at your new school. They will be happy to have you. St. Agnes will miss you as a student." Claudia nods, wanting to give him the finger, but doesn't push her luck. Who knows what kind of power he has over her transcripts. She goes to her locker and cleans it out, dumping its contents into her bag.

It's -20 Celsius outside, and snowing. Claudia's parents want her to go home with them, but the last thing she wants to do right now is sit around and feel sorry for herself. She promises them that she'll enroll at the public school first thing tomorrow morning, but for now, she is going to the library, a couple bus stops away. She'll stay there for a couple of hours, work on her admission essays, and get her mind off things. They relent, and plan for Mr. Young to pick her up on his way home from work.

As planned, Claudia starts at her new school the very next day. The school happens to be named after her favorite Canadian heroine: Laura Secord. She arrives at the main office before eight in the morning, ready to register and get into the swing. Surprisingly, few questions are asked, and once the principal gets a look at her pristine academic record, they have her enrolled in no time and a locker is assigned. A class schedule is printed for her on a piece of green paper, spelling out the same classes she would have taken at St Agnes.

While she had been required to wear a uniform at St. Agnes, Laura Secord High School has no such requirement, and she now finds herself spending a good ten minutes each morning in front of her color-coordinated closet, searching for something to wear. She has resorted to borrowing from her fashion-forward mother, who is delighted by the change in her daughter's attire; she had never been a fan of the dowdy plaid skirts.

"You have good taste." She says, nodding approvingly, on days when Claudia pairs her mother's expensive cashmere sweaters with her own tank tops and jeans. Claudia smiles at her mother sweetly, happy to please.

Claudia jumps right into her studies at her new school, and Mr. Percy is right – by the middle of the term, she's received notice of early admission to her school of choice: The University of British Columbia in Vancouver, armed with a full scholarship.

With only three months of high school left, she is focused solely on scoring well in her Advanced Placement classes – they count for University credit, after all. While her last school was highly competitive and full of over-achievers, it seems that here, apart from the stereotypical nerd crew, most of the students are focused only on dating, hanging out by their cars, and school sports.

In her advanced classes, the brainy kids give her the cold shoulder. On her first day in AP math, they eye her up and down in her flared jeans and fitted grey sweater with a giant black pi symbol woven on the front. She had worn it, thinking it would give her some nerd cred. One girl even holds up her textbook and points at it, mouthing the letters "AP", assuming that Claudia had sauntered into the wrong class.

A boy sitting near the back of the room gives her a warm, genuine smile, and subtly nods at the desk in front of him. Smiling gratefully, she walks over and slips into the desk. She introduces herself to him and he tells her that his name is James Cooper, and that he likes her sweater.

James is also in her physics class, so she sits in front of him then, too. Over the next few weeks, it turns into a comfortable habit, with her back to his front, no matter who gets to class first.

Halfway through the term, Claudia has to take a couple days off school in order to get her wisdom teeth removed. When she returns, James teases her about her swollen cheeks. "Chubby bunny," he names her.

She overhears that James is on the basketball team. The season finished in late February, but apparently he had steered the team to win the provincial championship. He drives a BMW, and parks it in the first spot in the student lot every day; he is an early bird. At 6'3" tall, he is more statuesque than most of his peers, and as much as Claudia tries to ignore it he is also quite good-looking. She avoids his inquisitive stares and looks away from him, blushing when he tries to catch her eye.

He likes to wink at her, which she decides is creepy. And he is always finding excuses to chat after class, often making her late for the next period, which annoys her more than she'd like to admit. He asks her questions about the math or physics lessons they just sat through, even asking to borrow her notes, though he knows as well as she does that his notes are way better than hers. Claudia is more of an auditory learner and prefers to listen and absorb, rather than take notes. James on the other hand, is always furiously scrawling into a moleskin notebook.

Their math class is the final period on Fridays, and one spring afternoon, halfway through the term, James follows Claudia out of the classroom and walks with her all the way to her locker, casually chatting about their last quiz. He'd lost points for not showing his work, which he disagrees with, he says, because these days, everything is done on computers anyway.

They are almost at Claudia's locker so she turns to him with a reserved smile. "Thanks for walking me to my locker James. Sorry about your quiz, but showing your work is the only way for teachers to know that you actually know your shit, and that you're not just copying off the person in front of you." She winks, giving him a taste of his own medicine. She immediately regrets it, feeling like a cheese. Or a tease, depending on how you look at it.

He's silent, watching her open her locker and pack her textbooks into her backpack for the weekend. When she is finished, the locker is completely empty. No old lunch bags, no extra clothes, not even a magazine clipping on the side of the door. It's like she doesn't exist on the weekends. For some reason this makes him feel sad. For the past four months now, he has been working up the courage to walk to her locker to ask her out. Now that he's here he feels like a dweeb. Surely she knows something is up. He decides to go for it.

Acting as if the idea is just popping into his head, and even snapping his fingers like he's in a bad after school sitcom, he says, "Hey! Wanna hang out...tonight?" He smiles expectantly. His perfect, straight teeth are a dazzling pearl-white against his tan skin and chestnut brown hair. He had just finished a box of Crest white strips. Suddenly self-conscious that they might be *too* white, he pulls his lips closed.

"What do you mean?" Claudia asks, innocently. "We're hanging out right now." She looks at him blankly, shrugging, watching him squirm.

"You know what I mean, you dork." He lowers his voice just in case people are around and he gets rejected. "Let's go to a movie. I'll pick you up from your house in a few hours. It'll be fun." He bumps her shoulder playfully with his own as he moves to stand beside her, their backs to the hallway.

It's Friday night and she has plans to study for the final exams that are coming up in a couple weeks. Knowing he won't want to spend the evening buried in books, she shrugs uselessly. "I kind of planned to study tonight," she says, not looking at him. She tucks some hair behind her right ear. "You should be studying too you slacker," She adds, teasingly.

"Okay cool, let's study then," he says, a bit too quickly, trying to sound casual. "Text me your address."

He touches her cheek with his knuckle briefly, excited by his success. "Chubby bunny," he says, shaking his head. "The swelling has gone down. I'll need to think of something new to tease you about." She flinches because his touch is a little too familiar, a little too soon. He notices and pulls back quickly, but recovers quickly, walking away with his head high, grinning. Cocky.

Slamming her locker door closed, she heads to the front exit of the school and proceeds to the crosswalk. Her mom always picks her up after school and waits parked on the other side of the road. It's kind of nice and also mildly annoying. Ever since the incident at her last school, her parents have become quite strict, demanding that she come straight home from school every day, just in case, God forbid, a couple of crazy girls decide to come beat her up again.

Her mom is across the street, waiting in the driver's seat of a black Lexus SUV, wearing large Gucci sunglasses, like some kind of Mafia wife. Claudia waves, squinting her unprotected eyes into the sun. She pulls her borrowed soft cashmere sweater tight against her body as she crosses the road, the dry wind whipping at her hair. She walks past a group of smoking Goths who stare her down, snickering. Really, she can't wait to graduate.

Claudia realizes on the ride home that she doesn't have James' number so she can't actually text him to confirm their plans. So instead, when she gets home, she settles into a pair of comfy yoga pants and a grey tank top, excited to hit the books and call it a day.

She's hitting the books by four, and before she knows it, it's eight in the evening and she's studied all the way through dinner. With Petey away at University, her parents are happy to let her eat what and when she wants, and they've begun to spend their Friday evenings out on a "date night." Her mom often comes home giggling, high off one too many glasses of pinot noir.

Her phone buzzes on her dresser, snapping her out of her zone. She gets up to read a text from an unknown number.

Unknown: You didn't text me your address. Still wanna hang out?
Claudia: Is this James?
Unknown: Yeah. I thought I gave you my number. My bad.
Claudia: No, I gave you mine a while back. Saving yours now.
James: If you text me your address, I'll come get you right now. If you still want to hang out that is.

Claudia pauses, thinking hard for a legitimate excuse she can use. She looks at her books and realizes that she could really use a change of scenery, so she complies.

She texts him the address and pulls on a pair of stretchy jeans that she thinks are pretty flattering. She releases her hair from a bun on top of her head – her typical study-style, an effort to keep her thick, espresso-brown hair out of her face. She shakes out the waves that have accumulated. She fluffs out her mane a bit to frame her round face, and grabs a hooded sweatshirt. No reason to dress up; they're just studying.

She peers at herself in the mirror on the wall. She still has makeup on from the morning, and she decides its good enough. Just a few swipes of mascara on her already long lashes and a hint of cream blush. She pulls out her lip balm and applies a layer rather hastily. Luckily she inherited her mom's pillowy lips so they don't take much work.

Her bedroom window faces the road and within ten minutes she sees James' blue BMW pulling up to the curb. She sees him getting out of the car, obviously coming to the door to greet her like the nice Canadian boy he is.

She quickly shoves her books into her backpack and runs out of her room and down the stairs, stepping into the converse sneakers she has sitting by the front door.

"GOING OUT TO STUDY!" she yells loudly to whoever is listening in the house. She'd heard her parents come home about twenty minutes ago. She opens the door and closes it behind her just in time, and turns to face James, his hand raised to knock. She finds herself so close that she has to put her hand out in front to keep from falling onto him.

"Whoa," he laughs, "Easy. Just studying, nothing to be that excited about." The proximity gives him an excuse to pull her into an awkward, but friendly hug.

She ducks her face away from him, breathless from the run down the stairs. "Just wanted to get to the door before anyone else did. The last thing you want is my dad asking you about where we're going, what time we'll be home, what we'll be doing..." she trails off.

He doesn't miss a beat. "What are we going to be doing, that I wouldn't want to tell him about?" He teases her and she flushes immediately, her ears hot.

"You know what I mean. It just gets weird with parents. Let's go." She tears her body away from the door and lightly jogs over to his car, backpack slung on her shoulder. He catches up in time to open the door for her and takes her backpack, which he tosses lightly into the backseat.

"Thanks, very gentlemanly of you," she says, with a hint of sarcasm. She doesn't want to encourage any date-ish behavior though admittedly it is quite charming.

He climbs into the driver's side and starts up the car, smiling at her casually. "So, where to, my studious friend?" he puts the car into drive and pulls away from her house.

"Well, the library closed an hour ago, so that's out...we could go to that 24 hour café by the movie theater. They have free Wi-Fi and a nice selection of tea..." she realizes how excited she sounds about going out to study. Really she has got to get a life.

"Sounds good," he says, glancing at her briefly, his dimpled smile challenging her to break her cool attitude. "I almost didn't have the guts to text you tonight, after I clearly told you to text me your address. Almost felt like I was being rejected. But then I thought, she's just being shy...am I right?" he shoots her his cocky grin, which she doesn't appreciate.

She looks at him blankly. "I'm not shy, James. You never gave me your number. And to be honest, our plans had slipped my mind. I was in my room for the past three hours, thinking about nothing but differential equations and integrals."

He raises an eyebrow. "I believe you," he says.

They pull into the parking lot of the café and she jumps out before he can even think about coming around to open the door for her. She opens the back door, hastily pulls out her backpack, and slams the door shut again.

"Ouch, you're hurting my baby..." James says, hearing the loud slam. "Do you know how many baskets I had to sink in order to get her?" he runs his hand over the hood of his car lovingly. "Be gentle to my girl," he says, winking at her.

Claudia doesn't know if he's talking about her or the car, she just mutters a "sorry" to him, though she finds it a turn-off when boys are so into their cars. She heads towards the café and waits for him at the entrance.

They push in through the double doors, side by side, like two doormen, Claudia not yielding to James' held door, and James not wanting a girl to open the door for him. Realizing how silly it must look, she laughs quietly. They find a booth in the corner and Claudia sits immediately, unpacks her things, opens a textbook, and uncaps a pink highlighter pen.

James throws his backpack into the opposite side of the booth but remains standing. "I'm going to grab something to drink. What would you like? It's on me." He adds the last part quickly, seeing that she is about to reach for her wallet.

She smiles politely. "Thank you. I'll have a peppermint tea please." He nods and goes over to the counter as she settles into her seat, breaking out her tortoise-shell glasses from their case. Rolling her shoulders up, back, and down, she's ready for some serious studying.

After a couple hours of complete silence, with the occasional cough or throat clearing from James, he sighs. Loudly. She peers up at him over her glasses from her book.

"Bored?" she says softly. She knows she's not a fun person to study with. She gets into her zone and barely says a word. Which is why she usually studies alone.

He's gazing up at the ceiling, chewing on a pen. She notices how his jaw flexes with the movement. His eyes are a piercing shade of blue, the kind of blue that some people wear contact lenses to achieve. She suddenly feels bad that she's been so cold to this nice looking boy, and even worse that he is spending his Friday night studying with her when he obviously has many better things to do.

"No, just finished studying," he says, looking at her with a smile. "But we can stay as long as you want, so you can finish too." His tone is challenging, as if he has just placed first in a studying competition.

She decides to let her guard down and lifts the corners of her mouth up in a hesitant smile. "I'm just reviewing this chapter now. I had about four hours on you. Would you like to go see a movie?"

His eyebrows rise in surprise at the suggestion. "Really? Little miss studious wants to do something fun and normal? I'm game!"

She immediately feels her heart drop. He doesn't think she's normal? Granted she has her priorities straight, maybe too much so for a teenager, but she still likes to have a good time. Her eyes fall back to her textbook and she grabs an un-used napkin from the table to mark her page. She closes the book with a loud thud.

"I am fun. I'm just very picky about how I have fun and who I have fun with." She stands up and starts packing up her things, a bit agitated. "So what's your idea of fun? You want to get high or something?" She shoots him a salacious glare, a weapon she learned from her mother.

He is immediately taken aback, and shakes his head. "Forget it. I can just take you home. I was just joking around. Man you're touchy, aren't you?" His ready smile is gone and he seems disappointed.

"Yeah, I am. Don't take it personally though, it's totally me, not you." She purposefully slings her bag on her back, guard back up at full force. She's waiting for him to follow suit. He packs his things slowly, muttering under his breath and flicking her disappointing looks.

They head out of the cafe, with her leading the way several steps ahead, and then unnecessarily holding the door open for him, trying to get under his skin.

"Why thank you," he says, purposefully striding towards his car. "See how I'm a nice person who just says thank you? And for the record, I don't get high. So what's your problem?"

"What's my problem? You said I wasn't normal and not fun. What's your problem?"

"Are you serious? I was just teasing you. You take everything so seriously. Is this why you keep to yourself at school? Does everyone piss you off?" he unlocks the car and gets into the driver's seat. She counts to ten, debating whether or not she should even continue this conversation, but her backpack is heavy and she doesn't feel like walking home. So she finally, slowly, gets into the car.

She turns in her seat to look at him. "No. I keep to myself because people are assholes," she says calmly. "And you just proved it. I thought you were a nice guy and we could be friends, but it turns out you're just a cocky asshole."

He lets out a grunt. "Wow. Cocky asshole? Really?" He rolls his eyes and turns to look at her. "Look, this is stupid. I'm sorry. I just like to tease you." The corner of his mouth curls slightly and he pauses thoughtfully. "You're pretty adorable when you get all worked up. Though you might be the most volatile girl I've ever met."

She can feel her cheeks getting warm and suddenly her heart is beating in her stomach. She's never thought of herself as volatile.

"Sorry. I know I'm a bit moody. I'm PMS-ing." She shrugs sheepishly. "But just FYI, I'm not looking for a relationship or anything. Not that I think that's what you want with me, just wanted to make things clear." She says the last part quickly, not wanting to appear presumptuous. "It's just that we're graduating, and I already know that I'm moving away for school, so it would just be a waste to start anything that would just have to end anyway."

He lets out a hearty laugh. "Wow, you really do say 'FYI'. I've heard you say it before but I thought it was just a glitch in the matrix. I thought people only write that in emails or memos or something. And thank you for telling me that you're, um, PMS-ing." He laughs again, a funny look on his face, embarrassed but relieved by her sudden openness.

"If there's one thing that'll shut a guy up, it's the female period. It's the only way I can ever get my brother to stop teasing me. He's relentless. But as soon as I say the word tampon he's running away from me, like, 'holy shit a fucking tampon!'" she laughs awkwardly. He's looking at her with an amused expression.

He pushes the issue a bit further. "So no relationship. Not going to lie, I was kind of hoping we could date, or something like that," he says, shrugging, his deep blue eyes twinkling. "But, I'm totally down for friendship. Especially with a smart hottie like you." He starts up his car, the sound of the engine drowning her out as she opens her mouth to object.

What the? Who does this guy think he is? Once she's had a chance to absorb being called smart, hot and adorable all in a matter of minutes by this extremely cocky son of a bitch, she realizes that in no way is he headed towards her house to drop her off, as was the plan.

She looks around frantically and sees that he is heading for the hills, literally. This area of the city is flocked with round, rolling green hills, and in the summer, the locals love to hike and explore them. James turns off the main road and starts up a dirt path, and the car ride becomes bumpy, as he dodges and drives over rocks.

Claudia looks around outside for a clue. "Where are we going? I thought the plan was to call it a night, since I freaked out at you."

He grins mischievously at her, with one hand on the wheel, and the other hanging out the window. She notices that he's dressed almost identical to her – grey hoodie and jeans, with black Adidas sneakers, against her own grey hoodie, jeans and black Converse. If there's one thing they do have in common, it's their unimaginative wardrobes.

"I want to take you somewhere. And you clearly didn't object when we were heading in the opposite direction, so I figured I'd just keep going..." he trails off, now second-guessing himself. "I can turn around if you want to go home. But we're almost there."

"No, it's okay. I wasn't paying attention, but it's fine. I'm up for a little adventure, I guess." She rolls down her own window, taking a deep inhale of the fresh night air and letting the breeze whip through her hair.

The hills are getting denser, and the path is lined with trees. They're weaving a bit, seemingly lost, until he finally finds what he's looking for. He pulls to a stop beside what looks to be a large dumpster, and gets out of the car. He pops opens the trunk and rifles through a few things, stuffing them into his open backpack. Lastly, he tucks a green plaid blanket under his arm.

She follows him, stepping over a chain held up by two posts, blocking a gravel path, which leads to a small clearing in the trees. "Hmm, a dumpster in the middle of the woods, tucked away high in the hills. If we were on a date, I'd think you were looking to either have your way with me or chop me up into a million pieces and leave me for dead...or maybe both." He looks at her in surprise, mildly shocked by the disturbing image.

"I thought you made it clear that this is not a date," he says good-naturedly. "And by the way, you're crazy."

He reaches back for her, and, as it is getting rather dark and she has no idea where they're going, she takes his hand. Together, they walk through the woods.

They stop in front of a giant rock, facing out of the side of a hill. It looks to be embedded into the hill from years of wind, rain and erosion, and the limestone surface is smooth, framed with moss and grass. There are a few trees around but the area directly in front of the rock is empty, grassy and flat, dotted with some early spring weeds and wildflowers.

He spreads the blanket out on the grass, and pats the ground for her to sit. She sits down, crosses her legs, and waits.

He immediately springs into action, pulling out an elegant, silver Apple Powerbook from his backpack and powering it on. Next, he plugs a contraption that looks like a camera but is much smaller, into one of the computer's USB outlets.

"What is that?" she asks, curiously. He is busy typing things on the keyboard, pulling up a folder of files.

"A projector. It's not even on the market yet. I got it from my dad, who's an investor in the company." He says this like it is perfectly normal to be carrying around a pre-market battery-powered projector on a Friday night. "I'm in the Science Club and have to give presentations sometimes, like with slides and shit. I like to have my own gear."

She laughs at him. "Gear? Like science is a sport, and you have to have your own equipment?" she continues to laugh until her stomach starts to hurt. "I'm sorry...that's just so nerdy. Do you happen to have your own lab coat and goggles, too?"

His face twitches with a smile. "Why in fact, yes I do." He seems a bit defensive but his tone is light. "And you should talk. Who studies on a Friday anyway? Plus, I'm on the basketball team, so I get a free pass for all things nerd-related." It appears he has finished setting up his "gear." He turns to her and asks her what movie she would like to watch. She shrugs, looking up at the sky that has quickly turned pitch dark, twinkling with a blanket of bright stars.

In a slight panic, she gasps. "It's so dark now. How are we going to find our way back?"

He whips out a flashlight and shines it at her face. She squints, swatting the flashlight away from her eyes.

"I brought two flashlights," he says, proudly. "Have you seen *When Harry met Sally*?"

She shakes her head no.

"Perfect. I have it downloaded." He double-clicks on a file, and a giant 80s-era Columbia Pictures logo is beamed on to the smooth giant rock in front of them.

"Wow…" Claudia breathes, taking in the setup. "This is like our own private outdoor theater…" she sprawls out onto her stomach, bending her knees and kicking her heels up towards the sky. "This is how the Ancient Greeks would have watched their movies, had they discovered computer technology instead of building the Parthenon." She is excited, looking at James with a wide smile. He cocks an eyebrow at her. She really is a nerd.

He plugs in a pair of headphones to the laptop and hands her one bud. She puts it in her right ear and he joins her on his stomach next to her, and puts the other bud in his left ear.

They watch Billy Crystal and Meg Ryan making their way through a story of love and friendship. Claudia and James stay side-by-side for the whole movie, chins resting in their hands, like two kids watching Saturday morning cartoons. The only physical contact is their shoulders, which touch out of necessity, since they are sharing a single pair of earphones. James is so close that she can smell his deodorant.

The movie ends and James closes the window but keeps the laptop on, serving as their light source.

"Well, that's just absurd." Claudia rips the ear bud from her ear and rubs it, sore from being stretched.

"What do you mean? That's one of the best movies from the late 80s, and I don't even like romantic comedies." He seems genuinely hurt that she did not enjoy the movie.

She rolls her eyes at him. "I'd hardly call that a rom-com. They're like, friends for ten years or whatever and then finally realize they should be together? How could you be with someone after knowing about all their intimate hang-ups and seeing them with all those other people? It's masochistic. Obviously, a dude's idea of romance. Like, *Oh, cool, you're an awesome girl...now let me sow my oats for a few years and wait around for me.*"

"Ooooh," he says with a smile. "Someone doesn't like to be strung along..." he gives her a knowing look. "And by the way, a woman wrote the movie."

She does a double take. "Strung – wait, what? Is that why we just watched that movie? Is that why we're here? Are you sending me cryptic messages?" She's spluttering. The nerve of him.

"No Claud, you're overthinking shit. It's just a cool movie." He is looking at her with that *you're crazy* look again. "Sorry you didn't like it. And for the record, if I had something to tell you, I'd say it to your face."

They're silent for a few moments, looking away from each other. He starts packing away his things.

"Sorry," Claudia starts carefully. "I keep freaking out at you. This was really fun, way better than studying all night. Thanks. And the movie wasn't bad, just struck a chord with me, I guess." She presses herself up to sit, shoulders aching from being in the same position for so long.

He shrugs. "No worries." He still doesn't look at her. He shuts down the laptop and puts it away in his backpack.

She waits for him to look up at her. When he does, she flashes him an apologetic smile, tilting her head sweetly. It works. He smiles back, showing his dimples.

She gets up and folds the blanket into a small square, and hugs it to her chest, shivering. It's gotten quite a bit chillier. He flicks on one of the flashlights, hands it to her, and turns the other one on as well. They start walking towards the car, Claudia following a few steps behind. Since her hands are full, he doesn't offer his hand to her this time, but she keeps her light shining on his back.

A buzzing noise greets them at the car as she opens the passenger side door. She realizes that she had left her bag in the car, and her phone as well. Fourteen missed calls and one unread text message are waiting for her. She reads the text first, knowing that the fourteen calls are probably from her parents.

Mom: Why are you not answering? Where are you?

Claudia sighs, and looks at James. "It's my mom. I have to get home. I'm never out this late." She quickly shows James her screen. He raises an eyebrow.

Fourteen missed calls? That's intense." He chuckles.

"It's past midnight," Claudia explains defensively. For most teenagers this is not an issue, but for her, it is an anomaly.

James expertly finds their way back to the main road in the dark, and gets her home within fifteen minutes. When they turn onto her street, Claudia sees a familiar car parked on their driveway.

How do I know that car? She wonders. James turns off the car, apparently ready to walk her to the door.

"No, don't," she begins. "Thanks for the ride. I had fun. You don't need to walk me to the door..." She looks at him, pleading with her eyes. She doesn't want to explain him to her mom, and she can already see the front hall light on, and her mother is surely peeking through the blinds.

"Alright, if you say so. But you can't say I'm not trying to be a gentleman." He gives her a friendly smile and reaches across her, bringing his body close. Claudia's breath catches at the contact, but he is only pulling the handle of the door, releasing it open for her.

She replies sweetly. "I appreciate the effort. Even though we're *Just Friends.*" She emphasizes the last two words.

"Just Friends? Or, "Just Friends"?" he uses his fingers as air quotes, challenging Claudia with raised eyebrows and a crooked smile. He knows he's pushing it but he can't resist. She blushes a deep shade of pink and narrows her eyes at him.

"Good bye James. See you Monday." She gets out of the car, feeling his eyes on her ass as she steps out.

The front hall light is on, and her mom pulls the door open before she has a chance to find her key.

She looks a bit mad, but mostly just worried, her pretty almond eyes wide as chestnuts. "Where have you been?" She scans Claudia's body and looks past her, outside, watching James speed away in his BMW. "I was so worried, I called Detective Bobby."

Claudia's eyes widen. "You called the *police?* Mom! I'm sixteen! It's not even one in the morning! Most kids stay out way later than this." She has no idea if that's true or not, but she figures, neither does her mother.

But the Police! That's a bit extreme. No wonder that car looked familiar. It belongs to Bobby Chan, the detective assigned to her case. Sure enough, on cue, Detective Bobby ambles into the front hall.

"She didn't exactly call the police," Detective Bobby says with a smile, obviously overhearing the conversation. "She called me on my cell. What's up Claudia? Everything alright?" Detective Bobby is in his early forties, half Chinese, half Irish, with a sprinkling of youthful freckles across his face, paired with deep-set dark eyes and black hair.

"Yes, just fine," Claudia says, straightening her spine. "I'm so sorry to bother you. I was just out studying...with a friend. I lost track of time."

"It's no trouble," the Detective says. "I live five minutes away. I was just getting off when your mom called, worried about you. I thought I'd drop by since I have some news for you anyway. Looks like you're okay, too, so that solves the emergency." He winks at Mrs. Young. She blushes at him.

"News?" Claudia asks.

"Yep. We found the girls who hurt you. One's the daughter of a known gang leader. Anyway, they confessed." He hands her an envelope. "I made a copy of the report for you in case you're interested. But just wanted to let you know, it's over."

Claudia nods, speechless. She hasn't thought about the attack in months. She more or less blocked the incident out of her head, trying to move on, but now, visions of those shrieking, psychotic bitches come rushing back to her. *Fucking bitch! You're gonna die!* She remembers the unforgiving crash of asphalt against her head as she fell to the ground.

She shakes her head to rid the image. "Okay," she says finally, exhaling. "Thanks."

"Sure. Let me know if you need anything at all. You too," Detective Bobby adds, signaling Mrs. Young. She smiles at him as he stoops down to put his shoes on. He opens the front door and leaves, shooting them a last smile and small salute.

Claudia now notices that her mom is only wearing a silk floral night robe, tied loosely around a white sheath nightgown. Even when her mom is ready for bed, she looks dressed up. On her feet she is wearing pointy mules that have a two-inch heel – her indoor shoes. Her face doesn't have a stitch of makeup on it but she still looks fresh and groomed, fifteen years younger than she is.

"Um, where's dad?" Claudia asks. "Were you already in bed?" She feels guilty, despite the overreaction.

"He is at the office," her mother says. "Some emergency at work. Anyway. I'm asking you again. Where were you?"

Claudia wonders why she didn't call her dad first, if she was so worried. Well, maybe she did, and he told her not to worry. As he should have.

"Sorry ma, I told you, I was studying." They speak a muddled combination of English and Mandarin, neither of them completely fluent in the other's dominant language. Claudia steps out of her shoes and starts towards the stairs, aiming to get to her room before any more questions are asked.

"Claudia, who dropped you off in that car? Was it a boy? I didn't even hear you leave the house. You snuck out." Her mom is looking at her with a suspicious stare. "You never go out late. It *must* be a boy. Tell me everything."

Making an exasperated sound, Claudia takes the steps two at a time the rest of the way. "Mom, he's just a friend," she says.

"And studying?" Her mother continues, exasperated. "If you go out, at least do something fun, Claudia. And don't walk away from me when I'm talking to you!"

Claudia stops at the top of the stairs and looks down at her little lady of a mother. "I'm tired mom, sorry for worrying you. You shouldn't have called the Detective. I did have fun studying. His name is James. We're just friends." And with that she goes into her room and closes the door.

The rest of the weekend passes by uneventfully. Spring brings unpredictable weather to Calgary, and after Claudia and James' pleasant night out in the hills, it pours rain non-stop. So, like all other weekends, Claudia diligently stays in the house, attends to her studies, and practices the violin for ninety minutes a day, as she has done since she was six years old.

She only leaves the house for dance rehearsal. She has been studying modern dance, jazz and ballet for over eight years.

She is preparing for a year-end recital with a group of eight girls, whom she has been dancing with for almost ten years. This will be their last dance performance together before Claudia goes to University.

When she was going through her plump, pre-adolescent phase, her mom had tried to get her to quit dance. Claudia was too chubby, she had thought, and it didn't make sense for her to surround herself with a bunch of skinny white girls. It would be bad for her confidence. She believed that instead, Claudia should focus on violin, and perhaps try her hand at the piano, too - a very refined, respectable skill for a young lady. But Claudia refused.

With the support of her father, who didn't see the harm in letting his daughter get a bit of exercise, she stuck with it. Studying dance has been her one rebellion against her mother, and also the reason for her good posture.

On Monday morning, sore from a weekend of grand battements and jetes, Claudia arrives a few minutes early to her Calculus class. She is usually the first one to arrive. She makes her way towards her usual seat, on the left side of the classroom, not too far back and not too far front.

To her surprise, James has beat her to class this morning and is sitting in his usual seat, one back from hers, with his textbook already open and pencil in hand.

"Hey friend," he says in his warm, friendly voice. "Ready for the quiz?"

"Of course." Claudia says, winding her hair up into a bun, and securing it with a hair elastic from her wrist. She sits down and peers back at him with a nervous smile. There's no doubt she'll ace the test, but she's still nervous.

She's wearing her tortoise shell glasses. They help her see the chalkboard crisply, and secretly, make her feel a little smarter.

"You look nice today," he says matter-of-factly. She glances down at her outfit. Jeans and a grey t-shirt, topped with one of her mom's cardigans. Black Converse sneakers with the laces tucked in. Definitely nothing to write home about.

"Thanks, man," she says casually, tucking a piece of loose hair behind her ear. "You look nice too." He's dressed just as plainly: A pair of dark-washed jeans and a black hoodie.

He smirks. "I try. So, did you get in trouble on Friday?"

Claudia rolls her eyes. "My mom called the cops. Or, *a* cop, I should say. But no, I'm not in trouble. My parents don't really believe in punishment, they just maintain a continuous level of scrutiny and are perpetually strict. I guess it's easier that way."

James laughs. "Wow. Cops, eh? Well, at least you know they care. My parents wouldn't even notice if I stayed out all weekend." His face fades for a second.

"You're in the Science Club. How much trouble could you get in to?" Claudia teases. James gives her a playful push on the shoulder.

She turns to the front and settles into her seat, taking a few even breaths to calm herself before the quiz. She fills her Bic mechanical pencil with new lead, and is about to put the eraser back on when he pokes her in the shoulder to get her attention. "Hey."

Claudia whips around. "Yeah?"

He clears his throat. "I wanted to ask you, um..." He looks around nervously, as their fellow classmates start filing in. He lowers his voice to almost a whisper. "Wanna go to prom with me? I mean as friends of course. Because we are "Just Friends"." He air quotes the last two words as he had on Friday night.

She freezes, her heart thumping a bit louder than she can control. She hadn't planned on going to the prom.

"Hmm…I'm not going." She looks at him apologetically, matching his whisper. She quickly adds, "but if I were, I'd go with you. You're pretty much the only person I talk to at school besides the teachers."

"Come on, you're going to miss your high school prom? It's a milestone. You need pictures to show your grandchildren one day. Plus, I was hoping to take the prettiest girl on the honor roll…" he chuckles nervously. He had obviously practiced that line, not knowing it would go to waste.

Claudia looks at him with a smile, but her eyes are expressionless. "No, thank you. You wouldn't have much fun with me anyway. I'm a bore." She turns back around and resumes fixing her pencil, slightly annoyed that he's distracted her right before their quiz.

James is relentless and leans over his desk to further convince her. "Just think about it for a few days. It would be fun." He sits back down as Mrs. Heidelberg, the large, intimidating calculus teacher enters the room and starts handing out the quiz sheets.

They decide to study together again on Friday at the downtown public library. Final exams are around the corner, and they both want to do well. This time, Claudia makes sure she is home by ten, and alerts her parents before leaving the house. They seem relieved that she is attempting to have somewhat of a social life, and applaud her for giving herself a curfew. They had never given her one before, since she never went out.

Claudia and James end up studying together every Friday for the rest of the term, and before she knows it, Claudia has found herself a real friend.

Claudia skips down the stairs, cell phone in hand, her backpack waiting at the front door. James will be picking her up in a few minutes for their last Friday night study session of the year. They have their last exam next week, and at the end of the month, they'll be receiving their high school diplomas.

Her parents are sitting on the couch in the family room. Her father is smoking a cigar in his armchair by the window, and watching the news on TV. Her mom is sitting on the loveseat, legs tucked under, playing some kind of video game on a hand-held device.

"I'm going to the library with James..." Claudia lingers in the doorway, leaning against the frame. Her mom is wholly consumed with the game and makes irritated remarks under her breath as she tries to maneuver her way through the game.

Her dad peers at her over his glasses, feet propped up on an ottoman. "You're spending a lot of time with this guy. Is he your boyfriend?" he raises an eyebrow at her. She knows that he's terribly uncomfortable with anything involving his daughter and another male, so she shakes her head frantically to ease his thoughts.

"No way. Just a friend. He's in my math and physics classes. He's really smart. He's in the science club. He's really nerdy..." she laughs nervously, talking too much.

"Ah, smart guy, eh? Invite him in so we can meet him." He turns his attention back to the television and Claudia suddenly feels nauseous. She had no intention of introducing James to her parents, ever.

Her mom pipes in as well, in between levels of her game and agrees that she should invite him inside. Not in the mood to argue with her mom, she sighs and sends a quick text to James.

Claudia: Could you come to the door when you get here? Parents want to meet you. Be nice.
James: I'm always nice. Be there in 5. Just getting gas. ☺

The next few minutes are excruciating, as Claudia sits on the leather loveseat with her mom to wait for James' arrival.

She tries to make light conversation. "Have you talked to Petey?" Claudia's older brother is at the University of Victoria on Vancouver Island. It's a short ferry ride away from Vancouver, and Claudia is eager to be closer to him.

"*Aiya*, he never calls me, you know?" her mom shakes her head, making a sour face. "Kids these days…so disrespectful." She sighs heavily and turns her device off. "Game over."

Claudia doesn't get a chance to defend Petey because she hears a rumbling noise, and a few moments later, a knock at the door. She jumps up and walks swiftly to open the door, her mother shuffling closely behind in her indoor mules.

She opens the door to a smiling James, wearing a grey t-shirt and jeans, topped with a fitted leather jacket. He is also carrying a motorcycle helmet.

Claudia's stomach drops to her feet when she sees that behind him, parked at the curb of her parents' manicured lawn, is a shiny, badass bike.

"Surprise, I got an early graduation present from my uncle. It's a Ducati." James steps inside and smiles at her sheepishly. "A surprise for me too, since I've never even met him. I was already on my way when I got your text. I would have driven my car if I knew I'd be meeting your parents," he whispers quickly.

Claudia turns to look at her mom, who is looking past James, at the motorcycle at the curb, a look of worry mixed with wonder projecting from her pretty eyes.

"Mom. Hey, *ma!*" She snaps her fingers to break her mother from the visions of motorcycle accidents that are clearly going through her head. She introduces a now nervous James to her mom, who eyes him up and down.

"Ah, James, good to finally meet you. We like to get to know Claudia's friends. Please come in." She smiles, confidently speaking her accented English in a singsong voice.

She can hear her father getting up from his chair in the family room with an overdramatic snort of exertion, and his even, daunting footsteps proceed through the hallway and towards the gathering at the front door.

Claudia stifles a giggle when she sees her dad. His cigar is still hanging out of his mouth, and he's biting on it like he's a pirate. He's wearing his "old guys rule" shirt he got on their last family vacation to Maui. His head is cocked to the side and it's now his turn to eye James up and down.

"Ah, I thought I heard a motorcycle," he says, perching a hand on his slim hip. "I once rode a motorcycle, but as a passenger. It was rather uncomfortable. How long have you been riding?" Having gone to College in the USA, Peter's English is near perfect.

James stretches his hand out to shake Mr. Young's hand. "It's nice to meet you, Mr. Young." The older man meets his hand in a firm grasp. "I've had my license for two years. I learned how to ride before I learned how to drive. I only take the local roads and I never get on the highway. My parents made me promise."

He says the word promise with a smile and a little bow of the head.

"Ah, very good," her father continues. "Very safe. It's good to listen to your parents. However, I'm sorry but I cannot allow Claudia to ride on a motorcycle with you."

Claudia is not surprised at all, but still looks at her father, narrowing her eyes. "Come on, dad, we're just going to the library, it's literally three minutes away."

"Ah, then you should walk!" her father says triumphantly, taking his cigar out of his mouth and using it like a finger, pointing it at them. "It's a very nice night for walking. Great meeting you, James. Next time, may I suggest you drive a car instead." He turns and heads back to the family room and his local news.

Her mother looks up at James, who towers over her by at least a foot. "Where your parents from?" she asks candidly.

"*Mom...*" Claudia warns. She knows where this is going. Her mom is never shy about asking personal questions.

"My mom's ancestry is Italian but their family lived in England, and my dad is English," he says, smiling at her politely. "They moved here before I was born. I grew up eating pasta and drinking a lot of tea," he says, chuckling. "Though I do love Chinese food..." he trails off when Claudia shoots him a glare. What's with the bowing and Chinese food talk? Is he mocking them?

But her mom is obviously drinking it up. "Oh, good! Chinese food is very good, especially when I make it. I will cook for you next time. Claudia, okay? Bring him for dinner next time." She looks at her daughter with a smile. "He's so handsome," she says in Mandarin, her eyes twinkling. "*Hao Suai!*"

Claudia can feel her face burning and she pushes James out the door, grabbing her backpack. "We're walking. See you later." They make it through the door just as she hears her mom making a final comment, reminding James one last time to leave his motorcycle at home next time.

James is laughing as he approaches his motorcycle. There is another, slightly smaller helmet strapped to the back edge of the seat, and he undoes the cord to also strap in the helmet he is holding. He snatches up his backpack, which has been perching on the seat rather precariously, and swings it onto his back.

"What were you thinking, coming here on a motorcycle?" Claudia asks him, shaking her head. "And what was all that bowing and Chinese food crap?" her second question comes off bitchy.

He shoots her an offended glance. "I thought you'd be excited to go for a ride." He brushes his hand lovingly on the body of the bike. He straightens, looking at her with his chin slightly lifted. "Had I known you'd want me to meet your parents tonight, I wouldn't have come looking like a greaser. I was already on my way. I told you that."

"They wanted to meet you. I didn't have any part in it, trust me. They want to know who I've been spending my Friday nights with and I figured they should meet my only friend at school. But anyway, back to my other question. Really, inviting yourself over for dinner, James. Were you trying to be funny?" she crosses her arms and looks at him.

"What? I hardly invited myself. I think your mom likes me." He puffs out his chest, gratified. "I do like Chinese food. And I didn't bow. You're being racist." He starts walking and softly checks her shoulder with his elbow as she falls into step beside him.

"*Me?* Racist? That doesn't even make sense. I know what I saw."

"I was just making an effort, Claud. Isn't that what guys are supposed to do when they meet a chick's parents? Make an effort?"

Claudia sighs. "Okay fine. You did well, I think my mom likes you. Do you really like Chinese food?"

"Who doesn't?" James smiles. He looks really hot in his leather jacket.

She kicks a couple of rocks and looks down as they make their way along the sidewalk.

She changes the subject. "Are you still going to the prom?"

He looks at her. "Yeah..." he says, hesitantly. "I'm going with my friends, and, um, I'm going with Tracey." He clears his throat. "Is that cool with you?"

Her heart drops a few inches at his answer, but she's in no way going to let him know it. She straightens her spine a bit and shrugs. "Of course. Cool. Good for you." If it's the Tracey she is thinking of, she is a tall, blonde, model-looking girl with sparkling green eyes and quite the reputation.

"Well, I wanted to go with you, but I assumed you hadn't changed our mind. Wait, did you change your mind?" His voice is hopeful.

Claudia pushes a button to cross the street. "Kind of. I was only going to go if it was with you, but since you're now indisposed, I'm back to square one. I'm not joking when I say you're my only friend." She smiles at him sheepishly, feeling like a complete dork.

He shakes his head. "Come on, no I'm not. You've gotta have some friends. I know you're new at school and all, but you're pretty cool. I guess you can be a bitch sometimes..." he laughs and runs across the street as she chases behind, landing a punch on his arm.

"Take it back!" She shouts at him, though she's smiling. "I'm not a bitch. I just don't have time for friends other than you," she says good-naturedly. "Between my AP classes, studying, violin, dance, and kicking your ass, I barely have time for anything else." She places the sole of her right sneaker right on his butt and pushes hard, sending him stumbling onto the library lawn. She laughs as he trips over himself, ungracefully catching himself from falling to the ground.

The library is only open for another 45 minutes by the time they get there. The walk had taken longer than expected and cut into their precious study time. Nonetheless, they both crack their books open right away, looking up only briefly to ask each other subject-related questions.

James is particularly engrossed in his textbook, so Claudia takes the opportunity to rip off a corner of loose leaf from her notebook, stick it in her mouth, and form it into a hard, soggy spit-ball. Without a straw she doesn't have great aim, but she effectively flicks the wad right on to his forehead, where it sticks for a moment, before falling off and onto his open book.

He swats at his head like there's a spider on it, shaking him out of his literary reverie. "Hey! Not cool. You're going to get a wet willy when you're least expecting it, mark my words." He shakes a finger at her. "Bad girl. Is that why you were expelled from your last school?" He's just teasing her, but realizes soon that he's hit a sore spot, as Claudia shoots him a cool glare.

"Sorry," he says. "It just came out. I am curious though. You're such a...*good* girl. I can't imagine you doing anything bad enough that would get you kicked out of any school. And there are all these weird rumors about you...." He trails off and his eyes lock onto hers, imploring.

Claudia knows about the rumors, and she hasn't made a point of explaining herself to anyone. So as far as anyone knows, they are all still rumors.

One rumor she has heard is that she'd slept with some gangster and his girlfriend had gotten mad and decided to beat her to a pulp in the parking lot at St. Agnes. Another rumor was that she was a drug addict, and owed money to some dealers, and that's why she was beat up. At least all the rumors got one part right: She was expelled because she was beat up.

Claudia sighs. "Yeah, I've heard all those rumors," she says with a shrug. "People will make up a lot of shit up when there's nothing to say." She hopes he'll believe her and leave it at that but she can see in his curious eyes that he wants more.

"So...what happened then? You know, I saw you on the bus...it must have been a few days after it happened. I didn't even know you then, but I remember it looked bad. They sure didn't take it easy on you." He shakes his head, looking sorry. "Whatever you did, it couldn't have been bad enough to warrant that."

She slams her textbook closed and meets his eyes, not wanting his pity. "I didn't do anything. I know it's hard to believe but it's true." Claudia bites a cheek. "They were a couple of loser girls who were looking for a thrill and I happened to be in the wrong place at the wrong time." She feels vulnerable, having not discussed this with anyone but her parents and the police for months. She gets up from the table, planning to go outside for a quick breather. "I'll be right back," she says, and heads to the large oak doors that lead outside.

The cool night air hits her as she steps outside and she inhales deeply, imagining her insides cleansing with the oxygen. As much as she wants to escape this city, she still loves how it smells. Fresh mountain air with a hint of pine, mixed with freshly cut grass. She would bottle it, if she could.

Getting beat up had been traumatic, physically painful, and a blow to her ego. But besides that, the worst part about the whole debacle, is that it made her lose trust in people. You never know when someone will decide to punch you in the face. Literally.

She's leaning against the library's brick wall, going to her happy place with her eyes closed, imagining a quiet green forest with rabbits hopping around, when a rustling noise jolts her lids open. James is standing in front of her with a worried look on his face, holding her backpack in one hand. His own pack is slung over his right shoulder.

"I thought it'd be good to start heading out, since they're closing in ten minutes anyway. I packed up all your stuff. Are you alright?"

She takes her bag from him, and nods once. "Yup. Thanks."

"I'm sorry for bringing it up. We won't talk about it ever again. I just wanted to know what happened. It doesn't seem fair that you had to leave your high school in the middle of Senior year because a couple of hoodlums decided to go Rambo on your ass."

"Ha," Claudia says, trying to move on. "Anyway, I'm fine. Just not my favorite topic of discussion."

"Fair enough," says James, a dimple showing on one side of his cheek. "The night is young, friend, what would you like to do? Considering we're on foot, I'd say our options are limited. But we could always walk back to your house and pick up the bike, though your parents would probably kill me."

For some reason, the idea sounds genius to Claudia just about now. If her parents find out, she'll already be on the bike and she can just deal with it later.

It takes them much less time getting back to the house than it did getting to the library. They ditch their backpacks and leave them by the front door of the house. No one's going to steal a couple of high school kids' textbooks, James reasons, though Claudia has her doubts. Her parents' geraniums have been stolen before.

James pulls the smaller of the two helmets carefully over Claudia's head, and clips the chinstrap. The helmet is black, with a reflective visor.

"I feel like a Power Ranger," Claudia says, flipping up the visor in the front. He does the same, and his pretty blue eyes are a jarring contrast to the black helmet. He climbs onto the bike and she gets on behind him, her knees jutting against his thighs.

"Okay, here we go. No jerking around back there, and wrap your hands around me...here." He takes her hands and places them right on his abdominal muscles, which she realizes are hard as a rock and ridged. She resists the urge to move her fingers at all. He pulls a pair of black gloves from his jacket pocket and puts them on.

"Just relax, and if you want me to stop because you're scared, or for any other reason, just squeeze. Ready?" He turns the ignition and revs the engine.

She squeezes with all her might.

He laughs and zips away from the curb, riding out of the quiet neighborhood, and into what's shaping up to be a very interesting night.

They ride about fifteen minutes towards the downtown area, and stop on 17th Avenue, a trendy street lined with bars, cafes and shops. Since it's nighttime, almost everything is closed, except the bars. Groups of teenagers mill around on the sidewalks, some smoking cigarettes, others riding skateboards.

James parks at an open meter and helps Claudia off the bike. They take off their helmets and he straps them to the seat.

"Aren't you afraid someone will steal those?" Claudia asks. The helmets look expensive.

"Nah...Believe in the good in the world, Claudia," he says with a wink. He pulls off his gloves and offers her his elbow. "Shall we, black ranger?"

Claudia hooks her arm through his with gusto and grins. She rises en pointe in her Converse, a favorite dancer trick of hers, to make up for their height difference.

James glances down at her feet. "Shit...does that hurt?"

"No," Claudia says. She does a couple turns, staying en pointe and pulling her arms up into a perfect fifth position, showing off. "This is why I love Converse sneakers."

"Wow," James says, impressed. "You're like, a real dancer."

"It's just for fun," she says, shrugging it off, and coming down on her feet. "So, what's the plan? What are we doing?"

He grins at her. "There is no plan. I figured we'd just grab a bite somewhere..." he glances around. Every bar on the street looks packed. "What are you in the mood for? Bar food? Hot dogs?" He points out a hot dog vendor parked at the next intersection, with a line of about ten people waiting for their fix of street meat. Claudia scrunches her face. She's not a fan of either suggestion.

"How about ice cream? There's a place a couple blocks down. It's organic." Not waiting for an answer, Claudia starts heading in the direction, pulling James along by the elbow. He follows without a word, lightly pulling his elbow out of her grasp, and instead, wraps his arm around her shoulders.

She looks up at him, giving him a questionable look. He shrugs nonchalantly. "I need a place to rest my arm," he says.

"Well, well," She says, playfully. "First, we're studying, then you get me on your bike, and now, I'm an armrest. Before you know it, you'll be buying my ice cream, too." She smiles at him.

"Hey babe, I'll buy your ice cream any day. Just name your flavor." He tightens his grip around her shoulders and he leans in to whisper in her ear. "As long as you let me lick – "

Claudia pushes him away. "Stop. That's too much." She feels like a prude, but she continues on. "Seriously, man. I don't mind a bit of harmless flirting but don't blow in my ear and shit. It feels funny." She crosses her arms, glaring at him.

"Funny, huh?" he turns to look at her, just as they've reached the ice cream shop. "I know we're just friends, Claudia. I respect that. But I've never pretended that I don't want more than that, if it were up to me." He runs a hand through his hair nervously, trying to look calm. "I know you like me too. I can tell." He looks at her, challenging her to deny it.

She sighs, leaning against the shop window. "I do like you, James. Mostly as a person and a friend, but I admit there's...something else, too. But I told you. It's just not a good time to start anything. I'm leaving for University at the end of summer. I don't want to start a stupid summer romance, and then get all hung up on you at the end. It's bound to work out that way. Maybe you're okay with having flings but I'm not." She exhales, taking a deep breath before looking at him evenly.

"Besides. You're going to prom with *Tracey*, right? I think she'd hardly approve of you licking anything of mine." She continues staring at him.

"Number one, I don't do flings. Hell, I've never even had a girlfriend." He looks away, embarrassed. "Two. Guess what? I'm leaving at the end of summer for school too, so big effing deal. You're not the only one going away for University, smarty-pants. And three, I told you that me Tracey are going to the prom as friends. Just friends."

"Right. Just like how you and I are Just Friends, James. Good one. And do you blow in her ear too?"

James can't help laughing. "You're ridiculous." He shakes his head.

"And by the way, you didn't tell me that you've decided where you're going to school next year. Some friend you are! Spill it James!" she glares at him, not even trying to hide her curiosity.

He tilts his chin up higher, shifting his gaze down at her, smiling smugly. "I'm moving to Vancouver. I'm going to UBC."

Claudia gasps, just as the door to the ice cream shop opens and a little bell jingles. A couple of teenaged girls push their way out, licking their melting cones.

James grabs the door on its way to close, and gives a shocked Claudia a teasing look. "Still want to get ice cream?"

They order their cones at the counter and go back outside to find a bench close to James' bike. Claudia insists on staying close by to keep an eye on the helmets, which James thinks is hilarious, and he laughs raucously, throwing his head back. He is way too cocky for a high school kid, Claudia thinks.

They settle onto a wooden bench and Claudia pulls her feet up into a cross-legged position. "Congratulations, by the way...on getting in to UBC. What are you planning on majoring in? And when did you find out you got in?" She talks between sumptuous licks of mint chocolate chip ice cream.

James is taking huge bites out of his scoop of chocolate, and has already started on the cone as he begins to answer her. "Biology. I want to go to med school when I graduate. But I also want to minor in something like Philosophy. I feel like you can't go to University without studying something completely useless like Philosophy." He flashes her one of his smiles, and continues, softly. "And I just found out today. Letter came in the mail. Between the excitement of the bike, meeting your parents and you freaking out at me again, I didn't get to tell you."

Claudia tucks a piece of hair behind her ear. "Cool. I guess I'll uh, see you around campus?" She focuses on catching the sides of her dripping ice cream with her tongue.

James is silent, having finished his cone. He stretches out his legs and arms, casually laying one arm on the back of the bench. This time he does not use her as an armrest, which surprisingly, kind of disappoints her. "Sure," he says, after a long silence. "See you around."

She knows she's being weird. They'd for sure see each other more than "around campus", considering the fact that they are from the same hometown, high school, and are actually good friends on top of it all. She's about to take her words back when he starts.

"I don't get you," he begins slowly, just as the silence is becoming too heavy. "I don't know if you're like this with everyone, or just with me. You're constantly rejecting me, even when you don't mean to." He laughs and continues in a less serious tone. "My ego can only take so much of a beating, dude.

My friends keep asking me what I'm doing every Friday and I keep telling them I'm studying with you. They think it's a huge crock of shit and that there's no way we're just studying together. I told them it's true, that we're just friends that study together."

He keeps going. "But the more I think about it, it is a huge crock of shit. I mean, I've been up front about my feelings about you from the beginning, and I totally respected your reasoning behind why you don't want to date. But now...after you've admitted that you do sort of have feelings for me, and I tell you that we're moving to the same city... going to the same fucking school...you don't even care. That sucks."

She looks at him, trying to express remorse through her eyes. "I do care! I think it's fantastic that you're going to UBC. I don't know anyone going there. Which honestly, I kind of like...but having you there will be...*fun*." She chooses the last word carefully. "We'll be college buddies." She gives him a hopeful smile.

He shakes his head and snorts. "OK, Claudia. Whatever you want. Study buddies, college buddies, whatever buddies. We can even be fuck buddies if you want." His face has taken on a scowl.

"What the fuck? Where did that come from?" Claudia is immediately fuming, like a struck match. She stands up and backs away from the bench. "That was totally unnecessary."

He shrugs, his face emotionless. "I'm just being straight with you."

Claudia looks up at the sky, uncomfortable. She may not want to date him, but she doesn't want to lose him as a friend, either.

She starts slowly. "I don't know what I want, James. This past year has not exactly been great. I was looking forward to finishing high school and getting out of Calgary. And then I met you. And you're so nice, and cool, and you don't care that I'm weird and nerdy, and that all I want to do is study. And you actually want to be friends with me." She looks away, insecure. "Well that's new to me, okay? I don't want to ruin it. What if we date and then we break up, and then you hate me? And then we'll be at the same school and I have to run into you with all these other girls and pretend I don't care, and..." Claudia stops, embarrassed.

James's face twitches with a smirk. "No, don't stop. Go on. I don't think I've ever heard you talk this much before about anything. I want to hear it." He crosses his left ankle over his knee. "You were saying...you'd have to pretend not to care about me dating other girls, *after* we've dated *and* broken up. Wait...how long do we date, before we break up?" He's wearing a shit-eating grin on his face.

"Shut up James. That's all I wanted to say. It's how my mind works. It projects forward and then pukes out of my mouth." She bites her lip, desperately wanting to change the subject. She sits back down next to him, not wanting to see his reaction. Slowly, she turns to look at him. He is staring at her lips, his eyes smoldering. He reaches over to touch her cheek as he did the first time he asked her out in the hallway. Her breath catches.

"*YO, JAMES!*" a black car squeals to a stop right in front of them, the tinted passenger window rolling down. DMX is blaring from the stereo. Claudia jumps and grabs on to James' arm with fear. She calms when she sees it is just some of James' friends from school. He gives them a little wave, almost a salute, with two fingers, and looks at Claudia nervously, almost apologetically. The car suddenly starts rearing forward, zipping a few meters away and expertly parallel parking into an empty space, a few spots down from James' bike.

Two guys and a girl tumble out of the car laughing, and the driver presses the alarm to lock it with a beep. They are headed towards James and Claudia, and they all have huge grins on their faces.

"Hey guys...what's up..." James says warily. One of the guys, the taller one with spiky black hair, cuts him off and reaches over to shake Claudia's hand.

"Hi. I'm Scott. You're Claudia, right?" He has a warm smile. "This is Tracey, and my man Brent. Don't worry, we're cool," he reassures her. "Didn't mean to interrupt your date..." he says the last word while wiggling his eyebrows, and proceeds to sit between the two of them on the bench, wrapping a friendly arm around each as if all three of them are old friends.

Tracey, a tall, pretty, blond girl, and the one whom Claudia suspects is James' prom date, rolls her eyes at the audacious Scott. "Come on Scott, leave them alone. They obviously don't want us around..." she tries to keep a straight face but suddenly erupts into giggles, and looks at Claudia, who responds with a blank, pokerfaced stare. She hasn't decided yet if she likes Tracey or not.

The leggy blonde is wearing cut-off denim shorts and a black t-shirt that says "Wild Child", and her hair is flat-ironed straight under a floppy, crocheted beanie pushed back on the crown of her head. Her nails are painted hot pink, and black ankle boots with buckles finish off the daring ensemble.

Claudia recalls briefly that she herself is wearing a pair of black leggings, a rather plain tank top, and one of her mom's cardigans. A chaste summer scarf is wrapped around her neck to hide any accidental cleavage. Luckily she left her glasses in her backpack, or she'd really feel like a dork.

"So I hear you won't be joining us at the prom," Tracey says to Claudia, sounding genuinely regretful. "I've stepped in as your

back-up...no hard feelings though. Anything for *Jamesy* here."
She kicks James in the shin playfully with her boot. "Luckily
these other dweebs found dates, so I only have to usher one
retard to the event." Her face reflects no signs of attitude, and
she is rather amusing, so Claudia decides to smile at her.

"Yeah, prom isn't really my thing," she explains, trying not to
sound like a snob. "But I sort of did change my mind..." she
stops, realizing that further divulging her change of heart will
sound like she's asking Tracey to relinquish her date.

Tracey squeals excitedly. "Yes! Do it! Come! We can all go
together. Going with a date is so lame, anyway. I only agreed to
it because these guys wanted to do it that way." She rolls her
pretty green eyes. "It's cause they think they'll get laid.
Anyway, we have one more spot in the limo. It'll be so fun! You
can be James' date, if you want," she adds, gently, touching her
arm.

Claudia looks at Tracey's hand on her arm, taken aback by
Tracey's forwardness. Does this cool girl want to be friends or
something?

She looks to James for help. He shrugs, with a smile on his face,
and looks at Tracey. "Thanks Trace. I thought you were gonna
lose it when you found out I was ditching you as a prom date."
He looks over at Claudia, beaming.

Tracey scoffs, flipping her long hair over her shoulder in a
sweep. "As if, bud! I was just doing you a favor. I'd much rather
not be your arm candy. I love you, but you're such a cockblock.
Anyway, you kids enjoy yourselves...we're out. Let's go." She
reaches down and pulls Scott to his feet by the wrist. Brent
trails behind a few paces back, playfully twirling his index
finger at his temple and crossing his eyes, behind Tracey's
back. He hasn't said one word but this makes Claudia smile.

James breathes out a sigh of relief as soon as they are out of earshot. "Sorry about that. My friends can be a bit much. Especially Tracey. She's Brent's sister, and thinks she's the boss of us all because she failed tenth grade and is a whole year older than us. But she means well. And she's a great friend." James stands up, stretching. "Well, Cinderella, we better get you home before my bike turns into a pumpkin, or your parents decide to call the cops on me." He cocks his head towards the waiting motorcycle and strides off, leaving Claudia sitting on the bench, wondering what just happened.

Tracey and Claudia become fast friends, mostly because of Tracey's persistent text messages, after she gets a hold of Claudia's number through James. Turns out, Tracey doesn't have many friends at school either – with the exception of James, Brent and Scott. They've all been friends since elementary school.

For Tracey, failing tenth grade was more a result of skipping classes and getting in involved with the wrong crowd than it was actual proof of her intellectual capacity. But the one debauchery-filled year left her with quite a reputation. The smart kids assume she's dumb; the preppy girls think she's a slut, and everyone else just follows suit. If anyone can understand the frustrating dynamics of senseless high school chatter, its Claudia.

"So, I want the real story," says Tracey, holding up a sequined mini tube dress from the sale rack at Holt Renfrew. They are shopping last minute for prom dresses since both girls realized late last night, forty-eight hours before the event, that neither had a dress to wear. Tracey's the kind of girl to have the booze and limo all organized, but a dress is last on her list. And Claudia's lack of enthusiasm requires no explanation.

"What story," mutters Claudia, though she knows exactly what story she's asking about. She sifts through the rack, skipping over the shiny, ruffled things. She seems to be drawn to the softer, flowing pieces, and safe, plain black.

"The *juicy* story," Tracey prods. "The one about you getting into a huge fight, getting put in the hospital and then kicked outta your last school. Trust me, when someone new mysteriously pops up in the middle of the year – especially senior year – people talk." Tracey pulls a blush pink chiffon maxi dress from the rack and shoves it at her friend. "This will look lovely with your bitch face."

Claudia pretends to be offended, but laughs. She's quickly learned that Tracey's favorite way to show affection to her friends is by calling them unwelcome names.

Opening up to her new friend, Claudia relays the story, minus a few gruesome details, and humors Tracey's nosy follow-up questions.

Tracey shakes her head, a cough of annoyance escaping her throat. "That really sucks. I mean, some people really deserve to get jumped. Like, me for example. I'm a total bitch to a lot of people. I am a bad student and I don't listen to my parents. I don't give a shit about a lot of things. But...no one beats me up. But you....I mean, look at you, no offense. You're such a goody-goody. I bet you play the piano too. It's so unfair." She gives Claudia a pouty, sympathetic look.

"Violin," corrects Claudia. She pauses before continuing. "I think I know why they did it. I think those girls could tell what I thought of them. I saw them pull in to the parking lot, get out of the car, sitting on the hood, acting all loud and obnoxious... they were picking someone up supposedly, a friend, or a brother or something. I think they could sense my judgment as I walked past them. I definitely looked at them and I remember thinking they were losers. They probably said to each other, *See that girl? She thinks we're pathetic. Let's jump her.* So they did. At least, it's pretty close to what it says in the police report."

Tracey laughs. "Fucking dumbasses couldn't think of a better reason to tell the police."

Claudia smiles, hoping this will be the last time she will have to talk about this. "Yeah. Whatever. Now they're in jail. And I," she says, doing a little pirouette, "am going to prom with the prettiest blond bitch in school."

Claudia convinces James not to go the prom date route, so that all three of them can go as friends. Tracey keeps insisting that she doesn't mind going stag but Claudia figures it's just a front. And while James and Claudia kind-of-sort-of talked through their feelings about each other that day on the bench, things are still up in the air and neither has decided to approach the subject again just yet.

But, date or no date, on prom night, James arrives at the Young Family's doorstep at six in the evening to pick her up. It's almost like just another Friday study date. Except this time, he is dressed stunningly in a fitted charcoal tuxedo, looking like he just stepped off the cover of a teen magazine.

Claudia went with the pink maxi dress that Tracey found, and her hair is loose in big waves that she has perfected with the help of a curling iron. On the left side, her hair is pinned back with a Swarovski crystal hair comb, borrowed from her mother, adding a bit of romance to the ensemble. Her makeup is light as always, but her eyes are lined with black eyeliner, giving her glamorous, piercing look that's borderline sexy.

James whistles, taking her in, when she opens the door. He smiles a half smile, the left corner of his mouth tugging up.

Claudia rolls her eyes at him as a warning. She can already feel herself blushing and her mom hasn't even taken pictures yet.

"Okay kids, one, two, three, say cheese..." her dad is using a point-and-shoot camera that still uses film, and the flash is astoundingly bright. Her mom is standing behind him with her camera phone, shooting video.

"I didn't get you a corsage," he says out of the corner of his mouth. "I thought you'd throw it at me since you've been insistent on this no-date crap." He continues smiling for the flashes. Claudia's mom has obviously changed her phone settings to camera as well, calling out her own spiels of one-two-three-cheese.

"Well, a corsage would have been...sweet." Claudia looks at him, just as another flash goes off. "But it's cool. I was pretty insistent. I wouldn't have bought me a corsage either." She smiles mischievously. "I, however, did get you a boutonniere..." she turns around to the entry hall table where there are two small cardboard boxes waiting. She takes one and opens it to reveal a creamy white rose with the stems neatly rolled in floral tape, with a couple of pins sticking out of it. She takes the pins out and holds the flower to James' lapel, and sticks the pins in from the back.

James is clearly touched, but embarrassed that he came empty-handed. "Claud...thanks. I feel like a jerk now. I'll make it up to you."

Claudia smiles brightly and shrugs. "No biggie. I got a flower for Tracey too." She grabs the other box that's waiting on the table.

She turns back to her camera-wielding parents. "We have to go..." Her mom is getting ready to shoot from another angle. She hams a big smile for her mom, showing both sets of teeth, like she is checking for food in her teeth.

"*Aiya*, Claudia, don't smile like that, it is so ugly!" her mom scolds, stamping her heel on the hardwood floor.

Claudia and James quickly push out the door and her parents follow, snapping pictures as they walk towards the limo at the curb, James leading the way. He pulls open the door just in time to reveal a shrieking Tracey popping open a bottle of champagne and pouring it directly into her own mouth.

Her parents pause in shock at the sight of their little girl getting into a limo with a bunch of high school boys, their scantily clad dates, and a champagne-guzzling blonde. Tracey sees Mr. and Mrs. Young staring at her and smiles widely, putting the bottle of champagne down. She wipes her mouth with the back of her hand shamelessly and gets out to meet them.

She is wearing the disco-ball sequined mini dress, with her signature black ankle boots. Her hair is crimped into zigzag waves and her makeup is heavy, especially on the eyes. Claudia thinks she looks smoking hot. Her parents on the other hand, may be thinking differently as, they gape at this beautiful monstrosity of a teenaged nightmare standing in front of them.

"Mr. and Mrs. Young, so nice to meet you! I'm Claudia's *best* friend, Tracey." She shakes both of their hands, talking a bit loudly, articulating each and every syllable, as if they are very old or deaf. Claudia suppresses a laugh. She has hardly known the girl for a month, but she's nothing if not enthusiastic.

"Don't you worry about her, I'll make sure she has a great time and that she is safe. No drinking and driving as you can see!" She motions towards the limo, hiccupping. Claudia shakes her head at her, hoping that she shuts up soon.

Claudia's dad sighs and puts a hand on his daughter's shoulder. "Have fun, Claudia. Don't drink. Too much." He gives her a scolding look.

Claudia looks at him in surprise. Since when were her parents so cool? The drinking age in Alberta is eighteen, but she has more than a year to go. Anyway, she isn't going argue with them about it.

She gives them each a quick hug and gets into the limo after Tracey. James follows after a quick word with her father about watching out for her. The limo door closes and a Top Forty radio station starts blaring. Tracey opens the box that Claudia passes to her, and gushes over the cream roses that have been artfully tied together into a wrist corsage. "Oh darlin'," she drawls in a very bad Scarlett O'Hara impression, "it is absolutely gorgeous. You are such a keeper." She holds out her wrist for Claudia to tie the roses on. When she's done, Tracey pulls Claudia's face to hers in a sharp tug and lays a fat kiss on her lips. She lets a bit of tongue slip, which makes Claudia yelp.

The limo cheers loudly, and Claudia's face is so hot, she is sure it has turned purple. She looks around for James and finds that he is sitting right next to her, his face a mix of amusement, shock, and perhaps, just a tinge of jealousy.

Someone passes her a glass of champagne and she sips it, enjoying the thrilling sensation of little bubbles going down her throat.

The prom is held at one of the new, fancy hotels downtown, built with the influx of money from the booming oil and gas industry. The ballroom is decked out in their school colors, an unfortunate combination of yellow and black. It's like being stuck in a beehive invaded by a bunch of noisy, dressed-up, drunk teenagers who are trying hard to act sober.

All of their teachers are present, and Claudia spends most of the night chatting with them, instead of her fellow classmates. She is forever grateful for her teachers, none of which had held her expulsion from St. Agnes against her, but instead, helped her get back onto her feet in the middle of a busy school year.

"I'll miss you, Miss Young," says Mr. Fields, her eloquent English teacher who is wearing a cheerful, forest-green corduroy suit with elbow patches. He has paired it with a floral dress shirt and the buttons seem to be on the verge of busting open. "Keep up with the writing. You have a real talent and I'd hate to see it go to waste." He eyes her up and down, zoning in on her cleavage. Obviously he's had a bit to drink as well.

"Thanks Mr. Fields. I will. And thanks for being a good mentor. You know, I got a perfect score on the written portion of the provincial English exam," she says, a proud smile on her face. "I didn't even know that was possible." She realizes she is gloating, but she figures it's okay, since he's the man that helped her get there.

"I had no doubt," her teacher says, glowing. "You're a smart girl with a good head on your shoulders. Now just don't let any boys get in the way..." he chuckles slowly, giving her creepy eyes.

She's about to hastily walk away to suspend yet another awkward moment in her life, when James strolls up next to her and casually throws an arm around her shoulders. "Heya Claud, hey Mr. Fields..." he is slurring a little bit but mostly just seems to be having a good time. "Mind if I steal away my little keener for some dancing?" he does a few comical hip thrusts to demonstrate what he means by dancing, and Claudia laughs.

She lets him take her hand and he pulls her to the dance floor – of course, just when a slow song starts. Groaning, she looks around for Tracey, and finds her quickly. The girl is wrapped around some dude who looks way too old to be at a high school prom. He is whispering in her ear and she is laughing, with her face buried in his neck.

"Who's that guy?" asks Claudia, pointing openly with disgust. "He doesn't go here. And he's certainly not a teacher. Don't they have security in here?" she looks around nervously, as if the guy is going to pull a gun at any moment.

James laughs and pulls her close, forcing her cheek to his chest, his chin resting on her head. "That's Warren. He's her on-and-off boyfriend. He's cool. Just relax and have fun. And now that she's clearly spoken for," he leans back and looks at her, his blue eyes shining, "I guess we're down to two. And I'll be damned if I graduate from high school without a date with the girl I've been chasing for months." He places a chaste kiss on her cheek, catching her by surprise. "And in case I forgot to tell you, you look absolutely, retardedly beautiful tonight," he says, his voice breaking, from the effort of speaking over the sound system.

Claudia smiles up at her own beautiful friend. "Thanks, Cooper. And you, I daresay, look absolutely ravishing. You'd give the eighteen-year-old James Bond a run for his money."

Feeling sentimental, she continues. "I'm glad I'm here and I'm so happy we met and became friends," she says, meaning every word. "And I'm excited that we're going to the same school next year. I didn't think I'd feel this way, but it would be pretty intimidating going to a new city and starting fresh without knowing anyone at all. I'm glad you'll be there." She stops her soliloquy before she says anything that her champagne-laden body refuses to filter.

Before the song ends, James is pulling away, his face mildly emotional, but smiling. He pulls her towards a table where she, Tracey and the other girls had left their things. "Grab your stuff," he says. "Unless you want to stay longer, which we can, but I kinda wanna get out of here," he says. He looks at her with a shy, hopeful smile.

Out of the corner of her eye Claudia sees Mr. Fields stumbling towards them, so she quickly snatches up her clutch and nods once. "Let's go, Bond."

The hotel is not far from 17th Ave, so they find themselves at the ice cream shop again. This time they sit at the counter indoors, facing out onto the street. Claudia gets a scoop of strawberry on a waffle cone. She figures, if she's messy, it won't look as obvious on her pink dress.

James is thoughtfully chewing on a mouthful of chocolate ice cream, when Claudia suddenly remembers Tracey.

"Shit!" she exclaims, pulling out her phone to text her friend. "She's probably looking for me. We were going to crash in a hotel room together. We booked it already." She quickly types in a few words and presses send.

Smirking, James turns to Claudia with a knowing look. "If I know Tracey – and I do – with Warren there, she is in no way thinking about sharing a room with you tonight. Sorry babe." He laughs to himself. "I'm glad you guys have gotten to be friends. She doesn't get along with a whole lot of chicks. Sucks for Brent because she pretty much scares off every girl he tries to date."

Claudia feels slightly miffed, being tossed aside for a guy, but brushes it off. "Oh well. I like sleeping in my own bed anyway," she says. She peers up at him. "What are your plans? Meeting up with the guys?" Last she'd seen, Scott was making out with his date outside the hotel bathroom, and Brent was tastefully slow dancing with his girl on the dance floor, a real contrast to the show his sister and Warren had been putting on.

"Nah. They're...busy," he chuckles. "I guess it's just you and me, Claud, until you want to call it a night." He continues to look at her, with that expectant look in his eyes. Claudia has had just about enough of this look, so she lays it out on the table.

66

"Okay James. I know I told you that you look like James Bond tonight, but I hope you don't think that you're going to get lucky. Tonight. With me, that is." She adds the last part quickly because she doesn't really know, or want to know for that matter, if he does in fact have other options.

"Fair enough," he says evenly, a favorite line of his. "But I have one tiny, teeny request." He has a glint in his eye. He stares at her lips.

Claudia's stomach flip-flops. "What's that?" She smiles coyly, because she knows what his request might be, and the thought of it kind of excites her. She bites her lip.

Without another word, James takes Claudia's ice cream cone from her, eats what's left of it in three bites, stands up, and throws her over his shoulder. He marches out the doors of the ice cream shop and on to the sidewalk, while she shouts at him. "You're going to ruin my dress, you asshole!"

He doesn't stop until they reach his car, which is conveniently parked about a block away. He puts her down. "Ah, that was fun. You know one perk about hanging out with a tiny girl like you? You make a guy feel fucking strong." He flexes his muscles theatrically.

Claudia laughs. "I'm hardly tiny, I'm like, 5'5. And you are strong. Look at you. You're ripped..."

She realizes he's smiling. "Stop fishing for compliments," she mutters. "And why is your car mysteriously here? Did you plant it so you could poison me at prom and dump me in the Bow River afterwards?" She is entirely joking, but James looks at her like she's a psycho.

"You have to let up on all that crazy psychopath shit. It makes me think that you might have a sick fantasy for something really bad like that to happen to you," he says, shaking his head. "Which would be really, really unfortunate. 'Cause then I'd have no one to study with anymore. And I hear University is a lot harder than high school." He grins at her. "Now, for my special request. If I may, of course."

Claudia crosses her arms, but he steps closer and uncrosses them. He puts his hands on her shoulders and gazes down at her, his eyes filled with adoration and mischief.

"Close your eyes," he says, softly. She closes them, tired of putting up her front. She parts her lips slightly, imagining his lips coming closer to hers. She feels one of his hands lift from her shoulder, and she tilts her head, expecting his hand to touch her cheek.

"*AHH!*" she shrieks. Something wet and slimy is in her ear and it shocks her out of her romantic trance. Her eyes snap open and she grabs the side of her head, cupping her ear.

She sees that James is keeled over and laughing so hard there is no sound coming out.

He finally catches his breath. "WET WILLY!!" he yells, like a maniacal seven-year-old. He attempts to stick another wet finger into her other ear, but she is ducking out of the way, screaming, and running from him. Still laughing, he envelops her from the back and pulls her to his chest. She is also laughing, but is quite disgusted, and involuntary wails are also sounding from her chest.

"Shh..." James says, still laughing. "If you keep screaming, people are going to think something's wrong."

Sure enough somebody from the apartment building across the road opens a window, switching on the light. An old woman with curlers in her white hair leans out the window. "What's going on down there? Is everything okay? Miss, are you okay? Do you need help? Should I call 911?"

"I-I'm fine," Claudia says, stuttering loudly. "I-I just noticed that my friend's face is so ugly, I had to scream. Sorry if I woke you!"

The old woman's face turns stern. "Keep it down out there, you hoodlums! Or I will call the police!" The window slams closed with an angry thud.

Claudia turns to face James. "You are soooo dead," she says, narrowing her eyes. She reaches up to grab his face, pulls him to her with an aggressive tug, and kisses him.

It takes a moment for James to realize what is happening. He has wanted this for a long time. Seriously, since he'd seen the gorgeous girl get on the bus six months ago, with bruises on her arms and a black eye, all he wanted to do was kiss that pretty cupid's bow mouth.

But it wasn't supposed to happen like this. *He* wanted to make the first move. Call him old-fashioned, but the guy is supposed to drive.

She pulls back, confused, and horrified. "You're not kissing me back," she says, stunned. "I just fucking kissed you and you're like a dead fish." She looks down at her nude pumps, peeking out from under her dress. "Well that's embarrassing," she says under her breath.

James shakes his head and runs a hand through his hair, looking at her. She is so fucking confusing. "Sorry, you caught me off-guard. One minute you're telling Betty White that I'm ugly, the next you're sucking on my face. You are so fucking...."

He steps closer to her and tilts his face down to hers. Her dark chocolate eyes stare up at him despondently, her pride obviously hurt. Her mouth is neither smiling nor frowning, but entirely kissable.

"You're so fucking hot." He leans down and brushes his lips against hers, teasing them open. He catches her upper lip between his lips and lingers there. His hand moves to the back of her head and she leans into it, as she lifts her face to give him a better angle. He feels her sweet tongue and welcomes it with his own, hungrily crushing his mouth to hers.

For minutes, they stand there on the dark street, next to his car, kissing. When they finally pull apart, they stare at each other, exhilarated.

"Well," she says, not breaking eye contact, breathing heavily.

"Well," he says softly, staring back at her, his face flushed.

"I....guess we should call it a night," she says, hesitantly. "It's getting late."

"Tease," he says. His eyes are playful, so Claudia knows he's kidding. "Get in the car....friend."

True to his word, James drives Claudia home. The champagne has worn off by now – he'd only had a couple glasses, anyway. He explains to her that all the guys had dropped their cars off earlier in the day so that they'd be able to drive home in the morning, in case they partied too hard at the hotel.

"I'm sorry you didn't get to spend the rest of the night with your friends," says Claudia. "I remember you saying how prom is a big deal and all," she adds.

"I just said that to try and get you to come," says James. "I guess it worked, huh?" he looks at her briefly, still smiling from their heated kiss. "And why are you sorry? I'm the one who wanted to leave. I'd rather spend my prom night with someone I can kiss good night." He reaches over the console and grabs her hand, squeezing.

She lets him hold her hand and even enjoys it. She sighs. "I don't know what's wrong with me. I don't want to say good night." She looks at him shyly. "No one's ever kissed me like that before…"

"Well, you could invite me in…or we could go to my house. Just to hang out of course," he says. "I heard your warning in the ice cream shop loud and clear." Claudia is breathing a bit faster, just the thought of possibly kissing him again giving her stomach butterflies.

"We can go to my house. I'll have to sneak you in," she says. "My parents are sleeping and they wouldn't want us to be hanging out this late, in the house. But we can make – um, hang out in the basement."

"Deal," says James. They arrive at Claudia's house a few minutes later, and he turns off the car. He turns to her in the dark, touching her cheek.

"Just wanted to let you know, that um, I'm really, really glad you decided to go to the prom," he says.

He gets out of the car, and since she's gathering her things he has time to cross over and open her door for her. She takes her shoes off before stepping out, since it's a short walk to the door.

"I hate wearing high heels," she says with a pained face. "They're torture devices invented by men."

Claudia unlocks the front door to the dark house, and they creep in silently. She can hear her father snoring soundly upstairs and she times each noise she makes with his snorts. James notices this and has to contain his laughter. She shoots him a sharp look and brings a finger to her lips to shush him.

The basement door is not far, and they quickly find it without turning on any of the lights. She opens the door and pushes James through, almost making him trip down the steps.

She follows behind, switches on the light, and closes the door. She lets out the breath she's been holding.

"This whole sneaking around thing kind of turns me on. You better be careful..." James says, only half-joking. The basement is fully developed, and covered with plush shag carpeting. A comfortable leather couch, a classic Eames chair and a huge, 70" television are assembled together in a cozy living area. She switches the TV on and turns the volume down low. She flips to a channel that's playing an old black and white movie.

She relaxes into the soft couch and James joins her, taking off his tuxedo jacket and vest. He loosens his tie and tucks it into the pocket of the jacket, and undoes the top button of his dress shirt.

Claudia has already taken off her shoes, and her dress is as comfortable as a nightgown. She removes the crystal comb from her hair and runs her fingers through, massaging the scalp. When she's done, James leans over and pulls her close, bringing his mouth down to hers for a deep kiss. She loves it. But...

"Wait," she says, pushing him away. She is dramatically gasping for air.

"What's wrong?" James says, pulling away, breathing heavily. His eyes are heated and full of lust.

"Let's just talk," says Claudia, as she catches her breath. Though talking is clearly what neither of them want to do right now, she suddenly feels an obligation to her future self to clear things up with this boy.

"I just want to set things straight, and know where we stand...before anything else happens between us." She speaks sensibly, looking at him directly in the eyes.

His eyes flicker nervously. *Not this again,* he thinks. "I'm an open book, Claudia. You wanted to be just friends. I gave you that. But we're going to the same school next year. We're going to be around each other a lot. I want to be with you. And not just some buddy that you kiss once in a while or study with..."

He pauses, thinking carefully about his next words. "I want you to be my girlfriend." He looks at her anxiously, waiting for a reaction.

Claudia's heart is pounding so hard she can feel it in her stomach. She curses herself for what she's about to say.

"I can't. I'm sorry." Claudia feels tears forming in her eyes, and she is angry with herself for letting them show. "I'm so stupid. I don't know why I asked you to come in and everything, and now we're sitting here, and you're telling me what any girl would want to hear and I'm just...." She trails off, shaking her head at herself. "I'm so, so sorry James."

James is shifting uncomfortably in his spot on the couch, looking at her with his mouth in a tight line, pissed off. "Uh, okay, this is kind of fucked up. Why am I here if you don't want me here? I thought we were on the same page. You kissed me first."

She looks at him and grabs his arm. "I *do* want you here...Look. I really, really like you. I never like guys. Ever. I'm so fucking glad that we're going to the same school next year because it means I get to see you, maybe even every day. But...we're starting a different part of our lives. We're going to be living in dorms! Do you know what dorm life is like? We're gonna meet so many new people and...things are going to change." She pauses and takes a breath before continuing. "We might want to be with each other now, in this moment, in our little world, here in Calgary. But what happens next year when one of us realizes that..." she doesn't know how to finish her thoughts. But she doesn't need to.

"Ah, I see," he says, with a sneer in his voice. "Yeah, totally makes sense." He gets up abruptly. "Let's not hook up all summer, then go away to University, and then you realize that there is someone or maybe a whole shitload of someones out there who are way better for you than I am. Right? Cool. Got it. I'm out." He picks up his things calmly and heads up the stairs. "I'll let myself out. Good night Claudia."

"Wait, James, that's not what I meant!" Claudia calls after him, but he is already opening the basement door. She considers following him out but doesn't want to wake her parents and make a scene. Her eye catches the window near the ceiling by the television and she remembers that it opens to the patch of lawn at the side of the house. She pushes the coffee table against the wall and slides the window open. Then, using all her strength, she pulls herself up and shimmies through, the narrow opening, snagging the hem of her dress.

Sure enough, she catches him just as he is getting into the car.

"James!" she whispers loudly. The dark silence allows for her voice to carry, and James looks over his shoulder to see her standing barefoot, on a patch of grass at the side of the house.

74

He stares as she walks to him, an ethereal vision of billowing soft pink that looks almost white in the moonlight.

Her small arms wrap around his neck, pulling him down. She hugs him, wishing that she hadn't said what she said.

After holding her for about a minute, he pulls back and gently pushes her away. His eyes are sad and he looks away quickly.

"You said your piece, Claud," He says. "And you can't take it back. You shouldn't. You can't help how you feel. No hard feelings."

He opens the door to his BMW, pausing as if he is about to say something else. He decides against it and shakes his head.

"See you on campus..." he says, and pulls the door shut. Claudia watches the BMW pull away, as James drives home in the dark.

The rain is pounding relentlessly against Claudia's large black umbrella as she hurries across the muddy UBC campus. She carries an achingly large canvas bag on her shoulder, which contains a laptop, two textbooks, a stainless steel water bottle and several power bars since she often doesn't have time to stop for lunch. Normally she leaves the umbrella at home and just pulls a hoodie over her head, but her mom just sent her this beautiful new leather jacket in the mail, so she decided to give it a try. A pair of dark blue jeans are molded tight and wet against her legs, and tucked into a pair of lace-up ankle boots. Her hair is braided loosely off to the side and it hangs over one shoulder, nearly reaching her waist. She has been growing her hair long ever since a very traumatic haircut in her first year of University, and she would sooner burn off her eyebrows than cut it again.

She's headed to the Student Union Building to meet Tracey. Excited to see her best friend, she speeds up her walk, splashing into puddles that have gathered on the sidewalk. Tracey is taking a few days off from her retail job in Calgary, to visit Claudia in Vancouver for the weekend. She will be staying with Claudia, close to the UBC campus, just a few kilometers away. The two friends have grown even closer after high school, despite the fact that Claudia spends less than two weeks in Calgary each summer and goes home only for the most important holidays.

Stepping into the warm, heated building that the students call the SUB, Claudia shakes out her umbrella, letting the droplets fall onto the red tiled floor. She unzips her jacket and loosens her scarf while squinting around to find Tracey. She sees her almost immediately; Tracey is hard to miss. The leggy blonde is in the gift shop, by the calendars, in a pair of skin-tight black jeans tucked into thigh-high, black leather boots. A bright fuchsia sweater hangs loosely on her torso, exposing one shoulder and a black bra-strap. Her platinum hair is tucked into a slouchy black beanie, and she is carrying a large duffle bag with her initials, T.M., embroidered on the side.

Claudia walks up behind her friend and wraps her arms around her. Tracey is much taller - close to 5'10", so the hug only goes around her middle.

Tracey spins around. "Hey!" She kisses Claudia on the cheek. "You found me! This is Trevor." She points her thumb to a big, lumberjack-type dude with a full beard, who is openly ogling Tracey's tight jeans-clad butt. "Trevor was just telling me about this new club in Gastown. We should totally check it out! Nice to meet you by the way – see ya!" She casually waves goodbye to Trevor, and he grunts a response, obviously not happy that Claudia has interrupted their little moment.

Eyeing an empty couch in the commons area, Claudia swiftly leads Tracey over before anyone can snag it. She drops her heavy canvas bag on the floor and relaxes into the musty couch with a sigh.

"I'm so glad you're here, Tee. Sorry I couldn't get you from the airport. I had so many classes today and then I had to tutor. I'm glad this semester is almost over, because I really need a break." Claudia is double majoring in English Lit and Math. One for her soul and the other for her mind, she likes to say, though she's not sure which goes with which.

"Always the bookworm," Tracey says wryly. "But listen, I don't want to hear anything else about school while I'm here. This weekend is strictly for drinking our faces off and having a good time."

Out of the corner of her eye, Claudia sees a familiar male figure heading their way. To her surprise, it's Brent, Tracey's younger brother. "Hey Brent!" she calls out, waving. "Is he here with you?" she asks Tracey, lowering her voice. "Not that I mind. I just didn't know he'd be here."

Tracey shoots her an apologetic look. "Sorry, I didn't want you to get your panties in a wad. He's here to see James, and we flew in together. Don't worry, he's not staying with us. James can't meet him until later on so I told him to hang with us while he waits."

"Oh! Cool." Claudia says brightly, just as Brent approaches. She really likes Tracey's younger brother; a quiet, considerate type that always has his sister's back. She has only seen him a couple of times since graduation, at their house in Calgary, since both siblings still live at home with their parents. It turns out that the blond twenty-one-year-old has really grown into himself. He's unshaved, and his wavy blond hair has grown long to his ears, with the front pieces grazing his hooded eyes.

Brent leans down to give Claudia a big hug. "Hey Claud," he says in his soft voice. "Good to see you. You look great, as always." He smiles at her, his green eyes just as deep as his sisters, but with little yellow flecks. He sits in a chair across from them and swings his own duffle bag to the floor.

Tracey turns to Claudia and sighs loudly. "Okay, look Claud. I don't want this to be weird, but James is my friend, too. I don't know what went on between you two, like, whatever, four years ago, but you need to get over it. I want us all to hang out this weekend, at least for a bit. I'm done with splitting my time between you dorks. You're graduating from University for God's sake. You can't still be hung up on stupid high school shit. Plus," she adds with a knowing look, "You guys practically live on the same street. Surely you've run into one another."

Claudia is engrossed with picking the nonexistent lint off her wet jeans. It's true, James lives in the basement suite of a little white house not too far from her own place, and she does sometimes see him riding to class on his motorcycle. When she sees him coming, she always turns her head away from the road in case he catches her face. The two had run into each other here and there during First and Second year, at parties, or just walking around on campus, but each time Claudia would try to get away as quickly as possible, wanting to avoid any uncomfortable conversations. After all, they'd only shared a kiss, and the rest was...well, nothing. And James never made a move to rekindle their friendship, anyway.

In fact, after prom night, she'd only heard from him once, and he hadn't even bothered to pick up the phone. James had sent Claudia a text message, two months later, in August. He told her he was driving up to Vancouver the next week, and offered her a ride, to save on gas or a plane ticket. It was a formal, courtesy message, spelled out in a couple of short sentences. Her brother Petey had already flown in from Victoria to drive up with her in her new Honda Civic, so she'd politely said no thank you.

"I see him here and there," Claudia says, finally. "I think he's pretty busy most of the time and our paths don't cross often. And he has a girlfriend, I'm pretty sure...." She clears her throat before continuing. "But we're cool. I mean, I don't avoid him or anything."

Brent chuckles quietly. "You're a heartbreaker, Claudia." She knows he is joking, but Claudia's heart does a flip. *Heartbreaker?* They hadn't even been dating.

"What do you mean? Barely anything – I mean, *nothing* happened between us."

Brent stares at her for a moment, twisting his mouth thoughtfully, as if considering whether or not he should continue. "He turned down a full scholarship to McGill to follow you here. The guy had it bad for you..." He stops, his sister shooting him a sharp warning look.

"We don't need to talk about that shit, Brent. It's in the past. They weren't even dating. And it's not Claudia's fault the guy never called. He's a stubborn shit sometimes. Right, Claud?"

Claudia looks at her friend guiltily. "Maybe not," she says, surprising herself. "We were in high school. Maybe I should have given him a chance. I wasn't ready for a real relationship, and I had all these funny ideas in my head. I thought that everything was going to change...who I was, what I liked..." She shakes her head and forces a smile. "Anyway, it doesn't matter. He has a girlfriend now."

Tracey and Brent look at each other, clearly scheming. Claudia narrows her eyes at them. "You better not be planning anything stupid. It would be a disaster. Please. Just don't." She looks from one flaxen-haired sibling to the other, looking for compliance.

"What would be a disaster?" A familiar male voice behind Claudia sends chills up her neck. She freezes momentarily, wondering how much he has heard. She turns around and gazes up into the deep blue eyes of a once-familiar face.

James is big. After high school he seemed to have taken a liking to the gym and his former lean 6'3" frame is now defined with muscle. Somehow, he still manages to look trim and sticks to his t-shirt, jeans and hoodie ensemble, topped with a leather jacket. Claudia hasn't been this close to him since last October, when they ran into each other outside the Main Library, on her way to her Literary Criticism class. He'd been with a pointy-nosed brunette whom he hastily introduced as his girlfriend, and then quickly walked away, with his hand on her lower back. Claudia had stared after them, feeling awkward and jealous. She'd proceeded to hit up the campus pub after class to throw back a few tequila shots with her friend Hannah, whom she'd roomed with in First Year. A few shots in, she successfully warded off her unreasonable, unrequited feelings.

And now he's here, staring at her, looking very serious, and his sudden presence leaves her mouth dry and her heart pounding into her stomach.

"Shoot, I was just about to tell the girls that you were on your way," says Brent, grinning, standing up to pull his buddy into a man-hug. "James finished early so I told him to meet us here." He's clearly explaining for Claudia's benefit. "Thought we could all grab a bite to eat."

James steps around the couch and Tracey squeals, standing to give him a big hug. "I've missed you, Jamesy," she says sweetly. "Good to see you. Haven't seen you since Christmas."

They smile at each other, old friends who've known each other almost their entire lives. Finally, James turns to Claudia.

"Hey…" he says carefully, his face falling ever so slightly. Claudia isn't sure if she should stand and hug him like Tracey did, or if she should stay sitting. Not wanting to be rude, she gets up abruptly and gives him an innocent, one-armed hug, avoiding any chest-to-chest contact. It's more of a pat on the back.

He chuckles. "You call that a hug? Come here." He pulls her to him suddenly, lifting her off her feet. Surprised, she wraps her arms around his neck, more as a safety precaution than anything. When he puts her down and they pull away, his amused eyes are pinned to hers, challenging. Claudia lifts her chin, refusing to look away.

Things are starting to get weird just as Brent clears his throat. "So…anyone hungry?" he asks, tickled by the standoff between his friends.

"Yeah." Claudia says, breaking her stare and grabbing her bag. "I can eat."

"Yes!" says James, smiling boldly. "I'm starving."

The girls decide to drop off their things at Claudia's place before heading out to dinner. Claudia's Honda is parked behind the SUB so they walk out in the rain, arms linked, under Claudia's umbrella. The guys follow behind, braving the elements.

James rode his motorcycle today, so Claudia offers to give the guys a ride to James' place. The boys cram into the small backseat after throwing everyone's stuff in the trunk.

It's a short drive from campus to Blanca Street, but the windows fog up quickly from all the talking going on in the car. James and Tracey are talking over each other, arguing about where to eat. They finally decide to go to Hell's Kitchen, a casual pizza place on 4th Avenue.

Claudia stops in front of James' house, and she catches a glimpse of his surprise in the rearview mirror. He didn't expect her to know where he lives.

"I see you still have the same car..." she indicates the blue BMW parked at the side of the street. "Probably safer to drive that in the rain than the bike." She can't help her tone.

James laughs. "Cautious Claudia. Some things never change." The guys get out of the car and before he closes it, he leans back in. "We'll swing by to pick you guys up in a bit. We'll take my car. Leave yours. Text me your address..." He pauses, perhaps noticing the déjà vu, but doesn't wait for an answer and slams the door shut. Claudia pulls the lever to pop the trunk open and turns in her seat to watch the two handsome men carry their things into the house. She is still staring at James' backside when Tracey smacks her in the arm.

"Come on horn dog, let's go. I need to pee, bad." She gives her a rascally smile. "You still like him..." she sings, taunting.

Claudia rolls her eyes and puts the car into drive, pulling into the parking garage of her building within a minute, just around the corner. "I'm not blind, Tracey. He's always been hot. Your brother's isn't that bad either," she adds, keeping a straight face.

Tracey laughs, unperturbed. "Yep, looks run in the family, I'm afraid. And if you want Brent, you have my full approval my dear. Though you better not break his little heart too..." she trails off, her face unmasking a hint of a warning.

Claudia rolls her eyes. "He's not my type, so don't lose any sleep over it. And really, I've had enough of this heartbreaker crap. I thought you were on my side! Like you said, he never called." She gets out of the car and pops the trunk to get their bags.

"True," Tracey confirms with a nod. "But neither did you." She takes her bag from Claudia and walks to the elevator. They ride it up to the two-bedroom condo on the eleventh floor. Claudia's parents bought the place a year ago, after getting sick of staying in hotel rooms on their monthly visits to see their daughter.

Tracey has been here many times, and she makes herself right at home, taking over the guest bedroom and hitting up the bathroom right away. Claudia can hear her peeing loudly for what seems like a full minute.

"You weren't kidding," Claudia shouts from the living room. "You're peeing like a racehorse!" She laughs, going to her own bedroom. She pulls out her phone from her pocket and scrolls to find James' number, which she still surprisingly has saved after all these years. She sends him her address.

The condo is cozy, with the main area comprising of the kitchen, living room and a dining room, which doubles as her desk. The master bedroom is on the far side, with an en-suite bathroom, and the guestroom is to the left of the front door. There are hardwood floors and floor-to-ceiling windows that overlook the Spanish Banks beach. Claudia knows how lucky she is to live in a place like this while going to school, and she studies extra hard because of it.

It's almost five in the evening, and she figures they'll be going somewhere to party after dinner. The key to dressing for spring in Vancouver is layering. The topmost layer will always get wet. She decides she will wear the leather jacket but strips it off first to change into a thin organic cotton t-shirt and a cashmere cardigan. She ditches the scarf and loosens her braid, shaking out her wavy hair.

She grabs her go-to black handbag from her dresser and transfers her necessities from her book bag: Wallet, lip-gloss, and cell phone. She notices a text message from James flash on the screen. She hasn't seen his name on her phone for years.

James: You live close. We're parked outside. Take your time.

She throws the phone back into her purse and checks herself in the mirror. Her skin's a bit pale, like she's seen a ghost. She dabs a bit of blush on her cheeks. Smiling at herself in the mirror she mentally tells herself that everything is fine. It's just a bunch of old high school friends, hanging out. He doesn't even care anymore, so why should she?

Tracey peeks into her room. "Ready? Brent says they're outside." She catches Claudia smiling goofily at herself in the mirror. "You look beautiful, dork. Let's go."

The boys are parked in a no-parking zone right in front of the building. Brent gets out of the passenger seat, insisting that Claudia take it instead.

"Shotgun for the lady," he says. Tracey smacks him, asking what that makes her, and he laughs.

The front seat of James' car is familiar. Claudia remembers the last time she was here. They were on their way home from prom, after their kiss. Just thinking about it makes her flush and she takes a deep breath.

James notices, and looks over at her when he stops at a red light. He catches her eye, and his lips twitch hesitantly into a half-smile. "Your hair is so long," he says, reaching over to flick a lock that has fallen loose from behind her left ear. "It looks nice."

"Thanks," she says, quickly. She's about to return the compliment but stops herself. Too trite. Though he does look good, in his dark jeans, white long-sleeved t-shirt and bulky Timberland work boots. But something is different about him. He looks older.

"How old are you now, 21?" She asks.

"22," he says. "Just turned. I started kindergarten late, so I'm a year older." he explains.

She nods politely, like they are strangers. "I didn't know that. I skipped third grade. I'm twenty. So, you're two years older than me."

"We never really got to know each other eh?" Says James. "You were more interested in your books than you were in me." He winks playfully.

Tracey and Brent are busy on their smartphones in the backseat. Tracey is snapping pictures of herself and Brent is texting someone, with a little smile on his face.

"How's Candice, man?" James calls out to his friend in the backseat. "Still going strong?"

Tracey snickers. It's no secret that Tracey detests every girl that dates her brother. She is extremely over-protective – and rightfully so, since Brent is just about the nicest guy in the world, and girls tend to walk all over him.

"Hmm, no we broke up," says Brent. "She went back to her ex. I'm seeing this other chick now, Malia. She's fucking amazing..." he scrolls through the photos on his phone, looking for a picture. He finds one, admires it with a quick smile and holds it over Claudia's seat to show them.

Malia is indeed amazing. She looks Indian, with big copper eyes staring suggestively at the camera, and a generous dose of cleavage pushed between her arms. Claudia can tell why Brent is smitten.

James lets out a whistle, after a quick glance. "Nice, she's a hottie..." Claudia sees him glance at her way quickly.

Hell's Kitchen has a covered, heated patio so they decide to sit outside when they get there. Tracey lights up a cigarette even though the city has a strict no-smoking policy for all public areas.

"You're going to get a ticket," Claudia warns, but does little to stop her friend. Tracey has a mind of her own and the more you tell her to not do something, the more she's going to do it. This might be the only thing the girls have in common.

Sure enough, the manager comes outside to tell Tracey to put out her smoke. Tracey glares in protest.

They order two pitchers of beer and two pizzas to share.

"Claudia says you never run into each other," says Tracey, raising an eyebrow at James. She is obviously trying to stir the pot. "I find that incredibly hard to believe. What's the deal, are you repulsed by each other?" She sits back with a satisfied face, eager to see how this plays out.

"Yeah. Completely repulsed," says James sarcastically, looking across the table at Claudia.

Claudia decides to ignore Tracey. "How's your girlfriend, James?" she asks, taking a sip of her beer. "Is she going to be joining us?" she looks around, as if said girlfriend is going to appear at any moment off the street.

James snorts. "No. That didn't work out. She freaked when she found out I was going to med school in Toronto, without consulting with her first. I felt bad for breaking it off, but she knew it was coming." He looks at Claudia with a smile. "Your turn. Seeing anyone?"

"Med school huh? Congrats! I can't say I'm surprised," she says, meaning it. James has always had his eye on his future. He nods his thanks, waiting for her to answer his question.

"Yes, I'm seeing someone," says Claudia, straightening. "It's not serious, but..."

Tracey gasps, interrupting. "You wench! You didn't tell me that! What else have you been keeping from me? And will this person be honoring us with his presence tonight?"

Claudia smiles weakly. "Well, it's not exactly public. We're not supposed to be dating." She avoids eye contact with James who is staring daggers into the side of her head.

She continues, realizing she'll only make it worse if she draws it out. "It's one of my professors." she spits out. "We've only gone on a couple of dates and we're really just getting to know each other for now."

Professor Quinn, or *Rob*, as Claudia now calls him, teaches her Senior-level Differential Equations class. He is young for a professor, in his early thirties, and could be easily mistaken for a student. They ran into each other off-campus at Starbucks one Sunday, a few weeks after the term started. Claudia had never noticed him any more than she had her other professors, but that day he was dressed in a casual hoodie with jeans, looking like a regular guy. They ended up spending the afternoon together, talking over cups of Earl Grey tea.

"A *prof*?" James asks incredulously. "You've got to be kidding me, Claud. Why are you settling for some old guy? Don't tell me you've got daddy issues."

The pizza has arrived and Claudia busies herself slicing it up and serving pieces to her friends. "He's not old. And please keep my daddy out of this," she gives him a glare.

"A prof..." Tracey muses. "That's...hot." She giggles, and gives James an apologetic shrug. "It's like a porno," she laughs. No one else is laughing, so she quickly shuts her mouth and shoves some food into it. "Sorry. Anyway, I'd love to meet him," she says, her mouth full of cheese pizza.

Claudia changes the subject while Tracey's mouth is still full. "Any plans for the weekend, Brent?" She gives him her sweetest smile. "Maybe a visit to the aquarium, or some biking along the sea wall?"

"As a matter of fact, I'm here for James," he says, clapping a hand on James' shoulder. "The team made it to the finals. I'm here to cheer on my buddy!" He ruffles James' hair.

Claudia vaguely remembers that James is on the UBC men's basketball team, but she doesn't know the details. "Oh, right," she says. Not knowing what else to say, she adds, "go, Thunderbirds!"

Tracey jumps in. "We're coming too. When is the game?" Claudia dies a little inside, and opens her mouth to object. Sitting through an entire basketball game is basically her idea of torture.

But watching James sweat in a jersey and shorts...

"Yes, what time?" Claudia seconds.

James beams at her. "Two in the afternoon. I'm so glad you guys are coming."

They pay the bill after cleaning off all the pizza and beer. They hop into James' car and decide to head back towards campus for a pre-game tiki party at Wreck Beach. Tracey lets out a whoop, ready to get her party on.

Wreck Beach is hidden behind the UBC campus, its entrance veiled between trees at the side of the highway. It's a nude beach - but not the glamorous kind. During the day, rain or shine, Vancouver's finest potheads and hippies hang out in their full glory.

It's close to nine when they arrive at the beach, and after a treacherous journey down the four hundred or so wooden steps that lead down to the sand, they arrive at a party in full swing. Coolers filled with beer and ice section off a generous area of the beach, and bright Mexican blankets are draped over logs. Glowing tiki torches staked into the sand provide a warm atmosphere despite the evening chill. About four-dozen basketball players, their girlfriends, friends, and friends-of-friends, are packed onto the beach, talking and throwing back beers. Tracey sees Trevor, the lumberjack from the gift shop earlier, and runs over to him to give him a hug. Claudia wonders if she's on a break with Warren, feeling slightly bad that she hasn't asked about him.

Brent is on his cell phone, talking to Malia, with a smile on his face, kicking the sand.

"You want a beer, or somethin'?" James asks, when it's just the two of them. He motions at the coolers. "Looks like there's some wine coolers, too, if you prefer."

"Um, sure. Whatever you're having," Claudia says, tucking her fingers into the back pockets of her jeans.

"Nah, I had enough beer at dinner," says James. "Tomorrow's the last game of the season, if we win – I'm not screwing it up with a hangover. Water?" He pulls out two bottles of Evian water from the nearest cooler. He hands one to her.

"Works for me," says Claudia, "I'm not much of a drinker anyway." She's already tipsy from the shared pitchers at dinner, to be honest. She twists off the cap of her Evian and takes a huge sip, causing some to escape her lips and dribble down her chin. James reaches over and wipes it with his sleeve. Claudia whips her head away instinctively. His lips twitch with a smile and he shrugs at her reaction.

"Sorry," he says, not sounding sorry at all.

They stand about a foot apart, watching the party, in silence. Claudia takes a sip of water every fifteen seconds, and screws the cap back on each time. It becomes a soothing activity for her.

James laughs at her. "Why do you keep putting the top back on?" He chugs the rest of his water in a few gulps and throws the empty bottle in a trash bin a few feet away. Claudia resists the urge to rescue it for recycling.

"This is weird," Claudia says, frankly. "You realize we haven't had a real conversation in like, four years right? And now all of a sudden we're hanging out like everything's cool."

"Everything *is* cool, isn't it?" he asks, looking at her, raising his eyebrows. The party is getting a bit rowdy, with some of the guys running around with girls on their shoulders and pretending to catapult them into the water. The girls are screaming and giggling.

"Whatever," Claudia says, despondent. "It was high school I guess."

A tall black girl with short, curly hair and a great bod catches James in the corner of her eye and sprints over to throw her arms around him. "Cooper! What is up?"

James hugs her back, a huge smile on his face. "I've missed you. Good to see you."

The girl glances at Claudia quickly. "Hi, I'm Nadine," she says, extending her hand. Claudia shakes it.

"Claudia and I went to high school together." James cocks his head towards Claudia. "And Nadine here," he places a proud hand on her shoulder, "Is my protégé."

Nadine laughs. "Don't you dare take credit for my natural talent." She turns to Claudia. "James helped me with my jump shot last year. We practiced every night for like a month. Must've worked," she adds, smiling.

Claudia nods slowly, recognizing Nadine. "Oh yeah, you're the Captain of the Ladies' team, right?" James looks at her, surprised that she would know such a thing. "I've seen you on the posters around school. You two make quite the pair," she says graciously. They must have hooked up, she thinks, spending every night together, sweating and shooting hoops, patting each other on the ass.

Nadine gives her an are-you-kidding-me look. "The pair of *us*? No way. Maddie would fucking kill me," she says, rolling her eyes.

"My ex. Maddie." James skates his eyes over Claudia briefly, giving his chin stubble a nervous scratch.

"Not cool, James, not cool," Nadine says, shaking her head and finger. "If you weren't so good at ball, I'd have to kick your ass." She turns to walk away giving them a quick wave. "Nice to meet you," she says to Claudia.

Claudia waves back, and turns to James. "Maddie! Yes, I remember her. She seemed nice. Why'd you have to go and break her heart?" she teases.

"I didn't want to lead her on," he says, matter-of-factly. "I'm leaving for med school across the country, and I know for a fact that she's not the one for me. She didn't see it that way though. Nadine's one of her best friends. That's how we met." He stops, looking at Claudia sheepishly. "You don't wanna hear this, I'm sorry. I'm sure you have your fair share of love stories gone wrong."

Claudia grimaces at the word 'love'. It hasn't happened for her yet. "Nope," she says. "I've never really been good at the whole dating thing." She gives him a knowing look and smiles. "You should know. I mean, I tried. In First Year, all the girls on my dorm floor were hooking up with guys. So I gave it a shot. I went out with a few but things always went terribly wrong. The only way I could get through the dates was to drink excessively. One time I got so drunk, I threw up in my date's lap." she laughs awkwardly, remembering.

"Lucky guy," James laughs, making a face. "Good thing you're not drinking any more tonight. So that's it? One year of trying and you gave up?"

"I'm busy," Claudia says, defensively. "I did have a boyfriend last year for about two weeks. We met at the gym. He was really tan, and I figured it was because he was on the Rowing Team. Then I realized he was going to the tanning salon every day. I could smell the burning skin on him when he'd pick me up. That really grossed me out. No one else has caught my interest."

"Until now," James interjects.

Claudia whips her head in surprise. "Excuse me?"

"Professor What's-His-Name." His face is straight.

Claudia shrugs. "I guess. I think I'm more attracted to our conversations than anything. He's um....he's really smart. I learn a lot from him."

James snickers. "Claud. He's your fucking prof. I'd hope you learn a lot from him. And if he's so smart, what is he doing without you on a Friday night? If you ask me, the fact that you're here with me, on a nude beach, sipping Evian means that he's missing a few screws. Not smart." He shoots her a cocky smile.

She stares at him with a frown. She does not want to be discussing her professor right now.

"Why didn't you call me?" Claudia asks, out of nowhere. "After high school, I mean."

James lets out a loud sigh. He palms his face with his hand. "Man, can we just let it go?" he groans. "I offered you a ride that summer, didn't I? Even after you made it pretty clear that you had no room for me in your very important future *university* life."

Claudia gasps. "That is not true. I wanted to talk things out with you. I thought you'd at least call me. All I got was that measly text message. Plus, I was confused. You were my first kiss. For all I knew I would have fallen in love with you and then you'd end up dumping me for some..." she flicks her hand around at the beach. "...Some basketball chick!"

"Good one. Basketball chick. You know what your problem is Claudia? You overthink everything. You think things to death. You can't just let it happen. We were these young kids, on top of the world, going to one of the best universities in the country – the *same* university. We clearly had feelings for each other. Yeah, maybe it wouldn't have worked out, but now we'll never know, will we?"

Claudia draws in a sharp breath. Never is a harsh word. But he's right, she thinks.

"But you know what really pisses me off?" James continues, his voice getting louder by the second. "I mean what really, really pisses me off?"

He steps closer to Claudia and leans in to her as he annunciates every word. "What really *fucking* pisses me off is that you didn't think I was good enough for you. So *fuck. You.*"

He straightens up, running a hand through his hair. He pauses for a brief moment, looking at Claudia, who is staring at him, her mouth agape. He walks away, heading towards Brent, who's still on the phone.

Claudia can feel the tears pricking her eyes but she refuses to cry. She turns to find the stairs to leave but remembers Tracey. She doesn't want to ditch off on her, but she knows she can't stay, not after that ridiculous display. She sees Tracey's blonde head poking out in the crowd, so she runs over and grabs her by the arm.

"Hey Trace, I'm not feeling well," she says, trying to sound genuinely sick, clutching her stomach. "Take my key, and let yourself in later." She thrusts her keys at Tracey. "I have a hidden spare, don't worry. I'm *sooo* sorry. I feel so bad for ditching out."

Tracey is a few beers in already and pulls Claudia in for a sloppy embrace. "CLAUUUDD you're such a party pooper. But I still love you," she slurs. "I'll seeyalater." Her lumberjack is already pulling her away.

Claudia sees Brent and James talking quietly over by the steps. She takes a deep breath, working up her nerve to march poignantly past them and up the long stairs. She stares straight ahead and starts to walk.

She decides to stop as she passes them to talk to Brent. "Hey. I gave your sister my key. I'm gonna head home first, but keep an eye on her...she's had a few drinks already. And that bearded guy seems to have a thing for her," she adds, wrinkling her nose. They clearly have very different taste in men.

"You can't leave," James says, pragmatically. "You didn't even drive. What are you going to do, hitchhike?" Claudia ignores him and begins walking up the stairs.

"Hey! What the fuck!" James starts after her as she pushes past him. He turns to Brent. "I'll come back for you guys after. Have fun." He takes the steps two at a time, and Brent heads into the party crowd, looking for his sister.

Claudia doesn't stop until she reaches the top of the stairs, and James is a step behind her the whole way, continually asking her to stop. It's a long climb, and when they reach the top they are both out of breath. "You…suck…." says James, breathing heavily. "I hate cardio."

Claudia smirks. "Better get in shape if you plan on winning tomorrow." Remembering why she left the party, anger floods back to her. "And fuck you too!"

She crosses the street towards Totem Place, a cluster of old dorm buildings that house First and Second Year students. She lived at Totem during her First Year, and the dorms have a reputation for being the rowdiest ones on campus. James had lived at Place Vanier, on the other side of campus.

She pulls out her phone to call a cab. James rips the phone out of her hand. "What are you doing?" he says, angry. "Who are you calling? Your professor boyfriend?"

"Not that it's any of your business, but no. I'm calling a cab. Go back to your party." She tries to take her phone back but he holds it up high, about a few inches too high for her vertical. He smiles triumphantly at her vain effort to reach it.

"I'm going to drive you home, if you really need to leave. You're not taking a cab. But first, you have to calm the fuck down." He puts her phone in his back pocket and she reaches around to try and grab it.

"That's very unnecessary, James, and stop saying the word *fuck*, please. I'm calm. I've taken plenty of cabs home so it's not big deal. In fact," she looks up, and points to the bus stop a few meters away. "I can just take the bus. The Four stops right here and will drop me off on my street. Phone, please." She walks over to the bench and holds out her hand for her phone.

James reluctantly retrieves the phone from his pocket and hands it over. "I'm sorry. I shouldn't have swore at you," he says.

Claudia laughs darkly. "I don't care," she says, making a careless gesture with her hand. "Say whatever you want."

It seems for a moment that James is going to leave it at that. He paces a bit, looking towards the road. Finally, he sits down on the bench next to her and scratches at a patch on his face.

"But it's true what I said," he says slowly. "You thought you were too good for me." He stares at her, daring her to refute him.

Claudia doesn't see a point to the conversation, but she answers anyway, with a sigh. "I'm sorry you feel that way. But I never said that, or even thought that. If anything, it was the other way around. I was this nerdy new girl who got beat up at her last school and I had no friends. I don't even know why you paid any attention to me..." She has always wondered that.

She continues. "It was never about you. It was always about me. I was scared. I didn't want to get hurt. I had this idea that I was moving away, and for some reason I thought my whole life was going to change. I thought that would happen to you too, and just couldn't see you being interested in me once we got here, and you realized there were so many other smart girls who were prettier or cooler than me." She stops, not wanting to divulge any more. "I'm sorry, though. For the record."

James leans forward and props his elbows on his knees. "Just to let you know," he turns to look at her and smiles. "There are a lot of smart girls here. But none as pretty and definitely none as cool as you."

Claudia scoffs. "Nice try. That's not true."

"And really Claudia, you have to get over yourself."

She laughs. "Me? Come on. You are still the cockiest son-of-a-bitch I know."

He shrugs, smiling. "Maybe I am. Anyway, are we done with this nonsense? Or are you really going to take the bus?"

Claudia agrees to head back to the beach with him, just as they see Brent and Tracey walking up the steps, winded.

"Holy drama," Tracey calls out to them as they cross the street. "Stomachache my foot," she says to Claudia with a raised eyebrow and a glare.

Most of the basketball players want to call it an early night, so the party has started to die down. They head home, with Brent driving. First, they drop off James at the SUB so he can pick up his bike, then Brent drops them off at Claudia's building, and the three of them make plans for brunch before the game.

Claudia and Tracey stay up late, popping open a bottle of red wine and catching up. Claudia finally asks about Warren, and Tracey's face turns cold. "He's a loser," she mutters. "I hate him. All he cares about is getting high." Claudia is relieved to hear this, but pulls her friend into a tight hug anyway, and tells her that she's sorry, but she can do a lot better.

It's nearly three in the morning when they decide to turn in. Not once does Tracey bring up James, and Claudia is glad for it.

Before they know it, Sunday has arrived after an action-packed weekend. In the late afternoon, Claudia and James drop the siblings off at the airport to catch their return flight to Calgary. The Thunderbirds had killed it the day before, taking home the championship, and a late night of celebrating followed. James and Claudia managed to get along famously, with no awkward moments or venturing into discussions about their past. A stranger would have thought the two were just old high school buddies rekindling their friendship after losing touch for a few years. Tracey ended up hooking up with lumberjack Trevor, and is now going back to Calgary with a disgusted Brent.

"You've been single for like, a week," he says to his sister. "I say this with all the love in the world, sis, but you are such a slut." He shakes his head.

Claudia cringes. She can't imagine her own brother calling her a slut. Petey has only ever called her by one nickname and it definitely isn't *slut*. He calls her Cloudie, a name that started when they were little and he couldn't pronounce her name. When they were a bit older and he still called her Cloudie, he said it was because she loved the rain. Claudia used to drop anything she was doing to run outside when it rained, and stick out her tongue to catch the raindrops. Her mom would shout at her from the backdoor to come back inside.

Outside the Departures Terminal, the girls say goodbye, kissing on cheeks, hugging and even shedding a few dramatic tears since they don't know when they'll see each other again. Claudia gives Brent a hug and James pulls Tracey in for a bear hug, telling her to take care of herself.

Afterwards, Claudia and James drive back in companionable silence. When they hit Granville Street, James clears his throat.

"So what are your plans after graduation?" He asks, rolling down his window. "More school? Find a job?"

"Hmm, I haven't decided yet," says Claudia uneasily. She doesn't have her future mapped out, and it bothers her. "I was planning on going to law school, but something just doesn't feel right about it. My parents are not very happy about that," she adds, with a small laugh. "I've deferred my admission so I can always go later, but for now I just want to take a break. I've been studying my whole life." She looks at James, biting her lip, smiling. "I can't believe I made you study with me all those Friday nights in high school. But it paid off didn't it?" She pauses for dramatic effect. "I'm very proud of you. You're going to be a doctor."

"Thanks, mom," he says. "I'm proud of you too. It sounds like you're taking a step back to think about what you really want in life, instead of just doing what's expected of you. That's cool."

Claudia shrugs. "Yeah, well. We'll see what happens."

It's a long drive home through the heavy traffic, and she invites James up when they reach her building. He parks on the street and follows her into the lobby. "Fancy place," he says, looking around. "How many math kids do you have to tutor to afford this?"

"Very funny. It's my parents' place," she says. "They plan to retire in Vancouver one day. And they visit *all* the time. Basically, I'm still living with them."

They take the elevator up to the eleventh floor. She unlocks the door to the condo and pushes it open. She sees a pair of familiar brown loafers and the smell of cooked garlic fill her nostrils. She freezes, looking at James. "Looks like my parents are here," she says, raising her eyebrows. "Told you. They're here all the time."

She wasn't expecting her parents until next weekend. Just as she is going to suggest that James leave, her mom rounds the corner, giant wooden chopsticks in hand, wearing an apron. "Claudia! You are home just in time for dinner. I made your favorite dishes. Who is that with you?"

Shuffling over in her indoor high heels, her mom's pretty mouth turns into a happy O shape. "James! Long time no see. You are even more handsome than I remember. Come in and have dinner with us. I made plenty."

James gives Mrs. Young a hearty hug. "Nice to see you, Mrs. Young. You look great. You and Claudia could be sisters." He flashes her a dimpled smile. Claudia rolls her eyes. He definitely knows how to turn it on.

Claudia kicks off her shoes. "I didn't know you were coming mom, otherwise I would have cleaned up. We just dropped Tracey off at the airport. She was visiting for the weekend…"

Her mom's face turns sour. She has never approved of Claudia's wild friend. "Hmmm, I see. Well, your dad and I are only here for a couple of days. Peter is coming in tomorrow. He will sleep on the couch." She freezes suddenly, and looks at James as if she's missing something. "Wait, where are you staying? What are you doing in Vancouver?"

Claudia quickly fills her in. "Mom, James goes to UBC. I guess I never told you. He lives close by. So um, he's not staying here. Overnight, I mean. You can stay for dinner. If you want." She looks at him quickly, hoping he doesn't feel obligated.

James reaches down to unlace his boots, giving her a wink on the way down. He'll stay.

Mr. Young is on the living room couch in an undershirt and boxers, smoking a cigar with the window open.

"Hi, Mr. Young," James says brightly, stepping into the room and walking over to shake his hand. "It's been a while. It's nice to see you again." He tries to act as if the man is not nearly naked.

"*Ba*, can you go put on some clothes?" Claudia pleads. She goes over to him and plants a kiss on his cheek. The older man grunts with annoyance, but retreats to the guest bedroom to get dressed.

The flat-screen television is tuned in to her father's favorite program – the local news. The reporter is at a live scene, the wind blowing through her hair, making whipping sounds in the microphone.

"...*The cause is unknown at the moment*," the reporter says in her perfectly poised voice, talking over helicopters. She presses a finger to her ear, trying to hear directions through an earpiece. Behind her, paramedics and stretchers are frantically moving around, people being wheeled to waiting ambulances and helicopters.

Claudia tries to piece the story together, moving closer to the screen.

The marquee at the bottom of the screen reads: VANCOUVER INTERNATIONAL AIRPORT in black letters against a white strip.

Claudia's breath quickens. It can't be...

"...*The airplane crashed during takeoff*," the reporter says, now re-counting the story.

"Oh my God..." Claudia's hand is covering her mouth, panic suddenly filling her body. "James....what was their flight number?" She is waiting to hear more information. James clues in quickly, and searches through his text messages for the info Brent had sent him earlier last week.

"1718," he says.

Claudia shakes her head slowly as the reporter finishes. "...*Flight 1718 to Calgary*."

"No. No way." Claudia pulls out her phone. "They've got to be okay. We were just with them." She looks at James for confirmation, but he is already on the phone, trying to reach Brent. No answer.

Claudia calls Tracey. It goes immediately to voicemail. "She must have switched off her phone before takeoff," she reasons out loud. "They're probably okay."

"Victims have been air-lifted to Vancouver General Hospital," the reporter is saying. *"No confirmations yet on fatalities, but about a dozen passengers have been reported injured."*

"We have to go, James. Now. Let's go." She goes to the door to put her shoes back on. Her mom is watching quietly from the small kitchen, her face stricken with worry. She glances at her mom, trying not to cry.

"Ma..."

"Go help your friend, Claudia." Her mom says. "Call if you need anything. We'll be here." She walks over and gives her daughter a firm hug. "It will be okay."

They leave the apartment quickly. They hop into James' car and head to the hospital. Not a word is spoken during the whole thirty-minute drive.

- 5 - Two Weeks Later

It's a ten-hour drive from Vancouver to Calgary. Right now, in the late spring, it's breathtaking. They pass through the Okanagan Valley, filled with cherry and peach trees, with signs promising "All You Can Pick!" and endless stretches of farmland. They pass by the Shuswap Lakes, pools of crystal green water with charming cottages lining the shores. James does most of the driving, and Claudia is in charge of snacks, water, and music. She's careful not to play any songs about love or death, which is quite a challenge. They end up sticking to Classical. In particular, Bach's Cello Suites, played elegantly by Yo-Yo-Ma.

Brent's funeral is tomorrow. He had been sitting near the back of the 737 when it took a nosedive, only minutes after takeoff. Tracey was in the aisle seat, he had the window seat, and there was nobody between them. On impact, Brent's head had crashed against the glass at top speed, knocking him unconscious and causing internal bleeding.

He'd gone into a coma on the way to the hospital, with his sister by his side. Tracey only suffered whiplash and a broken wrist.

James and Claudia arrived at the hospital just when the paramedics were wheeling Brent in on a stretcher, with hysterical Tracey attached to her brother's hand. The nurses were trying to get her to let go but she was screaming at them. Her baby brother, her best friend - the first boy she had ever loved – she couldn't let him go.

Claudia ran over to her and wrapped her arms around her chest from the back, trying to hold her back, so that the doctors could take Brent away and try to save him. Tracey had struggled against Claudia, accidentally ramming her into the wall behind.

James was able to restrain Tracey, and held her in his arms, hushing her, telling her to let Brent go. He was going to be okay, he said. They had to trust the doctors.

"No, he's not okay, he's just a baby..." she cried, her face drenched, saliva coming out of her mouth at the corners. "It should have been me, I made him switch seats with me..." She sank to the floor, her knees collapsing, her forehead slamming into her kneecaps, over and over, as if trying to wake from a bad dream.

Claudia crouched down beside her and held her while the nurses and doctors wheeled Brent away, speaking in urgent voices. Tracey's wrist was treated in silence, and afterwards, they stayed at the hospital all night, only able to coax Tracey away from the waiting room with a cigarette and coffee the next morning.

After twenty-four hours in the ICU and two surgeries, the doctors were losing hope. By the time they pronounced Brent's death, Tracey had completely shut down, not speaking to anyone, her face a sheet of stone. She wasn't even crying anymore.

All flights to and from the Vancouver airport had been shut down for hours after the incident, so Tracey and Brent's parents, Mr. and Mrs. Monroe, weren't able to get to Vancouver until the next morning. Their helplessness over their only son's future, and then their grief, was unbearable to watch.

The funeral will be at the Presbyterian Church, next to their old high school. James and Claudia arrive in Calgary just after sunset on Sunday, and he drives to her parents' house first, to drop her off. James' family lives on the other side of town. Claudia's parents are still in Vancouver, and since she doesn't want to be alone, she asks James if he'd like to stay the night. James' family lives on the other side of town, and since he's exhausted from the drive, he agrees easily. He carries their duffle bags into the house, following behind Claudia.

"It's been a while," he comments, as she unlocks the door. She punches in the code to disarm the alarm system, the code permanently imprinted in her brain after all these years. "The last time I was here, we were sneaking down to the basement to make out," he says, jokingly.

Claudia shoots him a cautionary look. She flicks on the lights and sees that his tired eyes are filled with sadness. He's still trying to make her smile, even through all this pain. This melts her heart and she feels the urge to reach out to him and pull his body close to hers.

She just takes his hand instead, intertwining their fingers. For the past week, any discussions about their unrequited feelings have taken a back seat to the events at hand. And for some reason, things between them have started to make a lot more sense.

"I'll make us some tea," says Claudia. She pulls him to the kitchen and motions for him to sit on a stool at the marble counter, as she puts a kettle of water on the gas stove. She finds a loose chrysanthemum and lavender blend in the drawer and reaches to the top shelf of the cupboard for one of her mother's teapots. James sees her struggling and gets up to give her a hand. He brings the pot down to her level, standing close, looking down at her small nose.

He cups the side of her face gently and he leans down to brush his lips against hers. Her eyes close and she exhales, leaning her face into his hand. He increases the kiss, pushing her lips open slightly with his tongue, drawing her top lip in between his, and bringing his other hand to the back of her head, scrunching her hair. Her arms encircle his waist and wrap around to his back, feeling his broad muscles underneath his soft t-shirt. She presses into his body and her insides feel as if they are going to burst at the seams.

The kettle whistles and they pull away from each other slowly. He brushes a piece of hair out of her face and kisses her on the forehead. She kisses his chest, and turns to the stove to remove the kettle and prepare the tea.

She arranges a couple teaspoons of tea leaves into the strainer, and carefully pours the steaming water into the pot. Replacing lid of the teapot, she presses herself up onto the counter to sit, and wait. The tea has to steep for about five minutes, to be perfect.

James moves over to her and stands in front of her. His blue eyes are crinkled, and he looks sad. He reaches down to open her knees gently, and reaches around to her lower back to pull her closer to him, her legs around his hips. She lets out a shallow breath.

"Don't think about it," he says, looking down. "Whatever is going through your head right now. We can talk about it later."

"Okay," she says. His lips find her neck, sending chills down her back.

He cups his hands under her thighs and she wraps her legs around him. "Where in this house can we make out?" he murmurs against her lips. "It's your parents house so I don't feel comfortable having my way with you just anywhere." His mouth pulls into a small grin that suggests that he is actually very comfortable doing anything that he pleases.

"The tea..." Claudia cocks her head towards the pot, her eyes half-open.

"Fuck the tea." He crushes his lips to hers and picks her up, heading for the living room couch, her legs clenching his hips.

He places her down lengthwise on the couch and leans down to lay with her. He pushes her tank top up to expose her stomach and kisses a trail from her belly button up towards her left breast. He moves the cup of her bra to the side and kisses his way to her nipple.

Claudia gasps. She arches her chest instinctively, giving him access to undo her bra in the back. She reaches down and pulls his shirt over his head, revealing his rolling muscles.

She bites her lip. "I don't think I've ever seen you topless. I think I like you better this way."

He laughs, pulling her up to sit. "I think I'll be saying the same." He pulls off her tank top in a smooth swoop.

Now only wearing a pair of jeans, Claudia feels incredibly vulnerable. She's not sure what to do next. "Take off your pants," she commands. He raises an eyebrow, surprised, but obeys, standing up to unbuckle his belt, and begins unbuttoning the fly of his jeans. He pushes them down to his feet and steps out, revealing a pair of black boxer briefs.

Claudia breathes in and out slowly, staring at him. She knows where this is going, and she knows she has to tell him. She sits up and pulls her tank top to her chest to cover up.

"I'm a virgin."

His mouth drops open. He sits down immediately, breathing slowly himself, trying to regain control of the situation. He's silent, staring at her in wonder.

Finally, he opens his mouth. "Serious?"

She shrugs, pulling her tank top back on to feel more at ease. "Yeah. I never met anyone worth doing it with, I guess." She looks at him, lifting her chin slightly. "I'm only twenty," she adds, defensively.

"I didn't mean it like that. It's just rare these days."

She nods. "Yeah. Sorry to spring it on you right now. Thought it might be a good thing to mention."

He turns to her. "Was I really your first kiss?" He asks her suddenly.

"Yeah."

"You were mine, too." He smiles gently. "Thought it might be a good thing to mention."

Feeling bold, Claudia climbs over James and straddles his lap, wrapping her arms loosely around his neck. "I want you to be my first," she says. "Again." She stares into his ocean eyes. "I want you." She kisses him once, pulling back to look at his face. His eyes are full of heat and anguish, as if she has just crushed him with her words. "It's a good thing, James," she says, cracking a smile. "It means I like you."

"Yeah," he says softly. "I just wish..." he doesn't finish his sentence because she is quieting him with her mouth, kissing him again, her fingers in his short hair, pressing herself into him. She can feel his body tensing up under her.

"I wanted you so bad," he says huskily, "I still want you so bad." His kisses are on her face, on her neck, behind her ears. He inches her tank top up once again, wanting to feel her skin.

She raises herself onto her knees and he undoes the fly of her jeans. He pushes them down her legs and he reaches under her lace thong. She stands to peel her jeans off all the way and she stands in front of him, nearly naked, with only a piece of black lace keeping her modest.

"Do you wear shit like that all the time?" he asks.

"My underwear? Yeah. They're comfortable."

He reaches for her hand and pulls her back down to him. "A virgin in black lace," he says. "In the middle of her parents' living room."

"Do you have a condom?" She asks.

He shakes his head no. "Are you on the pill?"

She nods. "I've been on it since high school. For cramps," she adds quickly. "Are you clean?"

He nods. "I just had my yearly check-up. Are you sure about this?"

"Yes," she says. She tugs at the elastic of his boxers. She pushes it down to reveal him. He slides them down the rest of the way and falls against her on the couch.

She clutches the sides of his face, her eyes closed. All she can hear is the sound of their heavy breathing. He pushes inside slowly, filling her. "Shit..." he breathes out.

She lets out a small cry of pain. She can feel him pushing against something – an inner wall of some sort. "I-I think you have to get past that," she says, breathlessly.

Letting out a groan, he pushes all the way in, breaking past her dam. She screams in surprise because it *really* hurts, and he pauses.

"I'm okay," she says. "Keep going."

He starts to move again, slowly at first but quickly building up speed. It feels raw and painful for her, but she doesn't want to stop. His thrusts become more insistent and he brings his forehead down to hers, sweating, and closes his mouth over hers. He comes with a groan.

He collapses on her, kisses her face, and pulls out. They are both silent as he sits up, pulling her to his lap, her hair rumpled and matted against her head.

Cradling her, he stands up, and carries her upstairs. "Where do you want to sleep tonight?" he asks her, when he's reached the top step.

She motions towards her childhood bedroom and he kicks the door open lightly, and lays her on top of the absurdly small twin-sized bed, pulling the soft green comforter over her. "I'm gonna go clean up," he says. "I'll be right back."

He finds a kitchen towel downstairs and wipes the blood off the espresso brown couch they just christened. He realizes how lucky he is that it is a dark, stain-resistant leather and not cream tweed as his own mother prefers.

Meanwhile upstairs, Claudia gets up from her bed and goes to the bathroom. She is staring at herself in the mirror, naked, dark rings under her eyes from the long day. Her cheeks are flushed, and her nipples are swollen. She turns on the shower and gets in, letting the steaming water wash over her face and body. Hearing the door open, she peeks out through the curtain. James is in his boxers, poking his head through the door.

"Everything okay, Claud? Sorry for leaving you so quickly after...I just wanted to make sure we didn't make a mess." Claudia realizes with horror what he means.

"Oh my God..." she groans. "How bad was it?"

He steps into the bathroom. "Not bad at all. Your parents have very forgiving furniture. I took care of it, though we'll have to dispose of the kitchen towel somewhere inconspicuous," he says with a grin. "Mind if I join you in the shower?"

Since he's already seen her naked, she nods, pulling the shower curtain open about a foot. He pushes his boxers off and steps in.

The steam curls around their faces. They speak in soft voices, only slightly above a whisper. He asks her if she is in pain. A bit, she says. She asks him if it was good, and he gives her a look as if to say, *do you even need to ask*? A Dove bar sits on a little dish, and they lather themselves up. Claudia washes her hair, her eyes wide open and staring straight at James as she rubs shampoo into her scalp. She leans her head back to rinse the suds out and when she's done, he pulls her to his chest, kissing her on the cheek beside her ear.

"I'm sorry," he says softly, into her ear.

"Why?" she asks. She is afraid to hear his answer. He's sorry he made a mistake. He's sorry, he doesn't want to hurt her.

He pulls away from her to look into her eyes. "I'm sorry that your first time was like this. If Brent hadn't died...and we weren't here for his fucking funeral," his voice breaks with emotion, "we wouldn't be here together. Someone had to fucking die. For this to happen."

She pulls away from him, not wanting to hear the rest. He holds on to her shoulders, tight, forcing her to look at him. "I'm not saying I didn't want it to happen. I just wish that...we were happy right now. Instead, we're so fucking sad...I'm just sorry about that." A single tear rolls down his face, or it could just be from the shower, Claudia can't be sure.

"Yeah, it is sad," she says, stretching a hand up to touch his wet hair and running her fingers down the back of his neck. "I'm sorry about Brent. He was my friend, too, but I know how much he meant to you. And I can't stop thinking about Tracey, and what she's going through. But...I'm glad we're here together," she says, looking at the water pooling around her feet. "I like being around you, even though we're so sad," she says, looking up at him, holding her tears in.

He pulls her back to him. "That's good," he says.

They dry off with soft, thick Turkish cotton towels, and Claudia dries her hair for a few minutes with a blow dryer. She finds an old Calgary Flames t-shirt and a pair of boy shorts in the closet of her old room, and pulls them on for bed. They are both beyond exhausted and collapse onto the tiny twin-sized mattress, her back to his front, facing the wall. His hand comes underneath her shirt, touching her stomach, and they fall asleep within minutes.

When Claudia wakes up in the morning, James is gone, and so is his duffel bag. Her heart drops, until she sees that he's sent her a text message.

James: Went home to drop off my stuff. I'll be back in an hour and we'll grab a bite to eat before heading to the church. X

If he's dropping his stuff off at his parents' house that means he's not staying with her again tonight. She childishly sticks her bottom lip out at the phone, since no one is around to see it. She enjoyed falling asleep with him. Oh well. She shrugs it off and decides to send Tracey a text message.

Claudia: Morning. I'll see you in a couple hours. Let me know if you want to meet up any earlier. I love you.

She keeps her phone close by as she brushes her teeth and takes a quick shower. She is running a curling iron through her hair when she hears a buzz. Expecting James, she gets a quick spurt of butterflies. She rolls her eyes at herself in the mirror.

But it's not James. It's Tracey.

Tracey: I can't go to this thing. I'm staying at home. Drop by after if you can.

Claudia had been planning to go by the Monroe residence after the funeral anyway, but she is shocked that Tracey is going to miss her own brother's funeral. She quickly texts back.

Claudia: Is everything OK? Is there anything I can do?

It buzzes back immediately.

Tracey: No. Thanks.

Claudia wants to cry. But she knows she has to be the strong one. Tracey lost her brother. James lost his best friend.

She finishes with her hair and puts on the black dress she'd bought before she left Vancouver. Her mom had insisted that she wear brand new clothes to the funeral, and that said clothes be disposed of afterward; something about death and clinging spirits. Claudia had been too tired to argue.

James arrives back on time within the hour, and they stop at a Denny's for breakfast. Neither seems to have an appetite so they end up just sipping their mugs of coffee and picking at their eggs. Claudia reaches across the table to touch his hand, her way of letting him know that she's here for him. He flinches in surprise and pulls away.

"Sorry," he mutters. "About last night…I really want to talk about it later. I just…we need to get through this, today, first. For Brent."

"We haven't talked about *it* for four years, James. I'm sure a bit longer won't hurt." She's not trying to sound sarcastic, but he gives her a *what-the-fuck* look.

She sighs. "I didn't mean it like that. I agree. We're here for Brent."

The service is brief and sorrowful. The enormous church is packed, including the second-floor balconies, and attendees spill into the foyer. Someone plays Green Day's *Time of Your Life* on the guitar during the procession, and Mr. Monroe gives a gut-wrenching eulogy. Mrs. Monroe is in the front pew, shaking uncontrollably with tears. Next to her is Malia, the girl from the picture Brent was showing off just days before the accident. She is wearing a tight, form-fitting, white strapless dress. She's dressed up for him, Claudia realizes.

James is stoic throughout the ceremony, and remains so as they leave, only nodding hello to their former high school classmates. Once outside the church, they find the Monroes to express their condolences. Claudia tells them that they'll be visiting Tracey at the house. Mrs. Monroe pulls her aside, eyes rimmed with red, her face ten years older than the last time she'd seen her.

"Tracey's taking it the worst out of everyone," she says, staring down at her hands in which she's clutching a wad of Kleenex. "She was there. And he was her baby brother." Her face crumples for a second, and she shakes her head to regain her composure. "He was everyone's baby. But, she blames herself. Try to talk to her. Please?" She places a hand on Claudia's shoulder, her eyes pleading.

Claudia nods, and gives the blonde woman a gentle hug. "I will, Mrs. Monroe. We all loved him so much. I'm sorry." She can't hold it in any longer and she breaks into a sob. Mrs. Monroe squeezes her tight. "Thank you," she says, tearing up again.

James and Mr. Monroe are talking quietly on the side. When Mrs. Monroe releases her, Claudia steps over to the men and reaches for James' hand, lightly grasping his fingertips. She looks at Mr. Monroe and her eyes fill with tears again. He nods at her, closing his eyes, his body shrinking into himself. He is a man of few words, and he had used them all for the eulogy.

A few relatives of the Monroes begin milling around, so Claudia and James move away to give them space. "Is there anyone else you want to talk to before we leave?" Claudia asks James softly, seeing that he is eyeing the car, looking ready to go. "I think I saw Scott somewhere over there..." she motions towards the large evergreen trees planted near the parking lot.

James shakes his head. "Don't really feel like talking to anyone. I haven't talked to Scott in ages. We kind of had a falling out. Let's get out of here."

Claudia explains to James that they have to stop at the Monroe's house to check on Tracey. He is just as concerned that she missed the service. They drive back north across the city into a suburb that was built in the early eighties, and pull onto the driveway of the Monroes' brick home. They ring the doorbell.

There is no answer, so they try the handle. It's unlocked, and they push it open, stepping into the familiar house. Both have spent a lot of time in this house – James in his childhood, playing video games with Brent while Tracey cheered them on – and Claudia, in more recent years on visits home, gossiping and catching up with Tracey in her room.

She can hear loud music blaring from upstairs and she assumes it's coming from Tracey's room. They head upstairs towards the noise and knock on the door.

No answer.

They look at each other, and James shrugs. He turns the knob and pushes the door wide open.

Tracey is sitting cross-legged on her bed with her back to them, wearing only her underwear and bra. Her body is pale and shrunken. She has lost probably ten pounds in just a little over a week.

The music is on so loud that she doesn't hear them approaching. As they make their way around her bed, they see that she's hunched over an old magazine, and with her one good hand, she is cutting up lines of white powder with a credit card into thin, even strips.

A twenty-dollar bill is rolled up next to her, and when she turns to pick it up, she sees James and Claudia looking at her with horror.

She seems momentarily panicked. Blinking twice, she continues where she left off, picking up the rolled-up bill, lining it up with the powder, and inhaling one line up each nostril. She takes her finger to wipe off the excess and rubs it on her gums. Claudia and James are too stunned to speak, and they stand there, staring at her for what seems like a good solid minute.

Finally, Tracey carefully moves the magazine to her desk. "Ever hear of knocking?" She spits.

She walks over to her closet, reaches in and pulls out a large Bush-X t-shirt and pulls it over her head. She finds a pair of gym shorts and puts them on as well.

"What the fuck, Tracey?" James breaks the spell first, turning down the music on the stereo sitting on the dresser. "You skip out on Brent's funeral to stay home and do coke? Are you retarded?" He is beyond angry. "You're allowed to be sad and fucked up, but...fuck! Coke? That shit is bad news, man."

Claudia chimes in with a different approach. "Tracey, we love you. Talk to us. Let's go downstairs and I'll make you some coffee, and we can – "

"NO!!!" Tracey shrieks at them. "I'M DEALING WITH IT." She turns to James, her voice calming only slightly. "Who told you to come here," she sneers. "The only reason why he was in Vancouver, was to watch you play your stupid FUCKING BASKETBALL GAME. And now he's DEAD." A sob escapes from her throat.

James backs away from her, shaking his head. "I know. I'm sorry, Trace," he says, his voice breaking. He doesn't blame himself, but it's true, and it feels like shit. Brent had been there for him.

"I'll wait for you downstairs," he says to Claudia. "Take your time." He looks at Tracey one more time before turning and leaving the room.

Claudia sits on Tracey's bed, trying not to look at the cocaine on her desk. "Tracey..." she holds out a hand to her friend. Reluctantly, Tracey walks over and sits with her, keeping her distance.

"It hurts so bad, Claudia," she says, in a detached voice. "Every time I close my eyes I see his face with all that blood gushing out of his nose...and his eyes are rolled back. I knew he was gone. Before the surgeries, before the doctors. I knew." She looks at Claudia. "It was supposed to be me. *I* was supposed to die. He let me have the aisle seat." She starts shaking and reaches to her bedside table for a pack of smokes and lights one.

She inhales deep and blows out through the side of her mouth. Claudia doesn't know what to say except the obvious. "It's not your fault, Tracey. You can't blame yourself. Or anyone else." She adds the last part hastily, for James' sake.

Tracey sighs. "I don't blame James. He'll get over it," she says.

Claudia nods, not speaking any more. She's here to listen. She lets Tracey talk for almost an hour, with intermittent silences that last for minutes at a time. Finally, she finds the nerve to ask Tracey about the coke. "Did Warren give that to you?" she tilts her head towards the desk.

"Yeah." Tracey lets out a heartless laugh. "He says it numbs the pain. For once I think he knows what he's talking about," she says, looking at Claudia apologetically. "Don't worry. We're not back together."

Claudia sighs. "It's bad, Tracey. You know that. I mean, drinking and pot is one thing, But this...Brent wouldn't want to see you like this." She immediately feels bad for dragging Brent into it. Tracey's eyes well up with tears and she looks at Claudia fiercely.

"I know that," she snaps. "He'd call me a fucking loser and punch Warren in the face. I miss him so much." Her face crumples and she starts to cry again.

She lets Tracey bleed her heart out in tears, holding her close. It is almost dark outside when Tracey's sobs turn to hiccups, and her breathing slows down. Claudia realizes she has fallen asleep.

Carefully, she maneuvers Tracey into a fetal position, and covers her with a quilt. Before leaving the room, she snatches the magazine, throwing it and its powdery contents into the wastebasket under her desk.

She sees a stack of post-its and a pen on the desk, so she leaves Tracey a quick note.

I'm sorry. Call me anytime. I'm here for you. Be good. xo

She sticks it on the pillow next to Tracey's face, kisses her like a child on the forehead, switches off the light in the room, and closes the door.

Downstairs, James is snoozing on the living room couch, with one forearm thrown over his eyes, blocking out the low light. Mr. and Mrs. Monroe have come home, and are sitting at the kitchen table still in their funeral clothes, sipping some kind of smoky-colored liquor. Both parents look ragged, withdrawn, and ready to join their child in his grave.

They offer Claudia a drink but she shakes her head, no thank you, though she actually could really use one. She knows that the Monroes probably want to be alone right now.

"Tracey's sleeping," she tells them. "We talked for a while. You're right, she's not...dealing with it well." She continues, biting her lip, thinking about the coke, but not wanting to betray their friendship. "I think it would be good if she talked to someone, eventually. A professional." She looks over at James, hoping he'll do the same.

"Thank you Claudia," says Mrs. Monroe, her voice tired, slow, and slightly slurred. "You kids better get a move on, if you're hitting the road in the morning."

Claudia goes over to the couch to wake James. Shaking him lightly, he wakes, squinting, forgetting where he is. Seeing Brent's parents in the next room, he sits up rather quickly, swaying.

"How long was I out for?" He rubs a palm over his face, and pushes himself up to stand, still wobbling.

"A couple hours, I think," Claudia says, holding his arm, doing what she can to steady him. "Let's head out. It's getting late."

When they leave the house minutes later, James is still in a foggy, semi-awake state, so Claudia offers to drive. He reluctantly hands over the keys, even though he is in no shape to drive.

"I can drop you off at home, and then drive your car to my house," Claudia says, being practical. "I'll pick you up in the morning and we'll head out from there."

James shakes his head. "I don't want you driving home in the dark by yourself. You can stay with me at my parents' place."

Claudia shakes her head adamantly. "I'm not going to spend the night at your house the first time I meet your parents," she says firmly. "I'll drive home."

"Relax, it's cool," says James, his eyes closed, leaning back on the headrest. Claudia starts the car and pulls out of the driveway.

James is dozing off when Claudia realizes that she doesn't know where he lives. "James..." she says. He doesn't answer. "James," she repeats, louder this time. "Wake up, I need directions."

He mumbles, turning towards the window "Hmm...shh...not so loud."

She sighs. She has no choice but to drive home to her own parents' house instead. Maybe he can take a nap and then drive home in a couple hours.

She manages to help James out of the car and up the driveway. He is acting rather strange. At the door, while she looks for her keys, and his arm is draped over her shoulders, she smells his breath. Alcohol.

"Great, Tracey's doing coke, and you're drunk," she murmurs, unlocking the door. He looks at her guiltily, and his eyes are so sad. She takes pity on him and decides to let it go. After all, she's not his keeper.

Claudia is wondering when he had time to get hammered, thinking for a second that he must have raided the Monroe's supply. A flask tumbles out of his blazer pocket as he's pulling it off. Knowing for sure now that he's not going to be driving anywhere, they get ready for bed.

They find James a new toothbrush from the medicine cabinet, since he doesn't have his duffel bag. They move like automatons, brushing their teeth, washing their faces, taking turns using the toilet. James strips down to his boxers and Claudia puts on a clean t-shirt and boy shorts for bed. When they get into the tiny bed tonight, Claudia lays a hand on his chest, and leans her head against his shoulder. Just when she thinks he's drifting off to sleep, she hears him breathing strangely. She touches his face and feels his wet cheeks. He turns away, facing the door. Rolling to face the same side, she wraps her arms around his waist, and presses her face into his back. She's a pathetic little spoon, but she holds him until he falls asleep. She cries her own silent tears, not knowing whom they are for.

In the morning, they leave the house before sunrise and stop briefly at James' parents' house to pick up his duffel bag. It's Claudia's first time to the Cooper property and she is floored by its palatial extravagance. James has never directly mentioned his family's wealth, and apart from his BMW, you wouldn't have guessed it.

They pull into an estate just outside of the city limits, with a private gate, long cobblestone driveway and acres of manicured green space surrounding the house. Well-tended rose bushes and large maple, oak and evergreen trees dot the property, and a giant terrace wraps around a grand Victorian-style home.

There is a guest cottage out back, James explains, where he stays when he comes home to visit. Claudia now realizes why he was so nonchalant about inviting her to stay over last night. Even in his drunken state, no one would have even seen or heard them. He leads her around the house, past a giant infinity swimming pool and unlocks the door of the white guest cottage. The inside is quaint and charming, obviously not decorated for James at all but for the guests of his parents. His black duffel bag is sitting on the bed, zipped and ready to go. He grabs it. He gives the place a quick once-over and turns to leave, pulling Claudia behind him.

She doesn't want to prod, but she is wondering why he's not stopping in for a word with his parents. Her parents would flip out if they knew she'd come by their house and didn't at least say a brief hello. She's getting in the car when she hears the front door open. A lady in her late forties, with James' unmistakable deep blue eyes and dark features steps out onto the doorstep, staring at them. His mother.

James turns to look at his mom. "We gotta go, mom. See ya." He gets in the car and closes the door. Claudia freezes, not knowing what to do. So much for a first impression. She looks back at Mrs. Cooper, who is wearing only a thin sweater and is holding her arms, shivering in the morning chill. She feels bad for Mrs. Cooper, and definitely doesn't want it to look like she's sneaking around with her son.

"Hi Mrs. Cooper. It's nice to meet you," she calls out. She looks between the lady and the car, feeling conflicted. Taking a deep breath, she closes the car door and scurries over to at least shake Mrs. Cooper's hand.

James rolls down the window "What are you doing?" He asks calmly. She looks back at him with a glare and stops in front of the house. Mrs. Cooper hasn't moved, and Claudia swallows, feeling nervous. She reaches a hand out. "I'm Claudia Young. I went to high school with James. We go to UBC together."

His mom takes her hand hesitantly, her hands cold and small. She frowns at her but nods. "Drive safe, you two," she says, loud enough for James to hear. She turns and goes back into the house, closing the door behind her.

Claudia stares at the giant door. Well, she tried. She makes her way back to the car and climbs in.

"What was that all about?" Claudia asks, closing the passenger door once she's in the car. "Your mom looked about ready to cry…"

He snorts. "She hasn't cried since my dad died, and she got over that pretty fast. I doubt she'll shed a tear about me driving back to school."

Claudia is silent. His dad is dead?

"I didn't know your dad died. I'm…so sorry." She turns to look at him. "What happened?"

James' jaw tightens as he starts up the car. "It just happened last year. It had been coming for a while. Cancer."

Claudia nods, shocked. "I'm sorry," she repeats. "That must be really hard." She realizes how true her words really are, especially given Brent's recent death.

It's James turn to be silent, driving towards the highway, heading west. He stares ahead at the road.

Finally, he speaks. "It was hard. It's still hard. He got sick the summer we graduated from high school. I remember finding out about the diagnosis the day after prom. He'd wanted to wait until after prom so I could enjoy myself." He shakes his head, letting out a humorless chuckle. Claudia feels like the wind has been knocked out of her.

"I didn't tell anyone, not even Brent or Scott. Then Scott found out, and he told everyone. Fucking guy always had a big mouth. I didn't want to be the kid with a dying dad, you know? It was hard enough seeing him lose himself to the disease. I didn't want to have other people feeling sorry for me. For him."

"That's why you and Scott don't talk anymore..."

He nods. "I guess Trace and Brent respected my wishes, if you never found out," he says. "They're good friends."

"I wish I had known, James. I feel like an asshole. How many times did we run into each other, and you were going through this, and I just kept on my way?" She shakes her head, mad at herself.

"It was my choice," he says. "Anyway. I guess now you get some insight as to why it wasn't so easy for me to just...call you again after prom. I just didn't need one more thing to deal with in my life."

Claudia feels a sting, but pushes it away. She steers the conversation back to where it started.

"So why are you mad at your mom? Don't you want to be close to her, after everything that happened?"

His face turns dark. "I love my mom. Don't get me wrong. But...some things you just can't forgive. She was in love with someone else. My dad's brother." He gives a heartless laugh. "And even after my dad got sick, they stayed together. They got married six months after he died. That's why I didn't go inside," he says, decisively.

He stops talking, and it seems he's done with the subject. But now that the gates are open, Claudia wants to know everything.

"Your family is very well off," she says, pushing it. "Your house is beautiful. I didn't even know they had houses like that in Calgary."

"Thanks," James says, relieved at the change in subject. "I love that house. I grew up in it. Brent and Tracey used to come over and we'd play hide-and-go-seek...you can imagine for a little kid how awesome that would be, with so many rooms and places to hide. My family is what you would call old money. My dad was sent to Canada to expand the family business after he and my mom were married. I hope you don't judge me because of our wealth." He looks at her quickly, his eyes wavering.

While her own family is not the kind to own a grand estate, or buy their high school kid a BMW, they live a very comfortable life, thanks to her father's hard work. Claudia has always known how lucky she's been to not have any worries about money growing up. But sometimes, being born lucky means you have to work even harder in life to prove yourself.

"I don't judge you at all," Claudia says. "If anything, I'm impressed that you're so driven. A lot of kids in your position would just be partying and driving nice cars at this age, not going to med school. Well...your car is nice, I guess, so I take that back." She smiles.

"I'm going to drive this car 'til the wheels fall off," says James. "My dad bought it for me after I set the provincial record for most points in a season. Even now when I play, I feel like I can hear him yelling my name."

Claudia's eyes tear up. She impulsively pulls one of his hands to her lips and kisses it. "He'd be so proud of you," she says.

They drive peacefully for the next few hours, each in their own heads. When they cross the Alberta/BC border and hit Revelstoke, a small mountain town, they decide to take a break. They both want to use the bathroom and stretch out a bit, so they stop for an early lunch at a Klondike-themed restaurant that promises "the best burger on this side of the border."

Claudia orders the French onion soup and James gets the burger. The server brings them two plastic glasses of water

"So, I'm moving to Toronto at the end of summer," James says softly, looking into her eyes. "I know I already told you, but...I just wanted to bring it up again. Seems like we have the most horrible timing."

Claudia looks at him confidently. "I'm so happy for you, James. You're going to be an excellent doctor. As for us...you're right. Our timing sucks. But look – we have the whole summer together, and I can always come visit, if that's what we want..." They haven't even discussed whether or not they want to start dating, let alone have a relationship. She clears her throat. "I realize it's hard to start something when you're about to make a big change in your life like moving across the country..."

"Luckily, I'm not a pessimist like you," James says, taking a sip of his water. "I'd like to try. Even though we don't know what'll happen when I leave. If you're willing."

She takes a deep breath. A second chance. With the only boy who ever came close to being her high school sweetheart. "I'm willing," she says.

James smiles exuberantly for the first time in weeks, his eyes crinkling at the corners. "That's the best news I've heard in a long time. But there's one thing I have to ask you first," he says.

Claudia panics. "What?"

"'What's the current situation with Professor Baldy?" He's wearing his cocky half-smile.

Claudia laughs. "He's not bald. And there's nothing going on between us anymore. Actually, never really was, just a few coffee dates here and there. We lost touch after what happened to Brent, and I missed a few of his classes." She pauses. "But, I do have to start going to class again for about one more week, if I want him to pass me."

"Somehow I doubt that you're in danger of failing any of your classes," James says. Their food has arrived and he starts on his French fries, putting two in his mouth at a time. "I'll give Baldy one more week in class with you, but after that, you're all mine." Claudia smiles, despite his possessiveness.

They make good time on the road, driving just slightly above the speed limit, and after nine hours they're catching glimpses of the Pacific Ocean and mountains, marking their arrival to Vancouver. Knowing her parents are still in town, she invites James over for dinner. "You'll finally get to eat my mom's Chinese food," she says. "I know she's just dying to feed a big white boy like you."

James laughs. "I'll try not to bow or be overly polite," he says. "I remember how that pisses you off."

Her parents are expecting them, as she'd sent a text letting them know what time they'd be home. Unlike her parents, she doesn't like to surprise people.

It is Claudia, however, who is still surprised when they get to the apartment. Her brother, Petey, emerges from the living room to greet her.

"Petey!" She runs to her brother, throwing her arms around him. "What are you doing here?"

Peter Young Junior, or, Petey, as only his sister calls him, is tall, slimly built, and wears a scraggly beard. His hair is long, just touching his shoulders, and he has an easy smile. His eyes are smaller and a bit more angular than Claudia's, and his cheekbones are slightly more chiseled, but when looking at them side-by-side, they are unmistakably siblings.

"Hi Cloudie," he says, hugging his sister back and kissing her on top of the head. "I thought I'd come up for a visit and see how you're doing." He searches her face. He makes it no secret that he is worried about her.

Claudia smiles. "Thanks. I'm doing okay. It's been rough. This...is James." James is bent down, unlacing his boots, giving the siblings a moment. He straightens up and reaches a hand out to the older boy. "Hey. Good to meet you. Peter, right?"

Petey nods, shaking James' hand, looking him up and down. Though Petey is tall, James has a good three inches on him, and is much broader. He smiles openly at Petey, showing his good intentions. "We drove to the funeral together. Brent was a good friend of mine," he says.

"Ah. I'm really sorry, man," Petey says sincerely. "Thanks for bringing my sister back in one piece. I don't know if you've ever seen her drive but you can't do moves like that on the highway." He deflects a playful gut-shot from Claudia.

The three head into the kitchen where Claudia's mom is cooking up a feast. Smells of garlic, ginger, and scallions make

Claudia's mouth water, and she looks over her apron-clad mother's shoulder to see what she's making on the stove.

"Whatcha making, ma?" She kisses her mom on the cheek. "It smells so good. We're starving."

"I made steamed sea bass, barbecue pork, drunken chicken, ginger beef, and lots of vegetables," her mother says brightly. "Enough for a week of leftovers!" Mrs. Young loves a steady supply of leftovers.

"Claudia, James, set the table," she commands. "Dinner will be ready soon. Peter, open the wine."

They set to work, James and Claudia tag-teaming the dining table. They make five places, each with a bamboo placemat, bowl, plate, chopsticks, and napkin.

James smiles, enjoying the intimacy. Claudia looks at him nervously. He's the first guy to have dinner with her family, and she's not quite sure what to expect.

Mr. Young emerges from the guest bedroom, looking fresh from a nap. He walks over and gives his daughter a big hug, kissing her enthusiastically on the cheek. Claudia tries not to laugh; her dad always gives the sloppiest kisses. James raises a hand in a wave from across the table. "Mr. Young," he says, with a smile.

Mr. Young nods at James kindly. "Good to see you again, James."

Claudia's mom has made so much food that the dishes don't fit on the table. Instead, they eat buffet style, carrying their plates to the kitchen counter to load up on food and returning to the table between helpings. Claudia eats like she's been starving for days (which she has been), and sees that James is doing the same. The boy can eat.

James and Petey do the dishes after dinner, and Claudia helps her mother clean the table and transfer the leftovers into Tupperware containers. Her dad announces that he is going for a walk and grabs his jacket, tucking a cigar into the inner pocket at the last moment, hoping to hide it from his wife.

She catches him. "*Aiya*, you said you were going to quit. You're going to die from those! And they smell so bad," she scolds her husband. "Tell him, Claudia. Tell him to stop smoking."

"You really should cut down, Ba," Claudia says obediently. Her father opens his hands in a helpless gesture.

"Come on. I work hard. I just want one cigar a day," he says. "Give an old guy a break. I'll be back soon." He leaves the apartment, locking the door behind him.

When the women are alone in the dining room, cleaning up the table, Claudia's mother begins the inquisition.

"So, is James your boyfriend? Don't lie." She taps her foot impatiently, waiting for an answer.

"I guess so..." Claudia says, answering in her typical mixture of Mandarin and English. "Yes. He is my boyfriend." She turns her chin up at her mom, expecting a lecture about her being too young, not to get pregnant and tied down, et cetera.

"Ah, good," her mom says cheerfully. "It's about time you had a boyfriend. I was getting worried you would never marry."

Claudia scoffs. "Mom! I'm only 20. And it's not like that. We're not getting married. Not yet. I mean, not now. Maybe not ever. And didn't you always want me to marry a Taiwanese guy?" She challenges.

Her mother shrugs, pursing her lips thoughtfully. "That would be nice. But James is good for you. He is tall, good-looking, and respectful." She stacks a few plates. "And, he tells me that he is going to be a *doctor*." She says the last word melodramatically, her eyes looking up at the ceiling as if imagining her daughter's future perfect life with the handsome Dr. James.

Claudia rolls her eyes. "Yeah, he's going to be a doctor. But he's going to medical school in Toronto. So, don't get your hopes up because we're not even going to be living in the same city."

She turns to carry more dishes to the kitchen, and sees James standing in the doorway, looking at them. He takes the dishes from her and returns to the kitchen.

"Were you listening?" she asks, following him.

"Kind of. But I only understood the words 'marry' and 'doctor'. Sounds like I have a lot of work to do," he says, teasingly. "Maybe we should tell her that I've decided to become a nurse instead."

Claudia laughs, heartily. "Don't. She'll have a heart attack."

James has an early class the next morning and decides to call it a night after they finish cleaning up. He thanks Mrs. Young for the delicious food, and she sends him home with a couple Tupperware containers.

"Study hard," Mrs. Young says to her daughter's new boyfriend, smiling sweetly.

Claudia walks him to the door and they hug goodbye. He gives her a kiss on the mouth, but she pushes him away just in case her mom is eavesdropping.

"Later babe," he says, giving her cheek a nudge. "I'll call you after class tomorrow."

She leans against the door behind him, taking a moment for herself. *I'm James Cooper's girlfriend*, she thinks. She looks at herself in the full-length mirror hanging on the wall. She turns to each side, looking at her body, flipping her hair over one shoulder, and then the other. She studies her face closely, lifting her eyebrows, sucking in her cheeks. What does he see?

She feels her mom coming up behind her. She stands next to Claudia, a few inches shorter, looking at her daughter's face in the mirror, then her own.

"We have the same lips," she says to Claudia, pursing her own pretty lips in the mirror. "Though yours could use some Vaseline."

Claudia's right hand flies to her mouth, red and chapped from a weekend of firsts with James. She blushes, and runs to her room to find her Chapstick.

- 6 - 1976, Taipei

Twenty-two-year-old Polly King has been waiting for five hours. She sits on a stool beside the rotary telephone in the kitchen, flipping through an English fashion magazine. There is only one telephone in the apartment, and she wants to answer it as soon as it rings. He said he would call, but it's late afternoon already.

Her Godparents, *Gan-Ma* and *Gan-Ba*, are elsewhere in the apartment. It's late afternoon, so old Gan-Ba, is likely in his office folding tiny origami animals. Gan-Ma is probably taking a nap, or smoking cigarettes on the balcony, while spying on the neighbors.

Their apartment is large, but not grand – it takes up the entire eighth floor of the inner-city building. They are not rich, but Polly's father, who had been a General in the army, had left a decent amount of money behind when he passed ten years ago, ensuring that his two youngest and unmarried daughters would be well taken care of, before they found their husbands.

Polly is the youngest of the four King sisters. She was born in the Year of the Water Dragon, and her mother had been in her late forties already. They had been hoping to conceive a strong male dragon heir. When Polly was finally pulled from the womb and announced a girl, her mother had turned her head away, exhausted and tired.

Nonetheless, little Polly grew to be a spirited child, charming the wits off her older sisters, and bringing new life to the family. Her father simply adored his sweet little girl, and took her with him everywhere, sitting on top of his shoulders, with her chubby legs dangling around his neck.

When she was four years old, her mother died of a rare flu. This brought her even closer to her father. Tragically, he passed away eight years later, when she was just entering middle school.

Her grown-up sisters all left Taipei before she came of age. Ting, the second youngest, was married at nineteen, only one year after their father's death. Ting moved to America with her new husband, reuniting with their two oldest sisters, Honey and Lily, who were already married and living in New York.

The phone finally makes a sound, and Polly picks it up before it gets through the first ring.

"*Wei*?" She demands.

"*Wei*, Polly?" A male voice inquires on the other end.

"*Si wo*." It's me, she says.

"*Ni hao*, Polly! You sound lovely on the phone. This is Peter Young. How are you?"

Polly doesn't like small talk, especially over the phone, when the operator overhears every word.

"What do you want?" She asks. "Do you want to go out again, or what?" She is straightforward, and expects others to be so as well.

He chuckles, taking his time with his answer. "Well. Let me think for a second. If I didn't want to go out again, why would I be calling? You are silly. Would you like to go bowling with me tonight?"

He pauses, but continues without giving her a chance to answer. "My friend will come pick you up in his car. He is staying in a house not far from you. Be ready at seven o'clock.

He'll be in a blue car in front of your building." He hangs up before she has a chance to answer.

His friend will be picking me up? Polly scoffs. How rude of him. Any decent boy from a good family would pick her up himself, no matter how far the drive or long the walk. *He's been living in America for too long*, she thinks.

The Young and King families had lived on the same street in Taipei when Polly was a child. Peter is the youngest in the family, but still six years older than Polly. He was sent away to boarding school at a young age so she hardly remembers him at all, but their families are tied due to one fruitful match already: Her oldest sister, Honey, is married to the Youngs' oldest son, Lee. Which means that Peter and Polly are already relatives, by marriage.

Gan-Ma had been awfully excited one day, coming home to report Peter Young's return to Taipei. She had overheard at her Mahjong match that Peter was home and looking for a bride. The news was quite uninteresting to Polly. She had no wishes to marry a boy who'd been living in America for the past ten years. Who knows what kind of horrid foreign habits he's acquired.

But when Peter Young himself had come knocking on their apartment door, with a box of fresh, expensive pineapple cakes tucked under his arm, she'd become slightly more convinced. At an even six feet tall, he is by far the tallest man she has known, and on top of that – he is downright handsome.

Polly does not use the word handsome lightly. There are well-mannered men, distinguished-looking men, and even pretty men. Peter may not be any of those things, but he is definitely handsome. His eyes are large for an Oriental, and his skin is the color of light copper, which is a dramatic contrast to her own smooth, porcelain skin.

She glances at the clock in the kitchen and realizes it is nearing five o'clock already. The nerve of him to make plans with her on such short notice. It must be how American girls prefer it.

Her hair is freshly washed from the morning, but the tropical summer humidity has made her sweaty, even though she spent her day indoors. She goes to the bathroom and runs a cold bath, stripping out of her sticky clothes. Sponging the cool water languidly over her bare skin, she thinks about Peter. She has only seen him twice since he's been in Taipei – the first time at the apartment, and the second time, last night, when he'd walked with her to a park and told her about all the girlfriends he'd had in America. She was terribly put-off by his attempt at conversation, but soon came to realize that he was in fact pointing out that the Western girls hadn't boded well for him in America. It was a strange, around-the-bush way of exposing to Polly that he is looking for a Taiwanese bride.

Polly also made it clear to Peter last night that she is strictly looking for a husband, and doesn't court men casually. She knows that getting married is the only way she'll be able to move out from under Gan-Ma and Gan-Ba's roof.

At seven o'clock she is standing on the sidewalk in front of her apartment building, looking like she is going dancing, rather than a bowling alley. She's wearing a powdery mauve silk dress that ties with a sash, accentuating her tiny waist. Her long hair has been set into giant curls that flare away from her face, and one side is pinned back with a barrette. She's wearing a full face of makeup, though she's good at making it look natural. Her nails are painted a bright red. She has left her lips bare, as they are naturally pink and full.

A blue car comes to a screeching halt and a tall, blond foreigner steps out of the car. He is handsome, Polly thinks. He has dark smoldering eyes. Brown like hers, but his are much larger and round like coins, framed with thick eyelashes.

"*Ni hao*, you must be Polly," he says in perfect Mandarin, which catches her by surprise. She is relieved, because her English is not very good and she didn't want to be making a fool of herself so early in the night.

"You must be Peter's friend," She says with a polite smile, stepping towards the car. "You speak Mandarin very well. Where did you learn?"

He doesn't answer. He just stands there, staring at her. She waits briefly for him to come over to her side and open the door for her, but he doesn't. Just as he notices her waiting and makes a move to come over, she pulls the door open and elegantly climbs in.

The car is a Jaguar with a buttery tan, leather interior. It must have cost a fortune. Polly adjusts her hair in the side-view mirror as the man gets into the car.

"I'm sorry, I haven't introduced myself," he says. "My name is Henry." They shake hands formally. Polly doesn't shake hands often, so she doesn't really know how to hold her wrist and it ends up being a rather awkward shake. Henry chuckles, and pulls the Jaguar away from the curb.

"To answer your question, I learned Mandarin years ago, when I studied at the National Taiwan University," he says. "My father also has a home here in Taipei not far from here. He works in shipping and this is one of their largest ports. I've been coming to Taipei since I was a child."

Polly nods politely. "How do you know Peter?" She inquires. Henry is weaving through the streets, driving like a madman, almost running a red light at one point.

She panics. "Are you mad? Don't drive so fast. There is no need to be in such a rush." She scolds him in a sharp tone. He just smiles.

"You Taiwanese girls are real cute," he says. "I've heard you make excellent wives."

Polly takes his condescending comment as a compliment. "Why thank you," she says.

The audacious blond man continues on in his perfect Mandarin. "I met Peter years ago in New York City. He was there for a wedding. Your sister's and his brother's, I believe. He's told me a lot about you," he adds, his eyes twinkling.

"I wasn't at that wedding. I was only a child at the time. However, I am curious as to what Peter could have possibly told you about me," she says, her tone challenging. "Our families are connected, yes, but I've only seen him twice since we were children, and two of those times were in the past week." She detests dishonesty.

He smiles nervously. "I apologize. Everything that has or has not been said about you is entirely positive." His turn of phrase is strange, throwing Polly off. She hardly understands what he means. He must be translating his thoughts from English, she thinks. Must be a nervous habit.

"So you're from New York, then?" Polly asks. She wonders if he lives anywhere close to her sisters.

"I'm British, actually," Henry says, with a wink. "If we were speaking in English you would be able to tell."

"You don't look British," Polly says.

"What do you mean? How am I supposed to look?"

Polly shrugs. "You just don't look British. I would have thought you were American."

Henry laughs. "Have you ever been to America?"

"No, I've never left Taiwan," Polly says, unabashed. "But you look like Ryan O'Neil, from *Love Story*."

"I've not seen that film," Henry says.

"It's very sad," Polly says. "The girl dies in the end."

They arrive within minutes at the bowling alley, which unsettles Polly. Peter really could have just come to pick her up himself.

They park in a crowded lot in the back, and they walk around to the front entrance, with Polly dodging pebbles carefully in her three-inch high heels. They push the doors open to the humongous space, which houses no fewer than twenty bowling lanes. Despite the crowds and the billowing cigarette smoke, Peter is easy to spot. He is easily the tallest man in the room and the most striking – though, with the blond Henry now present, this could be contested. Peter sees the two of them enter and waves across the room enthusiastically. He has already claimed a lane, and is holding a twelve-pound ball in his right hand, and smoking a cigarette with the other. Polly notices his skin-tight, bell-bottom jeans. His striped polo is just as tight, pulling across his chest. The neck cuts low into a deep V, with two buttons he has left undone, revealing a couple straggly chest hairs.

He is also wearing glasses, which is a surprise. "Peter," she addresses him curtly. "You're wearing glasses."

He grins at her. "Yes. They are for reading – and bowling," he says. "I can't let this British bastard beat me, can I?" He nods at Henry smiling, and switches to English. "Thanks for picking her up, Henry. I owe you one." Henry nods, and moves over a few lanes, looking for the perfect ball.

"My car is in the shop," Peter explains to Polly. "I walked here but didn't want you to suffer the same. I hope you didn't mind riding with Henry."

Polly softens, relieved that there was a reason behind his bad manners. "Thank you. That was very considerate."

Henry has found a ball, and announces that he is going to rent some shoes at the counter. "What size do you wear?" He asks Polly. "I'll get yours too." Peter is already geared up to go, slipping around on his rented bowling shoes.

Polly shakes her head quickly. "Oh no. *I'm* not bowling," she says, as if the idea is preposterous. "I'm not dressed for it. I will just watch you boys play."

Peter shoots her an odd look, his cigarette pinched between his teeth. "I told you we were going bowling. Why didn't you come prepared?" He stamps out his cigarette into an ashtray.

"I'm not in the mood to play," she says coolly, narrowing her eyes. "I would have told you that if you didn't hang up the phone in such a rush." She sits down, carefully smoothing out the skirt of her dress, and crossing her legs at the ankles. She pastes a genial smile on her face. "It's not a problem. I will sit here and watch you throw as many balls as you would like across the room. Perhaps we can talk after."

Peter shrugs. "Okay. Do you want to drink something? There's a concession stand in the back. Go get yourself something. He hands her some money. And get a *Heysong* for me."

He turns to the lane and rolls the ball down the lane, posing in a smooth stance. Unfortunately, the ball veers to the right, falling into the gutter.

Polly sighs heavily and walks over to the concession stand. She runs into Henry on the way back. He's holding two pairs of shoes. One pair looks extremely small in his large white hands.

"I guessed your size. They're the smallest they have. You have very small feet, I noticed." He hands her the pair. She hesitates for a moment before taking them from him. They are in fact the right size.

She thanks him. "*Xie xie*," she says, nodding graciously.

"Where are you going?" He asks her. She indicates the concession stand, and he motions with his head that he'll come with her. They order two cans of *Heysong* soda for him and Peter, and one can of *Apple Sidra* for her. It's her favorite – extra fizzy and fruity. He pays for it all and they head back towards Peter.

"Ah, you decided to play after all," Peter says happily, seeing Polly with the bowling shoes. Polly doesn't answer, and hands his unused money back to him. She sits down to put the shoes on, feeling slightly ridiculous pairing her beautiful silk dress with these ugly shoes. She's decided to play just one game to appease everyone. Really, she would rather be going dancing.

She uses a seven-pound ball. Surprisingly, she is quite good. Her throws are controlled and even, and her aim is impeccable. Though she does not have enough power to strike, she is able to clear the pins on subsequent throws almost every time with her incredible accuracy.

It turns out that both Peter and Henry are horrible at bowling. She ends winning two, then three games, attracting the attention of their lane neighbors and other bystanders. Soon, a small crowd has gathered around to watch, which distresses the losing men. Eventually Polly loses interest, so they decide they've all had enough.

They turn in their shoes and step out into the humid night. Polly asks Peter why he wanted to go bowling, if he wasn't very good at it. Shouldn't he be at least trying to impress her?

"Henry is leaving tomorrow and I wanted to see him," he explains, as Henry walks ahead to give them some privacy. "He's a very good friend of mine. I also wanted to see you. I figured bowling was a good activity to do in a threesome, and that no one would feel left out. I hadn't expected you to be so good." He smiles sheepishly.

Polly straightens. "It was my first time," she says, rubbing salt in the wound. "It's not very enjoyable when it's so...unevenly matched." She smiles.

Peter laughs. "Okay. Next time, we'll do something that I am much better at," he says.

"Like what?" Asks Polly, curious.

"Badminton!" he says enthusiastically, imitating the swipe of a racquet. Polly smiles. She is quite sure she can beat him in badminton as well, having played competitively in high school.

Henry is waiting by his Jaguar. He offers to give them a lift home, but since the bowling alley is so close to Polly's building, Peter tells him that he'll walk her home instead. Polly wants to object since she is wearing high-heels, but closes her mouth when she remembers that they've not had a chance to be alone all night. She shakes Henry's hand goodbye, and takes Peter's arm when he offers it to her. Before they turn to go, Henry pulls a camera from the backseat of the car and asks to take their picture.

"But why?" Asks Polly, exasperated. She abhors having her picture taken. But Peter thinks it's a great idea and straightens for the camera.

"Make it a good one," he says to his friend in English, teeth clenched in a ready smile.

"She could make a boar look good," Henry says, still in English, winking at Polly. Knowing she won't understand, he adds, "you lucky bastard."

Peter laughs as the camera flashes, delighted by the company of his good friend and this beautiful, cunning girl. He claps his hand on Henry's back to say goodbye. Henry gives them a last nod, and steps into his car, speeding away.

Finally alone, the two make their way down the quiet road, heading back to Gan-Ma and Gan-Ba's apartment.

Peter begins talking immediately. "Polly, I'm leaving next week, back to America. Since I don't have much time, I want to talk to you about something. I have been living in America for quite some time and it really is a great place. There is so much opportunity there. The future is there. Now, I know this is forward, but...have you considered what you want for your future?"

Polly is walking steadily, placing one high heel carefully in front of the other, like she's walking on a tight rope. She does this with ease, and could in fact balance a dictionary on her head, thanks to years of practice. She is holding on to Peter's arm, which is a challenge, as he is a man who talks with his hands.

"I am almost thirty years old," he continues with his speech. "I do not want to live here, in Taipei. I want to live in America. However, I do not wish to marry an American girl. They are...too progressive, for my tastes." He cocks his head lightly to the side, hoping that he does not sound too chauvinistic.

"What I'm saying is," he removes his glasses and tucks them into the breast pocket of his polo and turns to look at her. "Polly, would you consider me for your future?"

"Consider you." Polly repeats, in a musing tone. She continues to walk straight ahead, not looking at Peter who has shifted his attention to her face glowing in the moonlight. "What do you mean? Make it plain, please."

Peter sighs. "*Aiya*. I am asking you if you would like to be married to me. To become my wife, and start a new life with me in America. You would not have to work. I am educated and will have a good career, I am sure of it. I already have connections in Texas, where there are big opportunities in the oil industry for an engineer like me."

Polly wrinkles her nose at the thought of Texas, thinking of the movies she's seen in the theater. She pictures cowboys, deserts, and cactus. A place with very bad *feng shui*.

He continues. "Our families are well suited to each other. Just look at Lee and Honey's marriage. Though your parents have passed, I think that if they were here, they would approve of this marriage. I have already talked to your sisters and they are hoping you will agree. And I am sure your guardians will be very happy with the match."

"And what do your mother and father think of this?" Polly asks. She has memories of Peter's father, old Mr. Young, a tall, lanky man with a severe face, parting the sidewalks as he walked intimidatingly to work each morning at the Congressional Building. Though her oldest sister has already married their oldest son, she can't help but think they may still have their reservations.

"My Mother wants more grandsons. And my Father thinks you are a beauty," he says, smiling at her timidly. "I must say I have to agree with his opinion."

Polly tries to hide her reaction. The King sisters are known for their well-bred, refined looks, but she has never thought of herself as a beauty. She holds her fingers to her lips and lets out an embarrassed giggle.

He stops, and turns her by the shoulders to look at him. Grasping her hand that's covering her mouth by the wrist, he pulls it down gently. "Never cover up your mouth, Polly. It is your best feature. I want to see it when you're happy, sad, and especially when you laugh." He touches a finger to her bottom lip. "It looks like a heart."

Polly is blushing uncomfortably. "Stop it, Peter." She says gently, pushing his hand away. "You're being inappropriate."

He laughs. "You are right. I am being very inappropriate. Let me try this again." He bends down on one knee, little rocks biting through his jeans. "This is how they do it in America, and it looks very romantic."

He looks up at Polly. "Marry me."

Polly closes her eyes, her nose suddenly burning with tears, like she's eaten too much spicy radish. She knows how to hold it in. She counts to twenty, slowly.

Finally, she opens her eyes. "*Hao.*" Yes, she says. "I will marry you. But under one condition. I do *not* want to live in Texas. If you can promise me that we will live somewhere else – somewhere very beautiful, with water, mountains, trees, and flowers outside my window – then my answer is yes."

Peter jumps up with a shout, lifting her into an embrace, twirling her around, the mauve silk of her dress billowing in a circle in the moonlight. She holds on to his shoulders, feeling light, feminine and suddenly free. He sets her back down and gazes into her eyes.

146

"We will be so happy, Polly. You can start planning the wedding while I go back to America to finish up some business. When I am back, we will marry, and we'll take an airplane to America together to start our new life."

For the rest of the walk back to Gan-Ma and Gan-Ba's apartment, Peter holds Polly's hand for the very first time, their fingers intertwined. Their palms are sweaty from the heat and excitement. When they arrive, Polly leaves Peter at the door, going inside first to tell her guardians about their engagement. She comes back, with the aging couple shuffling behind her together, and invites Peter in. They pour four shots of Remy Martin XO into small colored glasses, and they toast the betrothal in high spirits.

Peter leaves the apartment at a respectful time and gives Polly a chaste kiss on the cheek at the door. She touches her cheek afterwards, which is moist from his mouth. They make plans for Polly to see Peter off at the airport in the coming week, and for a formal dinner with his parents, to make the announcement official. Peter promises that his mother has a beautiful diamond and jade ring sitting in a safety deposit box in the Taipei Central Bank. It will be Polly's.

Retreating to her bedroom, Polly lets out a shaky breath. She is engaged. She will be moving to America. Her husband's name will be Peter, and she will become a Young.

She falls back on her bed, staring up at the ceiling. She grabs a pillow and holds it tight against her face, muffling the uncontrollable sounds escaping her body.

She is so happy, that she cries for the first time since her father died.

- 7- Summer 2008, Vancouver

The days are long and balmy. Claudia finds herself swapping out her jeans and sweaters for sundresses and shorts, letting the sun kiss her light copper skin into a deep bronze. Her hair has grown even longer, which she wears loose in waves that fall to her waist.

James and Claudia finish their last round of final exams at UBC, and join the rest of their graduating class in a week of well-deserved celebration. There is a kegger almost every night. By Sunday, the day when Claudia is expected to walk the stage with her fellow Faculty of Arts graduates, she doesn't want to look at another red plastic cup filled with beer for the rest of her life.

Mr. and Mrs. Young, as well as Petey, have arrived in town for Claudia's graduation ceremony. James' mother and stepfather are in town as well, having attended James' graduation from the Faculty of Science the day before. The Youngs and Coopers will be having a commemorative dinner together tonight at a waterfront restaurant at Granville Island.

It had taken quite a bit of work to get James to include his mother for dinner. Especially after he found out that she would not be coming to Vancouver alone, and that her new husband would be joining her. Claudia however, was adamant.

"Why do we have to include my mom? She's not even staying at my place," James had said. "They probably won't want to come anyway. I like having dinner with your family alone. My side will just make it awkward."

"James, she's your mom. You're moving to Toronto in a couple of months and who knows how often you'll be seeing her. Plus, she's come all the way here to see you get your diploma. The least you can do is invite her to dinner." Claudia had pulled him close for a kiss to halt the argument, and James had conceded, in a moment of weakness.

And now, after all her goodwill and hard work, Claudia finds herself staring into her closet at the apartment, flashing back to her high school days, not knowing what to wear. This is her first time seeing James' mom after the early morning run-in outside the Coopers' house in the spring. Hours later they had officially become boyfriend and girlfriend in that little restaurant in Revelstoke, after learning about the death of James' father, and other shocking details, including the fact that Mrs. Cooper is now married to the late Mr. Cooper's brother – still a Mr. Cooper, nonetheless.

Claudia's family has always been stable and almost too normal sometimes, so this kind of family drama is on a whole new level for her. She has filled her own parents in on enough of what happened so that no uncomfortable questions will arise, but she is still nervous. *What if his mom doesn't like me? What if she doesn't think I'm good enough for her son? What if she's racist?*

Pushing her doubts to the back of her head, Claudia settles on a fitted, black tank dress and a deep red cardigan. She puts on a strand of pearls and touches up her makeup. She normally doesn't wear any, but she's made an exception tonight. The blush, mascara and lip-gloss highlight her best features, and she smiles at herself confidently in the mirror.

Her mother and father are waiting for her in the living room, already dressed. Mrs. Young's hair is perfectly coiffed, and her skin looks like it has been airbrushed to a flawless porcelain. Her eyebrows are perfectly groomed, her lips bare but rosy. She's wearing a demure green sheath dress and classic Ferragamo pumps. She looks absolutely stunning, she is clearly excited for the night's celebration.

Mr. Young is dressed in light grey slacks and a black sweater. He does not look as excited as his wife, but appears rather worried, with two vertical lines creased between his eyebrows. His daughter is clearly growing up, and tonight he is being forced to meet her boyfriend's parents.

Claudia smiles at the exquisite couple that is her parents. "*Hao piao liang*," she says to her mom. "You look so pretty."

She gives her dad a quick kiss on the cheek. "Are you ready? Petey says he'll meet us at the restaurant." Her brother had a few errands to run after the graduation ceremony, and had gone his own way. The three of them climb into Claudia's Honda and head to Granville Island, where Mrs. Young has made reservations at La Mer, a restaurant with one of the best waterfront views in the city.

The restaurant is simple and charming, elegant in a relaxed West Coast way. The tables are made of solid oak, and crystal chandeliers hang from the ceiling. Ice water is served in mason jars and the wine is poured out of large barrels. Their round table is in the back of a large heated patio, overlooking the Pacific. Sea gulls are soaring close by in the cool breeze, and boats file in from a day out on the water, docking for the night.

Petey is already there when Claudia arrives with her parents. They seat themselves strategically around the table.

Just as the Youngs are settling in, James arrives with his mother. A tall, greying man follows a few steps behind, with a nervous smile on his face.

Everyone stands to say hello. James embraces Claudia first, giving her a kiss. He shakes Mr. Young's hand and gives Petey a high five. He hugs Mrs. Young as he always does, and Claudia does the same with Mrs. Cooper, for the very first time.

"Good to see you again, Mrs. Cooper," Claudia says, smiling politely. She turns to the older man. "Hello, it's nice to meet you, Mr. Cooper." It's mildly confusing that he is not *the* Mr. Cooper, as in James' father. She extends her arm to shake his hand. His attention, however, is focused somewhere else. Claudia follows his line of sight and looks over her shoulder, and sees that he is staring at her own mother and father.

Claudia's parents are also staring back at the man, looking astonished.

"Henry?" Claudia's father's voice is both shocked and confused. He walks closer towards the man. "I almost didn't recognize you!" he is exuberant, and the men are embracing. "I haven't seen you in over twenty years! What are you doing here?"

"This is my mom's husband," James says slowly, stepping forward. "How do you two know each other?" He looks between Mr. Young and his uncle, trying to figure it out.

Everyone is silent and curious. Everyone that is, except Mrs. Young, who has an indecipherable expression on her face.

"Henry and I are old friends!" Mr. Young says. "This is just wonderful! Sit, sit! Please." Mr. Young leads everyone back to the table and they all settle into their seats. The conversation quickly turns back to Henry and Peter Senior, everyone wanting to know the story.

"We met years ago in New York City," says Mr. Young. "I'm sorry to say, we lost touch after Polly and I left Taiwan. Where are you living, nowadays?"

Henry seems confused for a moment. "I'm living in Calgary."

Mrs. Young chokes suddenly on her water, and Mr. Young turns to her, rubbing her back tenderly. "Well you should have told us!" Mr. Young laughs, after his wife's coughs have ceased.

"How long have you been in our city without us knowing? My, what a surprise!"

Henry clears his throat. "Yes. It has been a very long time. It is so good to see you both," he looks from Peter to Polly, nervously, but his tone is genuine and warm. "I had written you a letter, years ago, when I knew I was relocating to Canada from London. My father needed me to help out on some business here. I never heard back...so I thought you had either moved or..." he doesn't finish his sentence but instead looks from Peter to Polly, once again. He shakes his head, smiling. "It doesn't matter. We're here now, old friends, and new. And your beautiful family." He looks at Claudia. "You look just like your mother did at your age," he comments.

"Well, this is just dandy, isn't it?" James laughs, sarcastically. "Here I was worrying that this was going to be awkward." His mother sends him a silent warning look. Claudia squeezes his leg under the table.

The waiter comes around to fill everyone's wine glass with a bottle of the local chardonnay Polly had selected earlier. Claudia notices that her mother is not quite herself, and rather quiet for a change. *Perhaps she is nervous*, Claudia thinks. Her father on the other hand, has seemed to loosen right up. Really, the evening has changed from a graduation dinner for Claudia and James, to a reunion for the older men - long lost friends who've found each other once again due to a twist of fate.

Petey ends up switching spots with Henry, so that the reunited men can converse. Fueled with wine, they end up chatting the night away. James' mom, now sandwiched between James and Petey, makes polite conversation with Mrs. Young, all the while sneaking curious glances at their husbands every so often.

The dinner conversation covers James' upcoming move to Toronto and his plans for medical school. They also touch on Claudia's plans to "play it by ear" for a year, which causes her mother to sigh dramatically. Petey shares that he's found a new job in Vancouver, which he is starting in August. He plans on moving in with Claudia and it will be the first time the siblings will have lived together since they were kids.

After the entrees are finished, Claudia, James and Petey decide to skip dessert, and escape the evening to go downtown for gelato. Claudia leaves the Honda with her parents, and they take Petey's car. On their way out, Claudia catches her mother's panicked face.

Are you ok? She mouths to her mom. Her mom smiles meekly and gives her a quick nod. Claudia gives her a quizzical look. Something is up for sure. She makes a mental note to ask her mom about it later, and leaves with her boyfriend and brother.

The gelato shop is on one of the busiest shopping streets downtown. It is especially packed on this Sunday night, with swarms of tourists and locals trying to get the most out of their weekend. They wait in line for fifteen minutes to get their scoops, and sit at a table on the sidewalk patio. Claudia steals spoonful after spoonful from her brother's and James' cones, like an over-indulged child.

"That's just crazy," says Petey, about their father and Henry Cooper. "When things like this happen, I always think the world is just one big mind fuck."

James nods. "Yeah, totally. So random. I even heard him and your dad talking in Mandarin at one point. I didn't even know he could speak Mandarin. It's like the Twilight Zone."

Claudia sighs. "I think it's romantic," she says. Petey and James look at her like she's nuts. "Not like that, I know they weren't involved in that way...but fate brought them together again and that is just so...beautiful," she says, licking her ice cream. "Imagine if we didn't see each other for twenty years," she says, turning her attention to James. "And then we just ran into each other. Do you think you would still recognize me?"

"Well I for one, hope that doesn't happen," James says seriously. "I'm moving to Toronto, not Mars, so I expect you to come visit me at least once every two decades." He steals a bite of her cone this time, grabbing her wrist.

"I wonder what's going to happen now," she continues. "Like, are they gonna be friends and hang out and stuff? Dad could really use a friend in Calgary. All he does is work, and hang out with mom," James gives her a look. He does not want his uncle/step-dad getting all buddy-buddy with his girlfriend's father.

"Mom didn't look happy to be sharing dad, that's for sure," says Petey, with a half-frown. "In fact she looked straight pissed that dad spent the whole night reminiscing with the guy." He shrugs. "Well, maybe they can double date or something."

James suddenly stands up from the table. "I'd appreciate it if none of us encouraged them to hang out," he says, crumpling his napkin into a ball in his hand. "I like your parents, but I don't like Henry, for obvious reasons." He turns and walks towards Petey's car, which is parked at a meter up the street.

"Your boyfriend has step-daddy issues," says Petey to his sister, when James is out of earshot. "I can't say I blame him." Claudia had relayed some of the Cooper family history to Petey, late last night when they stayed up talking. "Hopefully he can get over it. You know how dad is." Claudia nods, knowing exactly what he means. Her father can be loyal to a fault. And how that he's found Henry again, he's going to make him his best friend.

"I'll talk to James," says Claudia. "At least he doesn't live in the same city as Henry. It makes it easier, I think." She changes the topic, looking up at her big brother, affectionately. "Thanks for coming up for my grad," she says. "I'm excited that you're moving here. It'll be like the old days. We can watch cartoons every morning and eat cereal together."

Petey gives her a droll look. "Unlike some people, I'll be working every day." Claudia frowns, feeling guilty.

He punches her in the arm playfully. "I'm joking, Claud. You deserve some time off. You already got into law school. And it'll still be there in a year, unless someone decides to burn it down."

"Yeah...we'll see what happens." Lately, Claudia has been seriously debating if she *ever* wants to go to law school. It's something she hopes to figure out, and soon.

They clean up the table, gather up their used napkins, and get up to relinquish their table to a family of four who are eagerly waiting to take their seats. The overzealous mother nearly tackles Claudia, after she trips over her own child. Petey and Claudia exchange a look of delighted horror.

They find James leaning against the passenger door of Petey's black 4-Runner. He has one leg bent, the sole of his shoe resting against the car's bumper, and he is smoking a cigarette.

"Since when do you smoke?" Claudia asks, appalled, and unable to hide the disgust in her voice. They have really only been dating for a month, so there are a lot of things she has to learn about him – but she figures that smoking is something she should have known by now.

He takes one last drag and throws the cigarette on the sidewalk, stomping it out. "I don't smoke. I bummed it off someone. Felt like a good thing to do at the moment," he says. Noticing Claudia's blank expression, he retracts his statement. "Sorry. That was dumb."

Claudia doesn't want to be the nagging girlfriend, but she hates the smell of cigarettes. Cigars are different because they remind her of her dad, but there is something about cigarettes that makes her think of a dirty back alley. Not to mention that the smell always triggers memories of the beating in high school. Those girls reeked of cigarettes.

"If you're gonna smoke, you'll need to find someone else to kiss," she says, her voice teasing but her face completely serious. "It's a gross habit and it'll kill you." She pushes James out of the way of the passenger door with her shoulder, opening it. "Shotgun."

Petey drops them off at James' place before heading back to the apartment. James' mom and Henry are staying at a hotel close by, so they finally get some privacy – something they haven't had all weekend. As soon as they enter the small basement suite, James closes the door behind them, and wraps his arms around Claudia, pulling her close, pressing his lips to her neck. His kisses becomes little bites, as he moves up towards her ears and finally to her waiting lips. She responds with a soft moan, letting him press her into the door, lifting her, and wrapping her legs around his waist. He carries her into his bedroom, past the small kitchen, bathroom, and hall closet. It is a tiny place, with the ceiling less than a foot taller than his full height. When Claudia had asked him why he didn't find a better place, knowing he could totally afford it, he had shrugged, saying it was good enough for him.

In his bedroom, there is a queen-sized bed, clothed only with a white comforter and two white pillows. There is one dresser, and one nightstand. Everything else is in his closet. The room is so clean it is nearly sterile.

They fall onto the white down comforter, glued together, with her on the bottom. James is kissing Claudia hungrily, his hands grasping the back of her skull. Her legs are still holding him taut to her body and she moves to unbutton his shirt, feeling his smooth, hard pectoral muscles against her soft hands. He shimmies the skirt of her dress up to her waist and brings his hand between her legs, stroking her. She moves her hands into his hair that is soft with pomade and she fists it between her palms, pulling his head slowly away from her face.

"James," she says quietly. "I love you." She pulls his face to hers again, not wanting him to answer or say anything he regrets because he thinks that's what he should do. She's been saying it to him for the past two weeks, because he is leaving soon and it is how she truly feels. She expects nothing in return. He exhales heavily, kissing her even harder, tugging her thong down her legs and removing it. He inserts a finger inside her folds, feeling her muscles clench around him, causing her eyes to roll and her hips to arch up towards his hand.

He can feel that she's close, and he pulls his hand out. She moans in protest, pulling him close. She reaches down to unbutton his jeans, as he reaches behind her and unclasps her bra through the thin jersey material of her dress. She helps his pants off with her feet, using her toes to push the waistband down. As soon as he's pulled the dress up and over her head, exposing her naked to him, she sticks her right hand down his grey boxer briefs, grabbing hold of him.

"Fuck...." He crushes down on her lips again, savoring the taste of her sweet lips. He kisses her throat down to her collarbone and moves to her breasts, drawing each nipple into his mouth with his tongue, grazing them softly with his teeth and drawing out her pleasure. She grasps the comforter with her hands, writhing with need.

Finally, pushing his boxers off, he pushes into her, filling her completely and making her gasp. He keeps a steady rhythm, bringing her to her peak and letting it flow out of her with complete abandon. Her mouth opens with a silent scream as she shudders. He comes moments later, slamming hard into her.

He remains on top and inside of her, supporting his weight with one forearm above her head. Pulling her to him, he rolls to his side, keeping her close.

"I've always loved you," he says. "Before you even knew about me." He kisses her on the head, and closes his eyes.

It's been a rough few months of high school for James. His mom is having an affair, his dad is sleeping with his secretary, and the only thing that keeps him going these days is basketball. With the season nearly over, he only has a few games left to prove his worth.

He's doesn't really care about winning games, but is a personal best kind of guy, setting goals for himself at the beginning of each season, and even the beginning of each game. Now, in his senior year, his goal is to set a record – and he has his eye on being the new provincial scoring leader. He only needs to score another 50 points, which he thinks is entirely doable in the three games they have yet to play.

Another motivation for setting the record is that his dad has promised him a sweet-ass new ride if he does it – a brand new BMW 3 series. Not that James cares about getting a new car – his current Lexus hand-me-down does him just fine – but there is something about getting his dad to care enough about something besides his new fuck-toy that gets him pretty motivated.

James' dad, Nathaniel Cooper, is not a bad guy, really. He was born into money, raised with money, and everything he does, says, or cares about, involves money. He loves his son dearly, but ever since James became old enough to form his own judgments about the world, it's been difficult for Nathaniel to connect with his son. Primarily because when James looks at his father, he sees the exact opposite of what he wants to become when he grows up.

James got his towering height and smoldering, debonair looks from his father's side of the family. His mom gave him her ocean eyes and thick chestnut hair, but really, he is his father's son in appearance. But personality-wise, the two men could not be more different. While Nathaniel Cooper has never left his skirt-chasing days behind him, even after marrying Elizabeth and fathering James, James could care less about scoring with girls. He finds that most girls his age are empty, self-centered and lacking in substance, and he is bored senseless most of the time trying to have a conversation. Then again, maybe he is just a jerk.

But differences aside, Nathaniel Cooper loves sports as much as the next man. And he loves to watch his boy play basketball. He never misses a game – a perk of working few and flexible hours, managing his family's Canadian assets and holdings – and he is often seen in the stands shouting his son's name, impressing his teammates' moms who have come to do just the same. *What a devoted father*, they say amongst themselves. *If only my husband were as involved with our kids.*

What they don't know is that after the game, once James is showered and changed, he climbs into his car by himself and drives home alone. It is a long drive, to the outer limits of the city, where larger properties are available. When he arrives at his family's sprawling estate, the wrought iron gates open for him, he makes his way up the long driveway, and he parks in his usual space under a large oak tree. When he unlocks the front door of the grand house, he is greeted by the dark. He goes to the kitchen, switches on the lights, and opens the fridge to pull out a plate of food prepared by their hired cook. While he heats it up in the microwave, he pours himself a glass of water. He sits at the counter and eats in silence, watching his own reflection in the window, past the large kitchen table.

After he eats, he studies and does his homework. He works hard academically so he can get into a good University far enough away from his fucked up parents. Somewhere on the East Coast is what he prefers. He goes to bed around eleven every night, in his boxers, with a nightlight on.

Some nights, neither of his parents comes home. Once in a while, he hears his mom pull in through the gates close to midnight, opening the four-car garage to park her Mercedes. He hears her enter the house, and then her light footsteps climb the winding staircase, and stop outside his room on the second floor. She opens the door a crack to peer in at him. He pretends to be asleep.

If his father ever comes home to sleep, he wouldn't know. Ever since James was in junior high, Nathaniel Cooper has stayed in the guest cottage behind the house, claiming to value his privacy and space.

But his father always comes into the main house for one thing: Breakfast.

Every morning, James gets ready for school, pulling on his usual combination of a soft cotton t-shirt and dark-washed jeans. If it's cold, he'll throw on a hoodie. In the winter he'll wear a toque. He then goes downstairs for the worst ten minutes he'll have all day.

He enters the kitchen with his head high and confident. There is always food on the counter: An assortment of fruit, pastry and bagels, laid out by the housekeeper. He takes his usual – a banana, bagel, and pours himself a cup of coffee. He then sits at the table, with his father reading the newspaper at one end, and his mother reading a magazine at the other, both acting as if they are a normal family, eating breakfast with their son. As if they hadn't both spent the night before fucking someone else. After silently eating his food, he gets up and grabs his keys. He'll catch his mother's eye, and she usually has a faint look of guilt set across her face. His dad doesn't look up at all for the most part, unless it's a game day. *See you at the game*, he'll say, on those days.

For those ten minutes every morning, James stews in the sham of family life his parents have committed to putting on. He hopes it makes them feel better, because it certainly makes him feel worse.

Leaving the house, he holds in his anger. He walks past his dad's Jaguar, wanting to kick a dent into it. But he doesn't. He makes it to his car, gets in, puts it in drive, and goes to school. Just another day for James Cooper, pretending that everything is just fine.

When in reality, everything is just a huge fucking lie.

January is the worst month in Calgary. Blizzards are a weekly occurrence, the snow is heavy, and the roads are covered in black ice. But even in the depths of winter, James refuses to wear a puffy down parka like his fellow schoolmates, and layers only a leather jacket over his hoodie, with the hood sticking out.

It's almost eight in the morning, and James is driving to school on the highway. He's eating a bagel with one hand and steering with the other. The car suddenly goes quiet. A few clicking sounds follow, and then the sound system and heat turns off. He groans, pulling over to the side of the road, throwing his half-eaten bagel into the cup holder of the console.

It's -20 outside, and he's not wearing gloves. Stretching the sleeves of his sweatshirt over his fingers, he pops the hood of the car and gets out to take a look. Not like he knows what he's looking for, it's just what people do when their car breaks down. He's not completely surprised – the car was due for service over three months ago and he'd ignored the light.

He reaches for his cell phone in his back pocket. *Shit.* He'd left it on the kitchen counter at home, in a rush to get out of the house. He thinks about flagging down a car to help him out, but decides against it. Seeing that the closest exit is only about thirty meters up the road, he grabs his backpack from the passenger seat, swings it onto his back, and decides to make a run for it. He'll send someone to pick up the car later.

Leaving his car on the shoulder, he sprints towards the exit, watching for cars, squinting against the icy snow cutting into his eyes and cheekbones. White clouds puff out of his mouth as his lungs fight the cold. It's so fucking cold it hurts. Luckily there is a 7-11 right off the exit across the street, and he steps inside, rubbing his hands together to warm them. He borrows their phone and calls his dad.

No answer.

He has an English test this morning that he doesn't want to miss. He checks the time and sees that he has twenty-five minutes to get to school.

"Do you have a bus schedule?" He asks the female clerk behind the counter. She hands him a thin piece of paper with a bunch of numbers and times on it.

He recognizes one of the bus numbers and asks her where he can catch it. She motions to the corner outside where there's a bus shelter and a group of kids huddled inside. He nods his thanks to her, and decides to get a small cup of coffee at the last minute. More as a heat source for his hands, than for the caffeine.

Amazingly, he has never taken the bus before. When the big blue vehicle stops and the doors open with the sharp sound of compressed hydraulic air, he gets on and has to ask the driver how much to pay for his fare. Two twenty five.

There's an empty seat in the middle of the bus, facing sideways near the rear exit and he sits down, slightly nervous. *How pathetic*, he thinks to himself, *that I'm nervous about riding the bus. I'm so fucking sheltered.*

He closes his eyes to enter a meditative state, but he can't seem to relax, with the bus coming to a jarring halt every couple of minutes.

On the third or fourth stop, a pretty Asian girl gets on. He notices immediately that she has a big bruise on her cheek, and one eye is completely bloodshot, as if a bunch of blood vessels had exploded. She's holding her arm in a way that shows she's definitely in pain. On her other shoulder, she's carrying a backpack.

Her eyes scan over the bus. Seeing nowhere to sit, she remains at the front of the bus, holding onto a rail and staying close to the driver. She is wearing a Catholic School uniform with a fur-hooded parka over it, and wool argyle tights. He notices that she had gotten on in front of St. Agnes High School. *That's where she goes*, he thinks logically. He wonders what she's doing leaving already. First period probably hadn't even started yet.

She gets off the bus a couple stops later, thanking the bus driver. James turns to look out the window at her, crossing at the pedestrian walkway in front of the bus. She is limping slightly, but from the look on her face you would not know that anything is wrong.

Her lips are turned up ever so slightly. She looks almost smug. To James, it looks endearing. The bus waits at the stop for a couple minutes, obviously ahead of schedule. He's not familiar with this side of town, and he watches curiously as the girl walks down the sidewalk, disappearing into a small grey building with large wooden doors. Squinting his eyes, he is able to make out the sign: *Public Library.*

He feels the urge to get off the bus and go after this elusive, beautiful girl, with the bruised face and swollen lips. But that would be weird. She's trouble, no doubt, looking like she'd gotten into a rough fight. And on top of it, she's skipping first period. No one skips first period, except to sleep in. Who goes to the library?

Imagine his surprise, two days later, to see the same girl walking into his math class, clutching an AP Calculus textbook to her chest, covering up the giant pi symbol printed onto her grey sweater. His classmates stare at her and whisper in hushed voices. *Who is she? Is she in the wrong class? Look at her eye.* He catches her good eye and gives her a small smile. He nods at the desk in front of him, indicating that the seat is open. She gratefully takes the seat and flashes him a smile. "Hi, I'm Claudia," she says, turning in her seat to greet him.

He feels like a little kid, when he sees that smile. He tells her he likes her sweater, feeling like an idiot. And all through class, as he sits back and watches her listening intently to the teacher, with her back straight and head tilted slightly to the right, absorbing every word as if her life depends on it, he thinks that maybe, he has found something else that will keep him going.

And it all comes crashing down on prom night. It's embarrassing, getting hardcore rejected by the only girl you've ever liked. But he figures he'll give her some space and revisit the issue in a few weeks. After all, they're going to be living in the same city for the next four years. It would hardly be prudent to leave things on a bad note.

After holding her in his arms in front of her house for what seems like hours, not wanting to let go, James hesitantly pulls back – for his own sake, knowing that she isn't ready to give him what he wants. He wants her to be his, to fall for him. The same way that he has already fallen for her.

He gets in the car, giving her a final look, urging her to change her mind, but he knows she won't, not right now. *See you around campus*, he quips, feeling like a douche.

He drives home with the music off, leaving his high school crush standing barefoot on the driveway of her house, light pink chiffon billowing in the wind. That bittersweet vision will remain in his mind for years to come. The last frame in a film from another life.

The lights are on when he pulls in to his family's estate. It's just past midnight, and he'd told his parents that he would be spending the night out with friends, so he's surprised they're home – they are rarely so.

Parking in his usual spot under the tree, he decides to go in through a side door, to hit up the kitchen. If he's lucky, he can avoid seeing them and go straight up to his room.

It turns out he miscalculated their whereabouts. As he unlocks and pulls open the door that opens into the hallway between the kitchen and dining room, he hears his parents' voices. There is a third voice - a man's voice, with an English accent, thicker than his parents'.

"We have to tell him," his mother is saying. "It's not fair to keep it from him, even if he is going away for University. He has a right to know."

"I don't see the point," his father says. "We've been through this. Nothing good can come out of it. He hates me as it is, it would only make him hate me more."

The third voice chimes in. "I know it's not my place – "

"You're right, it's not," snaps his father. "This has nothing to do with you. "

"This is a very complicated situation, Nathan. Henry is here for support. He's been a part of our lives in more ways than one, whether you've liked it or not. And, frankly...we need him right now."

James looks at a mirror hanging above a console across the hall, reflecting the dining room. He can make out the three figures sitting at the dining room table, with glasses of wine. He sees that his mother is holding the other man's hand. Her lover. What. The. Fuck.

"Thank you, Elizabeth," the Henry guy says, patting his mother's hand. "Nathan, I know this is very hard for you...for both of you. But you have to think of James. Put yourself in his shoes. Wouldn't you want to know?"

Silence. James can hear the grandfather clock ticking behind him. He doesn't want to draw attention to his presence and decides to back out of the house the way he came in. The front door would have been a better option.

Retracing his footsteps, he ends up outside again in the early summer night. He can smell a bonfire close by, which makes him think of roasting marshmallows and drinking beer – normal things that high school kids do at night. What's not normal is eavesdropping on a conversation between your father, mother, and her fucking boyfriend.

He goes around to the back by the pool and sits down on one of the lounge chairs. Kicking off his shoes, he stretches out onto the chair, cupping the back of his head with interlaced hands. He can feel tears pricking in between his eyebrows, making him feel like he needs to sneeze, so he closes his eyes instead, willing himself to sleep. He can deal with everything in the morning.

He's not sure how long he has been asleep, when a hand is on his shoulder, shaking him awake.

A voice speaks. "Son..." James blinks his eyes open, still blurry from sleep, to see his father standing over him, a look of concern on his face. "Sorry to wake you. You're going to freeze out here." It has gotten a few degrees cooler, and James notices he is shivering slightly. Damn Calgary weather.

He sits up, swinging his feet to the grass. Without a word, he stands up and walks towards the house. When he reaches the house, he turns to look at his father. He sees him heading to the guest cottage, both hands grasping his hair, as if his head is going to explode.

My head would explode too, thinks James, *if I had to shoot the shit with my wife's lover.*

He crashes into his bed and sleeps for a few more hours. When he wakes up, he wishes that it were a weekday so that he can escape to school. But it's Saturday. He checks the clock – barely nine in the morning. He debates whether or not he should go downstairs to breakfast. Surely they are waiting for him, wanting to break the news.

They're going to tell them that they're not in love anymore, and that they're going to get a divorce. They will expect him to be surprised, or maybe just act like he is. He has known for years that his parents had turned cold – he has even felt guilty at times about being the glue that forces them together. Their marriage is complicated, he knows – their union was more of a business transaction than anything, forced upon them by their families. James had learned as much from their terse conversations over the years.

He knows this was coming, and he always guessed they were waiting for him to finish high school. But there is still a little part of him that feels like a scared child, who wants more than anything for his mommy and daddy to stay together. He shakes his head at himself, cruelly laughing inside at the absurd thought. He decides not to delay the inevitable, and he throws on a pair of sweatpants, a hooded sweatshirt, and goes downstairs.

There is a generous spread of English muffins, jam, fruit, cheese, and cold cuts on the counter in the kitchen. He makes himself a sandwich and scoops a few slices of fresh honeydew onto his plate. His parents are sitting at the table, at either end, both sipping coffee. His dad is without his newspaper and his mom is staring at her hands, so he knows he's right. They want to talk.

He sits down, sighing, and takes a giant bite of his breakfast sandwich, surprised at his appetite. His mother clears her throat and looks at him, her eyes that are so much like his own, already rimmed with tears. She gives him a meek smile. He stares back at her blankly.

"James," his father begins steadily, seeing that his wife is already emotional and losing her composure. "I – your mother and I – we have something to tell you."

James nods slowly, astutely. "Yep," he says.

Nathaniel Cooper sighs heavily, putting down his mug of coffee. "As you know, things have not been quite...ideal between your mother and I," he says. "And I am to blame. Ever since we were married I've been preoccupied with other things.... commitments...and I've been a terrible husband." He swallows, his jaw tensing.

"Nathan, let's not get into that..." His mother gently tries to change the course of the conversation.

"No, this is important, Elizabeth. I'll get to it, don't worry." His father turns his attention back to his son. "I'm sorry if I have not been there for you, son," he says, his eyes glassy. "You deserve so much more and I've never been the one to give it to you." He looks away, composing himself.

James shifts uncomfortably in his seat. He would rather they just come out with it, instead of putting on this theatrical performance. He crosses his arms over his chest. "I get it, dad. You and mom aren't in love. You don't want to be together anymore. Just say it, and stop torturing yourselves." He feels angry, that he has to be the facilitator in this conversation. But he's always been a good son, and understanding, even at the worst of times.

His father shakes his head. "No, James, that's not it. I mean, yes, we aren't...in love, your mother and I." He looks up at James guiltily. "But I think you've known that, haven't you? I'm sorry about that. But this is not about us, or our marriage."

James tenses, confused. "What is it then?" He looks from his father to his mother, suddenly anxious. "Is someone dying or something?" He is only half-serious but when he sees his mother's face crumble, he knows he's hit it on the nose.

"Oh my God...Mom?" He drops his fork. She shakes her head. "No darling, not me."

James turns to look at his dad, whose face is as devastated as he feels. "Dad? What's going on?"

"Pancreatic cancer," his father says. "I have a surgery scheduled for next week. The doctors say it's pretty far along." He looks up at his son. "They think the surgery will give me a few more months. Maybe a year or two if we're lucky."

"When did you find out? How long have you been keeping this from me?" James asks. "And what was *that guy* doing here last night, when you guys were deciding whether or not to tell me?"

He glares at his mother. She closes her eyes, not able to look at her son.

"I found out on Wednesday, James. I didn't want to tell you until after your prom. It didn't seem fair to ruin that for you. And it's only been a few days but... Let me just say, finding out that you're dying is...eye opening, to say the least. I don't expect you to understand right now, though I know you will one day." Nathaniel clears his throat. "Henry is your mother's...friend. And he is my -"

James cuts him off, pissed. "You're right, I don't understand. First you tell me you have cancer, and now you're saying that this guy that mom's clearly sleeping with, is her *friend*? And you guys are all cool or something?" He shakes his head. "This is fucking ridiculous," he mutters.

"James." His mother's voice is even. He turns to look at her. "Listen to me. You are old enough to know this now. That man. His name is *Henry*. Henry *Cooper*. He's your uncle. He is your dad's brother. He and I were...are...in love." She takes a deep breath before continuing. "It started a long time ago, when I was just a young girl in London. I was with him first. But I was promised to your father. We married, and moved to Canada, as was expected of us. Henry remained in London." She sighs.

James' father continues. "As you know, James, our family controls a large amount of wealth. Properties, companies, stock, investments...and, I haven't exactly done a great job of managing it all these years. I always thought I would be around for a long time to clean it all up, and never gave it the attention it deserved. And, well..." he doesn't finish.

"Your father asked Henry to come here last year, to help clean things up, despite our...complicated circumstances," his mother says, finishing for her husband. "We rekindled our flame." She says this almost defiantly. "I'm sorry I kept it from you but it didn't feel like the right time to tell you."

James scoffs. "And this is the right time? And by the way, you didn't do that great of a job of 'keeping it from me'. I have a brain for God's sake. When my mom is suddenly spending the night somewhere else for most of the week, I can put two and two together." He cuts into his honeydew with his fork, viciously. "And you," he stabs his fork in the air at his father, rather rudely. "You're okay with this? "

Nathaniel Cooper is silent for a long time. "He is my brother," he says finally. "He loves your mother, I know that. He always has. And I've never been a good husband. I've had my affairs. The least I can do now is...be gracious." He sips his coffee. "I'm dying, James. There are bigger things to worry about. I've given them my blessing."

Now it's James' turn to be silent. "How long?" He asks his father, after a few long, tense moments.

"A year. Maybe two, if the surgeries prove to be successful."

James nods. He gets up from the table and throws his plate and fork into the sink with a clatter. He runs up to his room and puts on a pair of Jordans, lacing them up loosely. He grabs one of his many basketballs from a shelf by the door, and runs down the stairs and out the front door, bouncing the ball in a methodical rhythm. One, two. One, two. He jogs to the park about a kilometer away from their house and shoots free throws for an hour, clearing his head.

Last night he was just a kid worrying about getting with some girl. Now his father is dying of cancer, and on top of that, he has to sit by and watch his parents make fools of themselves in some kind of perverse romantic scandal; his father's idea of a final salvation. It's all just too much. He almost wishes they hadn't told him any of it.

He returns home and spends the rest of the day, and most of Sunday in his bedroom, browsing the Internet for articles on pancreatic cancer. His findings both scare him and fascinate him. He is horrified that this vicious disease has found its way into the body of his father, but at the same time, he finds it astounding that a mere disease can wreak such tragedy, as he reads patient testimonials and blog posts from family members of cancer victims. Sometime during the weekend he realizes that in order for him to be okay with everything that's going on, he will have to find a purpose in it.

He has always toyed with the idea, but he becomes more confident than ever, now, that he will be become a doctor. Deciding to make peace with his father, he goes outside and knocks on the door of the guest cottage. It takes a while for his dad to answer the door, and when he does, he seems to have just woken up from a nap.

"James," he says, smiling. "Hello. I take it you've had some time to think things over. What can I help you with?" Nathaniel Cooper is horridly formal, even with his son.

"Yeah," says James. "I wanted to let you know...I'm going to be an oncologist." He lifts his chin, looking his father in the eyes. "I just thought you'd like to know." He feels suddenly silly, standing out here, telling his dad about his plans.

"That's excellent, son," his father says, placing a hand on his shoulder. "I'd expect nothing less." Father and son stand staring back at each other for a good minute.

James finally breaks away. "Well. I'll see ya later." He turns to go back to the main house.

"James." His father calls after him. James turns. "See you at supper?

Trying to hide his surprise, James nods. "Yeah. Sure." He jogs to the house and closes the door behind him.

That night, the Coopers sit in the dining room and eat the first dinner they've had together in over two years. It is awkward, and unnatural, but James would not have traded it for anything in the world.

The surgery the following week is a success, and afterwards, James' father is started on radiation and chemotherapy right away. Within weeks his hair has fallen out in clumps, and James helps his father shave his head clean. Too weak to venture to and from the guest cottage every day, he moves back into the main house, into one of the empty bedrooms on the first floor. James decides to take over the guesthouse, thankful for the distance and privacy.

When he's getting ready to leave for Vancouver in August, his father is in stable condition, for now. His parents are the most cordial he has ever seen them – though he knows his mother is still involved with Henry. To James' relief, Henry has not made an appearance back at the house since prom night. Though he is technically his uncle, to James, he is firstly his mom's lover, and hence his father's rival, even if no one else sees it that way.

On a whim, he decides to send Claudia a text message and see if by chance, she'd like to drive to Vancouver with him. He could use the company, and she has crossed his mind more than a few times over the summer. He's been so preoccupied with his family that he's gratefully not had much of a chance to mull over the embarrassing rejection, but part of him has been hoping for, even expecting something from her - a text message, a call, even an email. But there's been nothing.

He tries not to overthink it.

James: Hey, you. Driving to Vancouver next Monday. Wanna join me to save on gas?

174

She replies within minutes.

Claudia: Hey…Good to hear from you. Thanks, but no, I'm actually driving down with my brother. Let me know when you're settled in Vancouver so we can get together.

He stares at the screen, analyzing her words. Then decides against the torture. He tosses his phone to the side. *So much for that,* he thinks.

Both his mother and father stay out of his way for the last week he's in Calgary. He's made it clear that he has everything under control and that he wants to do this on his own, even though it's the first time he's moved anywhere in his life. He figures it's similar to summer camp as a kid, except way longer, and he gets to bring his car.

On Monday morning, ready for his long drive, he kisses his mother goodbye on the cheek. She hugs him without a word. His father, who is weak from chemo, supports himself against the doorframe, giving his son the best smile he can muster.

"I'm proud of you," he says to James. His eyebrows and eyelashes have also started to fall out, and he has lost almost 30 pounds. Only months ago he had been a gallivanting, womanizing millionaire at his son's basketball games, without a care in the world. James wonders where his secretary is, now.

He gets into the car, waving a final good bye to his parents. His most important things – his laptop, a camera, and some other gadgets – are packed safely into a black Northface backpack, which he keeps in the passenger seat. Two duffel bags full of clothes and shoes are thrown into the back seat, and a tow bar on the back of his BMW holds the front wheel of his motorcycle off the ground, strapped in and ready for hauling. He almost decided to trash the bike, after figuring out that the bike had been a gift from Henry, but decided that it would be useful to have for getting around campus.

He makes it to Vancouver in nine hours. It's nighttime, but he is still able to check in to his dorm, located on the far side of campus. Place Vanier, it's called. He lucks out with a single room, since there are an odd number of First Years on his floor, and he happens to be the first to arrive. Everyone else will have a roommate.

He's able to lug all of his stuff to his room in one trip. He brought nothing of sentimental value, and figures that anything else he needs he can buy. Dumping his things onto the bare bed, he realizes immediately that he'll need sheets.

School doesn't officially start for a whole week, after Labour Day. He wanted to get to the city early and settle in, and check out all the buildings where he'll be having classes. Tonight, he is tired from the drive, so he crashes in his clothes on top of the bed, bundling up his leather jacket as a pillow.

The next day he drives into the city to get a few things. He has never before in his life had to buy bed sheets, so he calls his mother and asks her where to go. She sounds so happy to hear his voice, but he quickly hangs up after she tells him to go to The Bay.

He finds a location downtown and parks underground. He ends up picking up new pillows, a comforter, sheets, pillowcases and a comforter cover, all in white. He sees towels and decides he will need those too, and before he knows it, he is hitting up every floor and buying all the things he had left behind in Calgary, thinking they would be provided for him at his new dorm.

I take everything for granted, he thinks, as the cashier swipes his credit card, the total coming to over a thousand dollars. He thanks her and pushes his shopping cart to the elevator, pushing the button for the underground parking garage.

When he gets back to his dorm, he clothes his bed with the new sheets, comforter and pillows. He fluffs out the pillows and smoothes every wrinkle out of the sheets. The comforter is extremely difficult to get into the comforter cover, and he realizes he's bought a queen size, and his bed is hardly a twin.

Besides the bed, there is only one built-in cupboard, a small closet for his clothes, and a desk. The window is above the bed and he pushes it open, breathing in the salty, piney air of the Pacific Northwest. He looks around beneath the window at the parking lot, busy with students moving in with their parents at their sides, helping them carry bulging boxes of who-knows-what.

Feeling a twinge of loneliness, he reaches for his cell phone. He goes to his photos and scrolls through them, flipping past a picture of him shaving his dad's head, another of him on a night out with Brent and the boys for a final hurrah, and other meaningless pictures taken during moments of boredom. He stops when he finds the picture he is looking for.

He'd taken it on their last study date, the week before prom. Her hair is twisted into a knot on top of her head, and she is wearing her glasses. She's holding a pencil to her lips, biting the eraser between her teeth, caught in a moment of thought, and she is looking straight at the camera.

He wonders where she is right now, if she's moving into her dorm, or driving into town with her brother, if she is thinking about him at all, or if she plans on calling him when she gets here.

He remembers reading in his welcome pamphlet that there are over 40,000 students and faculty at UBC and that it is more of a small city, than a school. *See you around campus*, he had said to her. He panics suddenly, thinking that he may never see her at all.

Deciding to go for a run, he changes into a pair of Nike shorts and a t-shirt. He puts on his shoes and grabs his keys from his desk, and heads out the door. On his way down, he shares an elevator with two girls who are complaining about the cafeteria food. They notice him and smile shyly, introducing themselves as Becky and Raina.

He nods at them, *hello I'm James,* but as soon as the elevator pops open on the ground floor he sprints away, not stopping until he's left the dorm grounds and is on the sidewalk. Rounding the corner to hit the path that runs parallel to the highway, he slows his pace to a comfortable jog.

He'd heard that the other First Year dorm is on the other side of campus. Not sure which dorm Claudia is registered for, and getting a sudden urge to find her, he heads in that direction. If he had brought his cell phone he might have texted her instead, but he is feeling spontaneous and goes with it.

The other dorm, Totem Place, is easy to find. It's named as an homage to the aboriginal colonies that lived in this area of Canada first, and the buildings are named after different tribes like Haida, Salish, and Nootka.

On the back lawn, a large crowd of students is gathered around a bonfire, and music is playing from at least two different sound systems. *No wonder they call this the Loud Dorms,* he thinks, remembering that he had specifically checked off "Quiet Dorms" in his residence request form. Knowing Claudia and her studious disposition, he can't imagine that she would have picked the Loud Dorms either, and he is about to turn to run back the other direction, when he sees a familiar backside out of the corner of his eye.

He would know that backside anywhere. He's stared at that ass every time she got out of his car and walked into her house, and he'd stolen a glimpse every day she sat down in front of him in class in high school, and when he followed behind her in the hallway after class. And here, he sees that same ass, except now it is sitting on top of a pair of broad male shoulders, and the legs that are attached to that ass are draped around the gnarly dude's neck.

He knows he shouldn't, but he feels his fists clench up and he is seeing red. There are a bunch of other girls sitting on the shoulders of a bunch of other guys, and it seems they are doing some kind of race, but still, the sight of it just pisses him right off.

It's not just that she's sitting on top another guy. It's also the look on her face. It's a look of complete abandon, as if she doesn't have a care in the world. It is the happiest he has ever seen her.

And while seeing her so happy and beautiful strikes a moment of endearment in him, it is quickly followed by disappointment. He realizes that she had been right.

We're going to meet new people, she had said, or something along those lines. *Things are going to change.* She had definitely said that.

He realizes that he hasn't met anyone yet. Besides the girls in the elevator, he hasn't spoken a word to anyone but his mother since he's gotten to town. Turning around to head back to his own dorm, he shakes off his past, and decides that he is going to get his act together and meet some chicks.

The days are hot, the nights are cool, and everywhere you look, there are delightedly happy people relishing in the best months the city has to offer, before the rain hits again.

At the end of this summer, James will be moving to Toronto. He's decided to ship his car and leave his motorcycle in Vancouver, parked at Claudia's place, so that he can ride it when he comes back to visit. When he leaves, he'll be taking a five-hour flight, and Claudia plans to tag along, to spend a few days in his new city, before returning to Vancouver to pursue her year of nothingness.

U of T has the best medical school in the country, and even with James' above par grades and soaring MCAT scores, he barely made it in. It was his involvement with the men's basketball team that made him really stand out and pushed him over the edge. Apparently, doctors need to be well rounded these days as well. He had also been admitted to the medical school at UBC, but chose Toronto for it's stellar reputation. It is a poignant turn of events – he is choosing his dream school over his dream girl, but she doesn't have it in her to ask him to stay.

They spend the summer in a romantic haze, spending every day and every night together. They are only apart when Claudia goes to work – she's picked up a part-time gig for the summer, teaching dance at a professional studio downtown. She is there three times a week for four hours at a time, choreographing routines and leading adult ballet classes. James spends this time working out, and reading ahead on books from the curriculum list that came with his U of T welcome package. He finds a human anatomy-coloring book at the university bookstore and supplements his studies by reviewing different organ systems of the body, meticulously filling in the spaces with color, carefully shaded in with pencil crayons. Claudia loves to watch him color, his face in a frown, concentration knitted between the eyebrows. For once in her life she is not the one studying, and it feels utterly liberating.

They know there is an expiration date on their time together in Vancouver, but they don't talk about it. They become lost in each other, hungry for each other, as if their years without each other had primed them for this insatiable summer. They spend entire days in bed, laughing, talking, watching movies, having sex, and taking naps.

In late July, Petey moves in to the condo, and starts his new job in Yaletown. It turns out he's seeing a girl who lives in Richmond, a small island city, connected to the south side of Vancouver by a couple bridges. Claudia suspects that this is the main reason why he's suddenly decided to move here. Petey has always been a small-town guy, enjoying the peace and familiarity, and he had grown to love Victoria after moving there for school, planning to stay forever. Obviously, a girl would be the only reason for him to leave.

Petey's girlfriend Sophie is a small, chatty Chinese girl, whose family had immigrated to Vancouver after the Hong Kong takeover. She's polite and nice enough, but Claudia can't seem to hold a conversation with her. She has nothing in common with the girl, and she can't imagine that her brother does, either.

Claudia and James stay at his place most of the time, giving Petey and Sophie the run of the condo. In the morning, Claudia will sometimes come home for a change of clothes, and one day she happens upon Sophie sitting alone on the couch, watching television in her pajamas.

"Hey Sophie. Where's Pete?" asks Claudia, opening the fridge to grab some orange juice. She pours herself a glass.

"He went to pick up a few things at the store," Sophie says, her English lightly accented. "We are going to cook breakfast." She looks at Claudia's glass of juice. "Have you eaten yet?"

"No, but I'm fine. James and I are going to get some brunch after I get changed here." She thinks about asking them to join, but since they have plans to cook already, she decides against it.

"How long have you been together, you and James?" Asks Sophie.

"Not that long," says Claudia. Even though it has only been a few months, he knows her better than anyone ever has. "I've known him since high school, though. We almost dated."

"What do your parents think about you dating a *gwai-lo*?" Sophie asks candidly with a smile, checking her cuticles. "My parents would kill me if I dated a white guy."

Claudia knows enough Cantonese to know what *gwai-lo* means, thanks to her mom's throng of Hong Kongnese friends in Calgary. Sophie's question throws her off. Race has never been an issue for her and James, and she's never really discussed it with her parents at length. As far as she knows, no one has a problem with it.

Claudia shrugs. "They don't mind. They just want me to be happy," she says, a diplomatic answer that she thinks is both reasonable and true.

Sophie scoffs lightly. "That's what you think," she says. "You're a pretty girl. You could get any Asian guy you want. Why settle for a white guy?"

Claudia raises an eyebrow at her. "Who says I'm settling? And what's it to you? I barely even know you. I just found out about you like, three weeks ago," she says. Her claws are out now and she can't help herself. For all she knows, Petey may have been dating Sophie for a while and keeping it quiet until he knew it was serious.

Sophie flips her glossy black shoulder-length hair over her shoulder. "Clearly, this is a sensitive subject for you."

Claudia rolls her eyes and turns away from her. She is surprised to see Petey standing in the doorway, a bagful of groceries in his arms. She gives him a guilty smile, not knowing how much he's heard.

"I didn't even hear you come in," she says. "I just came home to change, and then I'm heading out, so I'll be out of your way."

"What? No! Stay. I bought plenty of food. I've barely seen you since I've been here. Tell James to come over." Petey is taking a carton of eggs out of the bag and placing them in the fridge. He has a wide assortment of herbs, cheese and meat as well. Just the sight of the ingredients makes Claudia's mouth water, but she has no intention to stay and chat with Sophie about *gwai-los* any longer than she has to.

"Nah. You guys enjoy. Thanks Petey." She gives him a quick hug and heads to her bedroom to change.

When she comes out, the couch is empty and her brother and Sophie are making out in the kitchen, against the fridge. She holds up a hand to shield her sight as she quickly walks past them and leaves.

James is walking towards her on the sidewalk when she gets outside. His face lights up when he sees her. She picks up into a light run and sends herself flying into him, wrapping her arms around his neck.

"Hey babe," he says, pulling her in for a long, luxurious kiss, as if they've been apart for way longer than half an hour. "I didn't feel like sitting at home and waiting for you so I figured I'd meet you halfway. Looks like you owe me since you didn't cover your half."

Claudia laughs, hugging him tight. "It's a good thing you did, because I'm starving. Let's go."

She pulls him by the waist, and he swings an arm around her shoulders. Their height difference makes her feel safe and protected when they're together. She feels downright tiny, even though she is average height, or even tall, especially for an Asian girl.

They walk up a few blocks to a small bagel place that's popular with students. They order at the counter. Claudia gets a smoked salmon bagel sandwich, and James opts for a bagel breakfast sandwich plus a blueberry muffin. They get two cups of coffee and take their food outside to sit on the patio.

"Mmm..." Claudia says, with a mouthful of bagel. "Carbs. You've been draining me," she accuses James with a sly smile.

"You know it." James also looks to be starving, jamming mouthfuls of sandwich into his mouth, and soon starting on his muffin before Claudia has even finished half of her bagel.

Claudia is still thinking about Sophie's question, even though she had tried to let it go.

"Do you wish I were white?" she asks James.

He shoots her a confused look. "What kind of question is that?"

"I dunno. Some Asian people have this thing about dating white people. It's not that they're racist, it's more of a cultural thing. Kind of like Jewish people. Some parents don't even let their kids date anyone outside of their ethnicity. I was wondering if

184

you ever thought about that." She takes another bite of her bagel.

"Well, your parents aren't like that, right?" James asks, a mouthful of blueberry muffin pushed to the side of his cheek.

Claudia shakes her head no. "It's never even come up. But just now, when I was at home, Sophie was there without my brother… and she made a weird comment. Something about how I should be dating Asian guys, instead of dating you. Just for the record, I don't like her very much."

"So you want to know if I think I should be with a white girl, instead of you? Because your brother's weird-ass girlfriend called me a *gwai-lo*?"

Claudia gasps. "How do you know that word? Has she called you that before?"

James laughs. "Come on Claud, we live in Vancouver. It's like forty percent Asian here or something. My Chinese friends call me that all the time."

"You know it means *ghost*, right? It's pretty derogatory."

"Yeah. I'm offended." He grins.

Claudia sighs. "And FYI, we don't say *gwai-lo* in Mandarin. That's Cantonese," she says. "We say….*wai guo ren*. Meaning a person of another country." She smiles, wincing at her horrible translation. Her Mandarin gets worse every day.

"*Xie xie,*" says James, bowing playfully. "Thank you for the lesson, wise master." He intonates a convincing Chinese accent. Claudia laughs.

"I'm glad you're not one of those guys who are just into Asian girls," she says. "Wait… you're not, are you?" She looks at him warily. "The only other girl I know of that you've been with is Maddie, but... wait, I don't think I want to hear about your past." She muffs her ears with her palms.

James has finished his food and he crumples the papers up, placing them all in the white plastic bag their food came in. He takes her wrists in his hands and pulls them away from her ears.

"You're the only Asian girl I have ever loved," he says. "You are the only *girl* I have ever loved." He looks at her in the eyes. "Now stop being crazy and finish your food, so we can go home and have sex."

Claudia's eyes flash with excitement, and she quickly finishes off the rest of her bagel. Her mouth full of food, she looks at James. "I'm done," she says.

He grabs her face and kisses it. "Chubby bunny."

Before they know it, it's time to pack up James' stuff. He's decided to bring as little as possible with him to Toronto, though this time he chooses to take his bed sheets and towels with him. He'll be renting a furnished apartment not far from his new school, so they hold a yard sale and sell off what little furniture he had accumulated over the years here. They make about eighty bucks, and blow it on a day at the PnE, a fair on the east side of town. They ride all the rides and eat blue cotton candy, and James wins Claudia a stuffed bear by smashing a bunch of plates with a baseball.

By the time they are done packing and getting rid of things, James' possessions fill up only one large Rubbermaid bin, and the same two duffel bags he'd moved to Vancouver from Calgary with, packed with clothes and shoes. One improvement is a sturdy leather bag from Roots – a gift from Claudia - to carry his laptop and electronics, rather than his worn black backpack, which he donates to Goodwill.

Looking at the bare basement suite sparks tears in Claudia's eyes, but she saves them, since she still has a few more days with him here in Vancouver, and then she'll be going with him to Toronto to settle in. She's thankful that she won't have to say goodbye here, at the airport. Instead, she will be the one leaving him, and selfishly, she prefers it.

James' landlord asks him to be out by the 15th of August, so he spends the remaining week in Vancouver living at the condo with Claudia and Petey. Sophie is a regular fixture there, even though Petey is away at work during the day. In fact, it seems as though she never leaves. Thankfully she keeps the place clean, doing loads of laundry, washing dishes, but not venturing far from the sofa otherwise. One day, Claudia decides to chat her up.

"Sophie, what do you do?" She asks, joining her on the couch and propping her feet up on the coffee table. "Do you go to school, or work?"

Sophie shrugs. "Not really. I didn't finish University, I wasn't very good at school. My parents don't mind. They don't want me to work anyway. They just want Peter and me to get married and have children. I'll be a stay-at-home-mom." She says this all very matter-of-factly, as if she has it all figured out.

Claudia is aghast. "Really? And Petey is okay with this?" She can't imagine her brother being with someone with no goals beyond getting married and having babies. He's an intellectual, and would need to be challenged on a regular basis, even at home. That's partially why she gets along with her brother as well as she does; he's just as much of a nerd as she is.

Sophie pauses thoughtfully. "We don't really talk about it actually. He doesn't ask." She doesn't pronounce the C in actually. She turns her stare to Claudia. "And what do *you* do? Will you marry James and have kids while he goes to medical school?"

Silently, Claudia reviews her game plan. She was trying to get a better read on this girl, who seems to have moved in with her brother – and as a result, with her, too. Now the discussion has turned into a question about her and James' future. How did that happen? But, Sophie does bring up a good point and she reminds herself to make it clear to James. She loves him, but doesn't plan on marrying him anytime soon and becoming a baby machine, no matter how successful a doctor he plans to be.

She turns to Sophie, with a big smile on her face. "Great question, Sophie. Maybe I will marry James, some day, and maybe even have children with him. But right now I am focused on me. What do *I* do? Well, I'm figuring that out. Next week I'm going to Toronto with James, and while I'm there, I'm going to look into a few schools and see what interests me. I've decided that I want to pursue choreography and stage production. It's something I've always loved." She leans back against the couch and exhales, looking up at the ceiling. "I don't know why I just told you all that. I haven't even told James."

"Told me what?" Says James, peeking his head out from Claudia's room. He'd been taking a nap and looks refreshed, though his hair is mussed up from sleep.

"Oh, nothing," Claudia says, her voice high. She'll tell him later. "Just some girl talk."

James gives her a look that says *I don't believe you*, but he leaves it at that. He goes to the kitchen for a glass of water, just as Petey walks in through the door.

"Honey, I'm home!" he calls out. Claudia and Sophie giggle, both thinking the salutation was meant for them. They look at each other strangely. Claudia gets up from the couch first and greets her brother. "Let's go out for dinner, Petey!" She says. "Double date."

The four of them decide to go for sushi, at a little place in Kerrisdale. It's a fifteen-minute drive away so they take Petey's 4-Runner. James and Claudia sit in the back, with Claudia resting her head on his shoulder, and Sophie takes shotgun, holding Petey's hand. The whole double dating thing is a bit banal for Claudia's liking, but she loves her brother and she loves James, and having Sophie around is a small price to pay for spending time with her two favorite men.

They order an assortment of rolls and a fresh sashimi plate to share, and in addition, the boys order bowls of ramen and more rice, to ensure that they are filled up. Petey's appetite rivals James', and Claudia watches them slurp their noodles, flabbergasted at their ability to put away so much food.

Petey is the one to bring up Claudia's plans for the coming year. "So, Sis, have you decided what you're going to do with your year in purgatory?" He likes to tease Claudia about her year off, though he knows she doesn't take it lightly.

"I have," says Claudia, eyeing James. "That's what Sophie and I were talking about earlier today."

James puts down his chopsticks and takes a sip of green tea, his attention fully focused on Claudia. "Well, spill it, buddy," he says.

"Alright." She puts her chopsticks down. "I've decided I don't want to go to law school. I've been spending the summer teaching dance and choreographing, and...I think I'm kind of good at it," she says. "Choreography, that is. And I really enjoy it, which I think is the most important. I want to pursue performing arts. Maybe even get a Master's Degree." She shrugs, looking at Petey with a worried expression. "Do you think mom and dad are going to kill me?"

He is silent, chewing on the inside of his mouth. "Yep," he says eventually. "They've always dreamed of you becoming a lawyer or some other fancy-schmancy elite occupation. But they'll get over it," he says. Petey has made his parents happy as a computer engineer, and his new job involves microchips and other things that are far too complicated to explain. But, they had originally hoped for him to become a doctor. They still wistfully cite Petey's high MCAT scores when bragging about their children's accomplishments.

James clears his throat. "Where are you planning to get your Master's, Claud?" he asks. He gives her an encouraging look, letting her know he'll support her wherever she chooses to go.

She smiles. "Well I haven't looked at any schools yet, so obviously haven't applied anywhere, but... I was thinking about checking out some schools when I'm in Toronto next week. No guarantees, though." She doesn't want to get his hopes up.

James jumps up from the table and picks her up in a big hug. "This is great, Claud," he says, a huge smile on his face, like it's Christmas morning. He hesitates for a moment. "But... do this for you. Of course I'd love for us to be in the same place, but you need to go where you need to go."

She nods, knowing that he genuinely cares about her future. "Toronto is the best place in the country for the arts," she says. "It's the cultural center of Canada. It just makes sense. But yes, I'll keep that in mind."

"Congrats, Cloudie," Petey says. "It's a huge thing to know what you want in life. Good for you." His eyes blink quickly at Sophie, not wanting to leave her out. "How about you, Soph? Have you decided what you'll do after the summer?" He obviously thinks that Sophie's couch potato life is temporary.

190

She looks at him and gives him a tight-lipped smile. "Nope," she says. "Definitely not going to law school, and I'm not much of a dancer. But I'm very good at other things." She wiggles her eyebrows at Petey, who seems to drink it up, and it makes Claudia want to barf her sushi back onto her plate.

James catches sight of her expression and holds in his laughter. He signals the waiter for the bill and pays for it, telling Petey to put his money away.

Petey shakes his head at James. "I know you're a spoiled brat, but I'm older than you," he says, jokingly. "I'll get it next time."

They drive home stuffed with food, and Claudia is feeling both buzzed and sleepy from the sake. She falls asleep on James' shoulder even though it's a short ride, and when they get home he piggybacks her up to the condo, with her brother and Sophie lagging behind. He doesn't put her down until they are in her bedroom, where he leans forward to flip her over and she lands on her back on the bed, barely awake, staring up at her gorgeous boyfriend. She looks into his deep blue eyes, filled with the promise of a future that seems too good to be true. He climbs onto the bed with her, spooning her from behind, with their feet toward the headboard. They fall asleep without brushing their teeth.

- 10 - Polly

Polly and Peter are experiencing empty nest syndrome. It's not new – they already felt the plight when their son left for University in Victoria, years ago, even though they still had Claudia at home for a couple more years. It was just suddenly quieter, with less to do. Claudia was a well-behaved girl for the most part, and besides the incident in Senior year that led to her expulsion from St. Agnes, she caused little to no stress on them.

The day of the incident will always remain in Polly's mind like a bad dream. She'd received a phone call from the school secretary, informing her that her daughter had been taken to the hospital. Imagining the worst, Polly had rushed down to Calgary General, in her indoor mules, hair in curlers, and clothes she'd only be caught wearing at home. When she saw her little girl with her face bruised, an eye swelled shut, and her head bandaged with bloody gauze, she had screamed at the top of her lungs.

The nurses had calmed her down, reassuring her that Claudia was not in bad shape, and that she would be able to go home with her that day after the police asked her some questions. The girls who had beat her up had luckily only caused surface damage, a few stitches, and a bruised rib. Even luckier - Claudia would only have one scar – on her scalp, which would be covered by her thick hair. Claudia leaned her head to the side as she let her mom part her hair to inspect the stitches, wincing with pain.

Soon enough, life returned to normal, with Claudia at Laura Secord and graduating at the top of her class. And with their second child now successfully admitted to a top Canadian

University, the two biggest projects in Polly's life – her two children – were complete.

Polly and Peter began an effort to rekindle the romance, which over the years had given way to carpooling, making lunches, planning summer vacations, and other parental duties. They even decided to purchase a condo in Vancouver during Claudia's Second Year at UBC, planning to retire there in a couple of years. They told themselves that anyway; it was, more than anything, a way to stay closer to their children, without being outwardly overbearing. When Claudia agreed to move into the eleventh floor condo, they were ecstatic, and made monthly visits out to see their kids.

When Polly hears from Claudia that she will be accompanying James to Toronto to help him settle in for medical school, she is a bit worried. She likes James. In fact, she thinks he is a perfect match for her daughter: Smart, handsome, and destined to be a doctor. She has only two concerns: His choice of location, and his mother's husband.

Polly had been as surprised as anyone to see Henry at Claudia and James' graduation dinner. Never in a million years would she have expected Henry Cooper, a ghost from her past, to show up dressed in a three-piece suit, reuniting with her husband after almost thirty years of separation. Ever since then, Peter and Henry have had weekly golf and tennis matches, becoming better chums than ever. As a result, Polly has been forced to befriend Elizabeth Cooper, often cheering on their husbands from the sidelines or having dinner as a foursome at restaurants downtown.

She tries not to judge the woman, but it is hard. Claudia had filled her in on James' mother's hasty marriage to Henry only months after the death of her first husband. She completely understands James' disdain for his mother and uncle, and she even applauds his unforgiving nature in this case. True loyalty does not give way to death; it lives on.

On their daily mother-daughter phone calls, Polly shares her concerns with her daughter.

"Claudia, *xiao xing.*" Be careful, she warns. "Keep your eyes wide open. I like James very much, but his family has a lot of money and there's always trouble when there's that much money involved. Your father and I knew Henry a long time ago, but since then many things have changed. I don't want you to get hurt."

"Yes mom," Claudia says, for what seems like the fiftieth time on this subject. "I'll be fine. James and I have talked about it. I wanted to know if he's expected to marry some kind of heiress or something. He said no. I guess his family saw what a disaster that had been with his parents." Claudia usually doesn't indulge her mother with this kind of gossip, especially if it involves James, but she wants to assure her mother that she's not being strung along. "Anyway. We're not even talking about marriage yet. For now we're just going to take it one month at a time. I'm hoping to find a good Master's program in Toronto."

Polly sighs heavily into the phone. "*Aiya*, Claudia. Toronto is so far. You need to stay close to your family. Maybe you should just wait in Vancouver for James. When he finishes school he can practice in Vancouver. *Hao ma?*"

Now it's Claudia's turn to sigh. "*Ma*, we've been through this. I'm not going to sit around and wait for him in Vancouver. That's just not me. And *if* I move to Toronto, I'm not doing it for him either. It will be for me."

"Law School *ne*? Don't throw away your future. You were never that good at dance you know," she adds, pushing a button.

"Yeah mom. You've told me my whole life. But I don't want to perform anyway. I'm going into production. Choreography, direction, behind the scenes kind of stuff. It's what I love," she says. "Anyway, I'm still young. If I decide I want to go to law school in a few years I still can. LSAT scores are good for like, six years." She had scored in the 97th percentile after weeks of studying. She had enjoyed the logic games and tricky reading passages, and spent hours writing practice tests, in a cozy coffee shop close to campus.

Polly finishes the conversation with her daughter with a promise to talk to her father, who is livid with Claudia's decision to pursue the Arts. He doesn't even understand what choreography means.

Hanging up the phone, Polly taps her manicured pointer finger restlessly on the kitchen counter. She has cleaned all the bathrooms in the house twice this week, and finished her daily dose of dusting. She has done the laundry, folded it, and put it away. A couple of hours ago she even mowed the lawn, even though it could have been left alone for another week. She checks her watch: Three in the afternoon. Still another three hours before Peter gets home.

She goes down to the basement, flicking on the lights. She loves it down here. The original Eames chair from her Godparents' apartment, shipped over after they were married in the 70s, sits in a corner of the entertainment room. The shag carpeting that she had picked specifically because it reminded her of a hotel in Paris she and Peter had stayed in on their 10th wedding anniversary, is thick under her feet. She rounds the corner, opening the door to a closet that makes use of the space under the stairs. She breathes in the scent of musty old wood, mixed with mothballs and faint hints of designer perfume. She had been quite the fragrance connoisseur in her twenties, always preferring the newest brand that would sweep the pages of Vogue magazine. She makes her way past the trunks and boxes filled with decades-old clothing, old books, and records, and finds the box she is looking for.

It's an inconspicuous box, with the word "BASEMENT" written on the side in black marker. She opens it and pulls out some of its contents. A faded silk dress, balled into a wrinkled bundle, sits on top. A small jewelry box made of redwood sits underneath. She takes it out, wiping away some of the dust with her fingers. The top opens like a book, revealing a shallow compartment. A short, red ribbon sticks out in a corner. She pulls on the ribbon, and the bottom of the compartment opens to reveal the rest of the box. A sheet of thin, waxy paper is folded into a neat little square, and she takes it out. A letter from another time.

It's written in Chinese, in black ink. The boxy scrawl is unmistakably masculine. She unfolds it and settles against the wall of the closet, to read.

December 5, 1977

Dearest Polly,

I hope you don't mind my forwardness, as we have only met once. I also must apologize that my written Chinese is not very good, so you must excuse my grammar.

I received news about your engagement to my dear friend Peter, and I must say it is a very good match. I am also aware that he has returned to America in preparation of your marriage, and I do praise his efforts in establishing a good home for your future. He is a good man and I congratulate you both.

I have a favor to ask of you. Do not worry, I have already mentioned this to Peter, and he encouraged me to ask you myself, which is why this letter is now in your hands. I will be in Taipei in two weeks to attend the Governor's Ball. It is not customary for a man to attend these events alone, and as I have not spent much time in Taipei as of late, I am without many friends in the city.

I would very much like to escort you to the Ball, if you would be willing. With a beautiful lady like you on my arm, I would be ever so grateful.

Please reply at your earliest convenience. I will be staying at my father's property and the letter can be delivered there. I will have arrived by the time you receive this letter.

Yours Truly,

Henry Cooper

#14 Heping Road Taipei, Taiwan

- 11 - December 1977, Taipei

Polly is sitting in her room, at her small, rickety wooden desk. She had ripped the envelope open without using a letter knife, thinking it was from Peter.

She reads the letter twice, remembering the blond foreigner's forward laugh and strange ways. Henry Cooper is a stranger. But she wants to go to the Governor's Ball. It's the first thing she has been excited about since Peter left for America.

She writes back immediately, eager for an adventure, if only for one night. After Peter's proposal and subsequent departure from Taipei, she'd been feeling a bit shafted. It's almost unfair, she thinks, that she is expected to remain at home like a helpless maiden, marinating in the hopes of her future, until her Prince decides to return and marry her. It has been over a year already, and it seems Peter is nowhere closer to establishing himself in America than he had been when he proposed.

There is only one dress in her closet that she could even think of wearing – the silk dress she wore the night of Peter's proposal. Even so, she hardly thinks it would be appropriate for a Ball, having worn it in a bowling alley. To be honest, she doesn't know what one does wear to a Governor's Ball.

She puts on her high heels, pulls on her best cashmere coat, and buttons it up to the collar. She fills her black leather handbag with lipstick, a handkerchief, and some money, and clutches it under her arm. She plans to deliver the letter personally, and perhaps, do a little shopping afterwards. She leaves the apartment, with a little hop in her step.

It's a brisk walk to Heping Road in the early winter chill, and her breath puffs out in light clouds between her rouge-stained lips. She passes by a few street vendors selling delicious smelling food. Chicken's feet, stinky but tasty tofu, fresh soy milk... her mouth waters at the fumes and she stops to get a bag of honey-roasted chestnuts. She decides to get an extra bag to give to Henry, as it is never polite to visit someone else's home empty-handed.

She finds the property easily enough. It is behind a metal gate, as are many homes in Taipei. She rings the doorbell, and waits. After a couple minutes a tiny older woman - the *amah* - scurries over and opens the gate an inch. She eyes Polly up and down.

"*Ni hao, Amah,*" Polly says politely. "I have a letter for Henry Cooper. Is he home?"

The woman's face relaxes at Henry's name, and she opens the gate, ushering Polly into the courtyard. She leads her to the house, past a fountain overflowing with water lilies, and in which red, orange, black and white koi fish are swimming around. The house is built in the English Colonial style, like a giant white box with a pitched roof. Square windows with green shutters line the house on two levels, and a porch wraps around the entire second level of the house. Most homes in Taipei are made of concrete and metal, but this one seems to be entirely made of brick. A few palm trees line the edge of the property, and some small fruit trees make up a tiny orchard in the front yard.

It's a world away from her Godparents' humble apartment flat, but Polly keeps a straight face, appearing to be unflustered by the wealth. The front door of the grand home opens to a waiting hall, where the *amah* asks Polly to sit and wait. She sits on the edge of a cushioned bench, crossing her ankles and angling her knees to one side, the way her sisters had taught her as a young girl. She checks herself in the mirror on the opposite wall, happy that her hair has managed to stay curled despite the damp weather.

She hears footsteps pattering down a giant staircase at the end of the hall, and she looks up to see the dashing Henry Cooper, walking towards her with a confident smile.

"Polly," he says, approaching her with his large, white hands open in a welcoming gesture. She is not sure whether this is an invitation to shake hands, hug, or kiss cheeks. Not familiar with the customs of his country, she simply stands and nods a small bow to him.

He smiles in response. "*Ni hao*, Polly" he says, returning her nod with a full bow and taking a step back. "*Hao jiu bu jian.* It has been a long time. It's very good to see you. Please, take off your shoes and make yourself at home." He holds out a hand to her.

"I can't stay for very long," Polly says quickly. "I just came to give you this." She reaches into her coat pocket for the letter she had penned on her new pink stationary. "Oh, and this," she adds, reaching into her other pocket for the bag of chestnuts. They are still warm and the fragrance fills the space between them. Had she known the home would be so grand, she would have picked up some pineapple cakes at the bakery. The wrinkled brown bag of chestnuts seems grotesquely out of place. Nonetheless, she straightens her shoulders and thrusts them towards Henry.

"You can read the letter. It says that I will accompany you to the Ball. Thank you for the invitation." Her job is done, and she decides it is a good time to exit. "Have a good day, Henry." She turns to leave the house, but Henry catches her by the arm.

"Polly, wait. Come in for some tea. We can enjoy the.... chestnuts you brought," he adds, peering into the craggy bag with a smile. "I have been bored all day. You are a sight for my sore eyes." He smiles.

"You are too kind, Henry," she says, trying not to sound too curt. She has no intention of spending an afternoon sipping tea with this attractive gentleman. "However, I was planning on going shopping. I do not have a dress to wear to the Ball and I would hate to disappoint you with my appearance."

"How wonderful!" Henry says, clapping his hands together. "I shall accompany you. Just give me a moment to put on my coat and shoes," he says. Polly looks down at his leather slippers. They look expensive, and are embroidered with the English letter C on each foot. His feet, like his hands, are quite large.

He doesn't wait for her response, but instead, turns and walks away quickly, and up the stairs, slippers clomping on the floor. "Give me five minutes," he calls over his shoulder.

Polly sighs quietly to herself. She has never shopped with a man, and she presumes it will be quite tiresome. Men are full of opinions and tend to be impatient. But of course she cannot be rude. She sits once again on the plush bench, and waits for Henry.

He returns wearing a wool coat, brown leather loafers, and he has changed into grey herringbone slacks and a crisp white shirt. Polly suddenly feels shabby in her casual plaid day dress and is thankful that she wore her good cashmere coat. He won't even see what's underneath. She stands, and straightens her coat.

"We'll drive," says Henry. He takes an umbrella from a stand by the front door. "It looks like it may rain."

He opens the door and gestures for Polly to step outside. She nods her thanks. He closes the door behind them and leads the way around the house, behind which, there is another building. Henry leads her through a small door and she sees that this is where the laundry is done. There is also a small kitchen.

"The cars are parked in the back," Henry explains.

Sure enough, at the back of the building there is a garage, and inside there are three sparkling clean cars waiting to be driven. Polly recognizes the blue Jaguar, and there are two other luxurious-looking cars, gleaming in the light. "How many people live here?" asks Polly. "I've never known a family to own three cars in Taipei."

"My father is a collector of automobiles," says Henry, choosing a pair of keys hanging from a hook on the wall. "He keeps an assortment at each property for his pleasure."

"I must say he has good taste," Polly says. "The cars are beautiful. How many properties does your family own?" She can't help her curiosity. Henry Cooper may be the wealthiest person she has ever known.

"Too many to count," he says, grinning. "My family is very rich. Don't think anything of it, please. I'm not sure what Peter has told you about me but it's something you should know if we're going to be friends. Do you have a problem with it?"

Polly's eyes are wide. "No, of course not. I think it will be fun having a rich friend," she says, daringly. "Do I get to choose the car today?"

Henry laughs, raising his eyebrows in surprise. "As you wish."

She indicates the small convertible, which Henry informs her is a Porsche. "It's going to get a bit chilly," he says. "Even with the top on."

Polly assures him she will be fine, taking out a pair of leather gloves from her handbag and pulling them on.

"*Hao ba*, let's go," he says, exchanging his set of keys for another on the wall. Polly opens the passenger door and climbs in.

They go to a department store located in the heart of the city, where Polly's friend Winnie works as a shop girl. Polly tells her that she needs a dress for the Governor's Ball, and her friend squeals with excitement.

"The Governor's Ball! So glamorous," she teases. "Is Peter taking you? I didn't know he was back in Taipei."

Polly shakes her head. "No, Peter is still in America. His friend is taking me. He is a *wai guo ren*," she whispers, looking around. "He's here with me. I will introduce you."

On cue, Henry finds the girls, mid-whisper. He flashes them a devilish smile, with his wool coat slung casually over one arm. "There you are," he says to Polly.

"Henry, this is my good friend Winnie," she says. Winnie smiles, showing her gapped front teeth, and she giggles, bringing her hand to her mouth and looking at Polly with a look of wonder.

Polly is embarrassed by her friend's reaction. Henry is striking, but she's acting as if she's never seen a foreigner before. She rolls her eyes. "Winnie, let's go. Please help me find a dress." She turns to Henry. "I won't take very long. You can go to the men's department if you'd like, which is upstairs."

Henry shakes his head. "I'll just wait right here," he says, motioning to a winged-back chair next to the dressing room. "Take as much time as you need."

Winnie and Polly get to work, pulling a few different gowns from the racks around the department. Polly likes the simple, elegant pieces while Winnie tries to push more daring dresses into the assortment. "Winnie, I am not wearing anything with sequins," Polly says adamantly. "Just put them away."

Winnie hangs the choices in the spacious dressing room and Polly steps in, pulling the heavy velvet curtain closed behind them. The first gown she tries on is made of red velvet, with a mandarin collar. She immediately dislikes it when she sees herself in the mirror. It is too tight and she feels like a prostitute.

The next few dresses are the same, tight cut, and Polly is exasperated with the current fashions. "Why do all the dresses make me look like a *zongzi*?" She asks her friend, referring to the plump rice dumplings that are wrapped tightly in bamboo leaves and tied with string.

Winnie laughs. "You are too conservative, Polly. Try this one." She hands Polly a light pink dress made of soft, thin silk, with a boat-neck and empire-waist bodice. "It's made in France."

Polly peers at the price tag and shudders. "You know I can't afford this, Winnie," she says, sadly. Her job as a bank secretary doesn't pay much and she gives most of it to Gan-Ma and Gan-Ba to help cover the bills.

"Just try it and see what you think," says Winnie. "I can give you a discount."

Stepping into the dress, Polly feels the soft silk encircling her body like a breath of air.

"It's too much," she says. But she lets Winnie zip her up in the back. Polly turns to the small mirror. She is in love.

Winnie whips the curtain open. "Come, the light outside is much better, and there is a full-length mirror." Polly had no intention of leaving the change room, but with the curtain wide open and Henry staring at her, she realizes she has no choice but to follow her friend out..

"Beautiful," Polly hears Henry say, under his breath, in English. She doesn't understand much English but knows that word. "Very pretty," he says louder, this time in mandarin. "Do you like it?"

Polly nods, biting her lip. "Unfortunately it is far too expensive, but I do like the fabric and the cut," she says. "I'm sure Winnie can help me find one just like it for a more reasonable price. Right Winnie?"

Winnie laughs, with her gapped teeth in full glory. "That's what you think. You get what you pay for." Polly glares at her friend.

Henry stands and walks over to Polly. "You look beautiful in this dress, Polly. I'll buy it for you."

Polly opens her mouth to protest. It is indecent for a man other than her fiancé to buy her such an expensive dress. "No Henry. Peter would not – "

"I owe Peter a few favors," Henry says quickly. "He would be happy to allow this…. transaction." He grimaces at his own choice of word. He turns to Winnie. "We'll take it, Winnie."

He pulls out his wallet and takes out a wad of bills, and hands it to her. Winnie looks at the money hungrily and counts the bills, handing three back to him. "I'll get you a receipt," she says, still stunned. "You are very generous."

They leave the store and stop at a café on the main level for a cup of coffee. Polly is still fuming about Winnie.

"How dare she," Polly says, more to herself than to Henry. "She knew I couldn't afford that dress but she wanted to embarrass me. I'm sorry you felt compelled to buy the dress. I will find some way to repay you."

Henry touches her arm. "You shouldn't be embarrassed. It is a beautiful dress and not easily affordable for a young woman. But I am happy to buy it for you, especially since you will be wearing it to accompany me. In fact, it would be horrible for me to expect your attendance without providing the proper attire. Shall we get you some jewelry next?"

Polly looks at him like he's crazy. "Jewelry? I am not an escort for you to adorn with silk and jewels. It makes me feel cheap." She takes a sip of her coffee, looking away. "Peter would not approve. You should not have bought me the dress."

"Why do you keep bringing Peter into this?" asks Henry. "He is the one who suggested I take you to the Ball in the first place, when I told him I didn't have a date. He is worried about you, you know. He fears you are bored in Taipei without him." He raises his eyebrows.

"Well, he's right," says Polly, honestly. "He has been gone for a year and I don't know when he will be returning. We're supposed to get married, but he does not want to do so until he is settled with a good job in America. I wish he were not so stubborn. I would happily join him in America right now. I could help him."

"Have you told him this?" Henry asks. "Does he know how you feel?"

Polly shrugs. "We barely talk on the phone. We write letters, but that kind of conversation should be had in person." She suddenly feels guilty, talking about Peter to Henry, and leaves it at that.

"Why didn't he take that job in Texas?" Henry presses on. "I heard it was a great opportunity and it would have provided a handsome salary."

Polly looks down at her coffee. "I told him I didn't want to live there. I detest cowboys and cactus," she says, feeling guilty. "Perhaps I should have been more open-minded."

Henry shakes his head with a smile. "You have a strong head on your shoulders and you know what you want. There will be no cowboys for you, not in this life." He raises his cup of coffee to her, in a toast. "Peter will be settled soon, and then you will join him, and start your perfect American life together."

Polly smiles. She hopes he is right.

On the night of the Governor's Ball, Henry picks Polly up at her apartment. Her Godparents greet him warily, not used to having a foreigner in their home, even if he is a friend of Peter's. They relax a bit when he speaks to them in perfect Mandarin.

"*Uncle, Auntie*, thank you for allowing me to take Polly to the ball," he says to them. "As Polly probably already told you, I am a good friend of Peter's, and I know his family. In fact, I believe his parents will be sitting at our table tonight."

Polly looks at him with surprise. She had not been aware that her future in-laws would be in attendance; she may not have been so eager to attend had she known. Too late to back out, she follows him out of the apartment and down to his car. Once outside on the street, she looks up to see Gan-Ma watching them from the balcony. She waves.

It is a chilly night, and she has paired her new dress with her mother's fox-fur coat and stole. The furs are the only things of her mother's that she received; the rest had gone to her sisters. She is wearing her best jewelry – a strand of pearls, and a pair of crystal earrings her sister Lily had sent from New York, a couple years ago. Her hair is curled in soft ringlets and pinned away from her face, and her makeup took two hours to apply. She even painted her lips a deep red tonight, lining them first with a pencil and then filling them in with a matching stain. As she gets into the car, she realizes that this is the first time she has been so elegantly dressed. The next time, she guesses, will be for her wedding.

Henry steals glances at his date as they drive to the ball in his father's white Porsche. She looks so delicate in the soft pink silk, and is draped in furs and pearls. She is as enchanting to him as she was the first time he saw her. And tonight, she has dressed up not for Peter, but for him.

He has always been a sucker for attractive, striking women. Such was the case with Elizabeth – the young Locarno family heiress whom he's grown up with in London. They had been sweethearts since he was seventeen and she was fifteen, sneaking around to the theater, for long walks in the park, even escaping to the countryside for picnics and long, passionate afternoons. But he had always known that she would not be his. It had never been a secret that she was destined to marry his older brother, Nathaniel, when she turned twenty-one.

Arranged marriages in families like his are common. Often, only the eldest son is of concern, as is the case with his family. In some ways he is lucky that he has the freedom to choose his own bride. Unfortunately, the only woman he has ever loved, happens to be the one married to his brother.

Elizabeth and Nathaniel had married two years ago, when she turned twenty-one. It was quite the ordeal, and guests from all over England and Italy came for the festivities. Shortly after the wedding, they moved to Canada – a move insisted by their father, to keep some distance between Elizabeth and his younger son.

Since then, Henry has taken on the role of a traveling steward of sorts, spending time at his family's different properties, overseeing new developments and investments.

When he mentioned to Peter that he would be in Taipei for the Ball, in place of his father, Peter had immediately suggested that he take Polly.

"It would be a great favor to me," Peter had said. "I feel guilty that I've left her waiting in Taipei all these months. I'd like her to have a good time." Henry had, in fact, taken a liking to the jaunty girl the time they had met, so he'd agreed to the arrangement quite easily.

But now, looking at this arresting creature beside him, with her long, glossy lashes and lips like cherry blossom petals, he thinks it may have been a mistake. As she turns to him and smiles, her large almond eyes mischievous, he feels a pull in his gut that tells him to turn the Porsche around. But it's too late.

"You didn't tell me Peter's parents were going to be there," she says, accusingly. "You're very sneaky. You knew I would have been hesitant to come had I known. Now I have to sit through a whole night with my future mother-in-law criticizing me."

"What," asks Henry, "would she possibly have to criticize you about?" She is like a watercolor painting, he thinks. They should be so lucky that their son will be marrying such a beauty.

"She thinks it is my fault that Peter is not back in Taipei yet," she sighs. "She holds it against me that I talked him out of taking the position in Texas. She wants us to get married as quickly as possible, and give her more grandsons. Apparently, I am too picky," she says, laughing softly.

"We'll spend most of the night dancing," Henry promises. "That way you won't sit long enough for her to goad on you."

Polly smiles. She loves to dance and her stomach flutters with excitement. "I am honored to be your date, Henry."

Henry feels heat in face, and is surprised to find that he has turned pink, when he looks in the rearview mirror. Henry Cooper, blushing? He needs a drink.

The Ball is at The Grand Hotel, a majestic structure in the northern part of the city. The main building of the hotel had been completed only a few years before, and it is built in the Classical Chinese style, looking like a giant temple. With its vermilion columns and sprawling staircase leading up to the entrance, Polly feels like an Oriental princess as the valet pulls open the door and she steps from the vehicle.

"*Xiao jie, huan ying*," the valet says, welcoming her as a lady and guest to the hotel. She nods graciously at him, gathering the skirt of her dress up in one hand as Henry rounds the car from the other side. He offers his arm to her and she places a gloved hand on its underside, as she has seen Queen Elizabeth do with King Philip in pictures.

"You look very pretty tonight, Polly," Henry says. "But I didn't need to tell you that. Surely you know what a beauty you are," he says.

Polly smiles uneasily. "Thank you, Henry. You are always too kind with your words," she says. "This dress is worth every dime."

He nods in agreement. "We should have a picture taken," he says. "For Peter," he adds quickly. He stops the valet before he pulls away, and reaches into the Porsche to pull out a camera.

"Please, could you take a picture for us?" He asks the valet. The valet complies, and the camera flashes once, capturing the glamorous couple in front of the magnificent building.

Decadent dragons, plums, and lion motifs line the interior of the hotel. It is Polly's first time in the building, and she breaks away from Henry in astonishment, gazing up at the gilded walls.

"*Wah*," she muses, enraptured. "This is truly stunning. Who knew there was a place like this in Taipei?"

Henry smiles. "I stayed here once as a hotel guest, when I was a child, before my father bought the estate. You know," he whispers conspiratorially. "There are secret passages. Perhaps if you're nice to me, I'll show one to you later."

Polly gasps. "Secret passages! You must show me!" Her eyes are glowing with excitement. He laughs, titillated by her enthusiasm, and leads her to the ballroom with his hand on her lower back. Her breath quickens at the unfamiliar touch.

There is a coat check at the entrance of the ballroom, and Peter helps her out of her furs and hands a generous tip to the attendant. He hands over his own overcoat, revealing an English tuxedo, tailored perfectly to fit his masculine body.

An usher escorts them to a table, where, as expected, Peter's parents are seated. "*Yang-Ba-Ba, Yang-Ma-Ma*," Polly greets them with a respectful bow. "It is a pleasure to see you again."

Yang-Ma-Ma gives her a saccharine smile, revealing gold molars near the back of her mouth. "Peter told us you would be attending with Henry. It must be nice to attend such an event, even while your fiancé is so far away. My son is quite thoughtful, isn't he?" she says, her voice sharp. Polly holds back the urge to roll her eyes. She nods, and turns her attention to Peter's father, instead.

"Yang Ba-Ba, you are quite handsome tonight," she says to her future father-in-law, giving him her winning smile. He rewards her with a wink, motioning for her to sit next to him. The tall, older man has always been kind to Polly, despite frightening others with his stern disposition.

"Henry, it's good to see you," he says, as Henry approaches the older man to shake hands. "Thank you for taking care of our Polly while Peter is away. Hopefully he will be home soon to relieve you of your duties."

Henry nods. "It's my pleasure, Mr. Young. Peter has chosen well. Polly is a lovely girl." He takes the seat next to Polly. A waiter hovering close by pours them each a glass of champagne.

Two other couples soon join the table. Sensing a window for escape, Henry stands, offering his hand to Polly. The rest of the table is involved in conversations about business, their children, and stock prices, and barely anyone – except Yang-Ma-Ma of course - even notice that they leave. Henry leads Polly to the large dance floor. A handsome Oriental man is singing with a brass band, in a Sinatra-esque voice. He smiles at the couple as they swoop past him, in a quick foxtrot.

They dance for nearly half an hour before Polly complains that her shoes are starting to pinch. Heading back to the table, they stop at the bar, where Henry orders a scotch.

"What are you drinking?" Asks Polly. The golden liquid looks delicious, like honey. "I'd like to have one as well," she says.

Henry raises an eyebrow. "Very well, another one for the lady," he says to the bartender. The bartender nods, expertly pouring a stream of liquor into a tumbler with one ice cube.

The first sip hits Polly hard. It burns down her throat, like a hot snake. She makes a face and looks at Henry. "This is poisonous!" She says, accusatorily.

He laughs. "You'll get used to it," he says. He clinks her glass to his and pours the rest of his drink down his throat. Not wanting to carry a glass of scotch back to the table like a harlot, she follows suit, throwing back the strong liquor.

The table has been served red wine, and shots of XO are placed in front of each seat. When Henry and Polly arrive back at the table, Mr. Young rises, holding his little glass of XO up in a toast. "*Gan-bei,*" he says exuberantly. Polly and Henry raise their waiting glasses, and drink the liquor quickly, on command.

Polly is plain drunk by the time the shark-fin soup arrives. She is trying not to sway and making a conscious effort to speak fluently when answering Yang-Ma-Ma's questions. She excuses herself and stumbles out of the ballroom as gracefully as possible. Finding the powder room, she sits down on a chaise inside, composing herself. An attendant asks if she can get her anything, and she asks for some water.

She is sipping on a glass when Henry pokes his head into the powder room. Polly's eyes widen in alarm. "What are you doing?" She whispers loudly, glancing at the attendant, who kindly pretends not to see Henry. "Get out! You'll be in trouble!" She waves her hand frantically, shooing him out. He doesn't budge.

"I came to make sure you didn't fall down the toilet," he says, grinning.

She scoffs. "I'm fine. Don't worry about me. Go back to the table."

"I was thinking," he says, still peering in. "Do you want me to show you those secret passages?" His eyes are twinkling. "Our company is quite a bore, and I've already made my appearance, so my work here is done."

Polly perks up, the dizziness of alcohol being replaced with excitement. Her face falls momentarily. "What shall we tell Peter's parents?"

Henry smiles proudly. "I already told them I was going to find you and take you home since you're not feeling well," he says. He cocks a blond eyebrow. "Really, you must learn to hold your drink a bit better."

"Wait outside," she hisses. It's not her fault she was forced to down three different types of liquor within an hour. She takes a cold towel from the impassive attendant and freshens up her face. Finishing her glass of water and popping a mint into her mouth from a bowl by the door, she gives herself an approving nod in the mirror before leaving, less drunk than she had been when she entered.

She steps outside the bathroom and nearly trips on her dress. Luckily, Henry is waiting a few paces away and catches her with one arm, laughing. "Easy, pretty lady," he says, pulling her towards him to steady her. Polly can smell the scotch on his breath. She notices he is holding another tumbler of amber liquid in his free hand.

"I'm already drunk," she says, making a face. "I don't understand how you can still be drinking." She brushes his

214

hands away from her. "You shouldn't drink so much," she mutters.

He laughs. "I'm double your size," he says, "and I'm English. I love that your cheeks turn rosy when you drink," he says, touching her warm face, his eyes glassy.

She pulls his hand away. "So, where is this secret passage you speak of? Or are you too drunk to remember where it is?" She puts her hands on her hips.

"This way," Henry says, quite soberly, motioning with his glass. He doesn't offer his arm, but instead walks briskly down the corridor, with Polly picking up her skirts and following close behind, being careful not to trip again. He leads her to the west side of the hotel, where it is rather empty, save for a few loitering attendants. Rounding a corner, he turns to her with a finger to his lips, motioning to be quiet. She nods, eyes dancing with excitement.

Henry looks around, making sure there is no one in sight. His attention is focused on the concrete wall. He runs his hand over a couple panels, and, all of a sudden, he pushes hard, a look of exertion on his face.

With a scraping sound, the wall gives way, pushing open like a trompe l'oeil door. Polly gasps. Henry quickly pulls her into the space with him, closing the wall behind them.

Polly's heart is pounding. It's dark, and their breaths are echoing, like they're in a cave. How well does she know this man? Well enough to be trapped in a closet with him, unsure of how she will escape?

Instinctively, she screams.

"Shh!" Henry switches on a flashlight and shines it at her. "Are you mad? We'll be caught."

Polly silences herself and takes the flashlight from him. She didn't even know he'd been carrying one. She shines it up at Henry, revealing a roguish grin and devilish brown eyes.

"Where did you get the flashlight?" She asks. "You planned this all along, didn't you?"

Henry chuckles, not answering the question. "Are you afraid of the dark?"

She shakes her head, lying. She shines the light away from his face and around the space. Her eyes have adjusted to the dark now and her heart beats even faster. "This is...incredible," she says. Everywhere she looks, there is concrete. They're in a tunnel, with stairs to her left, leading somewhere deep underground. Beside the stairs is what looks to be a smooth metal slide made of a giant pipe.

"How did you know this was here?" She bends down to touch the slide. Her hand comes away covered with dirt.

"I was twelve when I first stayed here," he says. He hands Polly his drink. She hesitates for a moment before taking a large sip of the burning liquid. She realizes she isn't very drunk anymore.

He continues. "I was here for two weeks, with my father. I was left alone at the hotel most days, while my father met with various dignitaries. I explored this hotel from top to bottom. About a week into my explorations, I found this tunnel. There's another one, on the other side of the hotel."

"What are they here for?" Polly asks. "And where does it lead to?"

Henry smiles knowingly, taking the tumbler from Polly and placing it on the floor in a corner. "Rich people are paranoid. I imagine the passages were built as escape routes, just in case the building came under siege. And as for your second question," he removes his tuxedo jacket and places it on the slide, "I thought you'd never ask."

He lowers himself down to the slide, sitting on his jacket, and grips the sides of the pipe with his legs sticking straight out. "You can take the stairs if you want, though I wouldn't recommend it," he says. "It's a long way down." He pats his knee. "I promise I won't bite."

Without hesitation, Polly climbs over him and sits. He's quite a bit bigger than she is, so it's actually quite comfortable. She locks his hands around her waist, like a seatbelt. She tucks the excess fabric of her dress in between her legs and holds tight to his forearms. "Let's go," she says, shuffling forward on his lap.

"You surprise me," Henry says. He pushes them off, squeezing her around the middle. Polly screams as they slide down in the darkness, with only the light of Henry's flashlight as a guide.

They come to a stop abruptly as the slide ends, sending them tumbling onto the floor in a clump. Polly grimaces in the dark, knowing just how dirty her dress and hands are going to be. Henry pulls her up to stand.

"Where are we?" Polly asks. She doesn't see a way out until Henry shines the light on a door. Unlocking it, he takes her by the hand, and pushes it open.

They spill out into the moonlight. Polly sees trees and grass, and the air is frigid.

"Welcome to *Jiantan* Park," says Henry. "We've successfully escaped the hotel."

Polly shivers, wishing she had had the foresight to get her furs, but she is also thrilled to be outdoors. This is more fun than she's had, ever. A sudden burst of happiness causes her to throw her arms around Henry.

"That was so much fun!" She says, laughing.

He hugs her, whole-heartedly, breathing in the scent of her hair. He feels her goose bumps from the cold and he shakes the dust off his tuxedo jacket and wraps it around her shoulders.

"It's a bit dirty, but at least you won't die of pneumonia," he says, matter-of-factly. She pulls the jacket around her, smiling.

"We'll have to go back for our coats, so I'm not sure how good your escape plan was." She says. Puffs of cold air give away her quick breathing.

"It's quite alright," says Henry. "I can have them delivered to my home in the morning. I know the manager of the hotel personally." *Of course he does*, Polly thinks.

She gazes around at the empty park. Kicking off her shoes, she digs her cramping toes into the moist earth and closes her eyes.

"*Ahh*, that feels so good," she says. "I love dancing, but I wish it were done barefoot." She spins in the grass, feeling the skirt of her dress balloon up beneath Henry's jacket. "Where should we go? How will we get home from here?" She is quite enjoying herself, but it is getting rather cold.

Henry steps closer to her, his brown eyes shining dangerously. He touches her face to brush away a piece of her hair that has caught between her lips, and moves it over her right ear. His hand lingers for a second, his thumb grazing her small rosy cheek.

He is about to pull away when her hand reaches up to touch his, and she leans her cheek into it, smiling sweetly. She opens

218

her mouth to thank him for the lovely evening, but he cuts her off by stepping even closer, his eyes piercing into hers.

Henry pulls her towards him, enclosing his mouth on hers, as she starts saying his name, to tell him to stop. She lets out a small yelp, stiffening. But he holds her firmly, pressing his mouth to hers, until finally, hesitantly, she responds, kissing him, a soft moan escaping her throat.

Pulling her even closer, he moves his lips and tongue to her chin, sliding over to her neck.

"I'm sorry," he whispers, as he kisses her neck, drinking in her floral scent. "This is all my fault."

"No," she says, pulling away, and looking up at him defiantly. "It's mine. We should go."

It's a short walk through *Jiantan* Park, up the road, and back around to the entrance of the hotel. Henry instructs the valet to fetch his car. The Ball is still underway, and the animated sounds of the band ring out into the night. Everyone is still inside, feasting, and dining. Henry and Polly are the only ones outside. When the car arrives for them, Henry opens the door for Polly and helps her in, before climbing into his own side.

They drive in silence. Her hands rest in her lap, as she stares straight ahead through the windshield. He taps the steering wheel to Stevie Wonder's *Superstition*, which is playing on the radio, tuned in to the international station.

When they arrive at the house on Heping Road, their silent breaths have created a layer of fog on the windows against the cold night. Henry parks the car in the garage, and leads Polly past the fruit trees, around the fountain, and into his elegant home. Once inside, he helps her aching feet out of her restrictive shoes, leads her up the grand staircase, and into his bedroom, where a king-sized bed covered in silk pillows and feather blankets await them.

Polly's pinned curls have long started to fall astray, and Henry gathers the long, silky pieces in one of his hands, holding them loosely at the nape of her neck. Firmly but gently, he pulls to tilt her head up towards him. He lowers his head to hers, and pauses when their lips are an inch apart, eyes searching her face.

He counts to three.

Claudia's not sure what she was expecting, but it wasn't a grey, muggy city filled with people rushing around. James' new apartment in Toronto is downtown on Bloor Street, and blessed with thick soundproof windows that block out the sounds from the streets below. Outside, the alleys smell of urine, and, due to a city worker's strike, rotting garbage waits in piles on the street, giving the whole city the stench of an old lunch bag. In the mornings, investment bankers wait impatiently at crosswalks, grimacing, before stepping over sleeping homeless bodies, desperate to get to their lake view corner offices.

Despite the stench, Claudia feels energized by the city. To her sheltered soul, even the graffiti is captivating. She feels a rush of excitement every time she steps on the subway, clutching her purse close to her side, staring at her fellow riders. She sometimes gets caught staring, and quickly looks away, only to continue staring after a few moments. While James goes to class at U of T, she explores the vibrant neighborhoods, buying handmade jewelry from street vendors, eating curry, visiting museums, and searching for sea glass at the rocky lake beaches.

She had planned to stay for a week. One week turns into a month, and finally, she decides to start looking at schools. After doing some research on the Internet, Claudia decides on York University's M.F.A. Dance Program and submits an application. On a visit to the campus, she finds a flyer on a bulletin board, for a small theater company on Queen Street. They're looking for a production assistant for a new avant-garde dance show that starts in a couple weeks.

If she gets into the Master's Program, it won't start until January. She figures it might be good to get some work experience in the meantime. Plus, if she gets the job, it means she'll be able to stay in Toronto until then. Claudia calls the number, and agrees to meet for an interview, and faxes them her resume.

She hadn't brought anything with her to wear for a job interview, so on the day before, she finds herself browsing the shops on Bloor Street, looking for an appropriate outfit. At times like this she wishes her mother were here. She always seems to know what to wear.

"Hi ma," Claudia says, calling her mom as she steps out of her fifth shop. "What should I wear to a job interview with a theater company?"

Her mom mumbles a reply on the other end, sounding like she has just woken up. Claudia quickly realizes that she's a couple hours ahead on Eastern Time. "Sorry ma, did I wake you?"

"Mmm. You did." Her mom says. "Wear something simple but elegant," her mom says. "If you're being interviewed for your dance experience, you should try to look like a real dancer."

"Okay," Claudia says, skeptically. She was counting on more concrete advice, but she lets her mom go back to her slumber and pulls open the door to Holt Renfrew.

The next day she is dressed in a black blouse with a scoop neck, paired with a knee-length, gray pleated skirt. She is wearing blush Chloe ballet flats and pulls her hair into a loose bun on top of her head. Her neck feels a bit bare so she drapes on a large charcoal silk scarf from her suitcase. She feels sophisticated, and does in fact think she can do a few pirouettes around the sidewalk as she makes her way to Queen Street for the interview.

She's decided to wear her tortoise shell glasses, for good luck. A beautiful black woman with a full head of spiral curls greets her at the small theater and leads her to a room in the back. Her name is Randi, and she is the theater owner as well as the director and producer of the current show. They hit it off and the interview becomes filled with laughter and storytelling, as Claudia relays her background, how she got to where she is, and her hopes for the future. Randi tells Claudia how she had rescued the theater ten years ago, days before it shut down. The former owner had defaulted on his payments, and Randi had put her life savings into buying out the premises and reviving its shows. Since then, with funding from the Provincial government, she has brought in acts from Montreal, Argentina, and Berlin, staging small-scale productions filled with dance, acrobatics, and live music.

"Your resume is skinny but impressive," Randi says, as their meeting hits close to an hour. "I know the studio you taught at in Vancouver. They don't hire just anyone. And one of our dancers trained at your dance school in Calgary, though it was before your time. If you want the job, it's yours. It doesn't pay much, but I don't get the feeling you're here for the money." She smiles, her bright white teeth sparkling against her dark skin.

"Thank you, so much," Claudia says, enthusiastically. "I would love to work here. You don't know what this means to me. I won't let you down." She stands and holds out her hand to shake Randi's, and the woman laughs, opening up her arms to give Claudia a hug.

"Welcome to the company, girl," she says. "See you next Monday."

Claudia leaves the theater smiling ear-to-ear. She sends James a text message letting him know the news. *He's going to be ecstatic*, she thinks. This means she's officially staying in Toronto.

She stops at a small market on the way home and picks up some bread, olives, cheese, and a bottle of wine. She figures they can have a snack when James gets home, which is often past dinner time, due to his heavy school and study schedule. He usually grabs food on his way home and Claudia gets hungry before then, so they've gotten in the habit of eating separately.

James' apartment building is fancy. No, it's downright extravagant. The revolving doors open up to a whitewashed lobby with a thirty-foot ceiling, filled with expensive Italian furniture and hand-blown glass figurines. There's a concierge in addition to a front desk, since it's attached to one of the most expensive hotels in the city. There is a full gym and pool facilities at their disposal. Claudia's sure the monthly rent costs more than most people can afford, but James won't accept her offer to chip in. To make up for, she makes a point of picking up groceries, keeping the fridge stocked with fresh food – a hefty task for an appetite like his.

She unlocks the door to the eighteenth floor apartment and is surprised to hear James's voice when she pushes it open. He is supposed to be still in class.

Then she hears a female voice. Her stomach drops.

"Well, where is your *girlfriend*? Don't tell me you live in this fancy place all by yourself." The girl's voice is annoyingly high-pitched and familiar. Claudia hates her immediately.

"She's at a job interview," James says, in an irritated voice. "What do you want, Maddie?"

Claudia gasps quietly, bringing her hand to her mouth. Maddie? What is his ex doing here? She tries to stay quiet. They hadn't heard her come in. She's usually not one to eavesdrop, but for this she'll make an exception.

"Nothing," Maddie says, defensively. "I just thought it'd be good to see you. Don't you miss me?"

Claudia drops her keys by accident, making a loud clanging noise. *Shit,* she thinks. *This was just getting good.*

"Is that you, Claud?" James calls out. He walks over to the door, rounding the corner from the living room. "Claud." His voice his relieved, but his face reads panicked. His eyes are crinkled with worry.

"I though you had class," Claudia says, accusingly, narrowing her eyes. She gives him a tight smile. "Did you get my text?"

"No, I haven't checked. It's been a rough day. Class ended early." He walks over to her, pulling her towards him in a rough hug. "Maddie's here," he whispers into her ear. "I don't know how she found out where I live but she cornered me downstairs on my way home. She wouldn't leave unless I invited her up first. I'm sorry."

Claudia is silent. She slips her shoes off, pulling away from James. She notices that Maddie hadn't bothered to take *her* shoes off. She sneers inside. Inconsiderate bitch.

She straightens, holds her head high, and saunters down the long entrance hallway, turning into the kitchen, and places the bag of groceries on the counter like she owns the place. Taking her time, she turns her attention to the living room. It really is a beautiful apartment, with dark oak floors, floor-to-ceiling windows, and a full view of downtown Toronto.

"Maddie," she says, good-naturedly, walking over. "I remember you. James didn't tell me you were going to be in town. I'm Claudia." She holds out her hand to the scowling brunette for a shake.

"*You're*...the girlfriend?" she scoffs. "I remember you too. I thought you were just some high school fling. Now you're full on dating?"

Claudia narrows her eyes. Apparently the bigger person approach wasn't going to work. "Look," she says, stripping her voice of all the friendliness she had mustered. "I'm going to let you and *my boyfriend* talk, because that's obviously why you're here. But I hope you don't plan to stay for very long. We have plans."

Claudia turns to James and glares at him. "I'll be at Starbucks. Once you've finished with your... *ex-girlfriend*, you can come find me there." She grabs her laptop bag from the couch. "You have fifteen minutes."

At Starbucks, Claudia orders a chai latte, and a brownie. She normally tries to hold back on sweets but she doesn't care about her waistline right now. She eats it in angry little bites, firing up her computer to pass the time while her boyfriend works out his issues with his besotted ex-girlfriend, up alone in his apartment.

She doesn't have long to fume because within minutes James is walking through the door, looking around frantically for her. He sees her and walks over, and sits down in the chair across the table.

"Claudia, I'm *so* fucking sorry," he says, remorsefully. "I had no idea she would be there today. I haven't even talked to her since we broke up. Are you mad?" His face is troubled, searching her face for reassurance.

"What did she want?" Claudia asks, emotionless, clutching her cup. "Did she move here, or is she just visiting?"

James puffs his cheeks, blowing out his frustration. "She moved here. Apparently thinking that we'd get back together if she did. God, I feel so fucking bad."

Claudia scoffs. "You feel bad? For who, her or me?" Claudia throws another piece of brownie into her mouth, crossly. "Because I feel pretty bad for me right now."

"You don't understand, Claudia. Things didn't end on good terms for us. I kind of just disappeared on her. I told her it wasn't going to work, and that I was moving to Toronto for med school. I guess I didn't make it clear that it wasn't going to work even if I *wasn't* moving to Toronto. It's kind of crazy that she'd move all the way here though, isn't it?" He looks up at Claudia.

"What, you mean like if *I* moved to Toronto? Would you think *I'm* crazy too?"

"We're different, Claud. I know that if you move here, you're not doing it just for me." He reaches over to take her hand.

Claudia pauses, mid-chew. "You're right, James. I wouldn't be doing it just for you." She resumes her chewing, washing down the rich chocolate with a sip of chai. "But let me ask you something. If I *did* move here, just for you - would you think I were crazy?" She looks up at him, eyes flickering.

James sighs. "I don't know. Yes and no. Yes because we've only been dating for like, a summer. No because I love you. Does it really matter?"

"Yes it fucking matters," says Claudia. "It matters because I *would have* moved here for you. Just like her. If you asked me to, I would have in a heartbeat. But you didn't." She looks away, disappointed. What a way to break the good news.

"By the way, I'm moving to Toronto," she says, shaking her head.

James looks up at her suddenly. "You are? You're staying? Did you get the job?"

Claudia nods, looking out the window. "I did. I start on Monday."

"That's fantastic! This is awesome!" He leans over to kiss her but Claudia pulls back.

"You know," Claudia says, her voice icy. "I was thinking. I really should get my own place." She gazes out the window again, not wanting to look at his tender blue eyes. "You're right. We've only been dating for a few months. It's moving too fast. It's crazy. I'll get my own place."

She turns to look at him, uneasy. "Then you won't have to worry if any other *crazy* ex-girlfriends decide to drop in at inopportune times." She knows she's being unfair, but she is feeling hurt, for more reasons than one.

James' face turns into a deep frown. "That makes no sense at all. Your parents are never going to let you live alone here in this city. It's dangerous. And there aren't going to be any more ex-girlfriends dropping in, you know that. I told her to leave me alone. She won't be back."

That's what you think.

"I've lived alone before, James. I'm a big girl. Plus it'll be good for us to have some space. We were together pretty much 24/7 throughout the whole summer. And then we came here together. Doesn't give a whole lot of perspective." She regrets the words as she says them, not wanting space from him at all. But some part of her, maybe it's pride or something, forces her to go on. She lifts her chin, daring him to respond.

228

"You want space? Are we breaking up?" James says, incredulously. "Seriously, think this through, Claudia. This is stupid." He looks at her angrily, fisting one hand, angling his body away from the table.

Claudia doesn't mean to break up with him. But somehow it's happening. Visions of Maddie in his apartment come rushing back to her. She pictures evenings spent eating alone in his expensive apartment while he is out studying and laughing with the new girls he meets at school.

"We need space." She says. Her voice almost breaks but she holds it together.

"*You* need space." James says forcefully, getting up from the table abruptly and exiting the coffee shop. The door closes loudly from his strength, and patrons turn to look at the commotion.

Claudia remains frozen in her eat, sitting with her laptop, silent tears running down her face. She didn't mean to break up with him. It just happened. She didn't think he'd let it happen.

After sitting for an hour, holding her empty cup, she finally packs up her laptop and walks one block to return to the apartment. She's not surprised to find that James is not there. For a second she considers collapsing on the couch and turning on the television, pretending like nothing happened, waiting for him to come home.

But that's just not something she would do. Instead, she starts packing up her things. She doesn't have much, since originally, she had only packed enough for one week. Just some clothes that all fit in one suitcase, and her toiletries.

She decides she should leave immediately, to make things less complicated. Perhaps she'll stay in a hotel until she finds an apartment. She's saved up quite a bit of money from her summer job, so she's in good shape. Her new job won't pay that much but it'll be enough to live on for a few months. Knowing she can't just leave without telling him about her plan, she pulls out her phone to send him a text message. Her fingers pause over the buttons, unsure of what to write.

Realizing that she's making the situation more dramatic than it needs to be, she sits on the couch and covers her face with her hands, trying to get a hold of herself. She grunts in frustration at herself, and starts to cry. She doesn't know how long her face is in her hands, but when she finally looks up, James is standing in front of her. She didn't even hear him come in.

He's holding a bouquet of red roses, still in his leather jacket, with tears streaming down his face. He looks from the packed suitcase to Claudia.

"Are you leaving?" he asks, softly.

She looks at him through her wall of tears and her heart wrenches to the gut. He is staring down at her with his devastating blue eyes, holding a dozen wilting roses, crying. She is reminded of prom night, when she broke his heart the first time, the day before his whole life crumbled.

She stands up from the couch and walks to him, gasping back her own sobs. She wraps her arms around his neck and crawls up into his arms like a small child. She presses her wet face into his neck, sobbing. He holds her tight, crushing the roses against her back. From that moment on, she will always think of him when she smells roses.

"I'm not crazy," she says, between her sobs. "I just love you too much."

His own sobs escape his throat, and he tightens his grasp on her body. "You have no fucking idea."

230

Later, after they've made up, and they lay naked in the bedroom, side-by-side on top of the covers, James rolls over to face Claudia.

"Remember when I told you I was moving to Vancouver for University?" he asks.

"Yes," says Claudia. She shifts uncomfortably, recalling how shallow she had been at that age, so eager to grow up, and so afraid of what she didn't know. She'd used every selfish excuse in the book to avoid dating him. But when she got to Vancouver, she was always looking over her shoulder, hoping James would be there, walking behind with a big smile on his face. She had even imagined that one day, he would sneak up on her and stick a wet finger in her ear, and she could then turn and smack him in the chest, and afterwards throw her arms around him and they could be friends again. Or something more.

"Do you know why I chose UBC?" James continues, his voice husky.

Claudia doesn't answer right away. She clearly remembers Brent's comment about James following her to UBC, but she doesn't want to be presumptuous. "No, not really," she says.

"I'd already gotten into a few schools," James explains. "I even got a full scholarship to McGill. I was set on moving east, to get away from my fucked-up family and our sordid life."

Claudia nods. He continues. "I'd applied to UBC as a back-up. It wasn't until you told me that you were going there, did I give it some serious thought. I got early admission." He glances at her. She remembers that he told her he had just found out, in May. Early admissions are announced much earlier.

He continues. "When you told me you were moving to Vancouver for school, and it sounded like that was the reason why you didn't want to date, I thought I'd give it a shot. I mailed my acceptance after the first night we studied together."

"I had no idea. You told me you didn't know where you were going yet."

"Yeah, I know," says James. "I didn't really know. I always thought I could change my mind at the last minute, if I wanted to. But after I told you, and said it out loud, I realized that I actually really wanted to go there."

"But you gave up your scholarship..."

"Yeah, but it didn't really mean anything. My education would have been covered either way." He shrugs. "I chose UBC. I chose you."

Claudia is silent. She had suspected something of the sort, but to hear James admit it makes her feel...rather lousy. "I'm sorry I was so...stand-offish." She says.

James laughs, pulling her to him, kissing her on the lips. "Stand-offish? That's one way of putting it. Anyway, I'm not telling you this to make you feel bad. It turned out to be a great choice. I love Vancouver. I love the friends I made on the basketball team. I wouldn't be here, or with you now, if I hadn't made that choice."

"Okay," says Claudia. "So why are you bringing it up now? Because I do feel bad." She hides her face in his neck.

"Because, I want you to know that I followed you. *I'm* the crazy one. Not you. I barely knew you and I followed you." He chuckles lightly.

Claudia pushes herself up onto her elbows and looks at her sweet, handsome boyfriend. He has not shaved for a few days and he is scruffy, but somehow his eyes look even bluer against the shadow. She brings a hand to his face, rubbing it with her knuckle. Lowering her lips to his chin, she kisses a trail up along his jaw to his ear, and breathes in the smell of his hair. She climbs onto him, cradling his torso underneath the cavity of her body, her knees against the mattress and clutching his sides. She lays herself flat against him, her cheek to his neck, and snaking her arms under and around his head.

"Am I crushing you?" she asks, kissing him.

"Yes. Lay off the fries, chubby bunny." He flips her over in one motion, pinning her to the mattress. She squeals, and tightens her legs around his waist, twisting, in an attempt to overpower his strength and flip him back over. He laughs, tickling her and blowing raspberries into her neck.

"Just give in, Claud," he says, whispering in her ear. "Just tap out." Eventually she tires herself out and falls limp, and he falls on top of her, his teases turning into caresses.

"I'm glad you followed me," she says, as he kisses a trail between her breasts and down past her navel. "I guess now we're even."

The next morning, Claudia unpacks her suitcase for good. She hangs up the few outfits she'd brought with her in the large walk-in closet in the bedroom. Calling Petey, she lets him know that she's going to be staying in Toronto, and he agrees to pack up some of her clothes to ship to her. She hasn't told her mom she got the job yet, so she calls her now, to break the news.

"*Wei*, Claudia," her mom answers cheerily, fully awake. "*Zhe me yang*?"

"I got the job, Ma," she says, matching her mom's upbeat tone. "I'm staying in Toronto."

Her mom releases a long sigh on the other side of the phone. "*Aiya*. I knew this was coming. Your dad will not be very happy to hear this."

"Is he home?" Claudia asks. "I want to talk to him."

"One second. *Peter! Claudia on the phone!*" Her mom has never been in the habit of covering the mouthpiece when yelling around the house. A few moments later another phone picks up.

"Claudia? Everything okay?" Her dad always thinks there is something wrong if she asks to speak to him specifically. It makes her feel bad, as if that would be the only reason why she would want to talk to him, but she knows he just worries.

"Hi Ba, yeah everything's great," she says. "I uh, got a job in Toronto. And I applied for a Masters program at York University that starts in January. So....I'm....staying here. In Toronto."

The line is quiet. Claudia can hear two sets of breathing. Not surprisingly, her mom hasn't bothered to hang up.

Finally her dad clears his throat. "Congratulations, Claudia," he says, surprising her. "I'm happy for you. But Toronto is very far away. And it's a very dangerous city. Are you going to live with James?"

This is the other part Claudia was nervous about. She knows her parents would prefer her living with James than living alone, but it's always been difficult for her father to come to grips with his little girl growing up. "Yes dad," she says, wincing. "He's right here, if you want to talk to him." James gives her a wide-eyed look from across the room on the couch.

She walks over and hands James the phone. He takes it, getting up from the couch and standing up straight, as if Mr. Young were here in the flesh.

"Hello Mr. Young. Yes, of course. I agree. Yes. For sure. Thanks so much, I'll take good care of her."

He hands the phone back to Claudia. "That was quick," she mutters.

He shrugs. "I told you they'd rather you live with me." He winks at her, almost smirking.

She gives him a playful glare. Ending the conversation, she tells her parents that she loves them, and promises to call every day.

There is small den in the apartment, which they've decided to make their office, since James will be doing a lot of studying and Claudia will need to as well, come January. They find a large, wall-to-wall desk at a nearby hardware store and install it along one side on the room. Claudia sets up her laptop on one side, with James' area a couple meters away. She smiles at the sight.

"What's funny?" asks James.

"I just think it's delightful that we're still going to be studying together after all these years. It's like we're doomed to be nerds for life." She giggles. She's wearing her glasses and they slip down her tiny nose.

"I wouldn't have it any other way," says James. "You know I'm only with you for your brains," he says, in a nasally pseudo-nerd voice.

"Well." Claudia says, sighing. "I guess that means I can start letting myself go." She puffs out her cheeks. "Speaking of which, I'm starving. Let's go get some food."

After a weekend of lounging around, Claudia starts her new job on Monday. Randi had told her to dress comfortably and to wear all black, so she wears black leggings, an oversized black sweater, and a large grey infinity scarf to protect from the cold. She pulls on her leather jacket and takes the Queen subway line from Bloor and gets off a few blocks from the theater. The hours are strange and erratic, with rehearsals from nine to two in the afternoon on weekdays, and performances six nights a week.

As a production assistant, she'll be filling the holes where needed. Sometimes she aids Randi with running rehearsals, or helps the costume department, and on most nights she helps set up and tear down. She even seems to be in charge of the catering which they order every Friday, and has the responsibility of remembering everyone's dietary preferences and requirements. All the choreography was finalized months ago, so she doesn't get to contribute much in that aspect, but as she watches the performers rehearse, she memorizes every step and detail in her head.

The show is called *Fuego*. It combines South American dance, percussion, music, and visual light displays. There is no actual stage – the theater is a large, open warehouse space, and the audience free-stands, moving around the room with the performers. The show involves spraying water and even some fireworks, which Claudia doubts has been vetted by the fire marshal. Needless to say, it is a far cry from the Nutcracker.

The dancers are all professionally trained, and they don't wear elaborate costumes. In fact they wear normal street clothes that have been specially fitted for them to move around easily. They glide around the room, suspended by cables attached to the ceiling, allowing them to be lifted like fairies off the ground.

The effect exaggerates their already beautiful steps and gives them a soaring, divine quality. The sometimes ambient, sometimes intense electronic music is played by a DJ in a booth hovering above the floor in a crane-like contraption, from which lights hang and shine in every direction, giving the audience the feeling of being at a choreographed rave or disco.

The DJ, Cory, is a couple years older than Claudia and has been involved with the company since he was a teenager. He started as a volunteer on show nights, and is now the lynchpin of the show, in charge of all the music and lighting. The dancers all rely on his timing. And, with his creamy mocha skin and shoulder-length dreads, the shy DJ is not without a few admirers, including, Claudia suspects, Randi herself.

On the third Friday after Claudia starts, Randi lets her take off early, since they have more than enough staff on hand. James is likely still at school, so instead of going home, Claudia decides to watch the show as an audience member. At intermission, the DJ booth is lowered to the floor, and Cory signals to her, inviting her to climb in. After catching Randi's eye at the side of the room and getting a brief nod of approval, she climbs in. She pulls the small door shut behind her, and Cory's green eyes smile at her as she settles in. He pulls a lever and the hydraulic system slowly raises the booth back above the warehouse, thirty feet above the ground.

The booth is soundproof, and Cory is wearing his headphones around his neck. He hands her a pair, with a smile. "I hope you're not afraid of heights," he says, his deep voice smooth and velvety.

Claudia grins. "It's not that high up," she says, looking down at the crowd. To her surprise, no one is looking up at them. She realizes that the DJ's role, while vital to the show, is of little consequence to most of the audience.

"This is awesome. Thanks for letting me come up." Cory nods, smiling, and puts his headphones back on. He holds up a few fingers, indicating that it's three minutes until the second half of the show begins. She nods and follows suit, putting her headphones on as well.

Seeing the show from this perspective is even more captivating. With a bird's eye view you don't miss anything, and it feels almost godly, sitting in a little box above the mini-universe of a show, and controlling its elements. Claudia is in a trance, following the movements below her that she knows so well, watching the waterworks fall from the ceiling in choreographed droplets, beading on the windows of the booth.

When the final sparks of fireworks flash, and the entire room goes dark, marking the end of the show, she explodes into applause, her adrenaline rushing. "Amazing!" she exclaims, pulling off her headphones. The booth is small and the soundproofing makes the booth completely silent, with the exception of her clapping.

The lights turn back on and she sees the audience slowly milling out of the theater, to the side of the building, where there's a full-service bar that opens after every show. Cory pulls the lever again, and the booth slowly makes its way to the ground.

"I take it you enjoyed it?" Cory asks, smiling.

"Oh my God," Claudia says. "That was fucking *insane*. I think the audience is getting ripped off, standing down there." She has an idea. "Hey, you know what would be cool? If you brought one audience member up here for each show. You could choose someone at intermission, just like how you got me to come up. Like, audience participation. People love that stuff."

Cory nods slowly. "Yeah, I gotcha. That would be pretty tight. I'll run it past Randi and see what she thinks. I'm thinking there would be liability issues though."

"Oh, I didn't think about that," says Claudia, mildly embarrassed.

"Yeah, this show has been tricky. It took a while for us to get all the licenses and approvals. We do some risky stuff with the fire and all. One bad move and we'll get shut down." Cory pulls a latch to slide the booth open on his side. He gets out first, and helps Claudia out, telling her to watch her step.

The cleanup crew is already sweeping up the floors, readying the space for tomorrow night's show. They don't rehearse on weekends, so Claudia will have the day off, only coming in at night for the performance.

"I'm going to go see if Randi needs any help closing down," she says to Cory. "Thanks again for the show." She smiles graciously, giving him a goofy wave. Feeling stupid, she tucks her hand into her pocket.

He chuckles, securing his dreads into a ponytail. "Meet me at the bar for a drink when you're done," he says. He turns, walking away in long, slow strides.

Claudia finds most of the company backstage, and Randi is talking to a few of the performers. "Great work," she's saying, wrapping an arm warmly around the shoulder of a catlike female dancer. "Best I've seen yet." She sees Claudia and smiles. "Did you enjoy yourself? Cory knows how to put on a show, doesn't he?"

"For sure," Claudia says, meaning it. She wants to be professional so she keeps her enthusiasm in check. She asks Randi if she needs any help closing up.

"I gave you the night off, honey," she says, giving her a squeeze on the shoulder. "Go enjoy it."

She stops at her cubby backstage to pick up her bag. It's a large pebbled leather tote bag that her mom sent a couple weeks ago, as a congratulatory gift. She always keeps a few extra layers of clothing in it, since it's almost Thanksgiving and the city gets quite cold at night, being close to the Great Lakes. She keeps her wallet buried all the way in the bottom, along with her cell phone. She takes out the phone to see if she's gotten any messages from James. Nothing from him, but one missed call from her mom. Making a mental note to call her back in the morning, she puts her phone away and goes to find Cory at the bar.

He is seated at one of the few stools, with two uncapped Heinekens in front of him. Seeing her approach, he cocks his head towards the stool next to him and angles his body towards it. She takes a seat.

Claudia is surprised he's by himself, and isn't being swarmed by admirers. "The DJ's all alone?" She teases.

He smiles. "Not anymore. Have a beer with me." He hands her one of the bottles. She takes it, thanking him.

"So. Do you have a boyfriend?" He deadpans. Claudia almost chokes on her beer. She hadn't expected shy Cory to ask about her personal life. But she is glad for it, so they can get off on the right foot. Boy-girl relationships can get complicated when things aren't out in the open.

She raises an eyebrow at him. "I do," she says. "His name is James. I've known him since high school and we we've been together for a few months. He goes to med school at U of T."

Cory's green eyes dig into her, and he whistles. "Med school, huh? Good for him." He leaves it at that. He swigs at his beer.

240

"How about you? Anyone special?" Claudia says. She takes a sip of her beer. The bubbles sting her throat.

"Yeah," Cory says, smiling. "My mama."

Claudia laughs. "That's nice. I love my mom too. Has your mom come to see the show yet?"

Cory shrugs. "Nah. She works a lot, so she hasn't gotten a chance yet. When I make it big she won't have to work ever again, and all she'll have to do is come watch me play." He smiles, looking at her. "She was a single mom. My dad left her when she was pregnant with me, and she worked almost every day since. I have her to thank for my green eyes and work ethic."

Claudia nods, imagining a beautiful woman with green eyes raising a sweet little dread-locked Cory, and her heart warms. "That must have been hard. I grew up with both parents. I can't imagine having just one around."

"Yeah, I hear ya. I can't imagine having two. Different people, different realities," he says, with a shrug. "It makes us who we are."

Claudia is silent, chewing on her cheek. She wonders if her reality has made her who she is, or if it's the other way around.

"How did you get into the industry?" She asks, hoping she's not talking too much shop, but she is curious. "It must be a dream to do what you love for a living."

"Yeah, I do love it. But it doesn't pay that great. Yet." He clears his throat, apparently not accustomed to talking so much. "My mom wanted me to get the best education. We lived in an all-white neighborhood and I was one of the only black kids at my school. Well, half-black, but didn't really make a difference.

Anyway, the school had a great music program and since I didn't really fit in with the rest of the kids, I spent most of my time practicing. I started playing the drums, started mixing, and my mom bought me turntables when I turned fifteen. The rest is history."

"Did you go to school for it?" Claudia asks. It seems Cory does a whole lot more than just mix tracks on a turntable, and she guesses he must have had some formal training.

"I have a couple degrees," he says, with a smile. "A bachelor's in music, and a diploma in production engineering. But education is bullshit. You either get it or you don't, and everything else comes with experience."

Claudia laughs nervously. All she's ever known is education, and studying, and exams, and degrees. She's not sure how else to get anywhere in this world. "Some people aren't as lucky to be so naturally capable," she says. "Education gives you a platform to grow and discover."

"Oh yeah, says who? What did you major in?" he asks, smirking at her.

She turns her face to him. "English literature and mathematics," she says smugly.

"My point exactly. I don't hear you reciting Shakespeare and we sure as well didn't hire you for your skills in algebra."

"You're right," she says, slightly defeated. "I don't know why they hired me at all. I barely have any experience. Though I guess I'm not really doing anything that requires real skill as of yet." She hopes she doesn't sound like she's complaining about her new job, because really she is very grateful.

"Trust me, Randi wouldn't have hired you if you didn't have potential. Everyone has to start somewhere." He raises his beer to Claudia. "To potential." They clink bottles.

They chat a while longer, finishing their beers, but when Cory offers to get them a second round, Claudia turns him down politely. "I should get home," she says. "Thanks for the drink. It's on me next time."

He nods at her, not getting up from his stool. "See ya tomorrow, Shakespeare."

Claudia steps outside into the biting fall wind, and walks towards the subway station. She pulls a scarf from her bag and wraps it a few times around her neck, shivering. She notices her phone flashing with a few unread messages and she pulls it out, seeing three from James, plus a missed call.

James: Headed home. Wanna go out and get some food or a drink?

Ten minutes later:

James: I'm home. Where are you?

Twenty minutes later:

James: I'm getting worried. Let me know what's going on.

She presses his name on her speed dial and holds her phone to her ear. She is almost at the station when he picks up.

"Claud? Are you okay?" He sounds anxious.

"Yeah, of course. I just stayed to have a drink with a friend after work. Why the sudden barrage of messages?" Had he known she'd been drinking beer with another guy? Does he have spies?

He sighs. "Sorry, I know you have a life. You're just usually home when I get here and you weren't...so I thought something might have happened. No biggie. Where are you? I'll come pick you up."

Claudia looks up at the street signs at her current intersection. "Queen and Dufferin. Are you sure? I'm right beside the subway. I'd get home faster than you'd get here."

"Stay there. Go into a café or a bar to wait, just text me where it is. We can grab some food, I'm starving."

She agrees, and hangs up. There are tons of bars and cafes around, and a place down the block catches her eye. She's walked past it a few times on her way home and has always wanted to stop in. There are colorful café lights strung on the front patio and there's a guy inside playing Spanish guitar. There's also a sign that reads "$3 Tapas" and that wins her over. James can order the entire menu, with his appetite. She sends him the address.

A sign says to seat yourself, so she finds a cozy booth on the heated patio so she can people watch while she waits. The pretty waitress has a pierced eyebrow and dark purple lipstick, and brings her a glass of water with a smile, snapping her gum. Claudia orders another Heineken, hearing her mom's warnings about mixing different kinds of alcohol loud and clear in her head.

A familiar figure walks by, head bobbing to whatever is playing on his headphones. Noticing his dreads, she calls out his name. Twice. On the second time he whips his head around, green eyes searching, lifting one side of his earphones. Finding her, his eyes light up. "Claudia. What's up? I thought you were going home."

"My boyfriend – James – he's meeting me here. Do you want to join us?" She points at her Heineken. "I owe you one, anyway."

Cory shakes his head slowly. "Nah, that's alright. I'm meeting some friends. Maybe another time." He glances around, Claudia notices, likely looking for James.

"He's on his way. We live on Bloor so there'll be a bit of traffic on a Friday night. He was uh, a bit worried that I wasn't home yet, so he offered to meet me down here instead." She knows she's talking too much, but for some reason, she really wants to be friends with Cory.

"Ah," says Cory. "I'd be worried too, if I didn't know where my girl was on a Friday night."

"He knows where I was," Claudia says, defensively. "I just stayed later than usual. Having a beer. With you." She doesn't mean that it's his fault, but it ends up sounding that way.

Cory is silent, but the smile hasn't left his face. "Sorry," he says. Putting the earphones back on, he points to his wrist. "Running late. Have a good time."

"Bye…" Claudia says, waving goofily again. She feels like such a dork. She doesn't really know how to be friends with guys. The only real experience she has with guys is with her own brother, and James, and neither of them falls in the friend category.

James arrives shortly, looking handsome, as always. He's wearing black jeans, black Adidas dragons, a crisp white Henley t-shirt and his leather jacket. A cashmere scarf that Claudia picked up for him a few days ago is looped around his neck stylishly.

"Hi Bunny," he says, bending down to give her a kiss on the lips. His face is cold and his lips are soft. He slides into the booth next to her, throwing an arm around her shoulders. He gives her another kiss on the cheek. "I've missed you."

Their busy schedules make it hard to spend any quality time together, except weekends, which they usually spend sleeping in and then running errands. In fact, this is the first Friday night since Claudia has started her new job that she and James have been out together.

"I miss you too," Claudia says, snuggling into his shoulder. "But it's almost Thanksgiving, and we'll get to spend an entire long weekend together." They've decided to take a trip back to Vancouver, so Claudia can pick up some more of her things. Her parents are meeting them there, and Tracey has also agreed to take the trip. They haven't seen each other since the funeral, and she's a bit worried that things will be strained between them.

"How is Tracey?" James asks, as if reading her mind. James and Tracey still haven't spoken since the day they caught her snorting coke. Claudia has stayed in touch with her, though mostly through text messages. Their once close relationship filled with phone calls and Skype conversations has dwindled into a touch-and-go friendship, mostly with Claudia doing the touching. Tracey has started seeing a therapist and it seems to be helping, though she is far from being back to normal. Granted, she may never be.

"She's as good as can be expected, I guess," Claudia says. "I don't think she blames herself anymore. I don't know much since we just text back and forth these days, but she's started using some smiley-faces. That's a good sign. Right?" Claudia smiles guiltily. "I feel bad that I'm so far away," she adds.

James squeezes her shoulder. "You shouldn't feel bad. She's going through a tough time. It's hard to lose someone in your family. Trust me, I know." He looks down for a second. "But.... she has to deal with it herself. Even if you were living in

Calgary, she'd probably be shutting you out. I pretty much shut out the whole world when my dad died."

Claudia looks up at him, seeing the sad memory clouding his eyes. She kisses him on the chin. She knows there's nothing she can really say whenever he brings his dad up. She just wraps her arm around and strokes him on the back, letting him know that she loves him. As for Brent's death, he hasn't talked about it much at all since they came back from the funeral. He seems to be fine, most of the time, but she decides to ask anyway.

"How about you? I know we don't talk about Brent much, but...we can, you know," she says. "You shouldn't keep it inside."

"There's nothing to talk about," he says, shooting her a look. "I miss him. But I have you. I'll be fine."

"Yes, but..." she starts, but the waitress comes back to take their order, cutting her off. James orders one of their draft beers, and as Claudia had guessed, almost one of everything on the menu. She grins at the waitress's baffled expression.

The food comes almost immediately and Claudia doesn't get a chance to resume the discussion. The whole table is covered in small plates, piled with cuts of meat, vegetables, potatoes, and little dishes filled with dipping sauces. Claudia realizes that she is also starving, since she hadn't had dinner. The show schedule has messed up her meal patterns a bit, and she's already lost five pounds since moving to Toronto.

"So tell me about your day," James says, between bites. Claudia fills him in, relaying her night off, watching the show, and her adventure in the DJ booth hanging above the stage.

James listens intently, clearly drinking in Claudia's enthusiasm. "And then we had a drink after the show," she says, finishing her story, without skipping over the parts about Cory. "There's a small bar attached to the theater."

"So this is round two for you, huh?" James says, taking a sip of his beer, a flicker of jealousy in his eyes. He blinks, and it's gone. "I'll have to meet this Cory dude sometime. He sounds…. Interesting." James is no sucker, but he's not one to be controlling, either.

"I invited him to join us, actually," Claudia says. "But he had plans. Maybe next time."

James nods slowly, moving on. "So, I ran into Maddie again yesterday," he says.

Claudia pauses, forking a potato. "Oh yeah? Where?"

"On campus. She's uh…going to law school here apparently."

"Smart girl," says Claudia, hiding the edge in her voice. She keeps eating. "Had I gone with plan A, we might have been schoolmates," she says. "That would have been quaint."

James bumps her shoulder playfully. "That would have been a disaster."

"So she's here for good, huh?" she says. "Maybe we should invite her over for dinner." She is being sarcastic, so she is shocked when James looks over with a hopeful face.

"Really? Claud, I think that's a great idea. She doesn't know anyone here. And I do feel bad about the way things ended with us. I was thinking about befriending her on Facebook. She could use a buddy. What do you think?" He looks at her, his blue eyes innocent.

"Are you serious?" Claudia gapes at him. "You want to be friends with your ex-girlfriend, the one who followed you to

248

Toronto and tracked you down? The one who called me your high school fling?" She wants to throw the potato on her fork at his face. "And *Facebook?*" She splutters. "Tell me you're kidding."

James shrugs stubbornly. "I don't see what the big deal is. She's actually a really nice person. You don't just throw people away," he says.

"Throw people away? "Claudia's voice has gone up a couple levels. "You mean like how you ignored me for *four years* after high school? Or how you won't even talk to Scott anymore because he told some people about your dad?" She pushes herself up from the table to stand. She moves over his lap across the seat and to the other side of the table, for better confrontation.

"If you want to be friends with her, go ahead," she says, sitting, leaning in to him, lowering her voice and faking calm. "Just see how long I stick around to watch your friendship blossom."

"Holy shit, calm down," James says. "I hate when you get so vindictive. I'll avoid her, alright? Is that what you want?"

"Yes, that's what I want!" Claudia says, throwing her hands up, exasperated. "Isn't that obvious? I mean would you be okay with me hanging out with my ex-boyfriend? Come on, James. Think about it."

"You sure don't have a problem climbing into booths with random DJs and letting them buy you a beer afterwards," he says, snidely.

She narrows her eyes at him. "That's completely different. And I made it clear that I have a boyfriend from the very start. Plus, I've never *fucked* Cory, so it's not even a legitimate comparison!"

"Not yet," James says. He raises his chin at her, glaring.

Claudia's chest is about to burst with fury. She can feel her face turning red, and her hands are shaking. She picks up her empty Heineken bottle and throws it hard against the brick wall behind James. It smashes into a thousand little pieces.

James ducks, not knowing where she was aiming. "Claudia! What the fuck!" He stands up, looking at the mess behind him. The rest of the patio is silent, staring at him.

The waitress comes rushing outside. "Is everything okay? She looks from James, to the broken glass, to Claudia, who is sitting, and clearly fuming.

"Are you okay?" The waitress asks her, bending to touch her arm, clearly concerned. She obviously thinks James had committed the bottle blast, and she glares at him. "You can't do that in here, asshole! Have some self control!"

James opens his mouth to protest, but nothing comes out. He looks over at Claudia to see if she'll come to the rescue, but she's just sitting there, staring at him. He thinks he sees her lips curl up in a slight smile. Bitch.

"Sorry," he mutters. "We're leaving." He pulls out his wallet, throwing a few bills down on the table. He stares down at Claudia. "Let's go."

Claudia takes her time putting on her jacket, wrapping her scarf around just so. Pulling her tote bag onto her shoulder, she stands. Without a word, she leaves the restaurant through the patio gate, stepping onto the street with purpose. She walks, not caring which direction she is going in.

She can hear James behind her. "You are a piece of work," he sneers. "That was totally unnecessary. Who does that?"

Claudia whips around to face him. "You basically implied that I am going to cheat on you. After you told me you wanted to hang out with your ex again. Am I supposed to just sit there and smile and act like everything is fine? Do you really think that would have made more sense?"

James sighs. "Okay, yeah. I was out of line. It just came out. It was an easy target with the issue at hand. I'm sorry."

Claudia nods. "Thank you."

"But you can't just lose it whenever we get into an argument," he says. "Seriously, it's pretty scary. You go from being the sweetest girl in the world to all-out psycho in thirty seconds. I never would have guessed you were the bottle-throwing type. You have pretty bad aim."

"Duh, I wasn't aiming for your head. I'm not stupid," she says. She walks a few more blocks, cooling off, sensing James' presence behind her the whole way. Finally realizing that she'll either have to get on the subway or follow him to his car, she stops and turns around to face him.

"Okay. I'm sorry too. I won't throw bottles anymore. Or anything made of glass for that matter. It felt really good though," she admits.

James looks relieved. "Thank God. It's fucking freezing out here and I was afraid I'd be following you all the way home on foot. So are we good?" James asks.

Claudia shrugs. "Not really. It's still not cool that you want to be friends with Maddie. Sorry, I'm just not that understanding of a person. I'm not willing to share you with your ex-girlfriend. If you're okay with that, I guess we're good. But it still bothers me that I have to tell you that."

"I would never let you share me, whatever that means. I was just trying to be a nice guy." He shoves his hands in his front pockets, looking at her with insistent eyes.

She steps closer to him. "The next time you want to be a nice guy," she says, "call your mother."

Suddenly, James bends down and throws Claudia over his shoulder, her tote bag swinging and in serious danger of losing its contents.

"You fucker!" She yells. "Put me down, James!" She clutches her tote bag tight, as he starts to run.

He's laughing. "Always trying to be tough. You're not that tough, babe." He finally sets her down a few blocks later, and she sees that it's where he is parked.

She straightens herself out, smoothing out her hair and clothes. "This isn't over," she says, pointing at him. "But right now, you're going to take me home, and we're going to have make up sex." She pulls open the door as James disarms the car. "And in the morning you're going to make me pancakes."

She gets into the car, smiling. He climbs in to the driver's side, pulling her into his lap, accidentally pressing into the horn. "I would never let you share me," he says again, as she eases off the wheel, bringing herself closer to him. "You're already too much to handle." He pulls her to him, delaying their drive home with a sweet kiss.

Thanksgiving weekend arrives, and they fly west to Vancouver on a Thursday night. Claudia is always anxious on airplanes, ever since the crash that took their friend, and she wills herself to sleep before takeoff with a cup of chamomile tea she picked up from the airport café. James pulls out a textbook and studies the whole way there. They arrive at one in the morning, and Petey is waiting for them at baggage claim, looking tired.

"Hey bro," James greets Petey with a man-hug. Claudia grins at the sight of her boys embracing.

She kisses her brother on the cheek, hugging him. "You look like shit," she says, giving him a concerned look. "Too much work?"

"Something like that," Petey says, smiling at his sister. "We'll talk about it later. How much luggage did you bring?"

"Just an empty suitcase," Claudia says, grinning. "I figure I have plenty of clothes here to last me the weekend, and I have to take some stuff back with me. Have you moved into my room yet?"

"You bet," Petey says. "But really I just sleep there. I still have all my stuff in the other room. I didn't touch your stuff except for what you told me to pack for you. I didn't want to find anything, uh...personal." He blushes. "You know what I mean. Girl shit."

Claudia laughs. She should have asked him to pack up her supply of tampons from under the bathroom sink.

It's a quick drive back to the apartment in the middle of the night, with no traffic. Claudia rolls down the window of the passenger seat, breathing in the pleasant marine air, letting the salty scent mix with her hair. Even though she grew up in Calgary, she now thinks of Vancouver as home, for some reason. "Is mom and dad here already?" She asks Petey.

"Yeah, they drove in this afternoon. Tracey came with them. I guess she's not too keen on flying anymore." He glimpses at

James through the rearview mirror, sensitive to his reaction. Brent was, after all, his best friend. "They're all exhausted."

It has made Claudia very happy to learn that her parents have forgiven Tracey for her wild ways and have developed a soft spot for her. If there's anyone who understands loss, it's her mother, who lost both parents at a young age. Tracey is even staying at their condo with the whole family this weekend. It's going to be a full house. Suddenly, she remembers Sophie.

"Is Sophie at the condo too?" She's trying to figure out how the sleeping arrangements are going to work. Petey coughs, switches through a few radio stations, and rolls down his window. He looks at her and gives her a sour look.

"What?" Claudia asks. "Are you guys... okay?"

Petey scoffs. "No. We broke up a little while after you left. We didn't see eye-to-eye on a few things. A lot of things. I found her to be a little ignorant." He looks at her quickly. "By the way, she never said anything....stupid...to you, did she?"

"You mean about dating a *gwai-lo*?" She asks carefully. She turns around to look at James, who winks at her. "Oh no, never."

Petey laughs, embarrassed. "Sorry. She's not a bad person, just stuck in her own reality, I guess. She moved back in with her parents."

Claudia doesn't bring up that she hadn't known Sophie had moved *in* in the first place. She figures it's a dead horse.

When they arrive at the condo, both her parents and Tracey rush to the door, and everyone is hugging.

Claudia hugs her mom first. She finds that she is sniffling back tears, not realizing how much she had missed her family. Her dad gives her a big kiss and then Claudia turns to Tracey, throwing herself at the tall blonde in a big hug.

"It's so good to see you, Claud," Tracey says, hugging her back. When they pull away from each other, the girls look at each other, and burst into tears. They hug again, laughing and crying.

Claudia's mom has prepared a hearty midnight snack – chips, salsa, guacamole, an assortment of cookies, and a large plate of fruit are sitting on the counter in the kitchen.

"Eat," says Mrs. Young, always eager to feed her troops. She opens the fridge and pulls out a carton of orange juice and milk, for the cookies.

"I think we need something a bit stronger than orange juice, mom," Claudia says. Petey grabs a case of Kokanee from the fridge, and takes a few beers out, flipping off the caps with an opener on his key chain.

"*Aiya*, I'm so tired," says Mrs. Young, yawning. "Now that you are all safely here, I am going to sleep. Claudia, Tracey - tomorrow we will go shopping, okay?" She smiles at her daughter. Claudia nods, giving her a hug good night, kissing her on the cheek. "I love you, ma."

Mr. Young retires as well in an act of solidarity, though it seems he wants to stay up later and perhaps smoke a cigar on the balcony. But a single look from his tired wife changes his mind, and he follows her into the bedroom, saying good night.

Claudia grabs a chocolate chip cookie and turns to Tracey. "You can sleep in the bed with me. James and Petey will take the couches. Right guys?" Her brother and boyfriend shrug.

"Just keep it clean in there," James says, winking. Claudia rolls her eyes at him. He might joke about it, but she knows that messing around with another girl would not be cool with him.

"Come on." She tugs her friend into her old bedroom. She sees that it is exactly as she had left it. The bed is freshly made in anticipation of visitors. Claudia feels a sudden pang of nostalgia, as if her University life had been years ago, instead of only a few months. She looks around, settling her gaze on her two diplomas, that have been framed, likely by her mom, and set on the dresser.

She jumps on the bed and Tracey joins her, laying back on a pillow and turning to her friend with a sweet, peaceful face. "Claud, thanks for inviting me for Thanksgiving," she says. "Things have been pretty rough at home. I'm sorry I haven't kept in better touch." Tracey isn't wearing any makeup and her eyes are greener than ever, against her pale skin and blonde eyebrows. Her hair is also bone-straight, and she's dressed in a silky navy t-shirt and jeans. She looks almost plain. But beautiful.

"I'm sorry too," Claudia says. "I should have come home to visit in the summer. And then I moved to Toronto. I've been in my own little world," she pauses, feeling guilty and thinking of James, just outside the room. "Are you mad at me?" She looks up at Tracey meekly. She has been dreading this conversation but now that the question has come out of her mouth she realizes how absurd it is.

"No way." Tracey says, smacking her on the shoulder. "If you had done anything else I would have given you shit. You and James are doing what you should be doing. You're going for it. Don't feel guilty about me. I'll be okay." She looks down at her fingernails. "Eventually."

"How's therapy going?" Claudia asks. "Is it helping?"

Tracey shrugs. "I guess. We're all going. Me, my mom and dad. Scott's been going too. Baby steps. By the way, hope that, uh, coke thing didn't freak you out to much." She smiles awkwardly. "You know it wasn't my first time, right? Warren and I used to do coke all the time."

"No, I didn't know," Claudia says. She can't help sounding chastising. "Is that supposed to make me feel better? It did freak me out. I hope you're not still doing that shit."

Tracey shakes her head. "Trust me, I feel fucked up enough every day, I don't need drugs on top of that. It numbs me out for a while but once I start coming down it makes things ten times worse."

"Good," Claudia says. "That shit will rot your brain." She decides to change the topic. "So. Me and James."

"You and James." Tracey repeats, a knowing smile on her face. "It's about fucking time. Brent would be so happy." She nods in affirmation. "He was always calling James a pussy for not going after what he wanted. But maybe it was better this way, eh?"

"I think so," Claudia says. "We've only been officially together for like, six months. But it feels right. We're living together, you know?"

Tracey nods, raising an eyebrow. "How do your parents feel about that?"

"Surprisingly they've been pretty supportive. I think they prefer me living with a six foot three, two hundred pound dude, than alone in the big, bad city." She chuckles. "The lesser of two evils, I guess."

"Well good for you," Tracey says. "Living in sin and ditching law school. You're shaping up to be quite the rebel, aren't you?

I couldn't be more impressed. Just don't turn into a pothead, or else I'll have to kick your ass."

Claudia laughs, getting up from the bed and pulling Tracey to her feet. "Speaking of pot... I think I have a little something hidden in the freezer that will make us all very happy." She can't help it, she literally giggles with excitement.

Tracey's shocked face makes Claudia laugh even harder. "This is B.C., Tracey. Don't tell me we never smoked up when you used to visit?"

"Never! All you ever did was get wasted after a few drinks and start asking about James. Since when did you start smoking weed?" Tracey shakes her head in astonishment.

"I don't. Just once in a while. And this is a special occasion. Come on let's get the boys." She goes to the kitchen to unearth their prize.

The four of them huddle together in the master bedroom, around an open window. Claudia has rolled a small joint, just enough to get them all a bit high, but not enough to completely stone them for the night.

"Where did you learn how to roll like this?" James asks, inspecting the flawless, smooth joint as it's passed to him. He holds it between his thumb and forefinger, inhales, and chokes back a cough.

"When I lived at Totem," says Claudia. "Hannah taught me. She was my roommate. I've always been good at origami and this was pretty similar. I ended up being extra good at it because of my small fingers. I was the resident joint roller. But I'd only smoke once in a while, like after a big exam or something."

Petey laughs. "Mom used to say that your little fingers were made for the violin. If she only knew! Oh man. Maybe we should wake her up and get her in on this action," he jokes, taking a puff.

Claudia rolls her eyes. "I'm pretty sure mom was no angel when she was my age. It probably explains why she's so over-protective. It's almost like she's thinking about all the scandalous things she used to do at my age." Claudia had found a few of her mom's secret mementos one rainy day in high school, when she was rummaging in the boxes under the stairs in the basement for some cool records. Among some letters written in Chinese that she couldn't read, she'd found an ivory cigarette holder, a soft pink dress that looked like it could use a good washing, and a picture of her mom with a good looking blond guy. In the picture, her mom was dripping in furs and the guy was wearing a classy tuxedo, and they both looked like they were having just a bit too much fun. Likely one of her former beaus, though she was surprised that her mom had dated a white guy.

Down the hall in the second bedroom, Polly wakes up in a daze. She sniffs the air, smelling something sweet and familiar, like popcorn. She glances at the clock: It's 3 AM. Too tired to get up, she falls back into her deep slumber, dreaming about a young Englishman with blond hair, dark brown eyes, and a penchant for unavailable women.

- 13 - 1977, Taipei

The bright morning sunshine peeks through the gauzy white curtains, waking up Polly, who squints at the pain of a pounding headache in the back of her skull. She groans, sitting up.

Looking around at her unfamiliar surroundings, she takes in the Western-style furniture: A giant wooden bedframe, a matching dresser and chest, and woven rugs that cover the bamboo parquet flooring so completely that it looks almost like wall-to-wall carpet.

She looks to her left and sees Henry Cooper lying next to her, with a feather quilt pulled up to his waist. He is shirtless, and she realizes with a start that she is as well. In fact, she's not wearing anything at all.

Memories of the night before come flooding back to her and she feels her stomach tumble. The Ball. A few too many drinks. A secret passage. A kiss. Oh no, and then she had come home with him, and they had drank some sweet amber liquid and smoked something that had made her extremely giggly and disturbingly at ease.

She sees her dress hanging over a chair across the room. Her shoes are nowhere to be seen and she guesses that they are downstairs and have likely been stowed away in a hall closet by the *amah* by now. Getting up carefully, trying not to wake Henry, she puts one foot on the floor and stands up slowly.

The floor makes a loud creak. Henry stirs, blinking his eyes open. He sees Polly making a move to leave, and he pulls her back down into the bed, holding her to his chest.

"Henry, I'm leaving," Polly says earnestly. "This was a very bad mistake. Peter will never forgive me." As she mentions Peter's name, she feels tears forming in her throat. She wheezes, as they start to flow. "What have I done?" She croaks, sobbing.

Henry sits up, still holding her. He gazes at her, concern filling his dark brown eyes. "I'm sorry, Polly," he says. "It's my fault. I won't tell Peter. It will be our secret."

Polly cries even harder, doubling over and burying her face into the feather blanket. "That's even worse," she says, sobbing. "He is going to be my husband. I can't start lying to him before we are even married." She takes a deep breath, gathering herself. "I will have to tell him."

Henry pulls away from her gently. "Was it very bad?" He asks. A sudden, horrible thought passes him. "It was not your first time, was it?" The color drains from his face. "Oh Polly..."

Polly shakes her head quickly. "No." She leaves it at that, not wishing to divulge any more of her private life to him.

Henry's not sure which question she answered. He stares at her for a few moments, and then decides to move on. It was just one night.

"Are you hungry?" He asks Polly, changing the tone. "I can have *amah* cook us some *xifan*." He knows the Taiwanese love to have congee for breakfast.

As much as Polly would love a bowl of hot *xifan* right about now, she doesn't want to complicate the situation further by staying. They have crossed a line. She should never speak to him again.

Polly gets up from the bed and crosses the room to the chair. She pulls on the dress, the fabric sliding coolly over her body.

"Henry, can you please drive me home?" She has no intention of walking through the streets in her current disheveled state. "I shouldn't have let this happen." She bites her lip, keeping in her tears.

"Of course," Henry says. He pulls a crisp shirt from his wardrobe and a pair of slacks. Polly imagines that she must look like a heathen, and she sneaks a look at herself in the mirror. Her hair is mussed up and some of her makeup has smudged onto the side of her face.

"May I use your washroom?" She asks. Avoiding eye contact at all costs, she moves toward the en-suite, not waiting for an answer. Once inside she splashes cold water on her face, and blots it with a towel she finds near the sink. Wiping her face down, she feels better immediately. She finds a comb on a shelf and tidies her hair, her efforts straightening some of the curls she had painstakingly worked on the night before. She swishes some water in her mouth and spits it out in the sink.

Henry is waiting in the bedroom for her, dressed and hair combed. He holds up a woman's blouse and wool skirt, offering them to Polly. "My mother's," he says. "They may be a bit big, but at least you will have something clean to wear."

Polly nods, thanking him. It's rather hard to be short with him when he's being so accommodating and considerate. *Are all Englishmen like him?* Polly wonders.

Taking the clothes, she goes back to the washroom, even though he has likely seen everything she is trying to hide, and gets dressed. The blouse is a bit loose but the skirt fits quite well. Her sisters have always teased her about having the body of a *lao-wai*, with round hips and a perky backside. Most Taiwanese girls are petite all over.

She re-enters the bedroom, and it is empty this time around. The door is open, and she can hear Henry downstairs talking to the *amah*. Bundling her silk dress into a ball, she tucks it under her arm and peers out into the hallway. Seeing that it's empty, she tiptoes to the stairs, and makes her way down.

As she approaches the landing, Henry appears and greets her at the bottom. He is carrying a paper bag with a few *yotiao*, fried donuts, sticking out. In the other hand he has a glass of water and an aspirin, which he passes to Polly.

"You'll need this, if you're feeling the way I'm feeling." He smiles at her painfully. "And have some *yotiao*. You need something in your stomach."

Polly drinks down the pill with the water in a few gulps, but refuses the donuts. "I'll eat something when I get home," she says. "Do you know where my shoes are?"

Henry opens a hall closet and pulls out Polly's beige high heel pumps. Polly puts them on, feeling immediately more refined with the height. She follows Henry out the front door and around to the cars. He doesn't bother letting her choose a car this time, and they drive away in the blue Jaguar, towards Polly's apartment.

It's a short drive since it is only a few streets away, and Polly thanks him for the ride in front of the building. She prays that Gan-Ma and Gan-Ba are not looking down from the balcony.

A gust of wind sweeps into the car as she opens the door, and she suddenly remembers that she'd left her furs at the hotel. She turns to look at Henry. "Henry, my furs..."

"I'll drop them off to you later today," he says, gently. "If that's alright."

She hesitates, not wanting to spend any more time with him than necessary, but the furs had belonged to her mother and she wants them back desperately. She nods. He thrusts the bag of donuts at her before she gets out of the car and she takes them, wanting to get inside as quickly as possible.

The apartment is empty when she opens the door. They must have gone to the market. She breathes a sigh of relief and runs to her bedroom. On her bed there are a few envelopes waiting and she feels both excited and guilty when she sees Peter's concise penmanship.

She tosses her dirty dress over her desk chair and takes off her high heels. Deciding that she needs to take a bath before she reads his letters, she strips out of Henry's mother's clothing and puts on a bathrobe. Trudging her way down the hallway to the bathroom, she feels ashamed.

But a tiny part of her feels just a little bit satisfied.

Henry is her first. She has yet to sleep with Peter, since they've had such little time together. She didn't want Henry to feel like he owed her anything, or that she was vulnerable. She had been too drunk and too high to think about the consequences, and she realizes in horror how lucky she is that she didn't bleed all over his sheets. That would have been quite unfortunate and embarrassing.

She sits down in the warm bath water and lathers herself with almond soap. The sounds of the water swishing around the bathtub are the only accompaniment to her racing thoughts.

Why did Peter want Henry to take her to the Ball? It was rather surprising, after meeting him only once, that he should want her to accompany him to such a high profile event. It seems almost as if Henry and Polly had been forced together by Peter, that he had some wayward plan up his sleeve to pawn her off to his good friend.

But that would be impossibly sordid, and downright ridiculous. Peter is a straightforward, decent man and he would never expect Polly to even entertain the thought of sleeping with another man. Which is probably why he thought it would be perfectly acceptable for the two of them to attend the Ball together. A good, happy time for Polly, and a favor to Henry. An elegant evening out as friends, and nothing more.

No, Peter would not have foreseen for any of this to happen.

But what did he expect? He has been gone over a year, keeping in touch with only a couple letters a month. Phone calls are sparse. Yet she is undeniably betrothed to him. She has dinner or tea with his parents at least once a month, and it is sadly the highlight of her life these days. Is she expected to just wait around and court his parents until he is ready to marry her?

Polly splashes her hand angrily in the water. It's his fault, the naïve bastard. He is the one who has been staying away, and then forcing her to go to a fancy ball with his dreadfully handsome, foreign friend. If he didn't expect Polly to fall into Henry's bed, then he might be just plain stupid.

Around three o'clock in the afternoon, the doorbell rings at Polly's apartment. Her Godparents are home now, and Polly has been hiding out in her bedroom for most of the day, avoiding them. Gan-Ma is busy cooking in the kitchen, and Gan-Ba is reading the paper at the table, keeping her company.

"I'll get it!" Polly scurries to the door.

She peers through the peephole. Upon seeing Henry's face, she curses to herself silently. Opening the door quickly, she closes it immediately behind her, stepping into the hallway. He is carrying her furs, which she takes from him hastily. She keeps her eyes down, not wanting to make eye contact.

"*Xie xie*," she says. "Sorry for the trouble." She turns to go back inside but he grabs her elbow.

"Polly, can we talk? Perhaps we can go for a cup of coffee somewhere?" Against her better judgment, she looks up at him. Henry's face seems genuinely concerned and Polly senses that he feels just as guilty for what they've done. She has finally decided that she won't be telling Peter what happened, and she figures she may as well tell Henry, so that he too will keep his mouth shut.

"Let me get my coat and handbag," Polly says. "Please wait downstairs, I will only be a minute."

Gan-Ma is already quite unhappy that Polly didn't come home last night. She has never been the kind to pry, since Polly has always behaved well, but she can only assume what may have happened. And now, her Goddaughter is leaving the house only hours before dinnertime, to do who-knows-what. "We will not wait for you to eat," she scolds Polly. "Where are you going?"

"I have to meet Winnie," Polly lies. "She has something important to tell me." Leaving it at that, Polly goes to her room and pulls on her cashmere coat over her shirtdress, and a pair of leather pumps. She exits the apartment quickly, not bothering to check herself in the mirror.

Henry is sitting in the car downstairs, smoking a cigarette. He is driving the blue Jaguar, which seems to be his favorite car. Polly gets into the passenger side and Henry pulls away from the curb without a word.

They drive for a few minutes before Polly asks where he is taking her.

"A place where we can talk in private," he says. "It's not very close though. Is that alright with you?" He lights up a new cigarette, offering one to Polly. She nods, keeping her words minimal, and takes the cigarette, rolling down her own window. He pulls out a Zippo and lights it for her, and then his own. They smoke in silence while Henry drives with one hand.

They are headed north towards *Yangmingshan,* one of four National Parks in Taiwan. It's a grassy mountain area that is relatively undeveloped. He begins driving up the winding roadways, passing by tall, wispy grasses, spotted cherry trees, and other broad-leafed trees and bushes that Polly can not identify. In the summer, people come here to see the butterflies. In the winter, it is rainy and cold, but beautifully green.

After about twenty minutes of winding roads, Henry slows and turns into a hidden, private driveway. It is unpaved, and the enormous building that sits beyond the dirt road looks new, modern, and posh. It's surrounded by trees and woodland, but looks rather empty and deserted.

"This is The Manor. It is going to be a spa, kind of like a country club," he says. "My father bought the property years ago and it's being converted. Eventually, people can come here to go swimming, and bathe in the hot and cold springs. Very good for health." He parks in front of the building. "No one knows about it yet. It isn't meant to open for another year or so."

Polly gets out of the car and follows him up the walkway to the front door. He takes a large key out of his pocket and they enter through the giant double doors. The interior is very impressive, with vaulted ceilings and filled with Ming Dynasty furniture. Red and gold carpets line the halls and there are touches of green in bamboo plants and paintings around the space.

"It's very beautiful," Polly says, wistfully. She fingers the wood of a chair close by. "However, I am confused as to why you brought me here. We could have found a place to talk privately not so far away." She is anxious and realizes that she is rather hungry. "I'm going to miss supper," she mumbles.

"I thought you might like to see this place," Henry says. "After all, you seem to like secrets..."

She glares at him.

"I-I was talking about the secret passage at the hotel. Honestly." He sighs. "Sorry. Follow me."

He walks through the foyer and down a long hallway. Polly follows a few steps behind. They pass by several rooms with closed doors, which he tells her will be used for private events or meals. There is a large banquet hall on the right, filled with tables for ten. Polly can imagine dignitaries and their wives coming here for a relaxing day in the pools and then dining in the grand room.

On the far side of the house there is another set of double doors, which lead outside. Henry unlocks the doors and pushes through, and they step out onto a large balcony. Polly gasps in awe as giant trees surround her, and she steps to the railing, overlooking a clear blue lake. The evening sun is setting and there is just a bit of fog, creating a cool, misty vista.

"It's beautiful, isn't it?" Henry asks, rhetorically. "This is the best of Taiwan, I would say." He motions towards a small table with two chairs. Polly sits. It is chilly, but it is so enchanting out here that she doesn't mind.

"Excuse me, while I go make us some tea," Henry says. "I've also brought along some *saobing*. Would you like some?" Polly nods, remembering her hunger. She pulls her coat even tighter around herself and pops the collar up. She closes her eyes, breathing in the cold air. It is so quiet here on the mountain, and when she opens her eyes, all she sees are deep green forests beyond the balcony. Despite the recent events, she is feeling quite content at this very moment.

Henry returns with a silver tray. On it, there is a Chinese teapot, two small cups, and a plate of layered, flatbread pastries topped with sesame seeds, and stuffed with red bean - *saobing*. There is also a cotton quilt draped over his arm, which he wraps around Polly after he puts the tray down.

Polly is quite distressed about how thoughtful he is being. Who carries pastries in the trunk of their Jaguar? What is he trying to prove? She pours tea into both cups without spilling a drop, and when Henry sits down, she raises her cup to him.

"*Gan bei,*" she says, tritely. Cheers. "Now that I'm wrapped up here like a warm spring roll and drinking the tea that you've so kindly made for me, perhaps we can talk. What is it that you want from me?" She takes a sip of her tea and stares into his now-familiar eyes. She softens her tone slightly. "You are Peter's friend, and I'm his fiancée. I feel awful that we've betrayed him. But you seem rather at ease, and I'd like to know why."

Peter takes a long sip of his tea and takes out a cigarette. He sees Polly eyeing them and he hands her one. Once he's lit both of their cigarettes, he exhales a plume of smoke through his nostrils, and finally opens his mouth.

"It's complicated, Polly. I do feel bad about Peter. Really, I do. I never meant for this to happen. I think you are an exquisite woman and I wanted to spend an evening with you on my arm, with the permission of your fiancé. But when I saw you last night, glowing with excitement and even willing to ride down that filthy slide with me in the secret passage, well..." he pauses to take another drag. "I think my loneliness finally caught up with me."

"Loneliness?" Polly inquires incredulously. "*You* are lonely?" She is quite sure that with his charm and good looks, not to mention the fortune of his family, he could surely win himself any company he'd want.

Henry sighs. "It's a long story. There was a woman. I was with her for six years. She was promised to someone else." He laughs darkly. "My brother, actually. They were married a few years ago, and ever since, I've been roaming the world, trying to feel useful and...not so lonely."

Polly nods. "Yes, it must be lonely traveling the world by yourself. But you choose to do this. Why not settle down with someone else, if that is what you want?" *And what does this have to do with last night?* She adds to herself, silently. She knows loneliness better than anyone. After her father's death, and with her sisters across the world, she always feels lonely, even though she is rarely ever alone.

"Perhaps that would be a wiser decision," Henry smiles. He continues. "I have a broken heart. And when I was with you last night, and you looked so beautiful, I just wanted to be with you. It made me feel not so broken anymore, not so lonely. I wasn't thinking about Peter." He takes a sip of his tea, and tapping some ash off his cigarette over the balcony. "I was only thinking about me and my loneliness. In a way I still am, enjoying this lovely evening with you here on the mountain."

Polly is astounded by his brazenness. "That is the most absurd thing I have ever heard," Polly says. "You use your loneliness as an excuse to do whatever you please? That is horrible. Shame on you."

"Well, what's your excuse?" he says. "Were you not lonely? Or do you often go around sleeping with your fiance's friends?"

Polly holds herself back from slapping Henry across the face. "I was drunk! And then we smoked whatever that was, that made me laugh like a hyena. And no, I do not go around – Nevermind. I'm not even going to answer that horridly insulting question." She looks away, over the tops of the trees.

Henry is silent. She continues. "Yes, I am lonely. But I wasn't myself, last night. I hope you won't tell Peter..." she drifts off, staring down at her cup of tea.

"I see no use in doing so," Henry says. "I was rather concerned this morning, when you said that you wanted to tell him. I was afraid that you already had when I came to see you this afternoon."

Polly shakes her head. "I can't tell him." She looks up at him. "That's why I agreed to come here with you, to tell you this. He must never know about us. Is that clear?"

Henry stares at her, with a sad smile. "Our little secret," he says.

"And I don't think you should continue with your friendship anymore," she says matter-of-factly. "I don't think it would be prudent." Her eyes flicker up to his, awaiting his response.

He drags on his cigarette. "I rarely see Peter as it is," he says. "We live in different worlds. And he will be living permanently in America soon, and you with him. I'll be returning to England. I will not cut him off as a friend. But I will certainly try to keep my distance."

Polly nods. "Good. I think we understand each other."

"We do," Henry says. "One more question."

"Yes?" Polly reaches for a *saobing*. She can never resist a good pastry.

Henry leans towards Polly across the table, refilling their teacups. "Now that I've told you what I want with you - and that is, just your company, for this evening, what is it that you want?"

Polly chews slowly. It is a fair question. After all, it took two to do what they did last night. And even though she was under the influence, she was quite conscious and aware of the situation. She swallows the delicious pastry and takes a sip of tea.

"Adventure," she says, finally. She wipes her mouth with a handkerchief. "I crave adventure."

"Ah," Henry says, nodding. "That is a very good answer." He gets up suddenly. "Come with me," he says. Polly looks at him reluctantly. Last time she went with him somewhere for an adventure, she had ended up in his bed the next morning.

Henry senses her hesitation. "Trust me," he says, looking into her eyes. "It will be worth it."

As always, curiosity wins out and Polly puts her half-eaten *saobing* down on the plate, gets up, and follows Henry down the balcony stairs, onto the grass, and into the forest.

They are walking for a few minutes, dodging branches and stepping over rocks, when Polly begins to protest. "My shoes are three inches high," she says. "I can not go much further."

Henry turns to her, several paces ahead. He hesitates for a moment, then walks back toward her, and scoops her up into his arms, with her knees bent and draping over one arm, and his other cradling her back. She lets out a squeal of surprise.

"It'll be faster this way," he says. He can't help drinking in her scent. He makes his way through the trees, navigating expertly and barely straining with the weight of her in his arms. When he finally stops, they are in a large clearing with a small steaming lake in the middle, surrounded by large wet boulders and rocks.

"The Secret Hot Spring," he says, putting her down. Polly is speechless at the sight. She has never bathed in a hot spring before, and definitely not one in the middle of a forest, on a mountain. She hears Henry undressing himself behind her. She freezes.

"What are you doing?" she asks sharply, without turning around. He laughs. She catches a glimpse of his nakedness as he jumps into the pool, and when Polly looks behind her she sees that he has draped his clothes carefully over a low branch, and his shoes are neatly placed close by.

"Come in, Polly," he says. "It's wonderful, especially right now, in the cold."

Without protest, Polly begins taking off her coat and shoes, surprising Henry. She strips down quickly into her modest cotton brassiere and underwear, and steps into the water. She momentarily thinks about how they will dry off later, but dismisses the thought once she feels the warmth of the spring enveloping her body.

"*Ahhh*," she sighs. The water is so warm that her toes and fingers tingle. She feels her body relax immediately. She leans back against a rock and closes her eyes. "Thank you for bringing me here," she murmurs.

Henry laughs. "You look like you're going to fall asleep. Look over there." She opens her eyes and he motions to a waist-high wall of rock on the far side of the pool, and wades over. He presses himself up and looks over, and Polly notices he is not wearing any underwear.

She diverts her eyes and carefully climbs onto a slippery rock to look over the rock wall. There is another pool, slightly smaller, surrounded by cherry trees.

"Another pool?" She asks excitedly. Getting out of the water, she plunges into the neighboring spring, and it surprises her with both its depth and its cold temperature. She screams.

"So cold!" She kicks her legs rapidly, pushing herself to the edge of the pool. Luckily she had learned to swim as a child so Henry doesn't have to dive in and save her. She gets out of the cold pool and steps back into the warmth of the hot spring.

Henry laughs. "It's a cold spring. I would have told you that had you not been so eager. You're supposed to go back and forth between the pools. It's good for the heart."

"Are these natural?" Polly asks. "They are incredible." She floats on her back, glimpsing at the darkening sky and feeling the coldness on her nose.

"They are," Henry says. "The heat in this pool comes from the earth's core. The cold spring is just a natural pool that happens to be right next to this one. Nature is quite dramatic, isn't it?"

Polly nods. She stands and spins around in the spring, taking in the beauty of the forest. Closing her eyes, she sighs heavily.

"What's wrong?" Henry asks, gently. He is leaning against a rock, his own eyes half-closed.

Polly moves over to stand a few feet away from him, leaning against the same large rock. She keeps her eyes ahead so she doesn't catch sight of any indecent body parts. "I don't know," she admits. "Things are complicated. I wish Peter would come home and marry me, so we can start our new life. While I am here without him, I feel trapped. Like I am buried in a hole and I'm waiting for someone to dig me out."

Henry nods, understanding what it's like to feel trapped by a person who is out of reach.

"But, right now, in this marvelous place," Polly continues, her eyes brightening, "I feel very happy. Like I am living. Is that wrong of me?" She turns to Henry.

"You're asking the wrong person," he answers. "My happiness once depended on another person. Perhaps it still does. So if you are asking me, I'd say live, no matter what you are waiting for." He turns to look at her, his light brown eyes sparkling with warmth. "But when he does comes back for you, give yourself to him fully. He deserves that."

Polly nods. They soak in the spring for a while longer, until the sun has almost completely set. They get out of the pool and quickly get dressed in the cold, shivering dangerously, their wet skin sticking to the fabric of their clothes. Henry picks Polly up without a word and hurries through the forest, beating the darkness back to the secret house. It is much warmer in his arms.

Henry finds towels for them back at The Manor. Polly rubs her hair dry, and does what she can with her clothes, but they remain wet from her body. She wraps herself in a blanket to keep warm, and Henry agrees to drive her home.

In front of her apartment building, she turns to him in the car to say goodbye, and he gives her an affectionate smile, as if they are old friends. He kisses her swiftly on the cheek and she gets out of the car, waving to him from the sidewalk as he drives away. It is the last time Polly sees Henry that winter.

She goes upstairs to the apartment, and dashes straight to her room to change out of her wet clothes. Her Godparents are already in bed, but she makes a bit of noise so they know she is home. She will have to be extra conscientious for the next week or so, after these past couple of days. She puts on a nightgown, ties on her house robe, and steps into her slippers. Her stomach is making hungry noises, so she goes to the kitchen to make a cup of tea, and takes a box of soda crackers with her back to her bedroom.

Lying on her bed, she sets the tea and crackers on her bedside table and reaches for the unopened airmail envelopes that are waiting for her. Tearing the first one open, she smiles fondly at the neat, impeccable penmanship. She reaches for a cracker, pops it in her mouth, and snuggles down into her pillow to read. The first two letters are short and civil, as if Peter is writing only out of obligation. She scans through them and tosses them aside. They are dated almost a month ago. The final letter is more recent, and after reading it, tears form in her eyes. As they roll down her cheeks, she holds her hand to her cracker-filled mouth, crumbs escaping out the sides.

December 7, 1977

Dearest Polly,

I hope you enjoyed the Governor's Ball with Henry. I am sorry that I was not the one to take you, but I wanted you to have a good time even though I am not there. Henry is a gentleman and I am sure he treated you very well.

I have some good news. I have found a promising position with a company in Canada. They want me to start as soon as possible, so I am going there in a few weeks. It is a beautiful, small city called CALGARY. I will find a house for us, get settled, and then return to Taipei in the fall and we will be married. You will then come with me to Canada, where there are mountains, rivers, and moose with large antlers. There are flowers in the summer, and fluffy white snow in the winter. And all the people are very nice.

Yours Truly,
Peter

It rains non-stop the whole weekend in Vancouver, so Claudia and James spend Thanksgiving cooped up at the condo with her parents, brother, and Tracey. On their last day, they walk down to Spanish Banks beach, with Petey and Tracey.

They bundle up with gloves, scarves, sweatshirts, and Claudia even puts on a down-filled vest for added warmth. It's extra nippy by the water.

The guys bring a football to toss around, and they venture close to the water while the girls sit on a large log. They watch the ball fly in perfect arcs, hurled across the sand.

Tracey is staying a day longer with Claudia's parents, and they will drive back to Calgary together, making a stop at the hot springs in Radium. Looping her arm through Tracey's, Claudia asks her friend if she has any other plans.

"Honestly, no," Tracey says. "I stopped planning after Brent died. I'm just taking it day by day. Eventually I guess I'd like to go back to school or get a better job but that seems a bit far away." She is peering into the distance.

"That makes sense," Claudia says, sensibly. "Although I was only asking about your plans for the next day or so." She smiles. "You have another twenty-four hours here with my family. Are you going to sit around with them and gossip about me and James?"

Tracey laughs. "Definitely not. I think I'll get enough of that on the drive home." She pauses to look at her friend in the eyes. "Your parents are great. My own parents are kind of MIA these days, as you can imagine. I hope you don't mind. I like spending time with them."

"Are you kidding?" Claudia squeezes Tracey's arm even tighter. "I love it. I'm so glad they've forgiven the champagne-guzzling Tracey from high school. By the way, I'm liking this…. natural look you've got going on lately," she eyes her friend up-and-down. Tracey looks as fresh as daisy, her creamy skin finally showing its true color after years of self-tanner and other unfortunate bronzing devices. She almost looks like a different person.

"Why thank you," Tracey says, genuinely. "It's a lot less maintenance looking like myself." She pulls out a pack of cigarettes and lights one, taking a deep drag.

Claudia holds her tongue, since it seems Tracey's on a pretty good path already. She moves over on the log a bit, not wanting to stink up her hair with the smell of smoke.

"Sorry," Tracey mutters, putting out her cigarette in the sand. "I'm trying to quit anyway. I'm down to only one or two a day."

"That's great!" Claudia says, enthusiastically. She impulsively inches over and pulls her friend into a tight hug. "I love you, Tracey. I'm so glad we got to spend some time together."

Tracey hugs her back. "Me too."

The guys are tired of throwing around the football and they head over their way. Their cheeks are rosy from the cold and exertion.

"Do you girls need a moment?" James asks, flashing his grin. "Looks like you're about to make out."

Claudia rolls her eyes at him and stands up. "We were just keeping each other warm." She reaches down and pulls Tracey up from the log.

278

"Let's go fill up on some food before we head to the airport," Claudia says, taking James' hand and walking away from the beach. They cross the seaside road and walk up a set of stairs that lead to Blanca Street.

Petey and Tracey lag behind, chatting quietly. Claudia looks over her shoulder to watch the two of them, walking closely, heads bent together. Tracey's blonde head is only a few inches shorter than Petey's. He's grown out his hair even more. It's past his shoulders, and so black, it's almost blue. He is also sporting a goatee these days, which their mom is always telling him to get rid of.

Tracey says something to Petey that makes him laugh, and then she looks at him, blushing and smiling. Their eyes catch for a moment.

They have only been gone for a few days, but when Claudia and James get back to Toronto, it seems the city has changed seasons on them. Evergreen wreaths and red bows line the lampposts on their street, and all the stores have their Christmas displays up already. The billboards on Yonge Street are covered in vibrant holiday advertisements, and there is a giant tree sitting in the middle of Dundas Square, looking ready to be decorated. Claudia always heard that Toronto was Canada's Big Apple, and she's beginning to see why.

The air has also changed. The humidity is still there, but it is now joined with a deathly chill, and when she gets inside their apartment and turns the heat up high, her clothes still feel damp. She strips off her layers and puts on an old, soft, sweatshirt and a pair of James' pajama pants. She is still on Pacific Time but she is so tired, she climbs into bed, and burrows under their down blanket without unpacking her bags.

James follows suit, stripping down to his underwear and joining her, spooning her from behind. Just the feel of his body cradling hers is enough to make her feel heated, and she turns to face him in the bed, sharing his pillow.

"Thanks for spending Thanksgiving with my family," she says softly, brushing his hair out of his eyes. His wavy chestnut locks have gotten long, curling at his ears, and she loves to run her fingers through.

"I love your family," James says, without hesitation, his blue glowing. "I love you." He pulls her to him, kissing her on the forehead. She inhales his scent, savoring it, realizing how much she'd missed this closeness, having spent the last four nights sleeping in separate rooms. Even though they had been together almost the whole time, they hadn't been intimate at all.

She throws a leg over his hip, pulling herself closer. She wraps her arms around him and he does the same.

"Happy Thanksgiving," she says, between his kisses. "Now give me something to be thankful about." He chuckles and leans down to kiss her.

The next day, Claudia receives notice from York University. She tears open the thin envelope, knowing intuitively that an acceptance letter should be larger and much thicker.

She didn't get in. It's a shock and a disappointment, and for a few days, she doesn't tell James. She continues to go to work at the theater, buys groceries on her way home, and stares at the television while James is in class, not knowing what to do next.

With the exception of being kicked out of St. Agnes, she has never been rejected by an academic institution before. For once, she was unable to study her way into something. When she finally tells James, he is sympathetic, and holds her patiently, stroking her back, as she cries for the future she had imagined.

At work, she tells Cory. He is less sympathetic, and tells her that she should stick to her plan, with or without schooling. If this is what she wants, she can get there with some hard work and maybe a bit of luck. He tells her he'll help her as much as he can, with the connections he has.

When *Fuego* ends its run in February due to poor ticket sales, Claudia is out of a job, though Cory is still employed for the next show. To help, Cory contacts a friend who is a director for a well-known entertainment company. He tells him about Claudia, thinking that he might be able to help her get a foot in the door. The three of them go out for a lengthy, schmoozy dinner, and Claudia gets so caught up with the intense conversation that she ends up pouring her heart out, talking way too much, expressing her raw love for dance and choreography. She goes home feeling embarrassed. Dramatically contemplating either swallowing a container of Tylenol or reviving her parents' dream of her becoming a lawyer, she picks up her cell to call her mom.

She sees a missed call from an unknown number. Usually she ignores unknowns, but something compels her to call this one back. When the voice picks up, she feels a jolt in her heart, and she freezes. It's the director from dinner. He'd gotten her number from Cory, he says.

Without beating around the bush, he offers her a job. She will have to work her way up, he says, starting as a choreographer's assistant, but it is a fantastic opportunity. One day, if she does well, she could be choreographing her own shows. Maybe even directing, eventually.

Not thinking twice, Claudia verbally accepts the offer over the phone. Her heart is pounding and she knows without question, that it is what she wants. Paul is delighted, and says they'll send her a hiring package in the mail with all the details.

The only problem is, the job is in Montreal.

When James gets home that night, exhausted from a long day of classes, she breaks the news to him.

"I got a job," she says, excited. "I can't believe it. It's like a dream come true. I start in two weeks."

His eyes light up. This is just what she needs, after getting rejected from York. He picks her up in a hug. "I'm so proud of you," he says. "That's fantastic."

"It's in Montreal," she says, in a small voice. She looks up at him with hopeful eyes. She wants him to be happy for her.

He stares at her wordlessly. A bunch of possible scenarios run through his head, and none of them make him happy. After a while, he gives her a small smile. "Congrats," he says. He goes into the bedroom. "I'm going to take a shower," he calls out.

James drops his leather bag on the carpet in their bedroom, and peels off his clothes. In the en-suite bathroom, he turns on the shower and lets the steam fill the air, while he does a few dozen push-ups, burning off some anxiety. He knows he is being selfish, feeling more upset than happy for Claudia, but it also hurts that she didn't think to discuss things with him before taking the job.

He steps into the shower and tries to clear his mind. Will she miss him? Does she still want to be together? How long is the train ride to Montreal? A part of him wonders if that DJ guy has anything to do with this.

He had gotten the chance to meet Cory, about a month ago, when he finally went to see *Fuego,* just before it ended its run.

He was pretty impressed with the whole production, and also with Cory. Claudia introduced them afterwards, at the bar, and he could tell immediately that the guy had a thing for Claudia. He was also totally cool, as much as he'd hated to admit it. Maybe he got a job in Montreal too, and they'll be working their way up together, supporting each other and celebrating their achievements together.

He laughs to himself darkly, shaking his head.

When he gets out of the shower he can hear Claudia on the phone with her mom, talking in Mandarin. She sounds so happy – elated, in fact. That fact alone makes him realize that he'll have to keep his feelings to himself. After all, he's here in Toronto, fulfilling his own dream of becoming a doctor. She deserves just as much.

Claudia's last two weeks in Toronto are a blur. James tries to be supportive but becomes increasingly distant, as he watches Claudia get more excited every day about her new adventure. At one point, he wants to ask her if she's sad at all that she's leaving him. But he doesn't. He keeps it to himself.

They spend their last weekend in bed together, barely talking, drinking in each other's physical presence. It's as if they are storing up enough of each other for a long winter apart. When Claudia finally gets on the train for Montreal on Monday with two packed suitcases, James truly believes that he has memorized every crevice and curve on her body. They hug goodbye, and kiss each other over and over again, even though they know they will see each other again soon. James promises to visit as soon as he has a break in his school schedule. Claudia nods, saying that she will try and work in a few vacation days as well.

When Claudia arrives in Montreal, she enrolls in French language classes at a community college to brush up on her speaking skills. Within months she is having successful conversations with strangers on the bus, and when she talks on the phone with James, he playfully accuses her of picking up a phony French accent.

He comes to visit her in Montreal for the first time in spring. Claudia's apartment is an artist's dream, housed in an old oak building with original crown moldings, fireplace, and stove in tact. This means, however, that it is poorly heated, and she has to wear bulky sweaters and giant scarves, even when she is indoors. She has decorated the studio apartment with sheer, muslin curtains, floor cushions, and mismatched furniture she picked up off Craigslist and yard sales. A queen-sized bed dressed in deep purple sheets sits smack in the middle of the large room on top of a large Turkish rug, serving as a multi-purpose area for sleeping, sitting, and general hanging out. It's a far cry from James' swanky downtown Toronto pad, but it feels warm, inviting, and a bit too easy-going for James' liking.

He meets her new friends and colleagues at a bar one night, and they all speak an expert combination of French and English. Cory is also there; it turns out he also landed a gig with the company, and he was the one who had hooked Claudia up in the first place. James pats himself on the back for being so perceptive.

When James gets back to Toronto, he runs into Maddie one night on campus. They decide to get a drink, and talk late into the night, catching up. He decides that she is just as nice as he remembered.

Claudia calls the next day, as she always does, probably to wish him a good morning. He doesn't answer, and switches his phone to silent. He ignores her call again in the evening, and texts Maddie instead, to see if she wants to get a bite to eat at his favorite Thai restaurant down the street. He could use the company.

He decides to write Claudia an email on a Friday night, while nursing a beer. His fingers freeze over the keys as he thinks about what he's going to say to her. He can't think of the right words, and finally just slams the computer shut, and grabs his phone instead. They've always been better at texting.

James: *Hey. I don't think this is going to work out. It's too hard. I'm sorry.*

He waits for a reply, but nothing comes. She is probably out partying with her new friends, he thinks bitterly.

He stays home that night, waiting for a response from Claudia. Part of him hopes that she will call him crying, asking him to reconsider, telling him that she needs him and loves him, and that she can't be without him. But nothing happens. He falls asleep on the couch during his fifth beer, with the television switched on to a re-run of *Friends*.

When he wakes up the next morning and realizes that she still hasn't tried to contact him back, he's worried, and decides to call her. Just to make sure if she is alright.

She picks up on the third ring. "Hey," she says, her tone even.

"Hey," he answers, relieved to hear her voice. He is quiet then, waiting for her to speak.

But she doesn't. She is silent, waiting for him to say something.

"I..." he begins. He rubs his hand over his face, trying to cork his emotions. "I wanted to see if you were okay." He lets out a quiet exhale.

"Ah. Sure. I'm fine," she says. He can hear her voice trying not to crack. "Is that...all?"

"Uh, yeah. I guess so." He feels like a fucking idiot. "So..."

"I have to go," she says abruptly. "I'll see you." She hangs up the phone and the line is dead.

Later that day James is in the library, surfing the Internet, unable to focus on his studies. He pulls up Facebook, wanting to see what Claudia has been up to. He almost wants proof that she's having a good time. He's sure she is happier without him, relieved of the tiresome boyfriend she has lurking around in Toronto.

When he logs on, he sees that there is a little red flag, indicating that someone has posted to his page. He clicks on it, and his own profile fills the screen. He has yet to upload a profile picture, but his name, school, and hometown is there. James Cooper; University of Toronto Medical Candidate; Calgary, Alberta, Canada.

The last he'd checked, his page was blank since he barely ever used Facebook. But now, on the "wall", there is a single picture, posted two days ago, by Maddie Thompson. It is a picture of him, holding chopsticks, about to dig into his green curry. His lips are in a half-smile, about to open in protest, not wanting his picture to be taken. He remembers telling Maddie to knock it off, just wanting to enjoy his food. She had giggled, which annoyed him.

While Maddie's not in the picture, it's clear that she's the photographer. The photo is credited with her name and she's written a caption, too: *Catching up with one of my favorite men over Thai food.*

James then notices a little thumbs-up icon below the picture. He hovers over it and it says *Claudia Young Likes This.* There is also a comment from Claudia right underneath. "Great picture. I've never liked Thai food." He sees that the timestamp is at 12:31 AM, late last night. Mere minutes before he sent her the text message.

He considers calling her to clear things up, but he figures there's no point. She hadn't seemed terribly upset on the phone. Maybe she has moved on already with DJ Cory, running to him with a sob story about her asshole ex-boyfriend. The thought of it makes him want to puke.

For the second time in the last twenty-four hours, he slams his poor computer into sleep mode. Packing up his things, he leaves the library for some air. He ends up pacing the streets for hours, until his shoulder becomes strained from the weight of his bag. Realizing he hasn't eaten in hours, he decides to get some take-out before heading home.

He is craving Chinese food, but decides to pick up a sandwich from Subway instead. He eats it slowly in front of the television, thinking that it tastes more like cardboard than cold cuts on bread.

He goes to sleep still hungry, and feeling empty. When he wakes up, he feels the same way. The summer comes and goes and he doesn't hear a word from Claudia. He briefly considers taking the train to Montreal and showing up on her doorstep, but he can't imagine what he'll say when he gets there. I love you? I'm sorry? Fuck that. She's probably forgotten about him by now. Plus, she was practically a different person the last time he'd seen her, with all her new Frenchie friends. She's probably living with Cory by now in some artsy shack in a historic neighborhood.

So, he decides to move on. He goes out with every girl who shows interest, and finally settles on Rebecca, a pretty redhead from med school who happily moves in with him after a few weeks of dating. She is a couple years older than he is, and ready to settle down.

He lets her fall in love with him. She never asks him about his past, so he doesn't tell her about Claudia, though they do run into Maddie here and there, and he introduces them. Strangely enough, Rebecca and Maddie become fast friends and his ex-girlfriend becomes a frequent visitor at his apartment.

One day, when Rebecca is putting away his laundry, she finds a framed picture of him and Claudia together from the high school prom, which he had tucked into the back of his sock drawer. When she asks him about it, holding it up curiously, he freezes for a fraction too long, staring at high school Claudia in her long pink dress, with a slightly annoyed, adorable look on her face.

"Just an old friend," he says, smiling at Rebecca. She clearly doesn't believe him, since guys normally don't frame pictures of themselves with friends from high school, and he suspects that Maddie had probably mentioned Claudia before. But she doesn't question him any further. Instead, she puts the frame on his desk in the spare room, right beside his computer, as if to test him. When he sees it, he throws it into a box aptly labeled "UBC stuff" and shoves it into the back of his closet.

Polly puts on her lipstick in the hotel mirror. She has used the same color for twenty years – a creamy raspberry, with just a hint of shine. Smiling at herself to check if she got any on her teeth, she turns her face from side to side, admiring her own reflection. Time has etched little smile lines to the sides of her eyes, and they have started to droop just the tiniest bit. Her skin is still velvety soft, and she has kept her body in great shape over the years playing badminton and hiking the hills with her husband on the weekends.

One of her children will be married today. Her own wedding had been a moderate affair, with less than 100 guests, which is low-key for Taiwanese standards. In comparison, the event today will be utterly miniscule.

Peter steps into the bathroom behind her, fixing his tie in the mirror. "You look wonderful," he says to his wife, smiling proudly. "The bride will be jealous."

Polly smirks at her husband. "Bullshit," she says in Mandarin. "I'm almost sixty years old. I can't compete with our beautiful bride."

He chuckles, leading her out of the bathroom with his hand on her back. They leave the hotel room and step out into the fresh mountain air. They are in the town of Banff, hidden within the Rocky Mountains of Alberta, and the hotel they are staying at is a luxury lodge surrounded by tall pines, rushing rivers, and wild deer. All the rooms have exterior entrances, like a motel, and everything is made of real, hefty, fragrant wood. Even their room boasts solid maple furniture, with vaulted ceilings, a crackling fireplace, two rocking chairs, and a balcony that opens up over a meadow. Every detail has been perfected with a combination of rustic charm and high luxury, down to the high thread-count sheets, lavender-scented beauty products, and complimentary gourmet teas. The couple has great taste, Polly thinks to herself, as she runs her hand over the wooden railing, proceeding to walk down the stairs from their room on the second terrace.

The ceremony is taking place in the meadow behind the hotel property, and they see Claudia headed up that way with a bouquet of pink roses in hand, walking up from her own room on the main floor. She is in a full-length, pale yellow chiffon dress, and a wreath of wildflowers circle her head. When she sees her parents, she waves heartily, smiling.

Polly is feeling the tears already, just seeing her daughter – and she is not even the one getting married. Claudia is Tracey's maid of honor. She flew in from Las Vegas earlier in the month to get fitted for her dress and to help with last minute preparations. Luckily, Claudia has a flexible schedule these days, working as a choreographer for Cirque du Soleil. Having both children back at home in Calgary has made Polly so happy, though she knows it won't last forever.

If you told Polly ten years ago that the boisterous, blonde wild child popping champagne in Claudia's prom limousine was going to be her future daughter-in-law, she would have laughed in your face. *How ridiculous,* she would have said. *There is no way that girl will marry into our family.* But things change, and now, Polly could not have picked a better match for her only son.

Petey moved back to Calgary a couple years ago, after he and Tracey started getting serious. By then, Tracey was a regular fixture in the Young house, coming over for dinner every Sunday. Her own parents moved to Florida, retiring early, and Polly suspects, wanting to get away from the sad memories of their dead son. They are here now, for their daughter's wedding, and it is the first time they've been back to Canada in years. When Polly saw Tracey's mother, Claire, at the rehearsal dinner last night, she could see the pure sadness in the woman's eyes, still mourning for her son, his absence at his sister's wedding almost too much to bear.

"You okay?" Polly asks her daughter as she approaches in her yellow dress, pulling her into a hug and bracing her own tears. The night before, James had flown in from Toronto for the wedding, and the two had reunited cordially at the rehearsal dinner, both sneaking glances at each other throughout the night. They had lived together in Toronto for a mere six months before Claudia had an opportunity with Cirque du Soleil in Montreal, and moved away. They had broken up soon after. Then, after getting the attention of a top director within her company in Montreal, Claudia was offered a position in Las Vegas the following summer.

James remained close with Petey after the break-up, and he's here today as the couple's Best Man. He is Tracey's oldest friend, a good friend of Petey's, and the only person in the world who could possibly stand in for Brent.

Polly has always liked James. Naturally, she is delighted to see him here, looking more handsome and dignified than ever, and hopes that her daughter feels the same.

"I feel great," Claudia says to her mom, adjusting her crown of flowers and grinning widely. Polly knows this is the truth. After all, her only brother is getting married to her best friend today, which is any girl's dream. After today, she and Tracey will be as close to sisters as they could ever be.

The guests have already gathered in the meadow. It is a breathtaking, panoramic view of Buffalo Mountain, one of the largest mountains in the area, and the ground is covered in late summer wildflowers and grasses. Majestic evergreen trees drape into a border around the meadow, framing the scenery. It is so beautiful, it looks unreal.

A harpist is playing Canon in D as Polly and Peter walk down the aisle, towards Petey, who stands proudly, his chin-length dark hair slicked back and away from his face. He is wearing a bespoke black suit, white shirt, and a black tie. Next, Claudia walks down the aisle accompanied by James. They look beautiful together, Polly thinks, gazing at them longingly.

Lastly, Mr. and Mrs. Monroe walk their daughter down the aisle. Her demure lace dress has a sweetheart neckline and a fitted bodice, accentuating her svelte body and model-height. She is wearing satin ballet flats, and a long cathedral veil that flows in the wind with her pale blonde hair.

It is a sweet and simple ceremony, and within ten minutes Petey is kissing his new bride, and the new Mr. and Mrs. Young are announced to the crowd. The older Mr. and Mrs. Young are the first to their feet, rushing to their son and new daughter-in-law, with tears in their eyes.

Claudia remains back, walking slowly towards the gathering crowd, giving all the other friends and family time to congratulate the bride and groom. She will have plenty of time to spend with the new couple in the next few days, since she is not due back at work until September.

She feels someone softly bumping into her shoulder and she looks up instinctually, knowing it is James. Even after all these years apart, she knows his touch.

"Hey you," he says, his familiar eyes crinkling at her. "Beautiful wedding, huh?" There are remnants of tears in his eyes, igniting Claudia's own emotions.

"The best," she says, her eyes welling up. Before she loses it, she inches her dress off the ground and runs to catch up with the crowd. When she sees that Tracey and Petey have a free moment, she throws herself at them, crying tears of happiness for her two favorite people in the world, who have just become one family.

There is a small lake down the road from the lodge, where a white tent has been constructed for the reception. Twinkling white lights are draped over the exterior, and wooden lamps are staked into the ground, creating a lit walkway from the road to the entrance. The inside of the tent is filled with wildflowers, and candles light up every table. The heady fragrance of the flowers mixes with the natural scent of the mountains, creating an intoxicating aroma that seems to be sweeping everyone up into a night of romance.

A four-piece band is positioned beside a small dance floor, and all fifty guests are mingling around the tables, chatting and laughing.

Tracey and Petey hit the dance floor before the first course is served, laughing as they dance to a Billie Holiday song that is just a bit too fast for their feet. A few bars in, they are joined by Polly and Peter, who dance the two-step, stealing the show. The guests cheer.

James' mother and Henry are also here, and when Elizabeth shakes her head with a smile at her husband, not wanting to dance, Henry taps Peter on the shoulder, playfully cutting in. Polly looks to be rather annoyed but obliges gracefully, not missing a step. She dances up a storm with her new partner, and they switch to the foxtrot with the new song. Claudia smiles, watching her mother from across the room, sipping on a glass of chardonnay. She hadn't known her mother was such a good dancer. She had never mentioned it. *She didn't want to encourage me*, Claudia thinks with smirk.

When the song ends, Polly leaves the dance floor rather quickly, heading towards the bar to get a glass of champagne. Henry follows her, and orders a scotch. They stand side by side, each sipping their own drink.

The band switches to an even faster song, and while the groom's father hits the dance floor with enthusiasm, tapping his feet and shaking his hips to the Rolling Stones, his wife slips out of the tent for some fresh air.

Henry watches Polly leave. Glancing over at his own wife, he sees that she is focused on her son, who surprisingly, looks to be confiding in her. He wonders if it has anything to do with the striking young Claudia, who reminds Henry so much of Polly in her younger days. Henry takes the opportunity to slip outside for a cigarette. He sees Polly standing on the dock by the lake, and he makes his way over.

"Polly." She turns to him, her face exquisite in the moonlight. She has changed into a knee-length, crimson brocade dress for the evening. She has hardly aged over the years, and even her body has remained remarkably pert.

"Henry."

He lights a cigarette, and offers her one. "I don't smoke," she says in Mandarin, shaking her head.

"You did once," he says, smiling. She scowls at him, and he quickly changes his demeanor. "I'm sorry," he says. "I don't mean to be inappropriate. I just wanted to have a quick word with you, alone. I hope you don't mind."

Polly crosses her arms. "Why would I mind?" She stares at him, urging him to continue. Her expression turns mildly pleading. "This is my son's wedding. Please, don't say anything to upset me."

Henry shakes his head. "No...whatever happened between us, all those years ago, doesn't matter anymore. I have never told Peter and I never will. I'm married to Elizabeth now, and you

294

have a beautiful family. I only hope that our families can continue to be good friends."

Polly sighs. "It was all a very long time ago, Henry. So long ago, that I might have even forgotten about it, had I not intercepted that letter you sent Peter before you moved to Calgary." She eyes him sternly. "You promised you would keep your distance from Henry. I shredded that letter."

"I figured something like that happened," Henry chuckles. "Which is why I didn't seek the two of you out when I arrived in Canada. I didn't want to cause any turmoil, in case he had somehow...found out."

"Found out about what?" The sound of her husband's voice causes Polly to spin around abruptly. Her husband steps onto the dock, cigar in hand. He likely hadn't heard much of the conversation, but she feels her cheeks flame immediately.

Henry looks at Polly for a moment. For a second, she panics, thinking he is going to tell Peter about their 35-year-old secret. It seems a good opportunity to do so, if he wants to come clean once and for all. But then he blinks suddenly, like an idea has popped into his head. "I was just offering Polly a cigarette," he says. "Once upon a time, she did have a cigarette with me. I don't know if she ever told you."

"Ah," Peter says. "Yes, Polly has always had a soft spot for cigarettes. She used to smoke those thin menthols when we first came to Canada. Which makes me wonder why she detests my cigars so much."

"They don't smell the same," Polly says, moving towards her husband, placing a hand on the crook of his arm. "Cigarettes remind me of Taiwan. Everyone smoked them. Cigars make me think of old men. Besides, I haven't smoked in years." She wrinkles her nose and Peter laughs.

"Excuse me, I'm going to get back to the tent. I only came outside for some air," she says, excusing herself. She gives her husband a swift kiss on the cheek and makes her way back towards the tent. Glancing back, she sees the two aging men talking, their heads turned towards each other in polite conversation. The only two men in the world that she has ever shared a bed with.

"*Aiya*," she sighs under her breath. She steps back into the tent. Seeing her daughter across the room, sitting alone, she makes her way over and joins her, just in time for the salads to arrive.

James watches Claudia talking with her mother from the comfort of the bar. He has parked himself close to the liquor after an upsetting chat with his mother. She had asked him about Claudia, and, feeling candid, he told her what he remembered about their falling out. His mother had listened intently, but in the end, only pursed her lips and told her son what he already knew: He screwed up.

He has not seen Claudia in over four years, since she saw him off at the train station in Montreal, returning to Toronto after that strange, disastrous visit. In retrospect, had he known the wouldn't be seeing her again for four years, he would have held her a little tighter, kissed her a bit longer, and maybe, just maybe, told her how he really felt.

But hadn't she known? Or maybe she hadn't cared. Either way, it's too late. He is still doing his residency in Toronto, and plans to move back to Vancouver to start his own private practice, when he finishes. And from what he can tell from his weekly visits to her Facebook page, she is happily living in Las Vegas, of all places, and apparently doing very well for herself, working for Cirque du Soleil. Gone are the days of her following him to Toronto, not knowing what to do about her future.

He looks at her smiling face, beaming in the soft light of the tent, and he wonders how it all turned out this way. They've been like sine and cosine graphs for years, intersecting at times but riding different waves, until one day she had decided to draw a tangent and follow it far, far away.

Or had he been the one to draw the tangent? He feels his cell phone vibrate, indicating a text message. He pulls it out, and sees that Rebecca has sent him a message.

Rebecca: *I miss you.*

He taps out a quick reply to her, something along the lines of "me too." He imagines that she is having a glass of wine with Maddie at the apartment, the two women gossiping about the one thing they have in common: Him. It still irks him that the two can be such good friends. He personally could never be chummy with a man who had fucked his girlfriend.

The salads are being served, and since it is a sit-down dinner, all the guests return to their seats and the band takes a little breather, playing some mood music. James takes his seat next to Claudia, which Mrs. Young relinquishes with a smile. She moves over a few seats to where her name card is placed.

"Take care of my daughter tonight," she says to him quietly, giving him a motherly pinch on the cheek. He smiles at her and nods.

The rest of the table is seated. The bride and groom, the bride's parents, Mr. and Mrs. Young, Claudia, James, Henry, and Elizabeth, make up the head table. It is a tight fit and cozy, but soon enough, the speeches begin and people are on their feet, laughing, clapping, and sneaking bites of their meal in between all the commotion. James makes sure that Claudia's glass is always filled, that her bread has enough butter, and he even invites her to dance a couple times, though she always declines.

She saves her dances for her brother and dad, and he watches her float around the room with the important men in her life.

As the last of the guests disperse from the tent, Claudia waits around, looking exhausted. Tracey has given her the task of tipping the servers, so she pulls out a stack of small envelopes from her satin clutch bag.

James stays behind, lingering at the bar. He watches Claudia distribute the envelopes to the servers and bartenders, feeling a twinge of jealousy when an especially grateful waiter pulls her in for an enthusiastic hug. Claudia laughs, taken aback.

Her hands free of envelopes, Claudia walks back to the table to fetch her clutch. James walks over, sipping on a drink. He takes a seat. Claudia sits down next to him, letting out a long sigh.

"What a day," she says, leaning back and closing her eyes. "So tiring. But so worth it." She opens her eyes and smiles at James. Their eyes catch and she quickly looks away.

"I should get to bed, we have an early brunch tomorrow," she says, getting up and forcing a yawn. "Night James."

"Wait, Claud..." He doesn't know what he wants to say to her, but he knows he wants to say something. Anything.

She turns back towards him and shakes her head, looking wistful. "No, James," she says softly. "Let's just call it a night, okay?" He watches her walk away, her backside a vision that is all too familiar.

His flight is scheduled for the next afternoon, since he could only get a couple days off. Petey and Tracey see him off to the shuttle bus that picks him up in front of the hotel lobby. It will take him straight to the Calgary Airport. His mom and Henry left a few hours earlier, after brunch.

He gives both friends hugs goodbye, congratulating them again, and promising to visit soon. He takes his time getting onto the bus, hoping that Claudia will turn up. Tracey sees him buying time, and she leans over to him, and speaks quietly in his ear.

"Sorry Jamesy," she says. "She left after brunch to run some errands in town. I'll tell her you said bye." She pulls away, giving James a squeeze on the arm, and a sympathetic smile.

James nods, stepping onto the bus. The door closes behind him and he sits in the second row, staring out the window, as the bus pulls away.

The bus stops at a red light at the base of the mountain, and James catches a glimpse of familiar dark brown hair. She is hovering by an ice cream stand, buying a scoop, pointing out which flavor she wants. The light turns green, and the bus pulls past her. As James looks back, he sees that she has gotten a scoop of mint chocolate chip to match her minty green blouse. For a moment, she looks up, and he thinks she sees him. He puts his hand up in a wave against the window, but she just keeps licking her ice cream cone, impassive. He gets the sudden urge to make the driver stop, so he can jump out, but his phone buzzes and he immediately thinks of Rebecca. Sure enough, when he pulls it out, her red hair and pretty face fill the screen, signaling her number. He presses the ignore button and stuffs the phone back into this pocket, and closes his eyes, cursing himself, feeling like a jerk. *Fuck me.*

Rebecca is at the airport in Toronto to pick him up, and she runs to him, hugging him as if he's been gone for months, rather than a couple days. "I missed you soooo much," she coos. He smiles at her, kissing her decently on the cheek. She had been at the hospital all weekend, unable to join him at the wedding. Not that he had asked her to come.

They take the expressway into the city, keeping the windows open in the BMW. Rebecca doesn't have a car, and James is generous with his things, so they share his car, apartment, and pretty much everything else that he owns. She even wears his clothes sometimes, since she is tall, and favors his sweaters over her own. When she wears them, James can't help but think about how much cuter Claudia had looked in his clothes – like a little girl borrowing her big brother's clothes.

They enter the dark, quiet apartment, and James flicks on the lights. There is a basket of fruit on the counter, and he grabs an apple, rubs it against his shirt and bites into it, starving.

Rebecca goes into the living room, and turns on the television while he wheels his suitcase into the bedroom with his free hand. He joins her on the couch after a few minutes, grabbing the remote from her and switching the channel to watch the news.

"Hey, I was watching that," she complains. "It's the final rose tonight." James rolls his eyes. He can't stand the dumb reality shows she watches. They're always about good-looking people trying to screw each other or screw each other over.

"I can't believe you watch that garbage," he says, chidingly. "It's all scripted, you know."

She shrugs. "It's entertainment. I don't care."

Throwing the remote down onto the coffee table, he gets up from the couch, goes to the kitchen, and opens the freezer. He is craving something sweet and the apple didn't do the trick. He frowns. They have no ice cream in the house. He realizes with a start that they never have ice cream in the house.

"Why don't we have any ice cream?" James wonders out loud.

Rebecca hears him. "I hate ice cream," she says, her eyes glued to the screen, which has now been switched back to her show.

"How can you hate ice cream? Who hates ice cream?" James mutters under his breath. She doesn't answer, perhaps because she hasn't heard him. It's still early, so he grabs his keys and tells her he's going out to get some food. He walks a couple blocks to the Haagen Dazs and gets himself a scoop of chocolate on a waffle cone.

Walking home in the humid, late summer heat, he passes by the Starbucks where he gets his coffee every morning. When Claudia lived with him, she would make him coffee in the mornings, but since she moved out all those years ago, he has gotten in the habit of getting a Grande Caffe Americano on a daily basis. He sees an Asian girl with glasses on, sitting by herself at a table by the window, and he does a double take, thinking that it's Claudia. Remembering that she's still in Alberta and in fact has not set foot in Toronto for years, he heads back to the apartment feeling stupid.

Rebecca is in the same spot on the couch when he gets upstairs. He finishes his cone, washes his sticky hands in the sink and stands at the counter, staring at his girlfriend. She is completely oblivious, enraptured with the shitty television show. He waits for a commercial break before he speaks.

"Rebecca," he says. Her attention is focused on a talking teddy bear in a laundry detergent commercial. He clears his throat loudly. "Rebecca, we have to talk."

Rebecca slowly drags her attention from the screen to look at him.

"Did you fuck her?"

When he doesn't answer, she turns her attention back to the TV.

"No," James says. "It wasn't like that."

"But you still love her. Right? You want to be with her? Maddie told me all about your little love affair with that Asian chick. It was her brother's wedding, wasn't it?" She says the word Asian like it's something disgusting. This pisses James off more than anything.

"You don't know what you're fucking talking about," James says. "We barely talked. I saw her, that's it. Yeah, I still love her. I always will. But I don't know what I want. But I do know that this," he signals between the two of them with his hand, and then making his tone slightly gentler, "this is wrong, Bec. We're not supposed to be together. You don't – you don't even like ice cream." He knows this is a petty thing to point out but for some reason, the fact bothers him immensely.

Rebecca snorts, flipping her red hair over her shoulder. "You're an asshole, James. You know what? Maddie warned me. She told me you fucked off on her to be with that bitch. And now you're doing it to me." She says this, shaking her head, like she should have known it was coming.

"Call me whatever you want," James says. "I am an asshole, you're right. Sorry about that. And I don't know what kind of fucked up friendship you've got going on with Maddie but she is full of shit. We broke up. It had nothing to do with Claudia."

"Ah, *Claudia*," Rebecca says. "To hear you say her name. It's a fucking anomaly." She gets to her feet, heading to the bedroom. "Don't worry about breaking up with me, James. Consider yourself dumped. I'll be out by Friday."

True to her word, Rebecca packs up her things, and James is living alone again by the next weekend. He did have to deal with two ex-girlfriends glaring at him while they dragged Rebecca's things out the door, but on Saturday morning, when he wakes up in his bed and sees a single strand of strawberry red hair on the white pillowcase beside him, he feels frighteningly fine. He strips down the bed and throws everything into the washing machine.

He doesn't pine for Rebecca, or check his cell phone regularly, hoping for a text message from her. In fact, he hopes he doesn't run into her ever again, feeling more than anything, ashamed for stringing her along.

Claudia returns to Las Vegas a week after the wedding, resuming her work on Cirque's newest show. She has partnered with another choreographer who is an acrobatics expert, and together, they've created one of the most popular shows on the Strip. She feels alive and gratified every moment she spends with the production, and almost all her hours are spent with the company.

She lives in a one-storey home, in a suburb a few exits down the 215, east of Las Vegas Boulevard. It's a buyer's market, and with her generous salary, she is able to afford quite a luxurious house, complete with a heated pool out back and a Japanese rock garden. The floors inside are all oak, and her furniture is leather, Italian, and chic.

Seeing James at Petey's wedding had thrown her off. It had taken her a while to get over him, after he broke up with her. It had come as a painful surprise; she'd thought they were strong enough to outlast the distance. But finding that picture on his Facebook page that Maddie took, changed everything. It broke her trust.

And she would even have let him explain himself. She could have even accepted the fact that he was going to be friends with her. But then she had received that text message.

He had broken up with her in a text message.

Just thinking about it makes Claudia angry, even now, four years later. He had called the next day, but had nothing to say. Claudia had gone easy on him, simply hanging up the phone. She didn't talk to him again after that.

Seeing him in Banff after all this time was beyond painful. It was cruel. He'd looked like he always had: Sweet, strong, and handsome. When their eyes met and they looked at each other, her heart broke. *He has a girlfriend,* she had silently reminded herself, over and over. She'd seen the pictures on his Facebook.

She kept her distance. They had walked down the aisle together, sat next to each other at dinner, but she had kept her head turned away from him, and refused every dance. He seemed eager to connect again, perhaps to apologize for how things had ended between them. But she didn't see the point. Knowing he would be leaving the day after the wedding, she conveniently ran some errands after brunch, dropping off things at the dry cleaner and returning vases to the florist in town. Walking back to the car, she had seen an ice cream parlor and bought a cone to cheer herself up. Mint chocolate. Her favorite.

The Banff Airporter Shuttle had passed by as she stood by the shop licking her cone. She guessed James was on it, but she couldn't see through the tinted windows. As it drove away, part of her wished that it would suddenly stop, and like it happened in the movies, James would rush out of the bus and run to her, scoop her up into a big hug, lifting her off her feet, spin her around, and tell her he loved her and that they were meant to be together. Her ice cream would get crushed between them, and they would laugh, not caring, with tears of love in their eyes.

But the bus had kept going, taking its passengers to the airport on time. And she had just stood there, licking her cone, while a single, pathetic tear dripped down her face.

After a long day of rehearsals on the Strip, Claudia drives home to her gated neighborhood, pulling into her three-car garage. It's kind of a waste of space since she only has one car, but she figures having room for three cars makes it look like more people live there. There are a lot of break-ins in Vegas, and even with the security gate, she always arms the house with a security system and double bolts her doors.

She has lost weight since moving to Las Vegas, always being on the go and not bothering to cook for herself. Most of her meals are eaten out at restaurants, so when she pulls open the door of her giant stainless steel fridge, there is little to choose from. She shuts it with a pout, opens the freezer instead, and pulls out a carton of Chunky Monkey. After softening it in the microwave for seven seconds, she eats a few bites directly from the carton, taking it with her to her bedroom.

Claudia owns a television but never turns it on. Instead, for background noise, she docks her iPhone into her Sony system and turns on Sigur Ros while she undresses. She pulls off her tight black skinny jeans, black t-shirt, and black blazer, and hangs them up in her closet next to their other black companions. She has an entire wardrobe of black that she wears for work.

She throws on an old t-shirt and a pair of yoga pants, plops onto her bed with the ice cream, and opens her laptop. Her phone rings, lighting up with Cory's face.

When she was with James, Cory had respectfully kept his distance. Then, Claudia moved from Montreal to Las Vegas for yet another job, and she had almost forgotten about her DJ friend. He showed up in town a few months ago, waiting backstage for her after one of her shows. He held a single yellow rose and she was shocked with his new look: Short hair, cropped stylishly close to his head, fitted grey slacks, and a tailored dress shirt. Not quite the Bob Marley look-alike she had known in Toronto. The new Cory was polished, well dressed, and downright hot.

He'd scored a position working as the Director for a huge nightclub in Vegas, responsible for overseeing all the music, DJs and celebrities that play there. A gig like this is like hitting the jackpot for a struggling DJ. The best part is that Cory even gets to spin, once a week, on his own accord.

That night after the show, they went out to celebrate their reunion and got pretty wasted. They were sitting in a booth at a swanky bar on the Strip, and Cory turned to Claudia, eyes glassy with drink, and in a few slurred sentences, confessed his affections for her. But they were drunk, and Claudia hadn't brought it up again when they were sober. A part of her though, was excited by the idea of being with Cory.

Apparently, Claudia wasn't the only one who approved of Cory's good looks. After he told her he was sweet on her, he also started meeting more women. Before Claudia had a chance to cash in on a date, Cory was seeing three girls a week on a regular basis, meeting most of them at his club. Instead, he and Claudia became close friends again. Best buddies.

Claudia goes on a few dates, here and there. Her friends in the industry are always trying to set her up with local Vegas men. The rich, successful ones who want to settle down are usually in their mid-forties, divorced, and have partied a bit too hard over the years. And they are all looking for a trophy wife, which is something Claudia finds appalling. The men closer to her age usually work as bartenders or club promoters, and they always assume that she does as well. And she can't count how many times she's been asked if she's a stripper, when she says she works in the entertainment industry.

She and Cory have started hiking Mount Charleston every weekend on a weekly basis. It's about a thirty-minute drive north, and the climate can be up to twenty degrees cooler there, which is a relief in the summer. Claudia likes getting away from the lights and action, and seeing trees and snow makes her feel more at home. Never in a million years would she have expected to miss snow, but she does. On these hikes, they talk about work, music, family, and once in a while, she indulges him with an entertaining story about an overly-tan hotel executive or slimy poker player that she's been recently set up with. He'll laugh, tell her she's too good for those guys, and run ahead a few paces, challenging her to keep up.

Lately, they have been seeing each other during the week, too. Sometimes they'll just cook dinner together and watch a movie afterwards, and other times they'll go out to dinner, or meet friends for drinks at a lounge. Claudia knows that some of their friends assume that they're dating, or at least sleeping together.

It's easy with Cory. She doesn't have to make an effort, she knows what to expect, and he's great company. But sometimes, she wants more than just company.

Claudia takes a sharp inhale and answers the phone. "Hey Cory," she breathes out.

"Hey beautiful, how was the trip?" She can hear that he's driving, with the car on speakerphone.

"It was lovely. The wedding was perfect. And I couldn't have chosen a better bride for my brother." Claudia says this with a smile, picturing her brother and Tracey on their honeymoon right now, in the Maldives, walking hand-in-hand in the shallow blue water.

"Awesome, good to hear. Did you see uh...you know? The ex?"

Claudia's heart picks up at the mention of James. She fakes a nonchalant tone. "James? Yeah, I did. We didn't talk much though. He has a girlfriend now and things are kind of weird between us. He only stayed for like, a day, anyway. Busy doctor and all," she says, a mark of sarcasm in her voice.

"Yeah. I get it. Whatcha doin'? Can I come over?"

"Uh..." Claudia looks around, her room in disarray. She hasn't had a chance to unpack from her trip yet. "I'm probably gonna crash soon but I need to clean up first. Maybe we can have lunch tomorrow instead?"

"Come on, I haven't seen you in over a week. I can help you clean. I'm good at it." He sounds so eager that Claudia relents, telling him to come on over.

He arrives within thirty minutes, with a bottle of Malbec in hand.

"Ooooh my favorite," Claudia says, looking at the label and rewarding him with a smile. "And here I was thinking I'd only be eating ice cream for dinner. Ice cream and wine is definitely a better plan."

"I would have brought you some food if you told me you hadn't eaten yet," Cory says softly, giving her a friendly kiss on the cheek. His eyes are full of concern. "You can't be skippin' meals, girl. You're gonna be thin as a rail." His light green eyes dance over her body. He pinches her on the waist. "Too skinny," he teases.

Claudia smirks. "That's not exactly motivation, Cory. Most girls want to be thin as a rail." She uncorks the wine and pours them each a glass. She hasn't bothered to fix her hair or change out of her comfy clothes and he doesn't seem to notice. They each take a glass of wine and Cory follows her into the bedroom to assess the damage.

"Whoa, looks like Hurricane Claudia came through here...." He says, looking from the clothes on the floor to the unmade bed and piles and piles of books around the room. Claudia does most of her research on the computer, but she still likes to get inspiration from heavy books filled with beautiful photographs. She always has at least ten books on loan from the public library.

"Yeah, it's my secret weakness. I'm clean but extremely messy. It used to drive James nuts." She frowns, not knowing why she brought him up. "That was weird," she mutters to herself out loud.

Cory cocks an eyebrow. "Got the ex on the mind, eh?" He has never lost his Canadian aphorisms, and Claudia loves him for it.

She sits down on the floor to sort through her exploded suitcase. "I don't really want to talk about it, but, it was strange seeing him after all this time. Anyway." She shakes her head with a smile, as if getting him out of her head. She turns to look at Cory. "Thanks for the company. I hate cleaning." She picks up her yellow Maid of Honor dress and throws it into a pile for dry-cleaning.

Cory is stacking up her books in a corner of the room. Claudia doesn't have a lot of furniture; she'd read somewhere that it's good *feng shui* to keep the bedroom simple with as little furniture as possible. The result of this is that she doesn't have enough surfaces to keep things on, and a lot of her stuff ends up on the floor.

The stack of books reaches Cory's eye level and they are leaning precariously against the wall. "Should I keep going?" He asks with a chuckle, holding up a hefty book of works by Degas.

"Two piles," Claudia says. "And could you separate the ones that have a library barcode on them? I have to return them in the morning. Sorry..." She sticks out her bottom lip to show him just how sorry she is.

With Cory's help, the room is quite tidy after only ten minutes. They go back to the kitchen to refresh their wine and plan on watching a short documentary. Claudia is turning on Netflix when she feels him beside her. He hands her a new glass of wine.

"So, I've been thinking," he says, clearing his throat. He turns to her, leaning against the back of the couch, looking nervous. "Remember that...thing I told you last year when I first got to Vegas? The night I surprised you at the show and I got really drunk?" He looks embarrassed.

Claudia rolls her eyes at him. "I remember. We don't have to talk about this. You were drunk and didn't know what you were talking about."

"No, I did know." He says, taking a sip of his wine. "I knew exactly what I was talking about. I thought you would have brought it up the next time I saw you, but..." he cracks his neck nervously from side to side – "You didn't. I was sort of glad but also sort of..." he trails off, looking at her. "Why didn't you bring it up?"

Shrugging, she looks him in the eyes. They are the color of moss, hinting at brown, with glints of hazel. "I didn't think it mattered. And it doesn't. You've been a dating machine ever since you got here. Don't tell me you've been hung up on that one conversation." She rolls her eyes and crosses her arms, looking away uncomfortably.

It's Cory's turn to shrug. His shoulders are wide, and his arms and chest fill out his white shirt. "No, not exactly hung up, but I've thought about it. Part of what excited me about moving to Vegas was that you were here. I wasn't expecting anything and I'm really happy we're friends, but...come on Claud. We've been beating around the bush with each other for like what, five years now?"

Claudia gives a little scoff, taken aback. "Beating around the bush? Is that what we've been doing? I just thought we were being friends, thank you very much." She can feel her ears turning red. "This whole time we've been friends you've just been wanting to get into my pants? You could have fooled me." She's pissed. What kind of game is this?

Cory's green eyes go wide with panic. "No, no no no.." he stutters quickly. "That's not what I meant. I just – " He shakes his head. "I'm really bad at this. I was just wondering if you wanted anything more. I don't know." He takes another sip of his wine and glances around anxiously, making a face. "Do you have any beer? I can't drink this. I need a beer."

She gets up and walks over to the fridge without a word, thankful for a reason to leave the room. She pulls out a Heineken, popping the top for him. He has followed her to the kitchen, and he takes the proffered beer, pouring a long slug into his mouth. "Thanks," he says. "Sorry, I can't take myself seriously sipping red wine so I don't think you can either." He takes another slug of his beer and leans forward on the counter, placing the bottle down.

"I didn't mean for it to come out that way. We're friends, for sure. Always have been. I guess hearing you talk about your ex – it just sparked something in me. I think I felt a bit jealous." He ducks his head, chuckling to himself.

Claudia takes her wine and moves to the center island of the kitchen, taking a seat on a stool. "There's no reason for you to be jealous," she snaps. "Because for one, we're just friends." She points between herself and Cory so he knows what she means by *we're*. "And for two, it's not like that between me and James. He's moved on. Way on. I wouldn't be surprised if he marries his girlfriend soon. She's a redhead, you know?" *A pretty redhead at that*, she thinks. *And a fucking doctor.* Thinking about James and his perfect new girlfriend makes her want to go hide under a bed and die.

"Hmm, nope, redhead, didn't know that," Cory says, giving her a small smile. "So, you're really over this guy? He'll go marry his ginger girl and you're going to be cool with it?"

Keeping a straight face, Claudia nods. Even though her insides are betraying her as she speaks, wrenching in pain at the thought, she is able to keep a calm façade. "Yup. Totally cool. They can go make a bunch of beautiful little redheaded children and..." She trails off and feels a frog in her throat, emotion about to explode from her face in the form of tears. "I've moved on," she says finally.

"Good." Cory steps toward her, eyes flashing. "So it wouldn't be bad if I did...this..." He leans forward and kisses her on the lips. "Right?"

She pulls back, shaking her head. "No..."

"No bad? Or just no?"

"No...I don't know." She bites her lip, looking at him, eyes welling with tears. "I don't want to lose you as a friend. You mean a lot to me." She touches his smooth cheek, tracing his jawline with her finger. *What am I doing...*

"You won't lose me," he says, moving forward again, this time kissing her more urgently. He smells sweet and musky, and his mouth is cool from the fresh beer. He pulls back one more time. "I can give you more time, if you want. I can wait."

She doesn't answer, just looks at him, with eyes wide, and tears on the verge of spilling out.

"Tell me what you want." He searches her face. They've known each other for years, but he has never looked at her this way.

Claudia keeps staring at him. She doesn't want him. She wants a lot of things, but he is not one of them.

But for some reason, she feels herself nod yes. She lets him kiss her a third time, because it makes her feel a little less shitty about the other things she is feeling. She kisses him back, losing herself, letting him gently push her against the counter, lifting her up by the hips to sit. She remembers being in another kitchen in another time, being lifted up in the same way, and she kisses him even harder, to forget. His mouth is insistent, and with her eyes squeezed shut, keeping her tears at bay, she finds that she is starting to enjoy the kiss.

Remnants of James are falling away, like old paint. They are being replaced by the warm strokes of a new, albeit familiar, man.

- 16 - Seven Months Later

"Who the hell is Cory?" Peter bites down hard on his cigar, near-shouting at his poor wife. "I've never even heard of him. How could this be happening? Is she pregnant?"

Polly sighs. "No Peter, she is not pregnant. He asked her to marry him, and she said yes. They have known each other since she lived in Toronto, when she worked for that small theater company. She told us about him a long time ago." She is also not at all happy about the news, but the last thing she wants right now is for her husband to lose his temper and push their daughter away. Who knows how far gone she is already.

Peter chews pensively on his cigar. Claudia; his baby girl. She is in her late-twenties now, but it's just not right that she is getting married to a man they have never met. And he works at a nightclub, for Christ's sake.

He gets up to walk down the hallway of their immaculate house, footsteps echoing against the wood floor.

"Where are you going?" His wife calls after him. "We're not done talking!"

"He didn't even ask for my permission!" He yells, closing the door to his office. He doesn't mean to take it out on his wife, but she is being a bit too diplomatic about the whole situation for his liking. She's always been strict with Claudia – why is she stopping now?

He sits behind his desk, staring at the phone. He wants to call his daughter, and demand that she change her mind. She is making a mistake. If this Cory were *The One*, she would have told them all about him before now, and perhaps even brought him home for a weekend. She has always been like that with her serious boyfriends. Well, granted, she has only ever had one serious boyfriend.

Peter remembers the first time he met James. The boy came over on a motorcycle, for God's sake, expecting to take his teenaged daughter out. He had more or less laughed in the young boy's face, and sent them walking instead. Claudia hadn't cared to hide James from them, and he hadn't exactly been an angel. So why start hiding now? There must be something very wrong with this Cory guy.

There's this thing Peter does sometimes, and he's not proud of it. He fires up his computer and pulls up Google. *Claudia Young Cirque du Soleil*, he types. It auto-fills, since he has done the search several times in the past year or so. Claudia's Facebook profile is one of the first links, and he clicks on it, bringing up her public page. He doesn't personally have a Facebook account, but he knows it's what young people do these days, and it does come in handy for him, when he wants to snoop on his children. He clicks on the tab marked "Photos".

The first picture is a profile shot of Claudia. She is smiling, wearing sunglasses, and resting her chin on her hand. So beautiful, his little pearl. The second photo is more of what he's looking for. She's with him. Cory. Undoubtedly, it's Cory. They're holding hands, standing on a sandy beach, in California somewhere, he figures. He's dark-skinned, with short hair. Nice eyes. Good-looking. He's not sure what he was expecting, looks-wise anyway. He didn't expect him to be black, of course. Is this why she has been hiding him from them?

In the next photo, she is with him again. It's a candid shot of them, sitting together at a table in a restaurant. Her face is turned away from him, staring out a window. She looks to be a million miles away. He is staring at the side of her head longingly. *Look at me please*, he seems to be saying.

The next photo is an actual photograph that has been scanned in. Peter sees that his daughter-in-law, Tracey, uploaded it a few weeks ago. *The good old days*, says the caption. It's from the girls' high school prom, and they are in a large group, standing in the lobby of a hotel. Claudia has her arm looped through Tracey's, and Tracey is leaning against her brother Brent. To Claudia's left, is James. He has his arm around her protectively, and she is beaming at the camera. The rest of their friends surround them, draped over each other, smiling. A group of high school kids with the whole world in front of them.

He doesn't know what he's looking for. Maybe some reassurance, that she's not making a big mistake, or some proof that she is. But a picture is just single moment in time. It tells nothing.

The photograph Henry took of him and Polly on the night of their engagement, is sitting on his desk. It was snapped only an hour before he proposed to Polly. She was a stunning girl in her twenties, a young woman streaked with the depths of loss and sorrow. Her beauty was raw and ignited with tenacity.

He takes the framed photo in his hands, wiping away the dust with his right thumb, and studies his young wife. She's smiling, but there's a hint of annoyance in her eyes. She probably wanted to get on with the evening, instead of wasting time taking pictures. She likely knew that the proposal was coming.

But it only took only a few seconds, and he couldn't say no to Henry Cooper. They had met in New York City years before, at his brother Lee's wedding. Peter had been dating a girl named Rose then - a cute, chubby, blonde-haired, blue-eyed beauty from Knoxville that he had met in his sophomore year at the University of Tennessee. She became pregnant, and Peter panicked.

He remembers he wasn't himself at the wedding in New York. His mouth was dry, and sweat beaded from his brow as he couldn't shake the image of himself, barely a man, as the father of the child that had begun to grow inside of Rose's belly. He cared for her, but he was not in love with her. And neither of their families approved. It was the seventies, and a Southern Belle with a "Chinaman" was just plain unusual to the average person.

Henry and Peter had met at the hotel bar, where the reception was taking place. Over cognac, Peter told Henry about his predicament, feeling bold from the alcohol, and needing someone to confide in. He had spoken to Rose earlier on the phone that day, and she had finally told him that she wasn't going to keep the baby, and didn't know what to do.

Henry knew what to do, and he agreed to help Peter. He arranged everything, kept it under wraps, and a week later, Rose took a bus up to New York City. The procedure was quick and she had recovered in a hotel room at one of the Coopers' hotels. Afterwards, she took an airplane home to Tennessee.

Peter never saw Rose again, and didn't hear from her either, unless you count the curt letter waiting at his apartment when he returned, asking him to stay away. Not only did Peter stay away from Rose, he continued to stay away from troublesome blondes from there on out.

But he and Henry thus began a friendship that was solid from the start. To this day, Henry is the only one who knows about Rose and the abortion. A secret like this made them close like brothers, even though they saw each other only once or twice a year at times, and came from such different backgrounds.

The day he received his mother's letter, accusing Henry and Polly of having an affair, he had crumpled it up in his hand, threw it in the fire, and pretended he hadn't read it.

But, Peter is not a stupid man. He loved Henry. And he was in love with Polly. He knew they went to the Ball together. He had arranged it, after all, feeling guilty for being away in America for so long, and wanting to make both his friend and future bride happy.

In the letter, his mother had written about the Ball. Polly was drunk, she reported. She became sick and left early, and Henry offered to take her home. Apparently Peter's mother had been concerned, so she followed, and witnessed them sneaking away towards a desolate wing of the Grand Hotel. That was all she saw, but it was suspicious enough. And his mother had always looked down on Polly.

But Peter's father liked Polly very much. She was beautiful, fair-skinned, and her late father had been a General in the army. Congressman Young approved of the match wholeheartedly, and Peter's mother was shushed when she tried to voice her disregard for the girl. Not surprisingly, she never mentioned anything about her suspicions to her husband. Over the years, it seems she forgot about it, and Peter never heard about it again.

Over the years, Peter had thought to bring it up with Polly. He has never doubted Polly's love for him, but there have been times when he just wanted to clear the air. He blames himself for being away for so long, engaged to a girl he hardly knew, expecting her to be waiting for him when he finally came back. But he never brought it up with her. He kept his head in the sand.

When Henry reappeared in their lives years later, at Claudia and James' graduation dinner, Peter saw Polly's reaction. Up until this point, he had never been sure of his mother's accusation. But now he was.

But it had been so long ago. And here was his old friend, back in his life after a thirty-year disappearance. Surely they could just all get along and pretend like nothing happened. And that's what they did. He got Henry back, he still had Polly, and to make things even more splendid, Henry was now married to his true love, Elizabeth.

He had seen Henry and Polly standing by the dock at his son's wedding, talking. He hadn't been spying; he had just wanted to go outside and smoke his cigar. He felt a twinge of jealousy when he approached them, but when he saw Polly's look of relief at his approach, he was immediately self-assured.

There just hasn't ever been a good enough reason to bring up the uncomfortable subject.

Until now.

Peter believes that if one does not conquer his demons, he will pass them on to his children. And while this secret has not caused any heartache or regret as yet, it is a demon nonetheless.

He picks up the phone to make two phone calls. The first, he makes to Henry, inviting him to lunch.

The second he makes to his daughter, but she does not pick up and it goes to her voicemail.

"Claudia," he says into the phone, recording a message. "It's your old man. Give me a call back. I have something important to tell you."

He hangs up, and leaves his office to find his wife. Henry is coming over for lunch, and he would like for her to join them.

Henry arrives with a fragrant pineapple from the local farmer's market. Peter smiles, nodding his thanks to his friend. Pineapples are good luck and make the house smell wonderful;

Polly will be delighted. He silently applauds his friend for never coming over empty-handed.

Polly is in the kitchen setting the table for four. "Henry," she says, greeting their guest with a brusque smile. She glances behind him and sees only Peter. "Where's Elizabeth?" She asks in English. "Will she be joining us?"

"No," Peter chimes in quickly. He switches to Mandarin. "Just three of us," he says.

Polly nods, giving her husband a raised eyebrow, taking one place setting away. "Please, sit. The food is almost ready." She motions to the table and the men take their seats as instructed.

Peter's doctor has him on a Mediterranean diet to help lower his cholesterol, so Polly has made a quick meal of sea bass, asparagus, rice, and a colorful salad on the side. They eat slowly. Peter's eyes are on his plate, enjoying his fish. Polly and Henry glance at each other cautiously, cutting up their food into small bite-sized pieces.

Finally, Peter clears his throat, wiping his mouth. He makes an appreciative sound. "Delicious," he says, smiling at his wife.

"Now that you've enjoyed your meal, Peter, what's going on?" Polly's hands are on her lap, holding steady. She stares at her husband for a response.

Peter takes a sip of white wine and refills everyone else's glass. Gently, he places the bottle back down on the table. "I wanted to talk to you both, because I have something important to tell you," he says.

Polly's hands shoot to her mouth, gasping. "Are you sick?"

"No, Polly. I'm not sick. I am quite well, despite all the cigars I smoke," he says, winking at her.

Polly's mouth is a straight line. "Then what is it?"

Peter takes a deep breath in. "I thought it was time I finally told you," he says. "That I know."

Henry stops chewing and swallows what he has in his mouth. He looks at Peter. "What are you talking about Peter? What do you know?"

"I know about the two of you."

Polly's eyebrows shoot up, in surprise. "Is this a joke?" She remains seated but her hands are shaking.

"Calm down, Polly." Peter pats his wife's hand comfortingly. "I know that a very long time ago, something happened between the two of you. I don't know what happened, and I don't care to know, but I know. It's been so long, and we are all getting quite old now. There is no use in keeping petty secrets between us." Peter takes a long sip of his wine. His wife is looking at him with what can only be described as seething anger. She pulls her hand away from him.

"I'm sorry to bring it up like this. I've always known. My mother..." he looks up slightly to pay his respects to her in heaven "...she wrote me a letter. I didn't pay much attention to it at the time, but even then, I knew. I chose to keep quiet."

Henry speaks up, though he is looking down uncomfortably. "I should have said something. But it only happened once –"

"Ah – I don't want to hear about it," Peter says, gruffly, eyeing his friend. "I just wanted to clear the air. We don't need to dig up old skeletons. Polly and I are happily married now, and you with Elizabeth. Let's just leave it at that."

Polly's eyes are wet with tears. Without a word, she leaves the table and goes upstairs to her bedroom. She is so embarrassed. And she is angry that Peter would put her in such an awkward situation. How dare he! And he has known all these years, and kept it to himself? What kind of man let's another man – a friend, for that matter – bed his wife, and remain cordial with him?

She hears the men's voices downstairs, talking. Henry is awkwardly apologizing, and Peter is telling him again and again to leave it alone. Eventually she hears the chairs scraping, the men getting up, and their footsteps heading to the patio door. She moves to the bedroom window, to watch them outside. Henry lights up a cigarette, and, to Polly's surprise, Peter takes one too.

Furious, she cranks open the window wide enough to stick her head out. "Peter!" She shouts frantically. Both heads turn to her in surprise. "Put that cigarette out right now!"

Peter's mouth curls up slightly, but he does as she says, and makes a show of bending down to stamp out the cigarette on the side of the porch. Polly pulls her head back in, but leaves the window open. She hears the men talking quietly about business, current events, even chuckling here and there. Astounded, Polly shakes her head. How can they just go back to the way things were?

Henry leaves soon after, and Peter comes to find her in their large bathroom, soaking in the Jacuzzi, reading on her Kindle. It was an early birthday present from Claudia, and she has been reading incessantly ever since she received it two weeks ago.

Careful not to drop her new favorite gadget into the water, she places it on a towel to the side and looks up, which is a silent invitation for Peter to enter the bathroom. He comes in and perches on the side of the tub, looking at his wife.

Her barely gray hair is tied up in a loose bun, held in place by a butterfly clip. Her skin is glistening with moisture from the bath, and her cheeks are rosy from the heat. Her eyes are tattooed with eyeliner so she looks perpetually perfect, and at this moment, her pretty, plump lips are turned down in a frown.

"You knew!" She starts on him. "You knew this whole time, and you let me make a fool of myself, thinking I had kept it a secret from you, to spare you. And you don't even care!" She splashes the water angrily. It is the last part that really makes her mad.

"Of course I care," he says calmly. "I did care. Had I been in Taipei when I received my mother's letter, I would have probably come over to your Godparents' apartment and demanded an explanation. Then I would have gone and punched Henry in the face." He laughs, causing Polly's frown to deepen even more.

He continues. "But I wasn't in Taipei. I was in America, and I had been away for a long time. I left you alone. I was thinking that it would be difficult, bringing you with me to start our lives while I hadn't yet settled myself. I should have taken you with me."

"So it's acceptable that I...was unfaithful to you?" Polly whispers, flummoxed. "Peter, that is absurd."

"No, it's not acceptable. But it was in the seventies, and I accepted it a long time ago. Today, you are my wife, we are married, we have two grown children, and...I love you." Peter looks away as he says the words. He does not often say those three words.

Polly is silent for a while. "It meant nothing," she says carefully. "I was young, curious, and seeking adventure. I wanted so badly for you to come home and marry me, so we could begin our own adventure. I became impatient." She looks down into the bath suds, tears welling up again in her eyes.

"I never even thought about him again," she says, fiercely. "When you came back, I was yours completely."

He nods. "I know that."

She looks up at him, still perplexed. "So, why now? We could have kept on the way we were. Why did you dig up this grave?"

Peter sighs. "I had to," he says. "Just in case we passed on any demons."

"Claudia," Polly says, understanding at once. He nods.

She gets up out of the water, dripping wet, and wraps herself around him, making all his clothes wet. He barks in surprise, but doesn't pull away. He turns his head to kiss her, and she runs her fingers through his short, salt-and-pepper hair.

He pulls a towel from a nearby rack and wraps it around his wife. She lets him rub her dry. He takes her hand and leads her out of the bathroom and into their shared bedroom, not bothering to drain the water.

Claudia cringes with worry, hearing her father's voice on the phone. She should have told Cory to call and ask him for permission, first. At the very least, she should have taken him home to meet her parents. Cory has never even met Petey or Tracey.

But it all happened so fast. After Petey's wedding, coming home to an empty house had been awful. Cory's presence was like a bandage, keeping the tears in and holding her together, even though on the inside, she was a complete mess. If it weren't for him, she imagines she would have completely fallen apart.

Eventually, it just made sense, being with him. After that night in the kitchen, they began spending all their weekends and evenings together, and before she knew what was happening, she was showing up at his gigs at the club, and he'd wait for her after the show every night to take her to dinner. They became the ultimate Vegas couple. And on New Years' Eve, alone on the sand in Newport Beach, after only four months of dating, Cory asked her to marry him.

She didn't tell her parents right away. She couldn't. And Cory didn't push her, though he did tell his own mother, who came out for a weekend visit, and whom Claudia absolutely adored.

It is now almost Spring, and they've been engaged for three months. She finally worked up the nerve to tell her mother over the weekend, and it was one of the most uncomfortable conversations they've ever had. She knows her mom has been holding out for her and James to get back together, so she wasn't surprised by her reaction.

Or, lack of reaction, that is. After hearing her daughter's news, her mom had stayed completely silent. Through the phone, Claudia could hear her drumming her fingernail on the marble countertop at home in Calgary.

Finally, she spoke, and she asked Claudia one thing: What about James?

James. Claudia deleted him from her Facebook shortly after she and Cory got together. She didn't want to witness any more of his life, or complicate her life even more. She had already come to terms with the fact that he would always hold a sore place in her heart, and she was just going to have to deal with it.

She replays her father's voice message. It sounds even more urgent this time around. Cory is at work, and she has the night off, so she's home alone. She dials her parents' number. Her dad picks up on the third ring.

Before she can say anything, he asks her to come home for a visit. Again, he says that he has something important to tell her. She asks if she should bring Cory, and he says it's up to her.

Claudia hangs up, scared. What if he's sick? She opens her laptop and books a plane ticket to Calgary, leaving the next day. She packs a suitcase, calls work, and texts Cory with the news. He insists that he should come along, but she tells him not to.

Cory comes over at two in the morning, after a long night at the club. They don't live together yet, but he's able to let himself in with the spare key she gave him. He wakes her up with a kiss, and she can see the hurt on his face already. He asks again if he should go with her to Calgary, to meet her family. He wants to do this the right way, he says. He knows he should have asked her dad for permission, but they were in this perfect place in their relationship, and he thought if he waited any longer, she would have said no.

Claudia is adamant about taking the trip home alone. She tries to explain, but there is not much of an explanation. He shakes his head sadly.

"Have a safe trip home," he says, leaving her bedroom. He is halfway through the door. Without turning around, he stops. "Whatever happens, you can keep the ring," he says.

She lets him leave, and pulls the comforter over her head, feeling horrible. The next day, she takes the early morning flight home to Calgary to see her family.

Petey and Tracey are waiting for her with a pink helium balloon in the arrivals lobby of the Calgary Airport. She hasn't seen either of them since the wedding, which was last year, and she tears up, seeing them together, welcoming her home. Petey gives her a big hug and takes her silver Rimowa suitcase from her, while Tracey kisses her on the cheek and thrusts the balloon into her hand.

"You spoil me," Claudia says, grinning at them. She ties the balloon to her wrist and loops her arm through Tracey's. She still can't believe that her big brother married her best friend. She feels like the luckiest girl in the world.

"Glad you're home, sis," Tracey says, pulling Claudia towards the parking garage. Petey follows behind, stopping to pay for their parking ticket.

"However," Tracey continues. "Though I'm stoked to see you, I'm pretty pissed that I had to hear about your engagement from your mother. Not to mention that I've never met the dude. What's the deal? And let's see the ring."

Claudia sighs, shaking her head. "There's no deal. Do we have to talk about this now? I haven't seen you guys in months." Petey's back, and she looks to him for help, but he is staring at her just as expectantly as his wife.

"Hmm, I'd also like to know the details," he says. "Spill it."

Claudia groans in frustration, but she knows she deserves the third degree. "I might not be engaged anymore," she says, blushing. "But he says I can keep the ring, if that's any consolation." She looks at Petey and catches a relieved look on his face.

"Sorry to hear that, Cloudie," he says, sincerely. "But honestly, I never met the guy so I'm not that sorry. I'm sure he was....is...great. Right?"

Claudia nods, sadly. "Yeah, he is a great guy. I haven't told mom and dad that it's off, but I'm sure they'll be just as relieved as you." She glances at Tracey, who looks overjoyed with the news of her broken engagement. "What's going on with dad anyway? He sounded cryptic on the phone. Everything okay?"

Tracey and Petey look at each other, shrugging. "He probably just wanted to talk you out of getting married. I'm sure everything is fine." He sees his sister's worried expression. "He's healthy as a horse. Don't worry."

They weave through the late afternoon traffic, past the expansive new suburban neighborhoods, and tidy parks. The roads are all newly paved, and there are strip malls everywhere, filled with outlet stores, movie theaters, and family restaurant chains. Calgary has been booming for the past ten years, and Claudia's old out-of-the-way neighborhood is now considered almost central. When she was growing up, she had to take two buses and a train to get downtown. Now there's a light rail stop within walking distance from the house, that stops right in front of the Calgary Tower.

Her mom is already at the front door, waving them onto the driveway, with an apron tied around her waist. She hugs her daughter ferociously, pulling her inside, where she is cooking up another one of her tasty feasts.

"Smells great, Ma," Tracey says, walking in with Petey, holding hands. Mrs. Young smiles with pride at her daughter-in-law and son. She knows she is lucky to have them living so close. She looks at her daughter longingly, silently wishing for her to return as well.

Mr. Young emerges from his study and pulls his daughter in for a big bear hug.

"Welcome home," he says, kissing her with a smack on the face. She smiles and wipes her cheek, trying not to sob, though that's what she wants to do.

She freshens up in her childhood bedroom, which is still crammed with plush toys and Babysitter's Club novels from an earlier time. She glances at the twin-sized bed and for some reason, thinks of James, and how she held him there, as he cried that night after Brent's funeral.

She goes downstairs and joins her mom and Tracey in the kitchen. Petey and her father are outside, shooting hoops on the small concrete court in the yard. Petey is right: Her father looks downright spritely.

She is setting the table in the dining room for dinner, when the doorbell rings. Her mom and Tracey are both busy, so she puts down the stack of plates she is holding to go answer the door.

Bright, piercing eyes catch her by surprise when she opens the door. Her heart drops into her stomach. He is holding a bouquet of lilies and he just stands there. His hair is longer now, pushed behind his ears and curling at the nape of his neck. He's freshly shaved and wearing a leather jacket over a white cotton shirt and black jeans.

She stares at him.

"Hi," he says, finally. He doesn't step forward, but waits for her to invite him inside. She keeps staring, forgetting her manners, but finally steps aside.

"James. What are you doing here?" She knows she is being impolite, but she has no idea why he is here.

"Your parents invited me for dinner," he says, sounding unsure. "You didn't know I was coming, I guess." He smiles awkwardly.

"Oh. No, they didn't tell me. I didn't even know you were in town. Come in, of course." She steps to the side, letting him in. "Petey's out back and Tracey's in the kitchen with my mom."

James steps into the house. "These are for your mom," he says, thrusting the flowers at her. Claudia takes them from him, and he bends down to unlace his shoes.

She forces a polite smile when he stands up again. "It's good to see you. You look great. How's Rebecca?" She can feel herself blushing hot, asking the question a bit too enthusiastically.

"You look beautiful," he says, finding her eyes, avoiding the question.

Claudia looks down at herself, to remember what she's wearing. She's barefoot, and wearing a black cotton maxi dress. Her hair is tied up into a loose ponytail, and she's not wearing any makeup. She feels like running upstairs to put on some mascara.

"No I don't, but thanks," she says, turning to lead James to the kitchen. "What are you in town for?"

"Family stuff," James says. He doesn't elaborate. "You?"

"Same." They enter the kitchen, and her mom rushes over to give James a hug, her mules swishing against the floor. She takes the flowers from Claudia and puts them in a crystal vase that she fills with water.

"Thank you for the lilies," Mrs. Young says, shooting James her illustrious smile. "I'm so glad you could join us for dinner. I know how much you miss my cooking in Toronto," she says, shamelessly.

Claudia rolls her eyes but can't help smiling. She'll chastise her mother later, for not telling her he was coming. James indulges her mother, paying compliments to the delicious aromas and her lovely apron.

He asks Tracey how her parents are doing, and sends his regards. Petey and Mr. Young come inside, and after everyone says their hellos, the six of them sit down for dinner.

No one brings up Claudia's engagement. It's the elephant in the room. James discusses the work he's been doing at the hospital in Toronto, and Claudia doles out some juicy tidbits about working in the Vegas entertainment scene. Petey and Tracey are like clockwork, finishing each other's sentences and refilling each other's plates with food, as they fill everyone in on the progress of their current home renovation. Only when Mrs. Young starts pressing for grandchildren, does the conversation start getting a bit strained.

After dinner, Claudia and Tracey clear the table while the guys wash dishes with Mrs. Young in the kitchen. Even Mr. Young chips in to help clean up, boxing up the leftovers and putting them in the fridge. For a moment Claudia feels like she is in high school, with her best friend and boyfriend over for dinner.

She refills her glass of wine and takes it outside on the patio for some much-needed air. James was sneaking glances at her all evening, and she knows there is more to his visit than he's letting on. Sitting on the steps with her maxi dress tucked around her, she hears the patio door swing open, and moments later, she feels James sit down next to her. He's drinking a bottle of beer, which he raises to her with a smile. "Dessert," he says, clinking her wine glass.

The sun is slowly setting, giving the sky a reddish hue. The yard is filled with evergreens, crabapple trees and wild rose bushes. It's still early in the year so nothing is blooming yet, but the carefully trimmed garden is sprouting with potential, anticipating the warm months. Claudia shivers, as a gust of wind blows. She clutches her arms, rubbing them with her hands to stay warm, not ready to go inside.

She feels James' arm press against hers and she allows her head to tilt to the side, touching his shoulder.

"So, I hear congratulations are in order," James says. There's a tremor in his voice, and he doesn't look at her. He takes a sip of beer.

"I don't think that's going to happen anymore," Claudia says carefully. "I think it's off."

"You *think* it's off?" James chuckles. "Marriage is a pretty serious commitment, so you might want to make sure."

Claudia pulls away from his shoulder and glares at him. "And how's your girlfriend? Put a ring on her finger yet?" her tone is harsh, but James doesn't seem fazed.

"No, but thanks for asking. We broke up a while ago, shortly after I got back from Pete and Tracey's wedding." He looks at her, waiting to see her reaction. Claudia takes a long sip of wine and smiles ironically.

"Well, here's to being single," she says with fake gusto. "I haven't talked to Cory – my fiancé – ex-fiancé, I mean, since he left my house late last night. He wasn't happy about me coming home alone, and that I wouldn't let him come. He's never met the family."

"Cory? DJ Cory? I always knew that fucker had the hots for you." He shakes his head slowly, like he had known this was going to happen all along. He turns to look at Claudia. "You were going to marry a guy who you've never introduced to your parents? I didn't think that was your style."

"It's not," Claudia says, defensively. "I've not really been myself lately. And please, he's not a *fucker*, James. He's a really good guy. If anything, I'm the fucker. We got engaged a few months ago and I just couldn't bring myself to tell my parents. I think I knew the whole time that I wasn't serious about it. But it felt nice to be engaged, you know? Even to the wrong guy." She frowns at her own words, feeling shallow. "I'm such a bitch."

James pauses for a while before answering. "Kinda, yeah. But I think I know where you're coming from. I was with Rebecca for a long time. I even planned on marrying her at one point. For no other reason than because she was there, and it seemed to make sense. And then one day I just couldn't do it anymore. After your brother's wedding, I saw him and Tracey together, and they just fit. I saw your parents, even my mom and Henry." He pauses to drink his beer. "And I saw you."

"You saw me, and what?" Claudia challenges. "Don't tell me you saw me and then rushed home to break it off with your girlfriend. Please don't. It's not cool."

He shrugs helplessly. "It's the truth. I don't know what happened between you and me. I mean, I do know what happened, in a literal sense, but sometimes I wake up in the morning and I don't understand why we're not together. We never had closure. Never had a real break-up. I feel like we've been together since high school, and we have these little pockets of time where we lost each other."

Claudia is silent. She can hear her mom puttering around the kitchen cabinets inside. Petey, Tracey and her dad have gone out to pick up some dessert. She knows James wants a heart-to-heart, but she doesn't want to do it here, with her mom listening in through the window.

"Hey, let's get out of here for a bit," she says, getting up. She gestures at his bottle of beer. "Are you okay to drive?"

James nods. "Sure. Where do you wanna go?"

Claudia shrugs. "Let's just drive. I need to clear my head a bit. Give me a moment to talk to my mom though." She goes inside to find her mom in the kitchen, loitering by the window.

"Ma," she says. Her mom pulls an innocent face. Claudia continues, speaking in Mandarin, just in case James is in earshot. "Why did you invite James over? And why is he in town?"

"Your father and I wanted you to see him again," she replies, matter-of-factly, not even trying to hide her intentions. "Before you make a big step in your life, we wanted you to remember some of your past."

"So you guys *asked* him to come to Calgary?" She is speaking English now, not caring who can hear. "You shouldn't have done that. I know you mean well but...he has his own life now. And I'm...was engaged." She shakes her head.

"*Hah*? Was?" Her mom's eyes sparkle with hope.

Claudia sighs. "I'm not marrying Cory, mom. I shouldn't have said yes."

Mrs. Young rushes over and hugs her daughter. "Oh, I am *so* happy to hear that, Claudia," she says, not bothering to hide her excitement and relief. "You can do so much better."

"You never even met him!" Claudia exclaims. "What's wrong with everyone? He's a very good person!"

"He was not good enough for you to bring home!" Her mom shouts back. Claudia keeps her mouth shut, because this is partially true. It's not that he wasn't good enough; it never felt right. Now that she thinks about it, she realizes how ridiculous she has been. Maybe in other families it's okay to marry someone you've never introduced to your family. In this family it's just plain crazy.

"Well, anyway, it doesn't matter anymore. It's not going to happen. So you can tell dad that too, so whatever you guys have up your sleeve, you can forget about it." She sees her mom stifling a smile, and she looks over her shoulder to see James in the doorway.

"Hey. Just checking to see if you're still coming." He looks a little embarrassed and Claudia guesses he has heard more than his fair share. "I'll wait for you outside. We'll go get some ice cream."

"But your dad is bringing ice cream home!" Claudia's mom protests. She wants to spend more time with her daughter.

"We won't be gone too long," Claudia says, giving her mom a squeeze on the arm. "We just need to talk for a bit."

James is waiting for her in the driveway next to a silver Mercedes. His mom's car, she guesses, since he's just visiting. He opens the passenger door for her to get in. He's about to close the door when he pauses and leans down towards her.

"Wanna go to our spot?" He asks, a mischievous smile on his face. "I'm not really in the mood for ice cream."

Claudia nods. "Sure. I didn't know we had a spot."

Minutes later, they are pulling into the foothills, up a dirt path, and stop to park behind a dumpster. Claudia recognizes the chain guard, and the clearing beyond. She gets out of the car and makes a run for the field, heading towards the large rock.

"Don't tell me you have a projector in your pocket," Claudia teases. "That was pretty smooth, as I recall."

James chuckles. "No, I don't have any gadgets to help me this time."

They walk over to the large rock and sink down, backs pressing against it. Claudia sits with her legs crossed Indian-style, and James bends his knees, keeping his feet flat on the ground. He waits for her to speak first.

"Why are you here, James?" Claudia asks him calmly. "I'm happy to see you, obviously. I know my parents probably called you, freaking out about my engagement. But why did you come? Were you planning on stopping me?"

"No," answers James evenly. "I just wanted to see you. Your parents didn't exactly ask me to come, but I'll let them take the credit," he says with a grin. "When they called me yesterday, they just wanted to find out if I knew anything about this guy you were marrying. They told me you were coming home for a visit and I knew I had to come. Even if you ended up marrying the guy, I still needed to see you first."

"Yesterday? You came on a day's notice?" Claudia laughs darkly. "So, I get engaged, and you fly across the country to see me. When I was a train ride away in Montreal, you couldn't even be bothered to call."

"I did call."

"Yeah, after breaking up with me over a text message. Thanks." Claudia shakes her head, sighing. "Okay, this is dumb. Let's not talk about that stuff."

"No, it's not dumb. We need to talk about this. When I saw you in Montreal, after you left Toronto, I snapped. You seemed different. You were living this new, exciting life, with all these super cool people. You spoke French, all of a sudden. It was a side of you I'd never seen before. I'd only ever known you as a bookworm and suddenly you were this dancer, artist type. I

336

remember seeing you out with your new friends and I just thought....man, I've lost her. I realize now that you were just growing and discovering things, doing the same thing I was in med school. It took me a while to realize it. But by then, you'd already left the country. It was too late."

"Dancer, artist type? James, I've always been a dancer. And I'm still an artist, and a bookworm too. I've never changed."

He nods. "I know that." He takes a deep breath, resting the back of his head into the rock. "Then, after I saw you again at the wedding..." he shakes his head, trailing off. "I didn't want to just show up on your doorstep, or call you out of the blue. I broke up with Rebecca and I needed time to myself, to sort shit out. But I lost my nerve. Honestly if I hadn't heard about your engagement, I might still be home in Toronto moping."

"Moping?" Claudia laughs. "I can't imagine you moping."

"Trust me, I've moped more than a few times over you." He says, his eyes earnest. He means it lightly, but remembering their on-and-off times over the years, Claudia feels regretful.

"I don't know what to say, James," she says quietly. "The last time I saw you, I didn't think I'd hear from you again. So I decided to finally, really move on."

James sighs and rips some grass out of the ground beside him, his face contemplative. "So, you're really not going to marry this guy? Or are you just saying that to appease your mom?"

Claudia shakes her head no. "Really not. I wasn't sure at first, but now being home and seeing my family, I know it's just not right. Sometimes when you're away from the people who are closest to you, you start losing yourself. I haven't been myself. Cory's a great guy and all but he's just not the one."

"The one? Do you believe in that soul mate stuff?" James asks, with a quick laugh, playing it cool.

"I do," she says, looking at him. "I think we have many soul mates. My brother, Tracey, my parents...they're all my soul mates. You..." She keeps her voice steady. "I mean it. You're like family."

Family. James' blue eyes flash fiercely against the dimming sky. He wraps an arm around her shoulders, pulling her towards him and sweetly kisses the top of her head. "I'm so sorry, Claud. About everything."

Claudia's eyes well up with tears and she lets them roll down her face. "Me too, James. What are we doing? We're so messed up. We're always playing these stupid games. We take each other for granted. It's like that awful movie you made me watch here all those years ago."

James laughs. "*When Harry met Sally*? That movie is awesome. Still one of my all-time favorites. So, am I your *Harry*?"

"No, I think it's more like I'm your *Sally*," she says, rolling her eyes. "Which is like, my worst nightmare."

"Is it so bad?" James asks gently, his mouth on her hair. "We're here now, together, right? Tell me what you want. I'm here, and I want you. That much is obvious. But I need to know what you want."

Claudia takes a deep breath in. "I want a lot of things, James," she says. "Where do I begin?"

"Start with me. Do you want me?"

"Yes," Claudia says, with no hesitation. "I've always wanted you. But this time – I mean, if we try this again, it's for real. No more ego games, and no more excuses. I know I'm just as guilty. No running away when things get weird, and no secrets. I think we owe it to ourselves, don't we?"

"We do," James says, brushing a piece of hair behind her ear. "But where do we go from here? You have your career in Vegas, I'm in Toronto..."

Claudia shakes her head. "It doesn't matter." She turns to him, her face vulnerable. "If I am yours and you are mine, we'll make it work, somehow."

James looks back at her. She is being so brave, putting her heart on the table again. He knows if he hesitates at all she'll lose her courage and then she'll be gone again, and this time it would be forever. He pulls her to him and kisses her softly on the lips.

"I've missed you," she whispers, wrapping her arms around his neck, tears tingling her nose.

"I've missed you," James says, smiling. "I'm glad you met me halfway."

Claudia is packing up the last of the boxes in the living room. This house - the first house she has ever owned, is on the market, and all the things that she's collected from this life in the desert over the past three years, are being crammed into the back of a moving truck, to be shipped across the country to her Aunt Honey's house, in New York City. She'll be there in a few weeks, when she and James arrive together, to start their new life.

James is finishing up his residency in Toronto and has decided to open up a private practice in Brooklyn. Vancouver had been the original plan, but he quickly gave that up when Claudia landed a directing role with an off-Broadway company in Manhattan. After seeing James in Calgary, Claudia returned to Las Vegas and put in her resignation with Cirque. Her director instantly recommended her for a position in New York City, which would be much closer to Toronto.

James was elated with the news, but being in the same time zone wasn't going to be good enough. So they decided that he would move to New York, too.

Claudia called Cory as soon as she got back. She wanted to see him in person, return the ring, and part on good terms, even though their friendship would likely be severed for the time being, or perhaps forever. Cory had been civil and accommodating. Maybe he had expected the outcome all along. Even when she told him she was getting back together with James, he was amiable, and not surprised in the least.

They briefly hugged goodbye at a coffee shop on Eastern Avenue, on neutral territory. Claudia promised to stay in touch and Cory told her to stay cool, to which she laughed. He took the ring back without an argument, and told her he'd be trading it in for a new car.

James has taken some time off and has come to Las Vegas to help Claudia with the move. They'll be driving across the United States and making a road trip out of it, stopping at a few National Parks, and hitting up all the sights on the tourist map. Claudia has promised James a twenty ounce steak in Amarillo, Texas.

She's sealing up one last cardboard box with packing tape when James enters the room, carrying two heaving crates from the bedroom, looking strained.

"I guess I know what you've been doing all these years," he says. "You were reading."

He drops the boxes on the floor with a thud. "For your next gift, you will be receiving a Kindle. Easier on the back," he says, wincing.

Claudia wrinkles her nose. "I don't do e-books. I gave away my Kindle to my mom for her birthday. I like the weight and feel of paper. Some things just can't be digitized."

James walks to the fridge and pulls out a bottle of water. Claudia admires his broad muscles through the back of his thin black t-shirt, and lets her eyes run down his low-slung jeans. He turns to her with a handsome smile.

"Lets get out of here for a bit, let the moving guys do their thing," As if on cue, one of the burly men Claudia hired from "Two Men and a Truck" comes through the door with a dolly, stacking the boxes of books James has just put down.

Claudia tosses James the keys to her Lexus – an emotional purchase she made last year after getting a big raise at work. Making more money had somehow made her feel emptier, and the car was a quick way to cheer up. She is glad for it now though – driving her old Honda across the country would have been a safety hazard.

It's starting to warm up outside already – in Vegas, summer starts in late April and by July it is painfully scorching. Claudia's property is beautifully manicured, kept in shape by Nico the gardener, who comes on a weekly basis. The neighborhood is quiet, and her realtor has assured her that the house should sell quickly, and for a small profit.

She climbs into the passenger seat, since James always insists on driving, and he starts the car. He speeds towards the interstate like he owns the city. He has only been in town for a few days but already seems to know his way around. Claudia relaxes into the plush leather seat, rolling down her window. There is something about being driven around in your own car that just feels so good.

When Claudia asks James where they're going, he just smiles and tells her he has it under control. He zips his way down Las Vegas Boulevard, past the giant pyramid at Luxor and the fake Eiffel Tower, and pulls into the valet lane at the Bellagio.

Claudia gets out of the car while James passes the keys to the valet.

"In the mood for Italian?" Claudia asks, raising one eyebrow. She hears the trunk pop, and a duffel bag materializes by their feet. James throws it over his shoulder with a smirk.

"Follow me," he says, with a cocky grin. He pulls her along into the hotel and straight towards the elevators.

"I snuck out earlier this morning to check us in," he says excitedly. He is terribly pleased with himself. "It's our last night in Vegas, so I figured we should do it up. Who knows how many crazy Vegas nights I missed out on while you were out here."

Claudia crosses her arms and narrows her eyes at him. "You know I hate surprises. All my stuff is packed. We were supposed to head out this afternoon. I had reservations in Albuquerque." She pouts her bottom lip. She doesn't like when things get off schedule.

James smiles sheepishly. "Do it for me? This is my first time in the lovely city of sin." Claudia can't resist his charms, and she lets a slow smile creep onto her face.

"Fine," she says. "No strip clubs, though."

The elevator stops on the top floor. James pulls her down the long hallway to the last door. The Penthouse. He pulls out a card key from his pocket and opens the door.

The room is opulent, with white marble floors and plush cream and brown carpeting. The furniture is modern Italian-style, all cream leather, with gold and emerald green accents all around. A crystal chandelier hangs from the ceiling, above a large dining table. The windows are floor-to-ceiling, with an expansive view of the Strip below. A giant flat-screen television hangs on one wall. Original oil paintings in vibrant red and orange hues adorn the walls.

A long hallway leads to another door, which Claudia guesses is the bedroom. She looks at James with a squeal and runs down the hallway to check it out. Inside she finds a giant king-sized bed, a small living room, and the best part – an exquisite bathroom with two separate areas – one for her, and one for him.

"James, this is too much!" She says, laughing, though she is thoroughly impressed with the space. "This is baller. Definitely not the kind of Vegas I've been living, that's for sure."

"It's just for one night, so I thought you would approve," James says, coming behind her and wrapping his arms around her. She feels his breath behind her ear and she closes her eyes, relishing in the closeness. She turns to him and lets him take her to the bed.

It is early evening by the time they are done with each other. They take a shower together, lathering up in the hotel's signature soaps and basking languidly in the shower, taking advantage of the large space. James sits on the shower bench and watches Claudia wash her long hair. She catches him gazing at her.

"Where have you been all my life?" She says softly, with a smile.

James doesn't answer but instead, pulls her to him and sweeps her mouth into a telling kiss.

While Claudia dries off in the "hers" section of the bathroom, James unpacks the duffel bag he packed earlier in the morning. Claudia is impressed with its contents: A cream silk dress with matching heels for her, and a pair of grey slacks and a black dress shirt for him.

They get dressed. Claudia dries her hair with the hairdryer and leaves it in loose waves, fluffy and fresh. She dabs on a bit of tinted lip balm but leaves the rest of her face naked.

James slicks his hair to the side and back, held in place with a pinch of pomade. He hasn't had a chance to shave, but it's the way Claudia likes it.

He eyes Claudia up and down. "Good choice," he says, while she turns around. It's a halter dress with a low back. The shoes have a four-inch wedge heel, and are surprisingly comfortable. Even so, she barely comes to his nose.

They take the elevator downstairs for dinner, at one of the hotel restaurants where James has made reservations. They are seated on a terrace overlooking the Bellagio fountains, and Claudia is giddy. She realizes with a start that this might be the first grown-up, romantic dinner she has ever had with James.

"Do you realize that this is our first real date in over four years?" She says, smiling. After they reunited in Calgary, they had flown to see each other every other weekend, but since they had such limited time together, they had spent most of their time indoors, in bed, and often, just ordering pizza. Not that they minded.

James is beaming as well, and he reaches over for her hand. "You're making me feel like a bad boyfriend," he says.

The waiter comes over to fill their water glasses and a pops a bottle of champagne.

"I went ahead and ordered for us," James says. "The fewer interruptions the better. After all, we have a lot of catching up to do. Four years is a long time."

"Cheers," Claudia says, raising her glass.

She is rather thirsty, and downs the first glass quickly. They finish the entire bottle before the main course arrives, and James orders a second. "Special occasion," he explains to the waiter, who nods politely and comes back promptly with a fresh bottle.

Claudia is famished and scarfs down her halibut within minutes of its arrival. She then finishes the mashed potatoes on James' plate. He tries to hide his amusement. "Slow down there, bud," he says, with a smile.

She shoots him her best glare. "If I don't eat, I'll puke. Two bottles of champagne before dinner is bad news."

She excuses herself to use the bathroom and freshens up in front of the mirror, smoothing her hair and touching up her lips.

When she gets back to the table, there is a small black velvet box sitting on her dessert plate.

She sits down slowly.

James nervously unbuttons the collar of his shirt and clears his throat. "I was going to hide it in your cake, but I thought it would be too cliché for your tastes," he says, with a small half-smile.

"James..." Claudia starts. She can't help herself. She is too curious, and snaps the box open. Inside there is a round-cut diamond the size of her fingernail, set on a simple platinum band. She inhales sharply.

"I called your parents and asked them," James says. "I know we've just gotten back together. But it you think about it, we've really been together since high school. I've never stopped loving you. I never will."

He gets up from his seat and walks over to her side of the table. He gets down on one knee. "Will you marry me, Claudia? Please?"

Claudia stands and pulls him up to his feet. "Yes!" She pulls his head down to hers for a kiss and the tables around them cheer lightly. Someone whistles obnoxiously and she snaps her head around at the offender. She gasps when she sees her mother, father, Petey and Tracey standing at the entrance of the restaurant. Behind them, James' mother and Henry are there as well. They are all staring at her expectantly.

"Oh my God!" Claudia shrieks. She runs over to their families, hugging her mom and dad first. Her mom is already crying.

James follows her over and embraces his own mom first, then shakes hands with Peter Senior. Claudia saves Petey and Tracey for last, and after letting her brother bear hug her, she and Tracey squeal and jump up and down like the excited girls that they are.

They are making far too much noise to be in the lobby of a five-star restaurant, and the hostess comes over and politely asks them to move outside.

"Wait! The ring!" In her excitement, Claudia had left it at the table.

"Got it," James says, holding it up. He presents the box to her once again. Claudia smiles up at him. "What do you say you put it on this time?" he teases. He slides the ring on to her left hand. It is a tiny bit loose, but she figures she'll grow into it.

They end up leaving to find another restaurant. Tracey tells Claudia that James had called everyone last week and filled them in on his plan, and they'd all decided to come join them in Vegas to celebrate.

"You are so sneaky!" She points at James. "How did you know I would say yes?"

James shrugs guiltily. "I didn't. I guess that would have been bad, eh?"

Claudia laughs. "You're good. I didn't suspect anything. I thought we'd be on our way through the Grand Canyon by now. I'm so happy you're all here." She tears up, looking around at her family.

James wraps an arm around his fiancé. "I'm happy you're happy," he says, kissing her on the temple. Claudia laughs. Since when did they become that couple?

Her parents, James' mom, and Henry are sitting at the far end of the table, and they seem to be talking about something intense. Claudia's dad is getting animated, in story-telling mode, using his hands. Her mom is laughing, and Henry and James' mom look amused.

"Look, everyone's getting along," Claudia says to James. "I used to think things were kind of weird between our parents."

Petey and Tracey are sitting across from her and James. Petey clears his throat. "So, Cloudie, I know this is your night and all, but um...Tracey and I have some news. We wanted to tell you first." He reaches over and pats Tracey on the tummy.

Claudia looks at Tracey, and sees that she is sipping on a glass of water with lemon, while everyone else is drinking wine.

"A baby?" She asks timidly. Her brother and sister-in-law nod, smiling. Another rush of tears pours from her eyes. "You told me before you told mom?" She thinks she has never been this happy, ever. She rushes over and hugs her siblings from behind, kissing them both on the cheeks.

"Congrats, you guys," James says. He raises his glass for a toast. "To family. And babies."

"Babies?" Claudia's mom interjects loudly from across the table. "Who's having babies?" Her face is alarmed.

"Surprise," Tracey says to her mother-in-law. "I'm pregnant. You're going to be a grandma!"

The grandma-to-be screams, and the entire restaurant turns to look at her. Tears of joy are spilling down her face yet again, and she knocks over a glass of wine in her excitement. Her husband is laughing, and holding her up to stand.

Later, when everyone has checked into their rooms and are resting from the eventful evening, Claudia and James are in their penthouse suite, sitting on the bed, sharing a pint of chocolate ice cream they bought from a gift shop downstairs.

"This was the best night of my life," Claudia says, between mouthfuls. "Thank you." She turns to gaze at him. "I can't believe you're going to be my husband."

James smiles. "It was a pretty good night for me too," he says. He takes a giant spoonful of chocolate ice cream and puts it in his mouth, chewing thoughtfully. "By the way, you know what's weird?"

Claudia shakes her head.

"I never liked ice cream until I met you."

They get an early start on the morning, stopping by the house to lock up and pick up the last of Claudia's things. When they are ready to go, the trunk is packed to the brim with everything they'll need for their cross-country drive. She turns to look at the house one last time. She didn't think she would be, but she's sad to leave.

James lets her take her time, watching her tilt her head reverently towards the sky, looking like she's saying a silent prayer to herself. She bends down to pick up a rock from the garden and tucks it into her pocket.

"You alright?" James asks gently.

Claudia nods. "Yeah. Every time I leave a place, I feel like I'm leaving a piece of myself. I'm excited for the future, but…" she trails off, looking away. "I'm going to miss this. My house, my life, me…" She gives him a guilty look. "Sorry, you probably don't want to hear that."

"Claud, you're not leaving yourself behind. You are still going to be you, except now I'm going to be around. I know life has been fine without me, " he pauses, trying not to sound wounded, "but maybe now it's going to be awesome. It better be anyway, or else we're both making a huge mistake."

"Shut up," Claudia says quickly, wiping her eyes. "It's not a mistake." she says. "I'm just….I'm PMS-ing. And I can never turn down a good cry. Let's go."

James gives her a squeeze and they get into the car. They have a long drive ahead of them.

Epilogue

Henry, Elizabeth, Peter, and Polly, are booked on the same flight back to Calgary from Las Vegas. The four of them share a taxi, and the driver heads northwest, towards the Youngs' home.

When they arrive, the Coopers come inside for a glass of wine, to unwind from the trip. Peter and Henry wheel in the suitcases while Elizabeth joins Polly in the kitchen, chatting excitedly about their children's upcoming nuptials.

"Polly, can you believe, after all these years, they are getting married?" She is glowing with happiness. "Nathaniel would be so proud," she adds quietly, her smile faltering a bit. Though he has been dead for over ten years, Elizabeth still thinks of him every day. They were never in love, but he was her first husband. And she is reminded of him every time she quarrels with Henry, and with every phone call with James, who, despite not having a British accent, sounds exactly like him.

She would never have guessed that she would be reunited with Henry later in life. Of course, it came with a price: Her relationship with her son, already strained before Nathaniel's death, became even more distant after she remarried. Granted, he had moved away for University, so the distance was also physical. But, he no longer came home for holidays, and didn't call on Sundays, as he'd used to. And she didn't blame him for it.

Only now, after Petey and Tracey's wedding last year, has James started to come around. He has started to speak to Henry, even.

It's hard to explain to your only child the reason why you've chosen a path that seems so blatantly wrong. While James has a general idea of what happened thirty years ago in England, there is so much that he doesn't know.

He doesn't know, for example, that his father had also been in love, before they were married.

Or, that on the day of the wedding, Nathaniel had been so distraught, he had taken ill and missed the ceremony. Henry had stood in as proxy.

It was like a cruel joke. Standing in front of hundreds of people, reciting vows to the only man you want to say them to, but having the words mean nothing.

And imagine, years later, having the freedom to say them again, but this time as the truth.

Perhaps now James understands. Now, he has Claudia.

Polly smiles warmly at Elizabeth, handing her a glass of Pinot Noir. "I am also very proud of our children," she says. She has grown to enjoy Elizabeth's company. After Peter revealed his knowledge of her and Henry's secret, Polly had assumed things would become more awkward than ever between the couples. She had felt especially guilty that poor Elizabeth would be left out in the cold, ignorant, like a chump.

But, Henry had returned home and told Elizabeth everything. She was shocked of course, and paid Polly a visit one evening, while Henry and Peter were at their weekly tennis match. Over slices of blueberry pie, they had discussed the complications, woman-to-woman. Both realized quickly that there was nothing to discuss, really. It had been so long ago, and Polly could hardly remember the details. Elizabeth was thankful. Claudia and James were finally getting along so well again; she was happy they could do the same.

Polly's iPad starts to ring, and she pulls it out of her Hermes travel tote. It's Claudia, on FaceTime. She swipes the screen to connect with her daughter. In moments, Claudia's beautiful face fills the screen. James is behind her, smiling with his sweet dimples.

"Hi Ma!" Claudia says. "We're in Denver. Just wanted to say hi. Is that Mrs. Cooper with you?" Claudia's eyes flicker to her future mother-in-law, who is hovering behind Polly.

"Hi kids," Elizabeth says with a wave. James waves to his mother. The connection is slow, and the audio transmission is a bit warbled. Polly blows them kisses and asks them to check in every day while they're on the road. Elizabeth chokes back a cough; she can't remember when she ever talked to James on a daily basis. She feels a slight twinge of remorse.

Polly senses Elizabeth's reaction and places a hand on the woman's arm, as she ends the call on her iPad. "I am an overbearing mother," she explains, rationally. "Most kids call once a month, or a week at best. I am lucky."

Elizabeth smiles. "Yes, you are. And I am lucky too, with James."

Polly nods. "And now they'll be married. I'd say we did quite well, didn't we?"

Sometimes, on a chilly afternoon, as Polly is soaking in her bathtub, with the cold air drifting in through the open window, she closes her eyes. She remembers sitting in a warm lake on a grassy mountain, after being carried through the woods by a blond foreigner with dark hazel eyes.

She wonders what would have happened if she had leaned into his arms a little more. Or, let him kiss her just one more time.

She opens her eyes.

Thank you so much for reading! If you love Claudia and Polly's story, please write a review and share the book with your friends.

You can also join me on Facebook,

Or write to me at: shen.lianna@gmail.com

www.liannashen.com

xoxo